KNIGHT RISE

QUOTE

"I have lost friends, some by death, others through the sheer inability to cross the street."
Virginia Woolf

Knight Rise

DL HAMMONS

Wild Lark Books

DISCLAIMER

For my wife, Kim. Owner of the first read...the last say...and my heart.

CONTENTS

| 1 |

The Client

Dianne

Everything unfolded on a Monday.

It was mid-July, and misty rain, the kind that drove the intermittent windshield wipers crazy, had been falling since early morning. I pushed my way through the outer front door, and then the matching interior one, walking into the small anteroom of Silent Sleuth Investigations. As I stepped up to the receptionist desk where Evelyn sat typing from notes pinned to a prompting pad, I took notice of an older woman dressed in a yellow waitress uniform sitting stiffly on one of the waiting room chairs and staring straight ahead. Her purse was resting on her lap with both hands holding the straps so tightly it was making her knuckles turn white. The blank expression on her face made me wonder what she was thinking about.

"Good morning, Evelyn," I said, plopping my notebook on the corner of the desk.

Evelyn was a couple of decades older than me, but with sharpshooter-like eyesight and hearing so acute she could detect a fly fart across the room. In her light-blue sweater, something she wore regardless of how hot it was outside, and her gray hair pulled back into a bun, she reminded me of my deceased grandmother. And much like my grandmother, I imagined Evelyn was the type of woman who tormented her grandchildren by assigning them an endless number of meaningless chores.

Evelyn stopped what she was doing and stared at the spot where I had laid my notebook. I quickly snatched it up.

"Good morning, Miss Williams," Evelyn replied with a weak attempt at sounding cordial. Evelyn had been with Silent Sleuth since its inception and made no attempt to hide her displeasure about the recent changes. "This lady is here to see you," she said, quickly followed by, "She doesn't have an appointment."

I glanced at the other woman again, and although I'm good with faces, I didn't recognize her.

Evelyn must have read my puzzled look because she answered my unspoken question.

"That is Mrs. Bennett. She's a longtime client of Mr. Cobb. She was scheduled for a meeting with him in June, but she didn't keep the appointment. Instead, she showed up unexpectedly this morning needing to speak with him. I explained the situation to her and that she'll have to reschedule, but she won't leave," Evelyn explained.

Aaron Cobb was the previous owner-manager of Silent Sleuth, and the *situation* Evelyn had referred to was the fact that he dropped dead in June. Massive heart attack. The part that irked Evelyn was that Aaron's last will and testament stated ownership of the agency was to be left to his sister, Tildy, which wasn't a surprise. However, Tildy's first act was to promote me to office manager, and that came as a shock to everyone, myself included. I was the investigator at Silent Sleuth with the least amount of experience since everyone stayed forever—my ten years still made me the novice. Getting the idea why everyone hated me?

In my mind, I began flipping through the open case files I'd been familiarizing myself with since taking over two weeks ago, and I recalled the basics of the Bennett file. This one was unusual and a bit sad. My caseload, along with the other cases Aaron had been working on before slumping over during a company picnic, left me swamped, and I really didn't have time for this. But I reminded myself that one reason I'd gotten this new position—according to Tildy—was that I focused on the client first.

I turned around to face the woman in the yellow uniform.

"Mrs. Bennett, I'm Dianne Williams. I understand you're waiting to see me." I introduced myself pleasantly.

Mrs. Bennett rose to her feet. "If it's not too much trouble. I have to be at work in forty-five minutes, so I won't take much of your time," she answered with a deep Southern accent.

"No problem at all. Why don't you come back with me," I replied, ignoring the sour expression on Evelyn's face.

SSI was founded in 1983 by Aaron Cobb. It had grown into a full-service detective agency with ten investigators on staff who served the Charlotte area and five surrounding states. The agency performed everything from background checks to criminal investigations to hidden assets searches. All of the investigators who worked at SSI had at least ten years' experience in the field they specialized in.

As I led Mrs. Bennett down a hallway toward the rear of the building, I passed the luxurious breakroom on the right, two closed office doors on the left, and paused before the entrance to the office farther back on the right just past the conference room. Using my key to open the lock, I pushed the door open, reached in, and flicked on the lights. I let Mrs. Bennett precede me into the room.

A plethora of sports paraphernalia, all belonging to Aaron, overwhelmed anybody entering my office. It dominated the decor. Framed hockey jerseys, a University of North Carolina football helmet, display cases holding autographed baseballs, and picture upon picture of various signature action shots took up every wall space or nook and cranny. Of course, I rationalized I had been too busy dealing with the day-to-day business matters to take the time to pack away Aaron's prized possessions and move in my stuff from across the hall. Still, the truth was I hardly spent time in my office, and it showed, so removing all of Aaron's decorations would leave the office naked. I didn't really care, but as the manager and the face of Silent Sleuth, I probably needed to.

I offered Mrs. Bennett a seat in one of the two captain's chairs in front of the enormous oak executive desk. I quickly stepped around to the other side and took a seat in the black leather desk chair, depositing my notebook on a computer credenza behind me.

"I was sorry to hear about Mr. Cobb," Mrs. Bennett said as she settled into her seat. "It must have been a shock."

"Yes, and it was quite sudden. We're all still trying to adjust. As Evelyn probably explained to you, I am taking over all Mr. Cobb's cases. Usually, whenever we move a case from one investigator to another, we like to have a conference with both investigators and the client present, but I'm sure you can understand the special situation here. I haven't looked at your case file in-depth yet, but I know the general facts. Evelyn told me you had an appointment scheduled for June that you didn't keep," I started.

Looking at the woman seated across from me, I now recognized her uniform from IHOP. A white name tag with Emily printed on it was pinned above her left breast. Her long hair had equal amounts of brunette and gray, held back from her face by a black plastic headband on top of her head. Unfortunately, the middle-aged woman's most prominent features were a pug nose, bushy eyebrows, and hazel-colored eyes that seemed set too far apart on her face.

"I've had an appointment with Mr. Cobb every year on that same date. Every June sixth. He would update me with any progress he'd made on my sister's case," the woman drawled.

"Your sister who was murdered in 1992?" I confirmed.

"Yes. My sister Pamela, Pamela Goodwin. Her murderer has never been caught, and the police stopped looking for her killer a long time ago. I employed Mr. Cobb and your agency to do what the police would no longer do."

I recalled what little I had skimmed in Mrs. Bennett's file. A pawn shop robbery that had apparently gone bad, ending with the murder of Pamela Goodwin and both owners. It happened in Easley, a small town just twenty-five minutes west of Greenville, South Carolina. There had been no new leads or developments in the case for over twenty-nine years, and the circumstances of her death offered little hope of a breakthrough. However, her sister would show up each year on the anniversary of Pamela's death, pleading—or in this case, paying—the agency to not let her sister's death be forgotten and go unpunished. From the documentation in the file, I remembered Aaron would log a couple hours of follow-up inquiries for show, send the woman a bill, and then file the case away to wait for her next annual visit. Aaron Cobb was generally a stand-up guy and a decent investigator. Still, as I started delving into the agency's past dealings, it became apparent he wasn't above padding clients' bills. This wasn't outstanding detective work, but then again, what could you expect from a twenty-nine-year-old case?

"Can I ask why you missed your appointment in June?" I inquired, already suspecting what the answer might be.

Mrs. Bennett's hazel eyes dropped to the purse in her lap, and the straps in her hands endured another round of twisting.

"My husband didn't...I...I had...I mean, we both had second thoughts. Second thoughts about...continuing." she struggled to say.

"Mrs. Bennett, I'll be candid with you here. The likelihood of catching somebody responsible for your sister's death is doubtful after twenty-nine years. I can understand your desire to see justice done for your sister, and your devotion in that regard is commendable. However, the money you would pay our agency might be better being put toward a remembrance fund for her."

Mrs. Bennett picked her head up and looked straight into my eyes. "Miss Williams, this isn't only about me wanting to see justice done, because that's not it at all."

That surprised me. "Then why don't you tell me what it is about?"

Mrs. Bennett hesitated. "I don't know if they wrote this in the file, but my sister and I both worked in that shop. I was supposed to be working that day, not her. I woke up with the flu that morning, and Pamela went to work for me. She worked and ended up dead. That should have been me. But what you don't know, what nobody knows, was that I only told everybody I had the flu."

A subtle tremor became evident in Mrs. Bennett's voice, and her eyes became moist.

"What I've told nobody was that I was out with my friends the night before and got home late. Pamela was covering for me...like she always did. I sent my sister to her death because I was hung over. I will never forgive myself for that."

The woman collected herself and returned her gaze to me.

"I need you to tell me the truth. Would you say that there was absolutely no chance of finding out who killed her?"

I looked long and hard into the woman's eyes, searching for a clue on how to answer. Was she here because she needed someone who knew about such matters to tell her it was finally time to stop? Or was she looking for a glimmer of hope, something to reaffirm what she was doing, had been doing for so many years, was the right thing?

Unable to find the answer in the woman's hazel eyes, I thought about the backlog of open cases, all with achievable results, stacked on the credenza behind me. I went with the truth.

"I'm not very optimistic, Mrs. Bennett," I answered. "But, I never say never."

The edges of the middle-aged woman's mouth tilted upward. She had heard the answer she was looking for.

"Do you still charge the same rate?" Mrs. Bennett asked, rising from her chair.

I extended my hand across the desk. "For such a longtime customer as you, Mrs. Bennett, this year, it's on the house. I'll send you a report with what I find out in a couple weeks."

Mrs. Bennett took my hand in both of hers and squeezed, smiling more widely now. I had the depressing feeling that smiles were scarce in her family.

I walked her back to the lobby and watched her leave.

"What did you tell her?" Evelyn inquired.

"I told her I'd look into it."

Evelyn shook her head and continued typing. "You're not doing her any favors."

The remark made me feel a twinge of guilt. Had I mistakenly given the poor woman hope where none belonged?

Little did I know that seven hundred miles away, events were taking place that would change my outlook...and my life.

| 2 |

The Blog

Lee

Lee Hamilton pressed Enter. That was that.

He pushed away from his desk, clasping his right hand over his left wrist, and stretching his arms taught over his head, making his muscles strain and his back pop. Finally, he relaxed and rolled back upright in the chair with a deep exhale, removed his reading glasses, and flung them onto the desktop next to the keyboard. He rubbed his eyes with his palms for a couple of seconds and wondered whether it was time to get his eyes rechecked.

Through his blurry vision, he looked at the display on his Dell monitor and could still make out the words Your Blog Post Published Successfully boldly written across the upper left-hand corner. Lee felt both relieved, and apprehensive. It felt good to have finally uploaded this blog entry after contemplating it for so long, but it was unlike anything else he had posted—raw and revealing. When writing it, like a good many of the things he wrote, he wasn't sure if he was going to post it at all. He had written the first draft in a single day and then spent the next two weeks fine-tuning it late at night or early in the mornings. Most of his struggles involved how much he should reveal, and what to keep to himself. It was an agonizing exercise.

There was only one other time he had posted an entry this personal since he'd started blogging, and he'd anguished about that post for a long time as well, changing his mind a dozen times before actually doing it. That decision turned out to be the right one because it garnered him the most traffic—or site hits—he'd ever achieved, and it put him on the map as far as the blogger elite go.

Lee had started the blog he innocently entitled *Cruising Altitude* back when blogging was relatively new and the general population was unacquainted with some of the more obscure goings-on the internet offered. He always felt the word itself, blog, seemed to unintentionally demean the concept it was meant to describe because it sounded so hokey.

Lee's blog was an outlet, a way to channel the creative side of himself. The style of writing he had gravitated to over the years typically revolved around articulating examples of the human condition shown in the simple events he witnessed every day. He'd turn those observations into entertaining slices of life stories and, fictionalizing certain aspects, make the tales funnier or more poignant. Sometimes he would step out of his mold and post entirely fictitious stories, being careful to inform his readers of that fact to avoid confusion. He always tried to drive home a central theme, one he hoped would make people feel good, whether writing about the world around him or making things up.

The popularity of *Cruising Altitude* turned out to be a double-edged sword. On the one hand, it flattered him that so many people enjoyed his writing and held it in such high regard, but on the other hand, it brought a type of stress he wasn't used to. He put pressure on himself to keep churning out meaningful and entertaining stories, and it wore on him. What he wished for was a type of anonymous fame, if there was such a thing. At times, he felt like he was producing material for his readers instead of himself, which was completely opposite from the reason he started writing in the first place. He was also continually being approached by marketing firms wanting to take advantage of his internet traffic, to which he flatly refused. It got to a point where he considered shutting down *Cruising Altitude* altogether, but even though he could never bring himself to do that, he did compromise by cutting back on the frequency of his updates.

Lee heard the door to the back deck open and close and then squeaky footsteps heading along the back hallway toward the kitchen.

"Are you finished with the backyard?" he called out, realizing that he no longer heard the lawn mower humming in the background.

His son Chase's voice answered from the kitchen, "Yep." The refrigerator door opened. "I still have to do the weed trimming."

It was mid-July, and true to form for summers in the South, it was the second time the lawn had needed attention this week. His son, who was home for the weekend from the University of Arkansas, surprised him by volunteering to do the chore. Although Lee was perfectly willing and able to mow the lawn himself, he let Chase help. The last few times his son had come home, Lee sensed Chase felt guilty for leaving him to grieve by himself. Lee tried to convince him he was fine and could handle being alone, but Chase still felt the way he felt. His son's way of easing his guilt was to do as many chores as possible while he was home. Lee was more than happy to accommodate by coming up with all kinds of odd jobs.

Thinking about Chase's remorse made him consider the months after his wife's death. It was a black period for Lee and something that still made him grimace whenever he remembered it. Terri's cancer had been aggressive. The doctors had diagnosed her in April 2020, and both children had choosen to forgo college that fall semester, much to their mother's strenuous objections, so they could help her fight the cancer and see her get back on her feet. Unfortunately, the speed at which her condition had deteriorated and her ultimate passing left the entire family devastated. She'd lost her battle in September that year.

Afterward, Lee withdrew from everyone and everything, even Chase and his younger sister, Chloe. Being a devout introvert, nobody but his children could see the difference since he was usually shy and brooding, anyway. His children knew him well enough to see through the emotionless outer shell he used to protect himself during times of stress, but what concerned them the most after their mother was gone was his clear lack of effort. They were deeply worried the loss of their mother, his wife, would cause him to stop trying to connect with people altogether, especially them. They were right to worry.

At first, Lee did the best he could to put aside his anguish and comfort his kids. In the short term, this succeeded, but it wasn't long before he felt himself becoming detached and more isolated than usual. The emotional void of his isolation became filled with numbness, and soon he couldn't even relate to the ones he loved the most.

Although normal was a thing of the past, Lee forged the path out of the pit he had fallen into over time, helped along by tiny nudges from his kids. It began with little everyday activities. Although painful at first because of all the well-wishers and unwelcomed attention, returning to work had been the first significant step. Then daily routines such as going to the athletic club and spending hours on the weight machines and treadmills, or sitting in front of his computer composing stories, all drove out the detachment and replaced it with minor accomplishments and a sense of renewed momentum.

The next rung of the ladder back was the most difficult of all. Lee needed to repair and redefine his relationship with his children. When they needed him most, he had withdrawn, something he hadn't forgiven himself for yet, so asking them for forgiveness was unimaginable. Yet, whether they forgave him or not, he had to develop some semblance of open communication with them, one that could no longer rely on their mother as the intermediary. To do that, he fell back on what he knew best—he wrote. Writing from a place in his heart that he had rarely put to paper, he composed a letter to his children that tried to explain to them just what their mother meant to him and how her loss left an emptiness he was ill-equipped to deal with. He told them he wished he could have been stronger for them, that the shame of who he had become weighed heavily on his soul. Not being able to mend their relationship and relate to them the way their mother always wished would be something he couldn't recover from unless he did something.

Once finished, Lee called his children to him and read them the letter. They shed lots of tears that night. Once they were dried, the three of them talked into the wee hours of the morning. They were a family again.

A month later, Chloe suggested posting the letter on *Cruising Altitude*. Lee admitted to having that same thought, but he hadn't been sure what Chase and Chloe would think. Chloe told him it would be a beautiful blog entry and a fitting tribute to their mother.

With his daughter's continued persistence, he finally posted the letter to his blog three days before Christmas.

The response was amazing. The post had gone viral. Although Lee had never installed a web traffic monitor on his site, one of the marketing firms that had tried to get Lee to link their advertising on his page told him that *Cruising Altitude* peaked at over nine hundred twenty-five thousand hits in one day.

The comments left for him on the blog were just as wonderful. The outpouring of support, from both men and women, genuinely touched Lee. Unfortunately, there were too many of them for him to respond individually to, so his first blog post after the letter was a thank-you to everyone who took the time to leave their thoughts and offer kind words. He pointed out that he had probably hit the high mark of his writing career with that letter, so they shouldn't expect the same quality of content going forward.

In the weeks following the posting of the letter, the traffic on *Cruising Altitude* fell off dramatically, but still maintained a respectable volume. A good portion of the people drawn to his blog because of the letter identified with his overall theme—humorous insights and observations of an average person about everyday life in small-town America. His style of writing struck a chord.

Lee glanced at his monitor screen and suspected that the story he'd just posted might bump up his traffic again, but he always found it difficult to predict what his readers would react favorably to.

Lee used the mouse to position the cursor over the button at the top of the page labeled Home and clicked. The web page where he inputted and posted his blog entry disappeared and was replaced by his blog home page, the name Cruising Altitude displayed across the top. Just below the block where the blog name existed was today's date, Monday, July 19, 2021, and directly below that, he could now see the title of his newly updated blog entry.

Slow Dancer (Part One)

Lee wondered if it would have the desired effect. It had been such a long time.

His fingers tapped the desktop. Finally, he took a deep breath and reached for the keyboard.

Now it was time to send the emails.

| 3 |

Mr. Brown

TJ

He almost missed it. He had been scrolling through lines and lines of data for nearly twenty minutes and had become muddle-headed, the result of a larger-than-usual lunch and an uncomfortably warm cubicle.

TJ had been pestering the maintenance department for weeks to increase the vent's airflow just above his desk because he couldn't feel anything coming out of it. When somebody finally showed up, they informed him that what he thought was a vent was an intake port. The closest AC vent was two cubicles away. To increase the airflow to his area, the thermostat for the entire section would need to be lowered, which would not happen since two of the older women in the cubicles closest to the actual vent were already wearing light wool sweaters. With the temperature outside today projected to go above the century mark, that only fueled TJ's imagined suffocation.

TJ decided to drown his sorrows in victuals. Food was the one constant in TJ's life that could always be counted on to comfort whatever ailed him. Unfortunately, that was also why he pushed the scales at close to three hundred and ten pounds and why his body temperature ran warmer than everybody else's in the office. As far back as he could remember, TJ had always been the biggest kid his age. In school or church, even at his college dormitory, TJ dwarfed everyone around him. His size wasn't because of an overactive pituitary gland or a genetic predisposition to obesity. No, that wasn't it at all. TJ just liked to eat. It was more of a passion. When his classmates were outside taking part in activities such as little league and soccer or developing hobbies like collecting baseball cards or building model airplanes, TJ was mastering his highly refined appetite.

TJ never had many companions growing up, but that wasn't something he dwelled upon. He was more of a loner, anyway. But what few acquaintances he spent time with withered compared to the number of friends he had accumulated online. A longtime avid player of *World of Warcraft* and other online computer games, TJ was an esteemed member of many internet communities that revolved around the games. Going by the profile name of LL&P (Live Long and Prosper), his popularity derived from his generosity with cheat codes and hardware hacks he'd collected over the years, something he had no qualms about sharing. He had also gained a reputation for his willingness to help fellow gamers troubleshoot their systems to squeeze out as much bandwidth as possible and improve a game's performance. All of his experience and helpfulness made LL&P a veritable icon on the internet.

TJ tried to improve his mood by eating a large lunch from one of his favorite restaurants nearby. Bite by bite, his mood improved, and after taking the full measure of his hour lunch break, he returned to his desk emotionally rejuvenated.

It didn't take long before his full stomach, combined with the warm room, went to work on his body and made him drowsy and less focused. The nature of his work didn't help matters either, as

KNIGHT RISE - 17

he found it both dull and beneath him. TJ had been with Homeland Security for just over a year and had been promised by Mrs. Jenkins that he was in line for a promotion to tier-one program analyst any day. Until that time, they relegated him to low-level data specialist tasks, which all new hires had to endure as a way of weeding out the less serious job candidates. Grunt work such as monitoring viruses, worms, trojan horse outbreaks, and scanning internet data reports looking for flags for a specific form of traffic was what his days were filled with. It was all menial work that came nowhere near challenging to him, and he couldn't wait until he moved to the second floor and started creating programs instead of being a simple watchdog.

TJ's large, round head jerked noticeably, and he realized he had nodded off. Even though the entrance to his cubicle faced an open wall, he still took an embarrassed look around to see if anybody had seen him doze. He paused his data feed and wrestled his large body out of the chair they'd had to special order for him, then lumbered down to the end of the hall to the water cooler. He took a sip of the cool water, and then took another before slowly returning to his desk.

With his head clearer, he gazed at the words still displayed on his computer screen and realized he had zoned out for a part of what he had already covered. Most of his coworkers would have simply continued without giving it a second thought, but not TJ. Even though his weight issues made him appear less than enthusiastic about everything besides food, and he felt the work was tedious, TJ still considered himself a conscientious employee. He knew you couldn't make it to the second floor by letting shoddy work go by. He depressed the Page-up button on his keyboard, and the pages of the report rolled back on his screen to where he'd begun when he returned from lunch.

He spotted it on the second page he reread. Any remnants of midafternoon grogginess disappeared, replaced by a burst of energy and a joyful feeling. It was like he had just won an all-you-can-eat pass to his favorite restaurant. He clicked on the Print icon. When it was complete, he snatched a yellow highlighter and lined over the report sections he felt were relevant. He then gathered the paper and headed down the hallway in the opposite direction from the water cooler.

Mrs. Jenkins's office was at the end of cubicle row, just before the elevators. When TJ entered her office, she was talking on the phone. A young woman was standing in front of her desk.

His supervisor was probably in her mid-fifties with pale skin and long, grayish-white hair. Her face was stuck in a perpetual scowl, which matched her mood around the office perfectly. A pair of reading glasses dangled from a chain around her neck.

The person in front of Mrs. Jenkins was another data specialist who had just started a couple weeks ago. She held a pen and notepad in her hands and stood at attention. TJ assumed she was still going through her orientation phase, which meant she would be at Mrs. Jenkins's beck and call for at least a couple more weeks. Poor thing. He considered her above average in the looks department, which was unusual for their line of work, and overly chatty, which was a common trait of most new hires. She gave him an amiable smile and nod. TJ nodded back and stood there silently, waiting.

"Hang on just a second," Mrs. Jenkins said to whoever was on the other end of her phone call, and then placed a hand over the mouthpiece.

She gave TJ an annoyed look. "Yes?"

"I've got a hit on one of my traces," he answered, showing her the papers in his hand.

"Which one?" She reached behind her and pulled a black binder from a bookshelf.

TJ looked to the top of the report. "Taylor/Panama City."

"Just another second," she said into the phone, and then placed the reading glasses on her face. She flipped through the black binder, looking for a particular section. When she found it, she ran her finger down the page, and then stopped about midway. Her face tightened.

"That's a priority file and needs to be reported at once. But I'm going to be tied up here for a while." Her mouth twisted awkwardly, and her eyes took on a distant gaze.

TJ seized the opportunity. "I could take it upstairs for you."

Mrs. Jenkins pulled the glasses from her face, holding them in her hand instead of letting them drop back around her neck.

"You are up for a promotion soon."

"Yes, ma'am."

"Okay," she said, and let her glasses fall, "report your findings to Mr. Brown on the third floor, room 3113, and then come right back here and tell me how he wants to proceed."

"Yes, ma'am!"

The new data specialist smiled more broadly now, sharing in his excitement. If the laws of physics could have been suspended, TJ would have bounded to the elevators.

When he reached the third floor, he stepped into the hallway and proceeded to the receptionist. The woman was in her fifties, dressed in a conservative blue dress and sitting behind a desk shaped in a semicircle with a black marble top. As he approached, he saw the familiar look of repulsion flicker across her face before she could hide her thoughts behind a generic smile. It was the type of greeting TJ usually received from strangers, but he didn't allow it to dim his elation about being anywhere other than the first floor.

"Mr. Brown's office, 3113?" TJ asked.

"Third office on your right," she said coldly.

He walked the sixty feet to the third office. The silver numbers of 3113 on the closed door confirmed he was in the right place. He glanced around and noticed that all the other doors in the hallway were open. Maybe Mr. Brown was holding a meeting or using his speakerphone for a conference call and needed the quiet. But this was a priority file, and it needed to be communicated at once, so TJ took a deep breath and knocked on the door.

No reply.

He waited a suitable amount of time and then knocked again with his beefy knuckles, slightly harder this time.

Still no response.

He looked back down the hallway to the receptionist. She was on the phone. TJ was about to walk back to her desk when he heard the knob turn and the door cracked open.

Before him stood a man in his late forties or early fifties, dressed in a sharp brown suit. Other than his clothes, the first thing TJ noticed about the gentleman was his sandy-colored hair cut in a military-style crew. His eyes were deeply recessed, green, and intense. He held the door partially open with a vacant expression. Even though the man was only an inch taller than TJ and probably only weighed one hundred ninety pounds—a full hundred pounds lighter than him—he still intimidated TJ.

"Mr. Brown?" TJ asked. Any other time, he would comment on the irony of the man's name and the color of his suit or ask him if his favorite NFL team was based in Cleveland, but he didn't feel particularly humorous in this gentleman's presence.

"Yes," the man replied. His voice was low and gravelly. The expression, or nonexpression as it was, still had not changed.

"Mrs. Jenkins sent me up to show you a hit from a priority file."

The man stared at him silently, his head moving ever so slightly as he gave TJ the once over from head to toe.

"Come on in," he finally responded, taking a step backward to give TJ room enough to enter. Once TJ had passed through the door, Mr. Brown closed it behind him. The uneasiness TJ felt al-

KNIGHT RISE - 21

most made him wish that he'd never suggested bringing the report up himself.

Mr. Brown made his way around the opposite side of the desk and took a seat. His movements were measured and purposeful. TJ perused the two chairs with leather cushions and metal handrails in front of the large wooden desk and realized he could never fit his massive body into either of them. A third chair, plain and armless, rested off to the side against the wall. He bypassed the leather chairs and took a seat against the wall.

Two flat-panel monitors positioned side-by-side were centered on the desk, with a keyboard and mouse just in front of them. Other than a multiline phone in the right-hand corner, there was nothing else on the desk. In fact, TJ noticed, there was nothing of a personal nature anywhere in the office. No artwork. No family pictures. No decorations. The man's office was eerily similar to his expression. Vacant.

Mr. Brown took notice of where TJ sat. "How much do you weigh?"

"Excuse me?"

Annoyance was the first emotion that TJ noticed on Mr. Brown's face since meeting him. It obviously perturbed the man that he had to ask a question twice.

"How much do you weigh?" he repeated in the same tone as before.

"Three hundred fourteen pounds," TJ answered honestly.

"Do you experience any breathing problems?"

"Only when the elevators are out and I have to take the stairs." He tried to smile weakly at his own small joke, but the lack of amusement on Mr. Brown's face made it clear that he was only interested in straight answers.

"Why didn't Mrs. Jenkins bring the report herself?" he asked.

"She was busy, but she knew this had to be brought up right away, so I volunteered to do it for her."

"Is that supposed to be an excuse?"

"No, sir. She...uh...I told her I could handle it." TJ wondered if this was what an actual interrogation felt like.

"Who's the report on?"

"Taylor/Panama City. File number 1075-03D."

The first signs of actual emotion surfaced on Mr. Brown's face, his eyes blinking rapidly. If TJ had to guess, he would say it looked like surprise.

Mr. Brown leaned forward and reached for the papers.

"This is it?" he asked, now more animated.

"Yes, sir."

Mr. Brown flipped through the papers, reading all the highlighted sections TJ had marked earlier.

"Remind me what markers we gave you to watch for?"

"Just two. Panama City, Florida, and the name Andi Taylor."

Mr. Brown nodded and continued looking through the papers. TJ sat silently, enjoying the coolness of the air on the third floor. He hoped that the temperature on the second floor was the same.

When he was finished reading, Mr. Brown laid the papers on his desk, got up from his chair, and turned to look out the window behind his desk. TJ could only admire the view of Washington, DC, from his chair.

"I want you to tell Mrs. Jenkins that from this point forward, I want all the raw intel from this IP address sent straight to me. As far as your department is concerned, this folder is now closed." He turned around and finished with, "Do you understand?"

"All intel?" TJ had never heard of raw data being forwarded beyond the first floor before.

"Everything. Emails, internet history, downloads, uploads, I want it all." Mr. Brown's clenched jaw demonstrated his irritation at being forced to clarify his instructions.

TJ rose from his chair. "Yes, sir. Everything to you, we will have no further involvement."

He turned and started toward the door, suddenly eager to return to his hot cubicle.

"Mr. Pickens?"

TJ stopped and turned to face Mr. Brown. "Yes, sir?"

"Good work," Mr. Brown added with a bland expression, then turned and faced the window again.

TJ was out the door and in front of the elevator so quickly that it surprised even him. When the elevator arrived, he stepped in and pushed the button for the first floor, suddenly wondering how Mr. Brown knew his name.

***

The Cat Lady

Once again, she had grabbed too many plastic bags and couldn't open the door leading into the kitchen. She always did this. It wasn't like she was in a hurry. It didn't really matter how many trips she had to make to get the groceries inside, so why did she always load up with so many bags? Especially on the first trip when the door needed to be opened? She tried to finagle her hand to the doorknob without putting anything down, but she could barely carry the bags she was holding, and she hadn't the arm strength to muscle them up even the six inches it would require for her to reach it. The strap of her purse slipped off her shoulder. Exasperated, she put down the bags in her right hand on the landing, reached and opened the door wide, and adjusted the strap of her purse higher on her shoulder.

Then she weaved her fingers back through the plastic handles and picked up the load, heading into the house.

It took her three trips to empty the trunk of her car and place her groceries on the small breakfast table in the kitchen's corner. She at once put the two percent milk and other cold items in the refrigerator but left the rest in their bags on the table. She could put them away later. Right now, she needed to get out of her work clothes and into something more comfortable.

"Whisper," she called out. She walked through the living room to her bedroom, undressing as she went, first kicking off her heels, and then unzipping her tan skirt.

"Whisper, I'm home," she called again as she went, looking around curiously. Her bedroom was brightly lit from the late afternoon sun that streamed in through the west-facing windows. Tiny particles of dust floated within the beam of sunlight, reminding her of white flecks gently suspended in the fluid inside the transparent sphere of a snow globe. Tossing her skirt and blouse onto her neatly made king-sized bed covered with half a dozen small pillows, she closed the curtains on either side of the bed. In the room's corner was a small antique desk with only a laptop on top of it. She raised the computer's cover, pressed the power button, and then disappeared through a door that led back into a walk-in closet.

After changing into a green T-shirt with a floral design stitched across the chest matched with gray sweatpants and a pair of furry green socks, she went directly from the closet through another door that led to the bathroom. She switched on the bank of lights above the large mirror, picked up the hairbrush from the counter, and started combing her long, nearly black hair.

She thought it was time to make another appointment to have her hair colored to eliminate the gray. It was peeking through again. If only some of the other signs of aging could be fixed as easily as her hair. If she had the money, she'd like to do something about the crow's-feet that had appeared around her eyes and some of the flap on her neck. And while she was dreaming, she may as well restore some of the bounciness to her breasts. She knew she could never afford it, though.

As she walked out into the dim bedroom, she noticed something stir on the bed.

"There's my Whisper," she said. She picked up a white Persian cat just awaking from a spot among the pillows. Whisper's blue-green eyes closed tight as the woman embraced her. A soothing purr indicated her pleasure with the attention.

Carrying the pet, she returned to the antique desk. The laptop was fully powered up and ready to receive a sign-on request. She sat in the petite desk chair and typed in her user ID and password. After the Windows logo had flashed on the screen and the numerous background programs had loaded, she clicked on the icon to bring up her email. Whisper's purring grew louder as she subconsciously stroked the cat's long fur while waiting for the next screen to display.

When she could finally access her inbox, she saw sixteen new emails, but one caught her attention. The subject line read, **Cruising Altitude Posted A New Blog 7/21/21 6:51:14 p.m.** She tossed Whisper back onto the bed, which drew an indignant look from the now fully awake cat, and then moved her mouse to click on the icon that brought up the Chrome browser. Once activated, she clicked on a phrase in the toolbar entitled Favorites, which brought up a drop-down box from which she then clicked on the words *Cruising Altitude*.

She could feel the excitement and anticipation building, and she cursed the speed of her internet connection as she waited for the screen to refresh. His blog postings had become so infrequent that she relished them when they appeared. Her students at Lincoln Junior High would say that her mood was considerably more buoyant for days after reading one of his postings. She couldn't disagree with their observation.

A couple of seconds later, her Yahoo home page was replaced by a page entitled **CRUISING ALTITUDE** with a sub-title of **I MAY NOT BE THE LIFE OF THE PARTY ~ BUT I'M CERTAINLY ITS SOUL.** As blogging sites went, she had to admit that this one was thin on the style and glitzy graphics that some of the more popular ones made use of, but that hardly mattered when it was the content that drew you in. Columns on both the right and left sides of the screen were emblazoned with a brown paisley pattern. The middle section had old faded yellow parchment that was darker at the edges, giving it an outlined effect. The far-left side of the middle section was an area that detailed the archives by month, with links to each. Directly in the middle of the page, it read:

MONDAY, JULY 19, 2021
SLOW DANCER (Part One)

When she saw the blog title, her blood ran cold in her veins, and her throat felt dry. Could he be writing about what she thought he was? Surely not. It had been so long ago, a whole other lifetime ago. Why would he be writing about that now?

Quit speculating and just read it.

By the time she reached the third paragraph, her hand had started tugging on the pair of gold studs in her right ear.

"Oh, God."

| 4 |

Slow Dancer I

MONDAY, JULY 19, 2021
SLOW DANCER (Part One)

Welcome back, faithful readers!

If you'll indulge me, today I've decided to offer you something completely different. Something other than my hokey observations about the world and homespun advice. We're all a bit tired of that, am I right? What follows is a piece that is incredibly special to me. Although everything I post always comes from honest contemplation, this slice is profoundly personal and a bit of a watershed moment for me. Thank you in advance for letting me bend your ear (or eyes, as it may be) to this.

This is a tale about a long-forgotten memory I unearthed a couple of weeks ago. It revolves around the people in that memory, the anguish it caused me, and how I ultimately dealt with it. It is a story of friendship, lost love, and seeking redemption. For reasons that will become obvious after completing the entire story, I debated long and hard the decision to post this. In the end, I decided it was something that I had to do for several reasons, which I will discuss afterward. For now, just enjoy the story.

This is rather long, so I've broken it up into six sections for ease of reading.

Hopefully, I won't bore you too much.

It started with a song.

I'd been sorting through another box of my old vinyl records, preparing to convert them to digital, when I stumbled across the album I now held in my hands. There was something curious about this one, something that went beyond music and wouldn't let go of my attention.

Most of the album covers in my collection had faded artwork with tattered and frayed corners from years of handling. This one was in pristine condition, even down to the shrink wrap that still clung to it.

An outline of the East Coast was on the cover, with a Polaroid picture superimposed on top of it, depicting a man and woman building a snowman together. It was the soundtrack for a totally forgettable film released in the spring of 1990. Along the top edge of the cover, the contributing musicians were listed - mostly country. These artists were out of place among the vast majority of hardcore rock 'n' roll I had collected over the years.

I was about to dismiss the album and place it in the stack with the others I'd designated as not worth converting, but something made me give it a second look. At first, I just stared at it because I was unsure why I owned it and how it was in my possession, but slowly I sensed that there was something deeper, something more significant about this record. There must be a song on the album that was important...especially important.

When I began converting my albums to digital, I discovered that besides reconnecting with hundreds of songs I hadn't listened to in years, I also uncovered a treasure trove of memories. Every night and on weekends, I could be found at my desk, the turntable spinning, headphones haphazardly positioned on my ears, reading the liner notes on the vintage album covers as I listened to the old tunes. When I started the endeavor, I knew it would be an incredible journey down memory lane, but I had not adequately prepared for the road I was about to travel.

I flipped the album over and quickly scanned the track listings. My eyes locked onto the last song on Side A, and my pulse skipped a beat, maybe even two. I suddenly felt a sense of despondency growing in the center of my chest, an aching like the one I felt whenever I thought about my late wife. Thinking back on it now, I believe it was a pang caused by the heart remembering what the brain chose not to.

I immediately stopped the album already spinning on the turntable, hurriedly removed the soundtrack from the cardboard outer cover and paper inner sleeve, and placed it on the platter. I positioned the stylus over the beginning of the last song on Side A, flipped the lever that allowed the tone arm to slowly descend to the vinyl, and raised the volume on my computer a couple ticks. I adjusted the headphones dangling around my neck until they covered my ears, and I sat back in the chair.

When the first couple of notes filtered through my headset, they engulfed me with a mixture of melancholy and nostalgia, and even more prominently, a sense of longing. This sudden flood of emotions rocked me, many of which I hadn't experienced in an awfully long time. I closed my eyes and was instantly transported back twenty-nine years to a place that was both physically and emotionally far removed from where I was now. As the song continued, more neurons in my brain fired for the first time in decades, awaking from their prolonged hibernation. The jumbled details of a four-day period during the summer of 1992 rushed back to me, and piece by piece, I slowly organized the fragments into a coherent memory. It was a memory I had unconsciously buried deep within myself and hadn't thought about since before my marriage to Terri.

My brain had finally caught up with my heart.

When the song ended and all that remained was the rhythmic clicking of the needle as it tried unsuccessfully to move to the end of the album, I awoke from the trance I had fallen into. I realized my eyes had filled with tears, while at the same time, I felt myself smiling. This was a bittersweet memory I had never shared with my wife. It was a memory, parts of which I had never shared with anybody.

I wiped the tears from my eyes, reached over to the turntable, and picked the arm up to return it to the beginning of the song. I wanted to go back again. I needed to go back again.

I owed her that. I owed all of them that.

What follows is where that memory took me.

**

During the summer of 1992, I had just completed my freshman year at LSU. I had already moved back home to live with my parents to conserve money and had a summer job lined up working construction at the naval base in New Orleans. But what I really wanted to do before I started earning money was take time to decompress from the long school year and have a little fun. Everyone was heading to the Florida beaches for a massive blowout, and I desperately wanted to do the same. There were a couple of problems, though. The first, I didn't have two quarters in my pocket to rub together, much less money enough to afford a trip like that. The second, I didn't have anyone to go with.

When I stepped onto the LSU campus, as I had done so many times at a new school while growing up as a military family member, I didn't know a soul. I laid my hopes for a dramatically different life on the belief that my pre-assigned roommate, whom I had never met, would be a person I might forge a friendship with, and things could grow positively from there. But unfortunately, it didn't quite go as planned.

Almost a week into the start of classes, I was still waiting for my roommate to appear. After checking with the floor monitor, they informed me that my potential roommate had a change of heart about attending school and wouldn't be coming. The school would assign me a new roommate as soon as things settled down, so I should be patient and enjoy having the room to myself. I spent the entire fall semester alone, and since I was both introverted and shy, friendless as well.

On the first day of the spring semester, I answered a knock on my door to see a boy about my height and weight with an enormous nose and loosely hanging straight hair cut in a bowl shape standing in front of me. He bounced into the room and started curiously checking things out as he went about introducing himself. His name was Mark Sigmar, and he told me he was transferring to this room from a dormitory that lacked air conditioning. Not only did he investigate the empty side of the room, but he also checked out my belongings, including the contents of my refrigerator.

Sitting on opposite beds from one another, we talked for a couple of minutes about random topics. It turned out Mark's parents had also recently moved to New Orleans and didn't live too far from my parents. He was a massive music buff, and when he asked me what kind of music I listened to, I couldn't give him an answer. That gave him pause, but then he said he could make it work as long as it wasn't country. The more he told me about himself, the more I became excited about his moving in. This was the type of friend I was hoping to find at LSU.

But once again, things didn't go as planned, at least at first.

I learned that Mark had grown up and gone to high school in the neighboring city of Lafayette before moving to New Orleans, and he hung out exclusively with four friends from that school. The five of them, Mark, Kent, Billy, Raymond, and Ebe, were inseparable. Kent and Ebe were roommates, as were Raymond and Billy, all in rooms in a different wing, and that's where Mark spent all his time. I hardly saw my new roommate.

Before breaking for the summer, I overheard Mark talking on the phone to one of the others about the possibility of a post-semester trip to Florida (that's kind of where I got the idea), but they were having difficulty arranging transportation. None of them had a car big enough or dependable enough to make the drive to Florida and back. That's when I formulated a plan.

I was the proud owner of a green 1966 Chevy van, ideal for transporting six people to Florida and back in relative comfort. Being a business major, I called Mark and made him a mutually beneficial proposition. My van would be the group's transportation to and from Florida, with me doing all the driving, and in return, they would take me along and cover all my expenses, including drinks! After a quick phone call to the rest of the group, they agreed, and the trip was set. We all rendezvoused in a church parking lot close to my house the first week of June, and then left for Panama City.

I learned a lot about my five companions during the six-hour drive, including something that instantly sealed our friendship.

Raymond James and Mark had been friends since childhood. Raymond was tall but thin, and that, combined with a jutting jawline, made him appear almost like a caricature. His face showed signs of a past acne problem, and his black hair was always perfectly combed. He was an above-average basketball player, extremely competitive—overly so sometimes. Raymond was in law school, which matched his opinionated disposition.

The athletic leader of the group was Billy Wister. Billy was rambunctious and full of nonstop energy. He was constantly dealing with injuries, such as skinned knuckles from trying to learn how to do handstands while skateboarding or a twisted ankle after trying to jump from a second-story window to the ground on a dare. Once a popular high school football star and consummate athlete, Billy now took part in every intramural activity he could find time for. He had curly brown hair, a perfectly chiseled body, and looks that would make most girls swoon. But seriousness in his athletic pursuits was as far as Billy could ever manage because his hyperactivity and inability to sit still plagued him in the classroom. I envied him the most because he could go up to any girl and start a conversation on any subject. However, he rarely took anything seriously, which is probably why he never had a steady girlfriend. The only time he was still and at peace was when he was playing his guitar. While the others enjoyed listening to music, Billy played it.

Kent "Shades" Jones was the jokester in the group. He was of Asian descent and not blessed with particularly good looks or physical stature. He had dark rings under his sunken eyes that he hid by wearing sunglasses, mid-length unkempt hair, an extremely thin build, a wardrobe most likely stolen from the set of *Hair*, and a carefree attitude.

Kent's laid-back personality was probably what attracted Ebe when it came time to choosing a college roommate. At first, it mystified me that Steven Ebe had fallen in with the group because he was so different from the others. Ebe's parents had moved to the United States from Belgium a couple of years before he was born. He grew up freckled with flaming red hair—which he'd let grow down to his narrow shoulders—completely unathletic, never made a grade lower than an A, and had a dry wit legendary for being razor sharp. He was the most challenging group member to figure out with a facial expression stuck in the thoughtful mode. He was the type of person adept at sarcasm but would never resort to ridicule, and he was probably the most serious-minded. A person of few words, Ebe's character traits were the closest to my own, which is why I couldn't understand what drew the others to him. That is, until the first time a song played on the radio that I didn't recognize.

Ebe's ticket into the group was punched at an early age. After hearing just thirty seconds of any song, he could quote the band name, song title, album, year of release, band members (including which instruments they played), and all of the other albums released. He was a musical historian.

Listening to everyone's banter as we drove, I found keeping up with their conversations difficult. They were all adept at lightning-fast comebacks and hysterical non sequiturs. I tried my best to hold my own, but I ended up just listening and occasionally answering a question. It wasn't until somebody mentioned Monty Python that things changed.

Monty Python's Flying Circus was a British comedy sketch show broadcast on the BBC from 1969 to 1974, but it found larger scope and impact in reruns, spawning many albums, stage shows, and five theatrically released films. I had stumbled across one of their albums when I was in high school and instantly fell in love with their non-traditional brand of humor. I started accumulating as much of their work as I could get my hands on. You can imagine my excitement when I discovered the others shared my love for the comedy troupes work, especially the film *Monty Python and the Holy Grail*. I earned my stripes with the gang as they tested me with Python trivia. It became commonplace for any of us to randomly quote something from Python.

After that, things changed. I had become one of the group, and it was a feeling that I hadn't felt in an extremely long time. As our van crossed the Florida border, I couldn't help but feel my fortune had finally traversed its own sort of boundary. Things were looking up.

What I didn't realize was for how short a time that would be.

| 5 |

Slow Dancer II

MONDAY, JULY 19, 2021
SLOW DANCER (Part Two)

Panama City Beach during the first couple weeks after college finals in the summer could only be equaled by Panama City Beach during spring break. For the uninitiated, it was truly a sight to be seen. The city's average population swelled to four times its size, and frenzied college students were everywhere looking for ways to celebrate their temporary freedom from lectures, tests, and round-the-clock cram sessions. Hotel rooms, motel rooms, cabins, condos, and campsites were filled beyond normal room occupancy limits. The two-and-a-half-mile Front Beach Road that ran parallel to the Gulf of Mexico and its glorious white sand beach was jammed with cars, trucks, vans, and motorcycles, most of them cruising for no other reason than to be noticed. The beaches were congested with sunbathers, volleyball games, and guys 'n' gals throwing Frisbees or footballs. The human overflow backed up into the nearby hotels where reclining chairs jockeyed for position around the pools and the chlorinated water churned from college kids escaping the heat or playing childhood-favorite games like chicken fights, belly flop contests, or Marco Polo. Half-naked bodies, suntan lotion, beach towels, sunglasses, coolers full of beer, and red smiling faces were at every turn. There was indeed a paradise, and I had found it.

Once we arrived and acquainted ourselves with the surroundings, it didn't take us long to fall into a routine. Waking around noon, we first ravaged the closest eatery, and then it was off to the beach. Billy gravitated to the volleyball matches, Raymond and Ebe did some tanning (with Ebe fully clothed), Mark and Kent body surfed, and I tried a bit of everything. No matter what we were doing, all of us scoped the girls, and they scoped us right back. Late afternoon or early evening would be time for a quick nap, and then it was off for more food before returning to the beach or pool for more girl scoping. Finally, around nine p.m., we started taking turns in the bathroom and in front of the mirrors, getting ready to head out to the clubs for the night. Usually, around ten p.m., we walked out the door for a long night of drinking and dancing.

After making the rounds of all the local clubs the first night, we settled on one club—the Sunset Club—as our favorite hangout. I could say we chose that one because it was where the most girls seemed to gravitate because of the club's humongous dance floor, or the bartenders didn't water down the drinks as much as some of the other clubs, but the plain fact was that they let us in despite being only twenty years old.

The Sunset Club sat on the back end of a large lot with limited parking in front and two smaller clubs on either side of it. Although it didn't appear like much from the curb, just a dark wood-paneled building with no fluorescent lights or any other glitz decorating its outside facade, what the club lacked in curb appeal it made up for on the inside. When you entered, it was a short walk down a hallway on the left side of the building, which opened into a dark, windowless room lit mainly from the lights illuminating the vast dance floor in the center of the room. The bar ran along the wall to the right as you entered the room. There were tables and chairs between the bar and the dance floor, with more along the walls on either side of the dance floor. The wall on the right side of the room was adorned with various paintings of beach settings and different seaside paraphernalia, such as boat paddles, ring buoys, and so on. The opposite wall was covered with hundreds of eight-by-ten-inch framed photos of people who were willing to pay the seventy-five-dollar fee for the privilege of having their photo hung on the club's aptly named Wall of Shame for prosperity. On the ceiling above the dance floor was a dizzying array of lamps, colored lights, strobes, and the requisite mirror ball hanging directly over its center. At the front of the room, behind a three-foot wall separating the area from everything else, was the DJ with all his special equipment. It would have been easy to believe that instead of just being used to boom out the latest dance tune, he was using all of that equipment to coordinate a NASA rocket launch.

It was late in the evening on our third night in Panama City, and I was sitting at a table up against the wall underneath an old volleyball net with Ebe and Kent discussing such highbrow topics as the proper technique for igniting farts. I couldn't recall ever laughing so much in my life. Meanwhile, Billy, Raymond, and Mark had endeared themselves to a couple of co-eds at a table closer to the bar.

Kent noticed I was looking over the crowd and asked, "Is it still the same girl?"

I paused a moment until I completed my scan and then said, "Same girl, orange tank top. No change."

"I still think you're nuts," Kent replied.

I had developed a ritual when we arrived at a club, where I would look over the crowd and choose the most beautiful girl there. Of course, none of the girls I selected realized the dubious honor bestowed upon them because I could never muster the courage to talk to any of them, but that was beside the point. After selecting the prettiest girl, I'd keep tabs on her in case she left, and a new girl had to be chosen. On rare occasions, sometimes a new arrival could even bump an earlier selection from her throne.

That evening, shortly after we arrived, I carefully checked the crowd, and my gaze kept returning to a girl who was about an inch taller than me, athletically built, and simply dressed. She was wearing layered tank tops with bright orange on top of plain white, dark-blue capris belted with a scarf that resembled a white handkerchief, and a pair of white skimmer boat shoes. She had either black or mahogany-brown hair cut in a wedge style made famous by Dorothy Hamill, a cute pixie-like nose that made a slight upturn at its end, and eyes that sparkled even in the dimly lit room. Her overall facial features, combined with a dark golden tan, suggested Mediterranean in her family heritage. But what really caught my eye was her smile. Her entire face seemed to light up whenever her perfect alabaster teeth, all thirty-two of them, peeked through her petite mouth.

"Orange tank top," I announced when I had made my decision.

"Oh, come on, the girl in the light green dress we saw on our way in is much prettier than that one, and her tits are twice as big," Kent protested.

"My game, my choice," I replied offhandedly.

"But what about the blonde at that table over there? The one with the fancy necklace," Kent tried again.

"She is stunning," I said, giving the blonde a second look, "but I'm sticking with the orange tank."

"I agree with Lee," Ebe interjected. "She's a viable choice."

"You both don't know how to appreciate a magnificent pair of breasts," Kent observed, and was off to get the first round of drinks.

Kent was right, but not about the breasts. Although there were girls at the Sunset Club that night who were maybe more "classically" beautiful or eloquently outfitted, even more anatomically gifted, there was something about the girl in the orange tank top. Perhaps the simplicity in the way she dressed or the way she carried herself set her apart from the others. She exuded a self-confidence that didn't come off as conceitedness, and when she smiled, it lit up the room. There wasn't any one thing I could point out to Kent that made her stand out, but she was definitely my number one.

When it came to clubbing, I was the proverbial wallflower. I'd gotten accustomed to my perpetual bashfulness, much unlike my friends who were approaching and carousing with girls they'd just met. As the night went on, I was content to sit back and watch everybody else enjoy themselves. I had constant company, though. Ebe apparently wasn't too keen on chasing girls, either.

"Why aren't you out there dancing?" I asked him finally.

With a straight face, he answered casually, "Because I'm gay."

That took me by surprise. "Oh," I simply replied.

"That's not a problem, is it?" he asked pointedly.

"No, not at all," I said.

If there had been silence in the room, it would have been an uncomfortable one.

"Is anyone else?" I asked, suddenly unsure.

"Anyone else what?"

"Gay?"

"Sure, there are loads of us."

"That's not what I mean. Are any of the other guys gay?"

"No, just me," Ebe responded matter-of-factly and turned his attention back to the dance floor.

We sat there for a minute, each with his own thoughts.

"You know," I began, "just because you're gay doesn't mean you can't still have fun and dance, right?"

Ebe smiled at that. "No, it doesn't. But my two left feet do. What's your excuse?"

"Me? I'm still working up the courage to ask someone."

"How long does that usually take?"

"I'm going on my twentieth year."

We both laughed, and then looked at Kent sitting at the other end of the table. He was scanning the crowd for what would ultimately be his one thousandth rejection. I had to admire his determination.

I spotted Billy and Raymond dancing just off to the right of our table with the girls they had become chummy with. Both guys were talented dancers, and the girls were working hard to not be overshadowed. As I watched them displaying their moves, I noticed the girl in the orange tank top was now on the dance floor next to them with the guy she had arrived with. Her partner was a decent-looking fella, a couple inches taller than she was, sharply dressed, and an adequate dancer. I was just about to see where Mark had wandered off to when I noticed something odd. The girl in the orange tank top was staring at me. When our eyes met, I immediately looked away and pretended to be interested in something else, my heartbeat pounding hard in my chest. However tipsy I may have been quickly dissipated, and I sat straight up in my chair. I discreetly looked around at the tables near ours, but there was just me, Ebe, and Kent. Could she really be staring at me? I waited a minute before I stole a second glance in her direction. The guy she was with was now whispering something in her ear, to which she laughed at. I told myself that the alcohol was playing tricks on me, and I was ready to declare myself the winner of the most shit-faced award. I peeked in her direction a third time and saw that they were moving to a table directly opposite ours across the dance floor.

I vaguely recall Kent and Ebe having a conversation at the time that involved a woman's bra and silly putty, but my attention kept being pulled elsewhere.

Once more, I glimpsed at the table across the dance floor, *and she was staring at me again.* This time I mustered all the willpower I possessed, as well as whatever courage the alcohol provided, to force myself to not turn away. My eyes locked onto hers, and, almost at once, I felt the impulse to do the complete opposite. I was about to lose it and look away when a small, almost imperceptible smile appeared at the corners of her mouth, and then she slowly looked away. *Oh, shit...oh, shit...oh, shit,* I said to myself. *I'm not that drunk... Am I? She's gorgeous, she's with a guy with obviously lots more money than I have, and she is staring at me!* And this wasn't just any girl. This was, by my own definition, the most beautiful girl in the club!

Still not trusting my own senses, I leaned over to Ebe.

"Ebe, is it me, or is that girl in the orange tank top sitting directly opposite from us over there staring at me?"

Even if Ebe hadn't been sitting next to me, I still would have gone around the table to ask him because I knew he could be discreet, no matter how much he'd had to drink. Kent would have leaped to his feet and marched right over to the other table to ask this mysterious girl why she was staring at his friend and then asked her if she wanted to have sex.

I watched as Ebe looked across the dance floor, struggling to make his eyes focus, and then he turned back.

"It's not your imagination," he said. "She's definitely looking over here."

I wasn't sure where all the blood in my body had disappeared to, but there definitely wasn't any in my head because I felt extremely dizzy. My ears were even tingling.

"Shit, what do I do?"

"Go ask her to dance, stupid," Ebe almost laughed.

"But I'm like you. I can't dance!"

And I couldn't. At least I thought so. I had always felt stiff and robotic when I'd tried it before, and since I couldn't work up the courage to ask anybody to dance, anyway, I abandoned any efforts to learn. Whether I looked stupid when I danced didn't matter. I believed I looked that way. But dancing would be my only chance at meeting this girl because there was no way I would be able to just walk up to her and begin a conversation. That simply would not happen. I was screwed.

At that very moment, the planets must have aligned because the DJ started a new song. And it was a *slow song*. Shit, even I could slow dance, I thought. I recognized the tune as an older song the clubs played that summer, and it had struck a chord with everyone because whenever it came on, the dance floor filled with couples. This was going to be my chance, but there was still one problem. The guy she was with. My briefly lifted spirits sank again as I thought her companion would surely take her back out to dance to this song. I looked over at their table, expecting to see them rising and headed for the dance floor, but it was only the guy who got up and headed toward the bar. *This is it*, I thought. *This is my chance! Go!*

"What's going on?" Kent asked.

"That girl in the orange tank is making eyes at Lee, and he's going over there to ask her to dance," Ebe answered.

As I got up and started across the dance floor, I heard Kent yell, "Ask her if she wants to have sex with me."

Later, I would say unequivocally that the walk across that dance floor was the longest stroll of my life. More couples were spilling onto the floor, delaying my progress. I wasn't even sure I'd be able to speak when the time came. The whole thing was all so surreal and dreamlike. Halfway there, I decided I might be making a grave mistake. Something suddenly convinced me that when I arrived at her table, she would stare at me like something she found stuck to the bottom of her shoe. Or even worse, the guy she was with would show up and try to stick me to the bottom of *his* shoe. The only reason I didn't reverse course was that I knew that Kent and Ebe were watching my every move, and to return without even asking meant evisceration by my new friends. I had put myself in a position where I faced either public ruin or private humiliation. Charlie Brown couldn't hold a candle to me!

I was just steps away from her table when she looked up, spotted me coming toward her, and smiled. And this time, it was a full-blown, honest-to-goodness smile. In the radiance of that smile, my chest puffed out, the curve in my back straightened, and I felt like I grew six inches. A feeling came over me I could not describe, other than to say that I could never remember feeling that confident. At that moment, I could have run through a brick wall or stood before hundreds of strangers, naked, to give a speech about syphilis. My nervousness was gone.

"Would you like to dance?" I croaked out.

"I thought you'd never ask," she replied as she rose from her chair.

We joined the others out on the dance floor, maneuvering to find a sliver of open space. I put my hands on her hips, and she clasped hers around my neck. Our eyes remained locked. For the first few moments, all we did was do as the song commanded, sway to the music. She was even more beautiful up close than I'd imagined. Her dark eyebrows and full lips stood out despite only the slightest hint of makeup. Her emerald-green eyes sparkled and instantly mesmerized me. The only jewelry she was wearing was a pair of gold studs, both in her right earlobe. Her smile remained, and I desperately hoped I appeared calm despite the Snoopy Dance taking place inside my head.

"Thought you'd never ask?" I finally said, leaning in close so I didn't need to shout above the music.

"I've been trying to get you to notice me for a while," she answered boisterously.

"Really? And what about the guy you came here with?"

"Mike? He's a local. My family and his family know each other, and I promised my parents I would let him take me out one night while I was down here this year." Her smile still hadn't diminished.

"Not your type, then?"

"Not really. He's just a friend."

The two of us rocked back and forth, looking into each other's eyes.

"Well, you're lucky this song came on when it did," I started again, surprised that I didn't have to think about what I wanted to say next. "Dancing isn't something I'm good at. I'm really just a slow dancer."

"Me, too."

I looked at her skeptically. "I've seen you dance. You do fine."

"I didn't say I couldn't dance. I just meant that I prefer the slow ones," she corrected me, the look in her eyes letting me know she wasn't the type of girl who agreed to something just to be nice.

"If your friend Mike hadn't gotten up to get a drink, I probably wouldn't be here right now," I confessed.

"That wasn't luck," she said, the intensity of her smile brightening ever so slightly. I could now see in her expression a measure of pride. "I asked him to get me a drink when I heard this song play, hoping you would take the chance."

"You're kidding."

"Nope. I tried to make it as easy as I could for you."

At that point, I started wondering when I was going to wake up because this had to be a dream. The incredible feeling when she first smiled at me had intensified twofold. Boldly, my hands reached a

little farther behind her, and I pulled her closer to me. She reciprocated by putting her head on my shoulder. Together we became one
with the music. It was truly a magical moment.

As the end of the song approached, I was unsure how to handle
what might happen next.

"Listen, would you and your friend want to come sit at our
table?"

She picked her head up from my shoulder and said, "Mike has
to get back, and I promised my roommates I'd be in by one o'clock.
Can you meet me at my hotel, and we can take a walk on the beach?"

"Sure. Where are you staying?"

"The Regency."

"We're staying at the White Sands cabins only a mile up the
beach from there. But I'm here with a group of my friends in my
van, so I have to herd all of them back to the cabin first."

"I'll wait for you."

"That's great. It would probably help if I knew your name, so I
don't have to call 'hey you' when we see each other again," I pointed
out.

"I'm Andi."

"Andy?" I asked, giving her a curious look.

"Andi with an *i*."

I smiled and said, "I like that. I'm Lee."

She smiled back at me, then returned her head to my shoulder,
and we continued to dance to the song that was quickly being etched
into a special place in my memory.

The music slowly faded away and was quickly replaced by C +
C Music Factory's up-tempo "Gonna Make You Sweat," but we remained on the floor a few seconds longer. Neither of us wanted to
relinquish the thank you/goodbye hug we had slipped into.

"See you in a little while," she said when we finally broke apart. I headed over to the group, fighting the urge to look back. As I approached our table, it surprised me to see all five of the gang sitting there watching my return.

"Hey, stud," Billy shouted.

"Man, that grin is going to leave permanent stretch marks," Raymond added.

"So, does she want to have sex with me?" Kent asked.

I grabbed an empty chair from a nearby table and pulled it over to ours, straddling it. For a moment, all I did was grin at the group. Regardless of the circumstances, being the center of attention wasn't something I was comfortable with.

"I don't think he can talk. His tongue is hard," Ebe observed, which elicited laughter from everyone.

"She turned him into a newt," Raymond said, making the mandatory Python reference.

"You guys ready to go?" I finally asked.

"No," they all replied in unison.

"Come on, guys, I'm supposed to meet her back at her hotel," I pleaded.

Billy looked across the room to where Andi and Mike were still sitting. "She doesn't look like she's going anywhere to me," he said.

I looked over my shoulder at them, and it was true. The two of them didn't give any indications they were about to leave.

"She's probably explaining why she was off dancing with somebody else while he was getting her a drink," Ebe offered in explanation.

"That is a good question. Why was she?" Kent pointed out.

"Because I asked her, Kent, and she said yes," I countered, a bit perturbed.

"Aren't you leery of a girl who's on the prowl for somebody else when she's already here on a date?" Mark asked.

"She's only friends with that guy. Their families know each other. Is that so impossible to believe?"

Nobody answered, but their faces weren't saying yes. I briefly considered giving up the argument and just leaving them behind and making them walk back to the White Sands, but my food, drink, and alcohol for the rest of the week depended on them, and I felt it better to not bite the hand that literally fed me.

Finally, after a considerable amount of begging and pleading, I got them to compromise by promising to stay just thirty more minutes.

Once we had an agreement, I looked over in Andi's direction just in time to see them getting up to leave, with a couple of untouched drinks left on the table. Before she disappeared down the hallway exit, she looked back and flashed me another one of her smiles.

This was going to be the longest thirty minutes of my life, I thought to myself.

| 6 |

Slow Dancer III

MONDAY, JULY 19, 2021
SLOW DANCER (Part Three)

Thirty minutes stretched into forty-five, and then an hour. Every attempt I made to get everyone rounded up to leave was met by some lame excuse. Kent was in the bathroom, Billy had just gotten a fresh drink, or Mark was dancing again. With every passing minute, I could feel my opportunity slipping away, and with it, my patience.

Finally, I couldn't take it any longer, and I tossed my keys to Ebe and told him to make sure everybody got back to the cabin okay—I was going to walk to the Regency. Ebe offered to drive me there, but finding a parking space at that time of night when he returned would be impossible, and then he'd be forced to leave the van on the street in an illegal parking zone. As we'd seen on previous nights, the Panama City police force took their parking violations seriously. I told him thanks, but no thanks; I'd rather not have my van towed.

Not long after I had set off walking, I suspected I had misjudged how long it would take me to get to the Regency, but going back would waste even more time. So even though I knew it would make me a sweaty, out-of-breath mess, I jogged.

The late-night ocean air was sticky, but the breeze from the beach felt cool on my slightly sunburned face as I ran. Passing by the other clubs, closed businesses, late-night delicatessens, twenty-four-hour liquor stores, and street vendors, I had time to think about the significance of what had happened at the club.

I didn't believe in love at first sight. Sure, there was the primal animal attraction thing, but saying a person could feel love for somebody before they ever get to know them demeaned the true meaning of love. What happened with Andi made me think twice.

Almost a full two hours after I told Andi I would meet her, I arrived at the Regency. Coming to a standstill in the parking lot to catch my breath, I stood there bent over with my hands on my thighs, huffing and puffing. I checked my wristwatch, and it showed quarter to three in the morning.

The Regency was one of the newest and nicest hotels along the Panama City strip, and one of the most expensive. Its seven floors towered over the much smaller hotels in the vicinity. With its own private pier out over the Gulf of Mexico and not one but three large pools for the guests to lounge around, the hotel was most certainly booked solid through the summer. And because it was one of the more expensive hotels along the strip, it wasn't the destination of choice for your typical college student.

As I entered through the swinging doors of the main entrance, a rush of cool, dehumidified air greeted me. The lobby was immense and decorated by large leafy tropical plants scattered throughout the room. Three of the four walls were solid glass, the lone exception being the barrier at the head of the room where the check-in counter stood. Just to the right of the counter was a hallway leading into the depths of the hotel. Tucked into one corner was a TV stand with a twenty-seven-inch television opposite a couch and a couple of chairs. The TV was tuned to a rerun of *Three's Company*.

Andi was nowhere to be seen.

I sat on the couch and pretended to watch TV, hoping that she might yet appear, not knowing what else to do. Finally, after twenty minutes of no movement, I walked around to see if maybe she was at one of the pools. I went over our last conversation in my head, and I couldn't remember if she specifically said meet in the lobby, so I decided not to give up just yet. I searched all the pools, hot tubs, and communal areas around the Regency, to no avail. Andi was nowhere to be seen. Finally, I reconciled myself to the fact that I was too late. I didn't know Andi's last name, so trying to find her room would be fruitless. I stood in the lobby again, trying to think of some way I could get word to her, letting her know I had shown up, that I didn't just blow her off. Short of pulling a scene out of *A Streetcar Named Desire* and standing in the parking lot screaming Andi's name, I didn't know what to do. Dejected, I began my trek back to the cabin.

Feeling sorry for myself, I thought what better way to sulk than trudging back on the beach. I pulled off my shoes and socks and descended the stairs alongside the Regency that led down to the beach, and I started making my way back.

I knew it was too good to be true, I told myself as I walked, and that something was going to mess it up. That was the story of my romantic life, or lack thereof. Anytime there was even a hint of something between me and a girl, life would slam the door right on my fingers. Frustrated didn't begin to describe how I felt. I could have easily been angry at my buddies for delaying me, but I couldn't blame them for not wanting to sacrifice their fun for my wild goose chase. I debated turning around and camping out in the Regency's lobby until she came down the next morning, but I discarded that idea because I felt it made me look too desperate, which I was, but I didn't want to appear that way. There wasn't a single stone, rock, bottle, or can on the way back to the cabin that was spared my frustration.

When I arrived back at the White Sands, I noticed my van had returned in one piece, and I found all the others passed out in their beds in various stages of dress. I felt around in the dark until I found the couch, which was what free room and board had earned me, and even though I wasn't tired, I lay down and hoped that sleep would numb my disappointment. My only consolation was the possibility of seeing Andi at the Sunset Club the following night if she was still around. I held on to that thought as I eventually drifted off.

At first light, I stopped pretending I was getting any sleep and decided to take another walk along the beach. I didn't mind being off on my own; in fact, I preferred it most of the time. I treasured my new friendship with Mark and the others and cherished their companionship, but I found the whole social dynamic exhausting and occasionally needed time to myself. Isolation and solitude were something I was used to, and it was never an issue. Maybe that was part of my problem?

I fumbled in the dark and managed to slip on shorts, a wrinkled T-shirt, and my flops before stumbling toward the front door. When I cracked open the door, the morning sun burst past me and lit up every corner of the room, seeking every dark recess. The brilliant light elicited more than a few moans and grumbles, so I quickly ducked out.

Even though the sun was still low in the sky, I soon regretted forgetting my sunglasses, and my eyes went into a perpetual squint. Then, as my vision slowly adjusted, I noticed someone sitting at the foot of the steps leading up to our cabin. The tank top was a different color, but the smile was unmistakable. It was Andi.

"Hey, you," was all I could say, in a state of shock. My heart was racing, and my eyesight instantly returned to twenty-twenty.

"Did you forget my name already?" Andi asked.

"No…uh…I was just surprised."

"I brought you some orange juice," she replied, rising from the stoop to hand me one of the two paper cups she was holding.

As I took the cup from her hand, I wondered how I had ever doubted my memory. In between my brief moments of fitful sleep, I'd let my mind run rampant with self-doubt and exaggerations as I relived every moment of our meeting in the club. I wondered if her beauty was only in my mind, embellishing the ordinary, playing tricks because this was the one girl who showed an interest in me. After all, my memories were formed in a dimly lit room with strobes and colored lights, and there was a fair amount of alcohol involved. But standing before me in the unforgiving morning sun, she still took my breath away. Despite the early hour, there were no bags or telltale sleepiness in her deep green eyes. The sunlight was obviously her friend.

"Thank you," I said, taking the cup from her. "How long have you been out here?"

"Not that long."

"How did you find me?"

"You said you were staying at the White Sands and you had a van. There are only two vans here, and this one looked more like your style," she answered, gesturing to my green van parked beside the cabin.

"I have a style?" I asked.

"Don't we all," she answered earnestly, taking a sip from her cup.

"I did come by last night, I swear, but it was really late. I couldn't get my friends to leave the club, so I had to walk."

Her face turned serious. "I wasn't there. I ended up spending the night with Mike."

My heart plummeted. I struggled mightily to keep the crestfallen look from my face. I turned my head away and stared off into the distance. A small, wiry dog was rummaging through a trash pile a couple of cabins away.

"I just wanted to come by and apologize, especially now that I know you had to walk all that way," she continued.

I could feel my resolve failing, but I was determined not to let her see my disappointment. I had obviously misjudged everything, and all I wanted to do now was get away as quickly as I could. The dog had scored what looked like an old steak bone and was carrying it away toward the beach. At least someone was having a good morning. I turned back to her and used my best poker face.

"Oh...okay...sure...I understand," I stammered.

She burst out laughing. "I'm joking, you goober."

I looked at her incredulously. She was kidding? I felt as if I had been gang-tackled by the emotion bullies, joy and jubilation hitting me high while anger and embarrassment took my legs out from under me. However unsure of myself I was before had just been magnified by a factor of ten. I eventually said, "Geez, that's cruel! I think I just got whiplash."

"I'm sorry," she reached out her hand and touched my arm. "I couldn't resist. You didn't really think I would do something like that, do you?"

"How would I know any differently? I barely know your name, much less anything else about you. And besides, you don't know my kind of luck."

The playful look made it impossible to be upset with her, but the joke set off alarms, warning me I needed to pay attention. Just take it slow and keep a certain amount of distance, just in case, I counseled myself.

"I fell asleep on the couch in the lobby waiting for you," she said. "We had been up the entire night before, and I couldn't keep my eyes open any longer. My roommate finally came down and took me back to our room. I'm really, really sorry." She seemed genuinely apologetic.

I stepped down to the landing and sat on the stoop next to her, careful not to spill my orange juice. She did the same, touching her hips to mine even though there was plenty of room on the step for both of us.

"So, I gotta ask. Why me?" I said, as I sampled the orange juice. It was lukewarm.

"Pardon?"

"Last night. You said you had been trying to get me to notice you. Why me?"

"Is there something wrong with you?"

"I don't think so, but I'm biased. I must admit, though, girls like you usually don't ask me to dance."

"First off, you asked me, I didn't ask you. And second, what do you mean girls like me?" The seriousness had returned to her face, but I interpreted it as a playful seriousness.

I hesitated a moment before I answered. *Remember, maintain distance.* I shouldn't let myself get lost in those amazing eyes...because I knew I could. And that would mean I would be setting myself up for a terrible fall if things went sideways, which they always did.

"Girls as pretty as you are," I blurted honestly. Screw the distance!

Her smile returned. She looked down into her drink as if she was trying to see through the orange pulp to the bottom of the cup. "You think I'm pretty?"

I looked off in the direction that the dog had disappeared in. Shrugging my shoulders, I said, "You're all right, but I really prefer older women. You know, late twenties to mid-thirties. I hear they really know how to have a good time."

Thud! The punch she landed on my upper arm surprised me with its power, but I did well to act as if nothing had happened. I glanced back, and the same playful seriousness had returned.

"You must have brothers," I reasoned.

"Nope, I'm an only child. Why?"

"Then where'd you learn to punch like that?"

"Did I hurt your wittle arm?" she mocked me in a childlike voice.

"No, but that was impressive, how you avoided answering my question," I said.

"What question was that?"

"Why me?"

Her gaze returned to the mystery beneath her orange juice. "No reason."

"Is that something you often do?"

She shot me a glance that told me the answer before she spoke. "No, never!"

"So then why me? Why last night?"

"Your laugh. Happy now?"

"My laugh?"

"Uh-huh. I was watching you with your friends, and you all were having so much fun. I don't know how to explain it, but every time I saw you laugh, it made me smile." Her eyes were still transfixed to the inside of her cup.

I took a moment to process that. "That's it? Just my laugh?"

"No, of course not." She gave me a sideway annoyed look. "Why are you so curious?"

"It's quite simple. There were probably over two hundred people in the club last night, half of them girls, and the prettiest one in the club, who already had a date, I might add, picked me out. In the world according to Lee, that's fairy tale stuff. So that's why I'm curious about what drew you to me?" I answered slowly and deliberately.

The way she looked at me made me think she was struggling to make her mind up about something. Then, finally, she said, "Okay. There were other things. One was the way you were dressed. You weren't trying to impress anybody and probably could not have cared less about what they thought about what you wore. But you weren't sloppy, just extremely casual. That told me you were at ease with yourself." She paused to see if I had any comment, and when I remained silent, she continued. "It was also the way you acted with your friends. I could tell you really listened to them when they were talking. You're not one of those people who just waited for their turn to talk."

She paused again and looked at me like she expected me to say something. I responded by saying, "This is me waiting for my turn to talk."

"Another thing," she continued while suppressing a smile, "was that you didn't ask a single girl to dance, nor did you try to strike up a conversation with one. That told me you were either very shy or gay. But I saw you checking out girls, including me, often enough. So, you weren't gay."

"I did ask you to dance," I countered.

"Only after I basically threw myself at you," she responded.

I grinned at her, and she smiled back.

"So, is that it?" I asked.

She returned her gaze back into her cup. "There was one other thing." She paused for a moment, "It didn't hurt that you're cute."

My grin turned into a full-fledged smile. "You think I'm cute?"

"Not as cute as your friend with the curly hair, but you're all right."

I balled up my fist and made like I was going to punch her on the arm. She recoiled.

"You wouldn't hit a girl, would you?"

"I'd hit one that could punch like you can."

I lowered my fist, and she righted herself, bumping softly against my side.

"Have any other questions, Mr. Fairy Tale?" she asked.

"Did you talk to Mike at all last night? I mean, golly, you sure are observant."

"Mike's a nice enough guy, and yes, we talked. Anything else?" she continued.

"I want to know where you get a smile like that. I mean, get a job with NATO or something, and put that smile to good use developing trade agreements with hostile governments. One look at that smile, and they'll roll over and show their belly."

She was trying desperately to suppress said smile. "I haven't seen your belly yet?"

Now it was my turn to suppress a smile. "The day's still young," I countered.

She couldn't hold it any longer, and her smile took control of her face, its brilliance giving the morning sun a run for its money.

"You know, there could be one other explanation why I didn't ask anybody to dance or hit on any girls last night," I offered.

"And what would that be?" she took the bait.

"I could have a girlfriend back home."

The twinkle in her eyes dimmed, and the contents of her cup captured her attention again.

"So, I've been doing all the talking and answering all the questions. I think it's your turn now to answer my questions," she said.

"Shoot."

"Do you have a girlfriend back home?" was her first question, looking straight at me for my response.

"Not even close," I answered. It was my turn to check out the contents of my cup.

"How come?"

"Well, as you so astutely pointed out, I have a severe case of shyness, and I just don't do well around girls." I could feel my face flush a bit.

"You're not that way with me." Her voice seemed softer now.

I looked into her eyes. "And I'm as surprised about that as anyone. All I can say is that it's more about you than it is me. Ever since you smiled at me when I asked you to dance, I have been totally at ease, relaxed, even confident around you. It's a feeling that, honestly, I have never felt before. Usually, I get all tongue-tied and clumsy around girls."

"I feel the same about you," she said, leaning harder against my side. "I feel relaxed with you."

The two of us were silent for a minute.

"So, how long are you in Panama City for?" I asked, already dreading the answer.

"We leave to go back Sunday. What about you?"

"Same day. I guess that gives us four days." It was Wednesday morning.

"I guess it does," she said, looking into my eyes again. "What do you want to do first?"

"When I came out here, I was about to take a walk along the beach. I owe you one from last night. Care to join me?" I asked as I rose from the step and reached my hand out to her.

"I thought you'd never ask," she replied, smiling, taking hold of my hand, and pulling herself up.

We headed to the beach with our hands still entwined.

| 7 |

Complications

Senator Brown

"Fifteen minutes, Senator."

Senator Theodore Roosevelt Brown, or Teddy as his close friends knew him, nodded his acknowledgment to the young producer. Then she disappeared again. He finished scanning the document he was reading and then placed it back in his briefcase, pressing the latches on the front until they locked in place. He took a last glance in the mirror his chair faced.

Distinguished was the word that flashed across his mind as he associated his reflection with the look he was striving for. He was proud of his near-perfect smile that displayed all his original teeth. His conservative dark-gray suit hung sharply from his five-foot, eleven-inch, one-hundred-eighty-pound frame and was rounded off against a cotton white shirt. His carefully chosen tie had a tinge of blue that not coincidentally matched the color of his eyes.

This was his second taping of the day and the eighth activity for the week. The pace was grueling, but he knew this was just the beginning, and it was only going to get more intense as the days started falling toward the first Tuesday in November.

He swiveled the styling chair a half turn away from the mirror so he could see the door to the anteroom without having to rely on the reflection. As he waited for the producer to come back and tell him it was time to take the stage, he looked around the room, surprised at how little it had changed since the last time he had been here.

In late 2002, he was in this same Miami, Florida, broadcast studio preparing for an interview in his first senatorial campaign. His seven years serving as the Florida Second Congressional District House Representative had prepared him well. During his previous years of public service, he often would suffer bouts of nervousness before speaking engagements. Of course, he would be fine as soon as he took the stage or the light on top of the camera turned red, but it was cold comfort minutes beforehand.

A graduate of Florida State Law School in 1987, he'd started his political career off in the academic arena, choosing to become a professor of political science at his alma mater instead of practicing law. He met his future wife, Bess, an undergraduate with a double major in sociology and psychology on the same campus, and they married two months after she graduated. Quickly realizing the teaching profession lacked a certain edge he quietly yearned for, he ran for and was elected as one of the youngest county circuit judges in Leon County in 1989.

The next six years tested the strength of his character, and there were more than a few times he wondered why he'd left the quiet comfort of helping to shape young minds instead of locking quite a few of them behind bars. The theological conventions he learned and taught in college of crime and punishment, right and wrong, good and evil, were all thrown together into this huge chaotic mess, and he struggled to keep his moral core centered. He searched desperately for an avenue that would lead him back to his idealistic existence before he went so far off track. His perseverance paid off when he was sought out by several key supporters who believed he would be ideal as the next mayor of Tallahassee. He won the honor in a close election in 1993.

For the next three years, like a flower blossoming in the morning sun, he became the public servant he knew he could be and helped shape the future of the capital of the state of Florida. He was appointed to the Florida League of Cities, the Tallahassee Economic Development Council, the Sunshine State Governmental Financing Commission, and the Economic Club of Florida. His energy appeared limitless and his devotion uncompromising.

Past success usually has a way of breeding future opportunities, and it was certainly the case for Mayor Brown. His achievement as mayor once again brought candidate hounds to his door for the Second Congressional District House of Representatives. This time, it took a little more convincing to get Teddy to believe he was the right man for the job. He was concerned about how a broader campaign would negatively affect his personal life and specifically the tolls it could put on his wife, who was still nursing their first-born son. It was Bess who finally urged Teddy into making the commitment, saying that she could never live with herself if she felt she had in any way held him back or couldn't live with him if he used her as an excuse. As a result, Teddy Brown won the congressional seat in a landslide in 1996.

In 2002, he didn't need a supporter urging him to take a chance at the next logical step in his political journey. That year he was the only Republican challenger to defeat a Democrat incumbent and the first Republican to win a statewide race in Florida since 1968. He made his first campaign appearance in the home city of his opponent, which was Miami. If memory served him correctly, he was wearing a suit similar to the one he was wearing now.

As he reflected upon his career and the choices he had made, or had been made for him, he was confident that the man who had sat in this chair sixteen years ago had had no idea of the heights he would reach or the possibility that he now pursued. If the polls were believed, and barring a major catastrophe, he would become the next vice president of the United States in just a few short months.

He could honestly say it surprised him when the Democratic presidential nominee, Senator Jack Fallon of Iowa, knocked on his door last month. Fallon was relatively young at forty-four years old for a presidential nominee, with only two presidents, Theodore Roosevelt and John F. Kennedy, younger. The party was looking for somebody with more maturity and years of public service to match with the rising senator from Iowa, and at fifty-six years old, thirty-two years of spotless public service, high opinion of not only his Democratic peers but Republican ones as well, Senator TR Brown looked like the perfect choice.

With the Republican National Convention just three months away, Teddy was once again on the campaign trail.

Senator Brown heard soft footsteps in the hallway outside the room and looked up, expecting to see the producer. Instead, a man in a brown suit with a military-style crew cut stepped in when the door opened. Senator Brown stood up and tensed.

"Teddy," the brown-suited man said after taking a careful look around the empty room.

"What are you doing here?" the senator responded tersely, ignoring the greeting.

"It's good to see you, too. You know you really should keep your itinerary a little more secret. Anyone can find out where you are and just show up," the visitor responded with mock concern.

"So, you flew thirteen hundred miles to give me a lecture on my security protocols?"

"No," the man responded calmly, looking past the senator and taking an interest in the mirrors behind him. "I thought you'd like to know there's been a development in one of our old cases, and I wanted to inform you personally. I don't feel comfortable having this conversation over the phone, so I came out here to see you." He closed the door to the anteroom.

"What case? What are you talking about?"

"The Taylor case. The one that's been an open sore for twenty-nine years now," he answered, making his way across the room

The senator's disposition suddenly changed. Below the layers of makeup on his face, his skin was turning pale. His shoulders drooped, and he appeared unsteady on his feet. He retook his seat in the styling chair. Even though the two of them were alone in the room, he looked around to make sure their exchange was private. His voice was noticeably lower and more reserved as he continued.

"What kind of development?" he asked after a long pause.

The visitor seemed unconcerned with the senator's sudden discomfort. "As you may or may not recall, we've had a data trap in place for several years now for anybody querying the name Andi Taylor. Two days ago, a Mr. Lee Hamilton, who lives in Conway, Arkansas, who is a fairly popular blogger, posted an entry to his blog that is particularly interesting to us."

"Go on," the senator prodded, his eyes closed.

"The gist of it involves a trip he made to Panama City, Florida, with a group of friends the summer of 1992." The man picked up and examined a device from the shelf used to curl eyelashes.

"And how does that affect us?"

"It's helpful because, as it so happens, he met and had a fling with Andi Taylor while he was there. So, it may be possible that he has what we are looking for."

"May be possible? You don't know for sure?" the senator responded tersely, now looking at the man in the dark suit.

"There's no specific mention of it in his writing. I've only just started to investigate, but he mentions a meeting between Andi Taylor and Stevens."

"You think that's significant?"

"Unclear. I'll know more soon, but I wanted to let you know about this right away." The man now was staring at his reflection in the large mirror.

"If he has it, why hasn't he done anything with it?" the senator asked.

"I'm not sure. Maybe he doesn't know what he has."

The senator perked up a bit and sat forward in his seat, turning it to face the man standing beside him now. "If he doesn't know what he has, then there's no need to do anything. So let it stay where it is, forgotten and inconsequential."

The man in the brown suit turned his head away from the mirror and stared down at the senator.

"Are you really willing to take that chance? I'm certainly not. What if he gets sentimental one day and decides to use it? What are we going to do then? I don't think we can count on it falling into the hands of a greedy public official again, do you?" His voice was sterner, but his facial expression had not changed at all.

The senator's chin dropped to his chest. *This can't be happening again.* He had spent the better part of his life making up for his one mistake, his one critical lapse in judgment, and he had finally reached a point where restful sleep was possible and he no longer feared the fateful phone call or knock on the door. Surely it couldn't be a coincidence. Just when his future was so promising and the opportunity to extend his positive influence further than he ever imagined just months away, that the horrible part of his past should re-emerge and remind him that redemption was an ongoing process. And in a world where signs and subliminal meanings were everywhere if you chose to see them, he didn't miss the one that was standing right in front of him.

Be careful who you make deals with.

Suddenly there was a knock on the door, and the young producer opened the door and stuck her head in. She glanced at the man in the brown suit and then addressed the senator.

"Excuse me, Senator, but it's time to take the stage," she said.

"I'm coming," he replied, and the woman disappeared, leaving the door cracked open.

Senator Brown rose from the chair, checked his tie once more in the mirror, and then moved to the door. He paused just before he exited and looked back at the man in the brown suit.

"Follow it where you need to. But Robert—"

The man turned and faced the senator.

"Nobody gets hurt this time!" the senator ordered and was gone.

| 8 |

Silent Sleuth

**Dianne**

Sitting in the reception area of Norwood Construction, I thought about why I was here and how I'd gotten myself into this position. I realized this was my doing, but a part of me wanted to lay the blame on Tildy—Aaron Cobb's sister—as well.

I could still remember my conversation with her vividly.

"You wanted to see me," I said, as I stuck my head into Aaron's office two days after his funeral. Tildy was sitting at his desk. At only five feet two inches and barely over a hundred pounds, the size of the desk dwarfed her, but she still exuded an air of confidence. I always liked and respected Tildy, even though I had no idea how she earned a living or passed her time. I think their family had money, and she played the part of a Southern aristocrat to a tee. She certainly dressed for the role with an endless supply of frilly dresses that would make Scarlet O'Hara envious.

There was a brown ledger open in front of her.

"I do," she said, smiling widely. "Have a seat."

I slid into the chair opposite her and relaxed. I was comfortable around Tildy, which I couldn't say when I was with most people.

"You've no doubt heard about Aaron's will?" she started, closing the ledger.

"I have. Congratulations. Were you surprised he didn't leave it to his wife?"

"Not really. Aaron wanted to make sure the agency remained in the family."

"His wife isn't family?" I asked.

"Hardly. The only reason they were still together was Aaron feared he'd get taken to the cleaners during the divorce, and he was right."

I chuckled. "That's why I'm never getting married."

"Oh, and here I was thinking it was because of your complete lack of social skills."

That's one reason I liked Tildy so much—her unwavering honesty. I smiled. "There is that."

"Aaron was just looking out for the business he loved by leaving it with me. He knew I'd do what was best for it, which is why I asked you here."

"I don't understand."

"Although I fully intend to honor my brother's wishes, I have no interest in running a detective agency. I want you to do it for me."

That stunned me.

After several moments of silence, Tildy continued. "You're not saying anything."

I squirmed in my chair. "I...uh...appreciate the offer, but I'm not a manager, Tildy. Besides, you have guys working here with much more experience. Let one of them do it."

"You mean guys like Mack Green?"

Mack Green was an ex-cop who had been with Aaron since the agency's formation. I considered him a dinosaur and the type of man people typically think of when they hear the phrase Private Dick, and not in a good way.

KNIGHT RISE - 69

"Maybe not Mack, but definitely one of the others."

"I don't want one of them. I want you to do it."

I was starting to feel trapped and found it difficult to meet Tildy's gaze.

"But, Tildy—"

"I once had a conversation with Aaron about the future of this agency after his eventual retirement. Do you know what he said?"

I shook my head.

"He mentioned you. He talked about all your hard work, dedication, ingenuity, leadership skills, and maintaining the business's excellent reputation. He said that if you were a man, he'd be tempted to tap you to take over for him."

Although hearing what Aaron said about me was a little surprising, he had always kidded around the office that one of the best things he had ever done for the agency was to hire a woman with a master's degree from West Virginia Criminal Justice. Even though I had relatively little experience in fieldwork, I had an exceptional understanding of computers and quickly carved a niche for myself, investigating and finding hidden business assets and performing background checks for civil lawsuits. My drive and determination led me to becoming familiar with all aspects of the agency's investigative techniques. I developed a reputation for never shying away from the less glamorous parts of an investigation, such as the endless phone calls, serving summonses, or even midnight stakeouts. My meteoric rise to senior investigator could have resulted in more than a few bruised egos in the agency, except for one indisputable fact—I brought in more business than any three investigators combined, which benefited everybody.

"I appreciate hearing that, Tildy, but the fact is, I am a woman. The lone woman investigator at this agency, and with the least amount of experience to boot. Silent Sleuth is pretty much a guys' club and putting me in charge would just upset a lot of people."

Tildy took a deep breath. "Do you think I care one iota about that sexist crap? I have a business to oversee, and you're the person I want in the driver's seat. This is your chance to make genuine changes."

I had never viewed myself as the person in charge before. Thinking about it now, I could envision the possibilities. I allowed the prospect to take root inside of me.

"But you said it yourself. I have no social skills. What kind of manager would that make me?"

"Why don't we find out," Tildy replied, smiling in the knowledge that she had me hooked.

A man in a tan sports coat pushing his way through the inner glass door interrupted my reminiscence.

"Miss Williams?" the gentleman asked. "I'm Chester Grant."

This was my first time meeting the owner of Norwood Construction, a longtime customer of Silent Sleuth, and I had to say it was a bit of a letdown. Norwood was one of the most powerful and influential builders in the state, the holder of a dozen government contracts with its name plastered on construction signs all around the city. Yet, its owner reminded me of somebody better suited to be a late-night shift supervisor for a dingy all-night fast-food restaurant. He was short, overweight, and partially bald, with his remaining hair combed over to hide it. Not what I expected.

I rose from my seat, expecting an offer of a hand in greeting, but when none came, I crossed my hands in front of me. "You can call me Dianne."

"Come on back, darlin'."

I nodded my appreciation to the perky receptionist and followed Chester Grant through the double doors. Trailing slightly behind the man down the bright hallway, I couldn't help but notice how he walked with his feet decidedly pointed outward, like a penguin.

"I must say, it surprised me when I received your call," Grant said as he walked, not bothering to look over his shoulder at me. "Should I assume this meeting is your way of introducing yourself as the new manager of Silent Sleuth?"

"In a fashion, yes," I responded.

The Norwood Construction offices were in the center of Charlotte in a recently completed building, erected by Norwood, and everything about it felt new. I wondered if the company had cut corners with their own building like they had been accused of in several high-profile legal entanglements of late.

"Take a seat," Chester Grant said, motioning to a pair of chairs in front of the desk. He made his way around to the other side. I sat in the first chair I came to.

"I imagine you've had a bumpy transition taking over for Aaron," Grant started as he took his own seat.

Overlooking the long hours, grueling schedule, and cold shoulders from the staff, I was warming to the idea of being the head of the agency I'd worked at for ten years, despite the timing and circumstances.

"You could say that," I replied.

"Well, we've always gotten along well with your agency, and I imagine that won't change."

"Actually, that's the reason I'm here today," I said.

Chester Grant's eyebrows rose. "Really? How so?"

"I wanted to inform you, in person, that Silent Sleuth will be ending our relationship with your company."

Grant's already narrow eyes narrowed even more. "Excuse me?"

"We will no longer accept Norwood Construction as a client."

"I don't understand. Our money's no good for you now?"

"That's not it, though some of your business dealings I've read about seem dodgy. But, no, it's simple. After reviewing your case files from the past five years—something I've been doing with all our clients—I've come across several that cause me concern."

"Which are those?" the man asked, but I could tell by the look on his face that he already knew the answer.

"Multiple times in the past, you've had Silent Sleuth engage the service of a personal assistant for you. Not unusual in and of itself, as we regularly perform background checks for prospective employees. However, the job requirements for this job are rather unique. Female, blonde, athletic with a specific body type, a negative drug test, a negative HIV test, no criminal record. The job has no required computer skills and no educational prerequisites whatsoever. The work address specified is a condo registered in the company name within walking distance of these offices. And there seems to be a lot of turnover in this position, since you give us an additional request every six months."

Grant adopted a smug smile. "There's nothing illegal about that."

I could feel the heat coming off the back of my neck. "That's debatable. But it is something we no longer offer at my agency."

"Your agency?"

"That's right. I speak for the company."

Grant sat back in his chair and put his hands behind his head. "I wonder, do you? I've heard there's a lot of unhappy folks in your camp."

"Fortunately for you, that's something you don't have to worry about."

"I do a lot more business than just this with you. You're going to pull the plug on it all just because it upsets some sort of moral code?"

"See, I knew you'd get it. Tildy told me you wouldn't appreciate where we were coming from, but I was confident I could communicate it to you in a way you would understand."

Grant dropped the hands from behind his head and jerked forward in his chair, fire in his eyes.

"Don't you smart-ass me, bitch. I'll stop payment on all your outstanding invoices."

I rose casually from my chair. "You won't do that. But if you do, I'll have to send a copy of my five-year audit to all of Norwood Construction's board members. Refresh my memory. Your wife sits on the board, doesn't she?"

Chester Grant remained speechless, the color on his face quickly approaching that of his red tie.

"I'll see myself out." I left him with his face red and his mouth agape.

As I made my way to the car, I reflected on the fact that I wasn't completely honest with Chester. Although Tildy agreed that cutting ties with Norwood was the right thing to do, it was a reluctant decision, and one that we both knew was sure to cause further upheaval in the office.

I couldn't worry about that now. We were doing brisk business, even without Norwood Construction, and every investigator was working on two or three cases, some more. Part of my job was to oversee the progress of each investigation to ensure it was being run up to agency standards and offer suggestions where needed. With all the cases I was now managing, it stretched me about as thin as I could go.

But there was one case that kept niggling at me—Emily Bennett. With everything on my plate, I didn't need a case that amounted to nothing but busy work and zero income. I knew I'd let my emotions get the better of me when the woman was in my office, which wasn't like me, but the one weak spot I will admit to is not knowing when to quit. The intelligent thing would be to draft a report based on what little work I had put into it so far and be done with it. But I had made a commitment, and I was going to follow through with it all the way to the predetermined, albeit tragic, end.

I reached my car in the parking garage and climbed behind the wheel. I didn't start the engine, choosing to just sit there instead, thinking.

Yesterday, I found the time to read the complete Bennett file and contact all of the relevant law enforcement agencies involved. I confirmed what I already expected to hear—no fresh developments. What did surprise me as I delved deeper into the backstory was that it wasn't a simple robbery gone wrong. It was something else altogether. It turned out the pawnshop owner had been in touch with the FBI the day before his murder—and there was a connection to the death of a bookie and the disappearance of a district attorney in Tallahassee, Florida. Organized crime was mentioned, which wasn't a complete shock given the lack of physical evidence at the crime scene. Everything pointed to a professional hit. But in Easley, South Carolina? Whoever was responsible even took the inventory log to prevent identifying what was stolen. There was enough reason for Aaron to send an investigator to Tallahassee to dig around for any leads the local police may have kept from the press, hoping that he could uncover something that could help explain the murders. Although their investigator came up with little, he established a connection with an informant.

The file listed Antonio Paretti as the source in Florida. Mr. Paretti's police record made it clear he wasn't exactly an upstanding citizen, but he was on the fringes of the crime family supposedly involved. I'd tried calling the number written by his name last night, but there was no answer. These weren't the type of questions you could leave in a voice message, so I had made a mental note to try back later, and now was as good a time as any. Hopefully, Antonio was a morning person.

I pulled out my cell phone and dialed the number from the file. After a half dozen rings, I ended the connection. I would try again tonight.

But right now, I had other things to deal with. One of those was keeping a promise I made to myself when Tildy dumped this job in my lap. It was time to hire a new investigator, and a female one at that.

| 9 |

Slow Dancer IV

MONDAY, JULY 19, 2021
SLOW DANCER (Part Four)

Andi and I spent the rest of that first morning together walking on the beach, getting to know each other. I learned she was born and raised in a small town named Easley, South Carolina, and was the same year as me at Clemson University. She was majoring in education with a minor in sports medicine in order to be a teacher and volleyball coach. Like me, she and two of her friends were there in Panama City to have fun before starting summer jobs. We took turns telling each other tidbits of each other's lives, and she took particular interest in the fact that I lacked the sense of smell. She found it fascinating and felt compelled to make a long list of aromas I had been missing out on.

We were so wrapped up in our talk that when we finally noticed where we were, we found ourselves in a deserted and undeveloped part of the beach. We turned around and headed back in the direction we came, picking right up where we left off in our conversation. Before we knew it, the time on my watch read just after noon, and Andi told me she probably needed to get back to her hotel to let her friends know where she was and that she was okay. I offered to drive her back to the Regency in my van, which she gladly accepted.

Even with midday traffic, the drive to the Regency took us only ten minutes. I parked my van in the south parking lot, and we entered the hotel from the beachside. Andi led me up a set of stairs and through a foyer, running alongside one of the three pools and into the hallway that came out next to the receptionist desk in the front lobby. I didn't bother to tell her I knew exactly where I was going because I had been through all those areas the night before, looking for her. We stopped in front of a pair of elevators around the corner from the lobby.

"Do you want to come upstairs and meet my roommates?" Andi asked, pressing the up-arrow button between the two sets of silver sliding doors.

"I don't think so. They might not be ready for company, and besides, I'll see them tonight, right?"

"Right." A soft ding signaled the arrival of an elevator. "Okay, I'll be right back," she said and disappeared into the elevator.

I wandered into the lobby and to the couch in front of the television, which was now showing some old movie. Leaning back and putting my hands behind my head, I reflected on how different my mood was now than when I'd in that very spot been less than twelve hours ago . I watched the people coming and going around the lobby. People checking in, or people checking out. Everybody was headed somewhere, and without exception, they all had one thing in common—a smile on their face. I knew how they felt.

I had been sitting there for fifteen minutes when a girl wearing a white terry cloth cover-up over what appeared to be a black bikini exited the elevator and turned the corner into the lobby, obviously looking for somebody. Her blond hair hung loosely about her shoulders, and a pair of dark sunglasses were propped on top of her head. I glanced at her, thinking momentarily it might be Andi, but when it wasn't, I looked away until I noticed the girl seemed to focus on me. She walked straight over to where I was sitting and stood in front of me.

"Are you Lee?" she asked.

"Yeah," I answered cautiously.

"I'm Andi's friend Gayle. I was wondering if I could talk to you for a minute?" Although her voice was cordial, her demeanor was businesslike.

"Sure, have a seat." I gestured to the chair next to me.

Gayle was a couple inches shorter than me, and although her cover-up concealed most of her body, I guessed that she was a little on the plump side. However, unlike Andi, she was a fan of makeup and made good use of it. Gayle sat down, turned slightly to face me, and placed her hands in her lap. I noticed she had different styles of rings on every finger.

"Andi wanted to take a quick shower and change, so she sent me down here to entertain you," she said.

"Oh…okay…thanks. I'll just hang out here—"

"But I also wanted to meet you and talk a bit," she continued before I finished.

"Sure, that's nice of you. Well, let's make it official." I extended my hand to her. "I'm Lee."

Her smile lacked warmth as she took my hand and shook it slightly. "Hi, I'm Gayle. Andi and I have been best friends since second grade."

"Wow, that's special. I can't even imagine having a friend for that long. It must be nice."

"It is nice. We do everything together. Have done everything together. They baptized us on the same day, we went to camp every year together, graduated from high school together, and are roommates in college. We are awfully close. We tell each other everything, and we watch out for each other. That's why I'm here now." The impostor of a smile had disappeared from her face.

"I...I don't understand." I sat up a little straighter on the couch.

"Andi doesn't normally do this, so I just want to make sure that you will not hurt her," she blurted out.

I stared at her, confused. "Why would you think I would hurt her?"

"You don't understand," she said, sounding a bit frustrated. She started using her fingers to comb her long hair back behind her head, where she funneled it into a circle and then flipped the end over her right shoulder. "As long as I have known Andi, she has never acted like this about a boy. Did you know she waited for you for over an hour last night, dead tired, and finally fell asleep on this very couch?"

I felt terrible all over again. "She told me. I couldn't get a ride."

"Well, I had to come down here and make her come to bed. But then this morning, she was out the door before the sun was up and determined to find you. That's just not like her." She started pulling her hair back again.

I sat there silently, not knowing what to say.

"Andi has never had a boyfriend," Gayle continued. "She's dated off and on, but nothing serious. She's always been focused on her schoolwork and sports."

"She told me. Volleyball. Is she good?" I asked lamely.

"All-conference three years in a row. Andi could have gotten an athletic scholarship to a smaller school, but we both always dreamed of going to Clemson, so she turned it down."

"Clemson, huh?"

"Better than some low-rent SEC team like LSU."

"I'm sure," I replied, with a grin on my face.

"You know it." She returned my grin, despite herself I suspected. "Anyway, suddenly Andi showed back up at the room last night, and all she can talk about is this guy she met at the Sunset Club. Lee this and Lee that. This from a girl who hasn't said more than a couple sentences about a guy in, like, forever."

"Wow, I can't believe a girl like her doesn't have a steady boyfriend or at least a whole slew of guys chasing her around."

Gayle again pulled her hair back behind her head, obviously a nervous habit. "In high school, all the guys knew she wasn't interested in anything serious, and they left her alone. At Clemson, she keeps to herself and studies a lot."

I thought for a minute, then asked, "And why do you think that I'm going to hurt her?"

"Because I know the kind of guys who come down here." Her voice had taken on a less friendly tone. "Get as many notches on your belts as possible before heading back to school to brag about it. I see guys like that everywhere. Hell, I've even been with guys like that, and I don't want Andi to be treated that way. She's not equipped to deal with it. She will be hurt!"

Gayle had stopped fiddling with her hair, and her eyes were fixed on me now.

"Gayle, I know now where you're coming from, and I'm not sure what I can say to persuade you that hurting Andi is the furthest thing from my mind, because it sounds like you've already made your mind up about me. But let me say this—from the moment I asked her to dance last night, I have never felt as relaxed around a girl as I do with her. I ran here all the way from the Sunset Club last night just to see her. All I am hoping for is that I get to spend as much time with her as she'll let me have while you guys are still here. That's all. No hidden agendas. No notches on belts. Just two people enjoying each other's company. I really hope that's okay with you because I wouldn't want to piss off her best friend."

Gayle didn't immediately say anything. She kept her eyes locked on my eyes, probably trying to see into my soul or read my mind.

Finally, she looked down at her hands, which had started playing with a corner of her cover-up.

"You wouldn't have any brothers, would you?" she asked, following it up with a meek smile.

"I do, but one is in the navy, and the other is still in high school," I answered, returning her smile.

"Too bad," she replied, and I felt as if she meant it.

"Andi is fortunate to have a friend like you."

Her small smile turned into a brighter one. "Thanks. But you're the lucky one. You're the one boy who Andi likes."

For the next several minutes, we continued our conversation, talking about previous trips to Florida (me—none, Gayle—one), college majors (me—English lit, Gayle—economics), and rooming arrangements (me—dorm, Gayle—apartment). We were debating the pros and cons of the Greek system when Andi and another girl suddenly appeared next to us.

Andi had changed into a red bikini that I found challenging to take my eyes off. She was holding her own terry cloth cover-up folded across her arm in front of her. The other girl with Andi, the tallest of the three at close to six feet, had on a royal-blue bikini and an orange T-shirt tied around her waist. She had her hair tucked up under an orange ball cap with a large blue C embroidered prominently on it.

"I see you two found each other. What are you talking about?" Andi said.

"About you, of course. Gayle was giving me all the inside scoop," I answered.

"She was, was she?" Andi replied, looking at Gayle and putting her hands on her hips.

"Not true, not true," Gayle countered. "We were just talking about fraternities and sororities."

"Sure, after she told me about your addiction to marshmallows and your irrational fear of pizza delivery men," I lied. The girl in the orange ball cap laughed.

Gayle was laughing as well. "I said no such thing!"

"Well, you can stop talking to him right now. He's all mine," Andi said as she walked around the couch and plopped down next to me on the opposite side of Gayle. The girl in the orange ball cap sat down in a chair catty-corner to the sofa.

"This is Trisha. She's our other roommate." Andi introduced the girl in the ball cap. I waved my hand and smiled at her.

Unexpectedly, I felt a twinge of my old nervousness ebbing back. Alone with Andi, I felt self-assured and tranquil, but now surrounded by three beautiful women with the focus on me, I could feel my confidence faltering. I was worried I would get tongue-tied and sound like an idiot again. Or I would assume every uncomfortable lull in the conversation was because of my inability to make small talk. I really enjoyed how I was when I was alone with her and desperately feared slipping back into old habits. I couldn't let that happen. I *wouldn't* let that happen.

Gayle was talking to Trisha about where they planned to eat that night when I felt Andi lean over and bump me with her shoulder. I turned my head and noticed a quizzical look on her face.

"Where'd you go?" she asked, no doubt referring to my trance.

I looked at her sitting there next to me, the eyes so friendly and curious, the way she was so comfortable in her skin and that beautiful body. I smiled at her, putting my weight back against her shoulder, and answered, "Not far."

We sat there talking about what we wanted to do the rest of the afternoon when Andi seemed to recognize somebody entering the lobby.

"That's Mike's dad," she said, surprised.

KNIGHT RISE - 83

I followed her eyes to an older man who looked out of place in a sharp gray suit, standing at the receptionist desk. Andi got up from her seat and headed off to talk to him. She tapped him on his shoulder from behind. He turned and smiled widely when he recognized her. They hugged briefly, then began talking. I saw Andi put a hand to her mouth and appear to be apologizing profusely to the gentleman. Finally, the two of them disappeared around the corner, heading back toward the elevators.

Ten minutes later, they both reappeared. Andi gave the man another hug and watched as he left through the lobby entrance. Then she walked back to where we sat and started shaking her head as she approached.

"That was Mr. Stevens, Mike's dad. I was supposed to give Mike something for his dad last night, and we totally forgot about it. I feel bad because his dad had to drive here from Tallahassee to get it." She held both of her cheeks in her hands, and her mood had soured.

"I wouldn't worry about it. He has it now, and he didn't seem too upset about it," I said, trying to cheer her up.

"He didn't look angry, did he?" She seemed to be looking for a way to get her good mood back.

Both of her roommates and I shook our heads convincingly. Attempting to change the subject, I asked, "So I hear the girl to guy ratio at this hotel is three to one. Any truth to that?"

"More like four to one," Trisha answered.

"Not like it should matter to you," Andi added quickly, punctuated with a shot to the arm.

Subject change accomplished.

| 10 |

Slow Dancer V

MONDAY, JULY 19, 2021
SLOW DANCER (Part Five)

For the next three days, Andi and I were inseparable. Morning, noon, and most of the night, we were together. I feared she would overdose on my company and think I was monopolizing her time, but every time I brought up separating for a short period, she quickly squelched the idea and wondered if I was trying to get rid of her. We shared both a sunset and a sunrise together, sitting on the beach next to one another, holding hands, her head resting on my shoulder and mine nestled against hers.

Each night, we made it a point to return to the Sunset Club. I introduced Gayle and Trisha to the gang, and the gang to Andi, and we all hit it off. Wednesday night was ladies' night, and they admitted girls free of cover charge, plus all bar drinks for them were only ten cents from ten until midnight. Andi and her two roommates became our new best friends.

About midway into the night, after returning from the bathroom, I found Andi talking to a guy I didn't recognize at first, but who looked familiar. As I wrestled my way back into the spot against the wall, the name of the person talking to Andi clicked. It was her friend, Mike.

"Hey everybody, this is Mike," Andi shouted to the group around the table. "Mike, this is everybody."

"What's he doing here?" I asked her when I was back in my seat.

"He called me earlier before we headed out for dinner and asked if I wanted to go out again."

She saw the look on my face and said, "Listen, we are just family friends, and he knows that. I told him I was already going out with someone, and he could meet us here if he wanted to," she explained further. "I think he has a thing for Trisha, anyway."

I looked across the table at Mike, who was already striking up a conversation with a couple of girls.

Andi's hands reached out and cupped each side of my face, turning it to meet hers. "You have no reason to be jealous!"

"Then I'm not." I couldn't stop myself from smiling at her.

She lowered her hands from my face, and we both took a sip of our drink. She had ordered a fruit drink this time, one with a cherry poised on top of it.

"Can I have your cherry?" I asked.

Andi coughed and snorted as if the drink had gone down the wrong pipe.

"Excuse me?" she asked, still choking.

"Can I have your cherry?" I asked again.

She cocked her head to the side and grinned smugly. "I don't think we know each other that well yet, do you?"

I looked at her, perplexed. Then the realization of how she interpreted my words slowly became clear to me. I could feel my face reddening.

I reached out and picked off the cherry from her drink. "I meant this cherry. I like cherries."

"I know what you meant," she said as she took the cherry back from my hand, pulled the stem from the fruit, then handed me back the fruit.

As I put the cherry in my mouth, she did the same with the stem. I watched as, keeping her lips together, she worked the stem around in her mouth, occasionally allowing a piece to protrude through her lips then disappear again. This continued for a minute until finally, her hand reached up and took the stem out of her mouth, complete with a perfectly tied knot in the middle. She placed it in my hand.

"Just so you know, I don't give my cherry to just anyone," she said.

I looked at the knotted cherry stem in my hand, then slipped it into my hip pocket.

"Just so that you know, I don't take just any ole cherry," I replied.

"That's good to know." Her smile was more brilliant than I had seen, more brilliant than I could have imagined.

Each night at the Sunset Club was spectacular. And thanks to Andi and her roommates, a constant stream of guys and gals hung out at our table. We even became friends with Mike, who indeed seemed to have a thing for Trisha. It was as if we were in the center of the universe.

As for me, my universe contained only one planet, and it was named Andi.

Whenever the foreshadowing of her imminent departure crept into my mind, I was quick to wipe it away with some diversion.

As the evening started winding down and the Sunset Club closed its doors for the night, Andi rode back to the cabin with the gang and me so I could walk with her on the beach and share more alone time. The guys let her have the passenger seat next to me, and they all sprawled into the rear compartment, which had no seats, just a carpeted floor.

As we were driving back, Mark poked his head into the front compartment. Even though I couldn't smell the liquor on his breath, the hairs in my nose burned.

"Andi, I just want to say that was our best night in Panama City so far, and it was all because of Gayle, Trisha, and you. Thank you for buying the drinks for us, inviting all those girls from the Regency," he said, slurring only a couple of words.

"You're most welcome," she responded, looking over her shoulder at him.

"And I also want to say that this guy here," he said as he slapped me on the shoulder, "he's a good one."

"Really? Because I'm still kind of on the fence about him."

"You shouldn't be. I've roomed with Lee for a semester, and although he doesn't say a lot, he makes a mean pancake."

"It's true. I make a mean pancake," I interjected.

Kent squeezed in beside Mark. And now I was worried that the alcohol fumes would somehow cause the engine sitting just below them to explode.

"Andi, if you're on the fence about our boy here, I would just like to say one thing," Kent added.

"And that is?" she asked.

"I'll be happy to take his place if you decide to dump him," Kent offered in a somber tone.

"Me too," Mark chimed in, laying his head down on the engine cover. From the back of the van, somebody was snoring loudly.

"These are some great friends you have," Andi pointed out playfully.

"I know. They've got my back," I agreed.

A soft, high-pitched "Ni" came from the back of the van, and we all busted out in laughter.

That's when the Knights Who Say Ni was born.

***

On Friday night, everybody was ready for a break from the Sunset Club, so we visited one of the other local attractions instead.

They built the Miracle Strip Amusement Park in 1963 just across the street from the beach. It featured several rides that were made uniquely spectacular by placing them within tightly enclosed spaces and adding pounding music and lighting effects. However, the park's highlight was the Starliner Roller Coaster, an out-and-back wooden coaster that delivered the biggest bang for the buck of any coaster east of the Mississippi.

We pulled into the parking lot across the street from the park as Andi and her roommates were piling out of their own car. Andi walked straight up to me wearing the same outfit she had on the first night we met. She had an odd expression on her face.

She said, "Give me your keys," which I did unquestioningly.

Taking my keys, she turned and exchanged them with the set that Gayle, who had walked up behind her, was holding. Gayle was grinning like the Cheshire Cat from *Alice in Wonderland*.

"What's going on?" I asked.

"Come on," is all Andi said and climbed behind the wheel of Gayle's Honda Civic, gesturing for me to get in on the passenger side. I looked back at the Knights, shrugged my shoulders, then did as I was instructed.

She drove the two of us out past the outskirts of the city to a secluded part of the beach, not saying a word despite my persistent questioning. She finally parked the car, got out, opened the trunk to remove a couple of huge blankets I assumed she had borrowed from her hotel room, and handed them to me. Then, still not saying a word, she took out a small ice chest, closed the trunk, and headed off wordlessly on a path toward the beach, leaving me no choice but to follow her.

What happened next only exists in the arcane minds of authors who write the improbable stories found in romance novels. Underneath a brilliant full moon, nestled in a cove that gave us a perfect view of the deserted surf, the two of us made love. It was my first time, and even though I didn't tell Andi, I could tell she knew. I was twenty years old.

Afterward, we lay in each other's arms wrapped in the blanket with a large R stitched in its corner. The only sounds were the rhythmic waves lapping against the shore and a slight warm breeze that constantly blew in from the gulf. Neither of us had said a word for several minutes. Then, finally, Andi spoke softly.

"I need you to give me something," she said.

"Anything. You can have the shirt off my back if you want it."

She lifted her head up, contemplating something, and then sat all the way up, keeping the blanket bunched up tightly around her.

"Okay, give me the shirt off your back, but that wasn't exactly what I was thinking of," she said.

I reached over to the pile of clothes resting a couple feet away and plucked out a gray T-shirt with the letters LSU boldly printed across the front. "What were you thinking of?" I asked as I handed her my T-shirt.

I waited as she slipped it over her head and then down over her body. She sat still for a moment, looking down at the hands in her lap.

"I need you to give me your word. Your word that no matter what happens between us, what we did here tonight will always be just between you and me. No stories or bragging to your friends." Her face was solemn.

"Wow, it sounds like you're writing us off already."

"No, that's not it at all. I'm just realistic. I live in South Carolina, and you live in Louisiana. We both have three years left to finish college, at least. Anything can happen in that time." She was looking at her hands again.

"Let me ask you a question then, and be honest."

"Okay."

"How many boyfriends have you had in the last three years?" I asked.

She paused for just a moment, then said, "None."

"That's funny, because that's my exact answer. So why is it so difficult to believe that we couldn't wait for each other for another three years?"

"Lee, I may be special to you, but I know that I'm not unique. You could meet someone else just like me."

"A girl who looks like you do who can quote Monty Python? Not going to happen," I countered, smiling now.

"I'm being serious. Just give me this one thing. Give me your word that this will be our memory and our memory alone. And do it not because you just want me to drop the subject, but because you really mean it."

I became serious again. "Andi, I wouldn't do that." It hurt me to think that she thought I would.

"I know you wouldn't now. But a year from now, five years from now, ten years, there might come a time when you might be tempted to tell a story about doing it on the beach in Florida with some long-forgotten girl." She lowered her head and looked at the sand in front of her. "I don't want to become that story."

I reached my hand out and touched her chin with my thumb and forefinger, lifting her head upward. Though it was dark, the reflection of moonlight from the moistness in her eyes told me what I needed to know. I leaned forward and gently kissed her on the lips, then again briefly on the tip of her nose.

"I promise. Forever." I assured her.

Andi took the edge of the blanket and wiped the tears from her eyes.

"Okay, now that you have something, two somethings actually, what do I get?" I asked.

She looked at me smugly. "I didn't give you enough tonight?"

Smiling broadly, I leaned over and gave her another kiss. "Yes, you did."

Andi reached into the same clothes pile and pulled back her Levi purse. She dug around inside the bag for a couple of seconds and produced a black cassette tape in a clear protective cover. She handed it to me, and when I examined it, I could see that the plastic case had a label affixed to it with hand printing that read Slow Dancing Mix.

"This is our song?" I asked, surprised.

"It's one song on there. I had a friend make it for me before we left home so we would have something to listen to during the drive down." She appeared proud of herself. "I told you I preferred the slow ones."

"This is awesome. Thank you." I leaned over and gave her yet another kiss, this one a tad more passionate.

We lay there together for a while longer, enjoying some of the Boone's Farm Strawberry Hill Wine from the cooler she'd brought along. As midnight approached, we packed everything up, said a fond farewell to our special spot on the beach, then headed back to the car.

Thirty minutes later, when we arrived back at the Regency, Gayle and Trisha were waiting in the lobby for us. They didn't seem to notice that I was shirtless and Andi was wearing my T-shirt.

"Andi, your father called and wants you to phone home right away. It sounded urgent," Gayle blurted out as soon as she spotted us.

Andi immediately headed to the hotel house phone on a small table next to the registration desk and started dialing. I went over to her roommates. Trisha was biting her nails nervously.

"Any idea what's going on?" I asked.

"Not a clue," Gayle answered. "Her father sounded really upset, especially when he found out Andi wasn't with us."

The three of us looked over at Andi talking on the phone. Although we were too far away to hear what they said, she was very animated, shaking her head several times. I wasn't sure what my role should be just then. Do I go over to her and hold her hand to support of whatever she is going through, or do I keep my distance and give her space. I decided I would follow Gayle's lead and hold back.

A couple of minutes later, Andi slammed down the phone and covered her face with her hands. The three of us looked at each other with concern, then Gayle walked over to her. Trisha and I followed. Andi must have sensed our approach because she began wiping away the moisture from her eyes, and she turned to meet us. Her expression was a mixture of sorrow and anger.

"We have to go home tomorrow morning," she spat out angrily. Selfishly, my heart sank.

"Okay, sweety, if we must, we must," Gayle replied supportively. "But can I ask why?"

"Yeah, why?" Trisha chimed in, obviously irritated.

"I don't know. My dad's a jerk, that's why. He wouldn't tell me," she answered.

The four of us stood there silently for a moment. Andi then walked over and embraced me in a hug so tight that I found it hard to breathe. Then she relaxed her grip slightly and kissed me on the lips.

"We are leaving at eight in the morning if you want to come and say goodbye. I have to go pack," she said, then turned and walked off toward the elevators.

I drove back to the White Sands in a funk, still reeling from the emotional roller coaster the night had become. I was only losing one day with Andi, but twenty-four hours with her were on a vastly different scale than any other measure of time.

At ten minutes to eight Saturday morning, we said our difficult goodbyes in the Regency parking lot. It took every ounce of self-control I had to maintain my composure, but nothing could keep the tears from welling in my eyes. Even when Andi was weeping silently in my arms and her two roommates were wiping the tears from their eyes, I still held it together. We held on to each other as if the world were crumbling around us.

We exchanged slips of paper with each other's address and phone number, promising to write and call often. Andi then pulled a plain white envelope from her rear pocket, made me hold my hand out flat in front of me, and then placed the envelope in it.

"This is for you, but you can't open it until I tell you to," she said.

"What is it?" I asked.

"The most important thing I could ever give you," was all she would say.

Realizing that further questions would be useless, I took the envelope and put it in my back pocket. I gave Andi one final long kiss and watched her climb into the passenger seat of Gayle's Civic. She was wearing a simple pair of jean shorts and the LSU T-shirt I'd given her the night before, and she was as beautiful as I had ever seen her. I waved goodbye as they pulled away, and then she was gone.

I stood there until the Honda was totally out of sight, then turned and walked down to the Regency pier. I walked past the morning fishermen and early risers, past the couples taking a morning stroll holding hands, to the bait shack at the end of the pier that was still closed. I sat against the far wall facing out toward the gulf where no one could see me and cried until there were no more tears to shed.

I did my best to enjoy the rest of our time in Florida with my friends, but everywhere I turned, something reminded me of Andi. Mark and the rest did their best to keep me occupied and distracted so I wouldn't mope, and I tried not to spoil the fun everyone else was still having. When Sunday rolled around, I was glad to be heading home.

As the Knights slept during the drive back home to Louisiana, my eyes were on the road, but my mind was miles away. I'd made friends with five incredible guys over the course of the week, but I felt lonelier than ever. The rest of the world was oblivious to the ache in my heart.

Even Andi's cassette tape played its part in mocking my sadness. The van's stereo only played CDs.

| 11 |

Slow Dancer VI

MONDAY, JULY 19, 2021
SLOW DANCER (Part Six)

My first couple of weeks back in New Orleans, I immersed myself in work, trying to keep my mind focused on anything other than the time in Florida. I volunteered for countless hours of overtime and weekend assignments I would normally turn my back on at my job. At home, I did projects for my mom, much to her surprise and delight. Whenever I'd sit still and let my thoughts drift toward South Carolina, I'd go wash a car or mow the grass for the third time that week.

The nights were the worst, and if I wasn't doing something with Mark, I would find myself sitting at the desk in my room with a legal pad and pen, rewriting the same letter to Andi over and over.

The magical feeling I had while in Panama City didn't take long to fade, and the self-confidence went with it. I started feeling unsure of myself again, questioning my perspective about everything.

Any time the phone rang, I secretly hoped it would be Andi calling to say she missed me terribly. I wondered if I should call but decided maybe a letter would be a better first step. Then I was unsure of what the proper timing should be. Wouldn't writing her first appear too needy? Shouldn't I wait until she wrote me first? There could be a letter waiting for me right now at my PO box at LSU, which was the address I'd given her so my parents wouldn't get curious and pry. But what if she was waiting for me to write first? Then I really started playing mind games with myself, thinking that maybe the whole thing was just a wild, crazy summer fling, and now that she was back to her everyday life at Clemson, she would forget about me. Could I have possibly misjudged her feelings for me that much? I was constantly fighting doubt and uncertainty. If I were to just follow my heart, I'd write her poems and sonnets, but I didn't want to appear as some lovesick child. Why was this all so damn difficult?

The cassette Andi had given me with our song trapped within it sat unused next to the curious white envelope in one of my desk drawers. I didn't own a cassette player. So, on the weekends, I scoured the local record stores searching for an album with our song. My hunt was hampered because I didn't know who the artist was or even the official name. I first found it on a forty-five-rpm version, but if the Knights had taught me anything, it was that any self-respecting record collector wouldn't own a forty-five, so I continued my search until I discovered the song on an obscure soundtrack album. I played that one track until I feared I would wear the vinyl thin.

Having waited as long as I could, I decided it was time to send the letter I'd rewritten over and over. In the final version, I settled on trying to sound witty and masculine while still admitting how much I missed her. I talked about my work and life at home with my family, filling in a few details we didn't get to talk about in Florida. I signed it *Your Love, Lee,* and in a PS requested a picture. The only things I had of her were a cherry stem, a cassette tape I couldn't play, an envelope I couldn't open, and my memories. During my lunch hour the next day, I took it directly to the post office and made sure it started on its way.

The following weekend, Mark and I made the hour-long drive to the LSU campus to check my PO box. It was empty.

The next three weekends, we made the trip to Baton Rouge to check my mail, and each week we returned empty-handed. The doubt and uncertainty I felt before I wrote my letter had turned into full-blown concern. Maybe the address was wrong? But Andi had written it down herself. Maybe I copied it wrong when I addressed the letter? I pulled out the paper with the address and made sure that was what I had written on the envelope. Even if I somehow used the wrong address, wouldn't it have been returned as undeliverable by now? Then why was she not writing back? Was the first letter too corny, too immature? I didn't think so—I'd worked hard to make sure it didn't sound that way.

It was now late July, and I would return to campus for the fall semester soon. Seven weeks had passed since we'd returned from Florida and the last time I heard from Andi. It was time to phone her and find out whether I should snuff out the flame in my heart and move on once and for all. I selected the time of my call carefully. It would be a weeknight because the chance of her being out late with her roommates and missing my call would be greater on the weekend. I would call between nine and ten my time, ten and eleven on East Coast time, when she would be off from work but probably not asleep yet. I made the call on a Tuesday evening after pacing nervously around the house for hours beforehand. I pulled the number out of my wallet and dialed the phone. After a couple of rings, I heard three sharp tones followed by a droll female voice saying, "This number is no longer in service," then the three tones repeated, followed by the same message over again. I hung up the phone, double-checked the numbers on the piece of paper, and dialed again. The same result. Now I was baffled.

Maybe she had moved? But if she knew they were going to move, then why give me the wrong address and phone number? Possibly because she didn't think they were going to move, I theorized. All sorts of speculation and possibilities ran through my mind, trying to understand her failure to respond to my letter and the disconnected phone number. Maybe the phone call from her father calling her home had something to do with it? Although Andi and I didn't talk about our respective families much, I didn't get the impression there was any problem there. But regardless of how many scenarios I thought about, they all ended with one undeniable conclusion—she had my phone number and address, and she wasn't using either of them. Whatever the two of us had for one another in Florida, for her, it had obviously waned.

I decided to write one last letter the week before I returned to school. Choosing my words carefully, I expressed my confusion regarding her lack of communication and the disconnected phone number. I told her that if things had changed for her, I could understand, but really needed her to say it directly by responding to my letters instead of simply ignoring me. I continued by telling her that the four days I spent with her were the best days of my life, and I would never regret them, no matter how things turned out.

I signed the letter, simply, Lee. Then, before I sealed the envelope, I inserted the small cherry stem with a knot.

The first couple of weeks back at LSU were exciting as Mark and I settled into a new apartment and reunited with the rest of the Knights. During the days before classes started, we would all congregate in somebody's apartment and take turns telling stories about their respective summers, with everybody's highlight always being the trip to Panama City.

Everybody asked me if I had ever heard anything from Andi, which I answered truthfully. They all thought that odd because the two of us appeared to be so tight in Florida. All I could do was shrug my shoulders. I was as confused as anybody.

When the semester started, I was a common fixture in the Student Union most mornings. When the bus deposited me on the steps of the union each day, I would check my PO box, get a cup of coffee and Danish from the cafeteria, and on fair weather days, take a seat on the patio overlooking the parade grounds.

One rainy morning, I hopped off the bus and sprinted down the steps to the union's lower floor. Shaking off the few drops I couldn't avoid, I entered the post office and made my way to my box at the end of the first hall. I stuck my key in the small lock, turned it to the right, and pulled the small door open. In the box was a six-by-nine-inch brown kraft envelope. I pulled it out and looked at the return address. There was no name, just a hand-printed address. The bottom line of the address read: Easley, South Carolina. Andi's hometown.

I found the closest empty bench and sat down, unceremoniously dumping my backpack on the ground next to it. I stared at the envelope with trepidation. *Is this Andi finally saying goodbye?* There was only one way to find out. I opened the envelope flap and let the contents spill into my hands. Out dropped a folded eight-by-ten-inch piece of paper and two regular size envelopes.

I looked at the envelopes first and was surprised to find my handwriting on them. They were the two letters I had sent to Andi, and both were still sealed. Shocked and confused, I turned to the eight-by-ten paper and unfolded it. It read:

Mr. Hamilton,

I'm sorry that I must communicate this terrible news to you in this fashion, but unfortunately, circumstances make this is the only avenue available to us. I am Andi's father, Richard. Not even the most gifted writers could find the right words to tell you what I need to say, but I will do my best.

Our beloved daughter, Andi, someone I believe you may have gotten to know in Florida, died on June sixth on her drive back home from her vacation in Panama City Beach. She and two of her roommates were killed instantly when another car crossed the median and struck them head on. The driver of the other car perished in the crash as well.

I'm sorry it has taken me this long to get this information to you, but I'm sure you can understand how distraught and overcome with grief her mother and I have been following that dreadful day. We are only now able to put Andi's affairs in order, and in doing so, we came across your letters. We are returning them to you, unopened. The fact that Andi was wearing an LSU T-shirt when she died combined with the LSU return address on your letters and the timing of your first letter led us to deduce that the two of you met in Panama City. We could have confirmed that by reading your letters, but we didn't want to invade your, or Andi's, privacy.

If you got to know Andi at all in Florida, then I know how devastating this letter is for you. I am sorry for you, for all of us who knew her and are now feeling her loss.

Write back if you so desire. I'd be glad to hear about any memories with her you'd care to share.

KNIGHT RISE - 101

Once again, my deepest apologies.

Sincerely,
Richard Taylor

I remained on the bench for over an hour before getting up and walking the almost four miles back to the apartment. I didn't attend classes that day.

I told nobody about the letter or its contents. I spent most of the next several days in my room, sleeping. On a dismal rainy afternoon a week later, I took the tall metal trash can from my room and positioned it in a covered walkway just outside our apartment. I deposited the envelope containing Mr. Taylor's letter and the ones I wrote to Andi in the can. Wanting a good-size blaze, I jammed a newspaper sitting around the apartment in the can as well, then set it all on fire with a kitchen match. Choosing to not stick around and admire my personal bonfire, I walked off into the rain I couldn't feel, leaving my feelings and memories burning behind me.

That semester ended up being a disaster for me. I found it increasingly hard to concentrate on my studies. I felt lost and unsure of the direction I wanted my life to go. More importantly, I couldn't find the motivation to do much past rising in the morning and going through the motions.

I also started drifting away from my friends—the Knights. They hadn't a clue to explain my sudden moodiness and lack of interest in anything fun. I told them I needed to study whenever they went out and spent a lot of time alone in my room. Mark tried to get through to me, but I wasn't having any of it. The worst part of it all was that I didn't even care what it was doing to our friendship.

Over the winter break, I dropped out of school and moved back home to New Orleans. My plan, what little there was of one, was to get a full-time job and take a couple of night courses until I could get my head together. My parents didn't question my decision or ask about what was going on in my life. I wouldn't have told them if they had. In their defense, how could they possibly have known?

While moving my stuff back home, I stumbled across Andi's mysterious white envelope, forgotten in a drawer of papers. I sat on my bed for the longest time, debating what to do with it. *Should I open it? Should I burn it like I did the letters? Or should I keep it?* Ultimately, I couldn't decide what to do, so I postponed the decision by sticking it in one of my yearbooks not yet packed.

With my van loaded to capacity and my mental health on empty, I headed home without saying goodbye or looking back.

Two and a half years later, I returned to LSU to finish my studies and earn my degree, my time with Andi finally a distant memory. Unfortunately, by that time, the Knights had either graduated or otherwise moved on.

I went through a couple of relationships until, in 1995, I finally met and fell in love with the woman I would ultimately consider my best friend. We were married in 1999 and shortly afterward moved from Baton Rouge to Atlanta.

We'd lived in Atlanta for a couple of years when I received a phone call from a familiar voice one night. It was Mark. He had tracked me down via the LSU Alumni Association, and since he happened to be in Atlanta for a couple days on business, he thought he would look me up. He came over for dinner one night, and I introduced him to Terri over lasagna. I was so happy to see him again. The two of us took turns telling Terri stories of our years in the dorms and our adventures at LSU, and she sat there, genuinely enthralled. Mark talked a lot about the Knights. He tried to make me feel better about my desertion by telling me that none of them were as close as they once had been, and Ebe had disappeared entirely. His attempt to cheer me up didn't work, though. I expressed my regret and vowed to try to see them again soon. When it got late, Terri excused herself, and the two of us continued to talk into the wee hours of the night. Not once did we bring up the subject of Panama City or Andi. He gave me all his contact information when we parted, and I promised to stay in touch. I have kept that promise.

In 2005, after we had our second child, we moved to Arkansas to be closer to family and later moved into the house I live in now. The eight heavy boxes filled with albums were carried straight from the moving van and carefully placed in the spare closet in the house's rear. In one of those boxes was an album that held a special song, patiently waiting for me to discover it again and trigger a memory. There it sat for sixteen years.

***

The stylus on my turntable was once again stuck in a loop at the end of the album. I did not know how long I had been sitting there listening to vacant noise. Returning the tone arm to its cradle and pulling the album off the platter, I read the song title printed on the record's center label. Track number five—"'Swayin' to the Music (Slow Dancing)' by Johnny Rivers, running time 4:00" was printed in black on a red background. I lowered the turntable's plastic dust cover and laid the vinyl disk, along with the paper sleeve and outer album cover, on top of it. My hands were shaking.

The emotions associated with that long-dormant part of my past coursed through my body, unhindered. The feeling I had when Andi first smiled at me, my unbridled joy and happiness for those four days, the agony of having to say goodbye, and finally, the desolation of learning about her death. They all grabbed hold of me. Then, amid all that, I was bombarded with emotions about the death of my wife, Terri. They started re-emerging and intermingling with the memories of Andi. I had never felt so powerless or such an utter loss of control. Two women, both taken from me much too early. I couldn't decide which was worse, the one whom I barely got to know—the first to show me the man I could really be—or the one whom I ultimately became one with and carved out our niche in the world.

Intermingled with all those emotions was one that I probably struggled with the most. Shame. A shame on multiple levels. Embarrassment at the fact that I let Andi's memory slip away and go ignored for so long. Her memory deserved a better fate from me. But there was another kind of shame as well. I had let my friendship with five great guys who had taken me under their wing and let me join their close-knit group deteriorate and fade away without as much as a struggle. For that, there was no excuse, only regret.

I had to let what I was feeling out. I had to tell someone. But I didn't know who or even how. It was tearing me up inside, like an old wound that never properly healed whose scab had just been torn off. I needed to talk about Andi and lay her to rest in my mind, much like I did when I grieved for Terri. A way of saying goodbye and then rejoicing the time together by sharing stories and memories about her with friends and family. There was only one person I had kept in contact with who had known Andi. Mark.

I picked up the phone and dialed Mark's cell phone number. It was time to tell him the truth. My hope for an outlet was crushed when I received his voice mail message telling all callers that he would be out of the country until the following week. I was still alone.

I paced the length of the house back and forth, trying to come to grips with my emotions. Who could I talk to? My children? No, they wouldn't understand. There was no one else. What was I to do?

The answer presented itself as I walked through the living room. Like a monolith casting an influence upon me, the computer monitor sat auspiciously on my desk. At that moment, I knew what I needed to do. I sat down, opened a new Word document, and started typing. I wrote and wrote until the following day when my red, blurry eyes couldn't take it any longer. I took a shower and a brief nap, and then continued writing. The details that poured out of me were amazing. I can't remember the pin number to my bank account half of the time, but I could recall the color of the shirt I wore twenty-nine years ago. I continued writing until I was done.

That concludes the story that I never told. A bittersweet memory that leveled me just when I believed I had come to grips with the loss of my wife. I don't know yet what I will do with this, but its existence has already served a purpose. I am at peace, mostly, with a short period of time that ultimately changed the course of my life forever.

The reason I can only say "mostly" is that I still have unfinished business with five old friends, if for no other reason than to simply apologize to them and say thank you. I'm not gullible. I know that life pulls people apart, and we sometimes make sacrifices in the relationships we choose to keep or not. But this isn't one of those cases. I walked away without looking back, and that is something none of them deserved.

This story was as much about them as it was about Andi. Andi's memory is alive again, both within me and here on the internet. Finding new life with all my readers.

All that remains for me to do now is to apologize to The Knights Who Say Ni. After I post this story, I intend to send an email to each of them, alerting them about this post, and my desire to reconnect.

Wish me luck.

| 12 |

New Hire

Dianne

"Miss Williams?" Evelyn's voice came over the intercom. I shook my head. No matter how many times I had asked that woman to call me Dianne instead of Miss Williams, she refused to comply.

"Yes, Evelyn," I answered, emphasizing her name.

"There is a Miss Timberlake here to see you."

"Oh, good, I'll be right there," I replied and excitedly rose from my desk.

The search for a new female investigator had been brief, mainly because I knew exactly what I was after and there were plenty of candidates to choose from. I wanted to give someone the same opportunity that had been given me when joining the agency, which meant they'd have zero real-life experience. Additionally, she had to be a recent graduate with a master's degree in criminal justice from a well-respected university and have a particular interest in cannabis security compliance. I viewed that as an opportunity for growth in our industry.

Briana Timberlake was the third person I spoke with, and I canceled all of my other Zoom interviews lined up after speaking with her. She was everything I wasn't. Outgoing, personable, an extrovert to the extreme. She immediately got on my nerves, but after reading her school résumé and glowing letters of recommendation, then listening to her talk about where she saw herself going if given a chance, I knew she was exactly what our agency needed. I offered her the position the next day, and she accepted right away and promised to be on the next flight to Charlotte.

My first new hire was standing next to Evelyn's desk when I arrived at the lobby. Briana was tall and athletic with shoulder-length brunette hair and thin lips. She was sharply dressed in a navy-blue blazer with three-quarter sleeves, a white top, and designer jeans.

"Briana, good morning. Have you introduced yourself to our receptionist?"

"Um...not exactly."

"Well, this is Evelyn. Evelyn, this is Briana Timberlake, our newest investigator."

I had a hard time deciphering the way Evelyn was looking at Briana. It was one-third shock, one-third dread, and one-third admiration.

"Let me show you around," I stated, before leading her back into the office area. As we were leaving, I was tempted to reach out and push Evelyn's lower jaw up to close her mouth.

At that time of the morning, most of the other investigators were already at their desks as we made the rounds, and Briana's introduction drew almost the same reaction from them all. It was those reactions that worried me. On the surface, they were friendly greetings and a welcome to the agency, but beneath it all, I detected a thinly veiled sense of contempt. I wondered if I had misjudged the depth to which the boys' club would close ranks. Being the way I am, I gave very little notice to that nonsense and concentrated on the work. But as a manager, I no longer had that luxury. I doubted

Briana had noticed. If she did, she gave to sign of it. Still, now I was worried about what I had gotten her into.

Together, we walked into the break room to grab a cup of coffee before beginning her orientation. John Stamata and Henry Billings, both ex-cops and two of the agency's most senior investigators, were sitting at a table near the entrance.

"John, Henry, this is Briana Timberlake. She just started today," I said.

Henry looked Briana over from head to toe and back to head again. John didn't bother to turn his attention away from his coffee.

"Starting as what, a filing clerk?" Henry asked, drawing a tiny grin from John.

I could feel heat building at the back of my neck. I opened my mouth to react until…

"No, I'm an investigator, just like you," Briana responded instead. "Well, maybe not *just like you.*"

That caused John to look up from his coffee and fix his eyes on Briana. "What's that supposed to mean?"

"Just that I'm sure we all have our areas of expertise. Take some of the other people I graduated with, for example. One was interested in financial investigations, another was into insurance fraud, but there was this one guy. Well, he was different. He was all about being one thing."

"Oh yeah? What was that?" John asked.

"A dick."

It took everything I had not to bust out laughing, but I couldn't suppress my smile.

Henry stared at Briana hard, but she didn't back down, returning the look with the same amount of intensity. After a couple of moments, Henry took a sip of his coffee.

"Where did you go to school?" he asked after swallowing.

Briana's demeanor relaxed as well. "Michigan State for my undergraduate, then Northeastern for my masters."

"A four-point-one GPA and Dean's list at both schools," I added.

Henry looked at John. "Doesn't your son go to Michigan State?"

John's eyes were still shooting laser beams through Briana. "Michigan."

Suddenly, a booming voice filled the room. "What's this bullshit I hear about us cutting off Norwood Construction?"

Mack Green bulldozed his way into the room, stopping just shy of stepping on my toes. Mack was a big guy, six feet tall and two hundred seventy-five pounds, most of it around his waist. He had one of those perpetually unshaven looks which contrasted with his shiny bald head. His eyes always seemed red, probably from his excessive drinking, but they also matched his contentious disposition. Rumor had it that he elicited most of his confessions during his time on the force from pure intimidation, and I didn't doubt it.

"Well?" Mack asked when I didn't respond.

"If you have a question about a client, you can make an appointment to talk with me in my office," I answered calmly.

"Screw that. We're both here now, and I want an answer."

"We all have wants. Right now, I want to continue my orientation of our new employee, so you'll have to see Evelyn about scheduling a time to discuss Norwood."

At the mention of a new employee, Mack glanced at Briana.

"What new employee? Sweet cheeks here?"

The heat rekindled on my neck, but I bit my tongue. Over the years, Mack and I had learned to avoid one another as much as possible. I'm sure he considered me a social misfit, refusing to play his games and endure his offensive jokes. I found him to be crude, abrasive, and an irritant to everybody, except Aaron, of course. By all accounts, he used to be an outstanding detective on the force and a competent private investigator, but that time was long gone. I'm pretty sure Aaron only kept him around because of his police connections. Now that Aaron was gone, I knew that I'd eventually have to deal with Mack's behavior, but I was hoping to let the rest of the crew get used to me being in charge a little more before that happened. I needed to diffuse this situation before somebody said something they'd regret, mainly me.

"Mack, I can see you're upset. Let's go back to my office, and I can explain everything."

Then Briana stuck out her hand.

"My name is Briana Timberlake, and you are...?"

Mack just stared at the offered hand. "Not interested in a blow job right now, honey. Can't you see the adults are talking? But hey, why don't you stop by my office this afternoon?"

The heat on my neck turned into a four-alarm fire.

"Your fired!"

I said it with so much force that I startled everyone in the room, including Mack.

"What did you say?" Mack asked, confused.

"I said you are fired. Terminated. Pack up your things and get out of here." I said it all through gritted teeth and noticed every muscle in my body had tensed.

Mack looked at John and Henry, then back at me with annoyance. "You can't fire me."

"Oh, I can, and you are. I'm not sure why it's taken me so long to do it. You're an embarrassment to yourself and the profession. Do you know how automobile dealerships hire former sports stars to hang around the car lot to draw in customers? Sad ex-athletes clinging to their glory days, collecting a paycheck for doing nothing. That's what you've become. So I need you to leave before I have you removed."

I at once regretted saying every word. It didn't matter that it was the truth.

Mack's annoyance turned into outright anger.

"This isn't over," he growled before storming out.

| 13 |

Loose Ends

_TJ_

TJ suspected that he could get fired for what he was doing and fooling himself if he thought that didn't concern him much because it did, but he continued his risky endeavor anyway.

What he'd been told to do made little sense, and that bothered him. He sometimes struggled with the legal and moral issues of what his job required, even though he understood that serving the greater good meant that sometimes individual freedoms might have to be infringed upon or sacrificed altogether. But this was the first time he had run up against the possibility of outright abuse.

After his meeting with Mr. Brown on the third floor, he had done some research. Nobody could ever recall a raw data feed from an IP address being forwarded above the analyst level, especially someone at Mr. Brown's security clearance. It would have to be of preeminent importance and highly classified national security material to bypass TJ's department. But what he had read from Hamilton's web traffic was anything but that.

When TJ returned from the third floor and informed Mrs. Jenkins of the change in status of the Hamilton file, she raised an eyebrow and asked him if he was clear about what they had ordered him to do. When he affirmed his instructions, she immediately updated her logbook and directed TJ to reroute the data feed directly to Mr. Brown's terminal address, which she provided for him. If his supervisor was concerned about what was happening with the data, she didn't show it.

Each analyst worked on one tasking duty and the relevant data stream that accompanied it within their department. The tasking duty number, the data stream number, the date it was originated, the badge number of the analyst assigned, the originator, and the response code for flag trips were all logged into Mrs. Jenkins's black book. The tasking duty explained the flags and triggers the analyst was to be monitoring along with possible variations. They coded each badge number on the repository in the data server. The analyst was then given the data stream number to gain access into the encrypted system on his computer, which was matched against his badge number in the repository. Of course, there were sophisticated supercomputers capable of accomplishing this in a fraction of the time with more reliability, and they handled many assignments that way. Still, the powers that be weren't ready to take tracks deemed as "sensitive" away from humans just yet.

Usually, when a tasking duty was completed, the IP address would be pulled from the collection register, and all old data would be transferred to a separate server for archiving. Meaning there would be nothing in the central server to access, even if an analyst desired to do so. But in this case, they handed the data stream over to Mr. Brown to access the information directly from his own computer. TJ knew that sometimes when data streams were transferred between analysts—something routinely done because of absences, vacations, or termination—the badge number of the original analyst wasn't always deleted from the server right away. The day after they had transferred the data stream, TJ typed the same number into his computer, and there it was. He could still access all the Hamilton information.

TJ had to be careful about how he went about this. He needed to avoid any files that hadn't been accessed yet because that would be a sign somebody else was viewing the material. And he still had all his regular workload to take care of, so during breaks and thirty minutes of his lunch (there was no way he could give up an entire lunch), he would devote himself to the Hamilton file. The first thing he did was pull up all the data he had already looked at and reread it. He rarely comprehended the material when performing a tasking duty because he was searching for specific words or phrases, and that was true with this file. But even though he did not truly understand what he was reading, he could still get a general sense of the subject matter and whatever criminal activity the IP address owner might be involved in. TJ got no such sense of that when reading the Hamilton file.

After a few days of rereading, TJ felt even stronger that something was amiss. Lee Hamilton wrote a blog that was entertaining but not really TJ's cup of tea. Nothing controversial or subversive. It generated above-average traffic for a blog, especially after posting his latest six-part sob story. Aside from that, Hamilton accessed his work computer from home a couple times a week, surfed some sports-related websites, and did little else. But around the time the tasking duty was put in place, he started spending a great deal of time using Google to search for old news accounts of fatal car accidents in June 1992 and the office of vital statistics in numerous states looking for a death certificate for an Andi Taylor. Andi Taylor and Panama City, Florida were two of the flags the tasking duty watched for. As far as TJ could tell, there was no reason for Homeland Security to track Lee Hamilton's online movement, much less be rerouted to a supervising director.

What was he supposed to do about it, though, TJ wondered? He wasn't even sure why he had gone this far, risking his career and giving up thirty minutes of eating time every day. If he showed this information to anyone in the building, losing his job would be the least of his worries. He doubted they had many three-hundred-plus-pound men incarcerated in federal prisons. Of course, he could simply just let it drop because there was no actual harm being done to Lee Hamilton other than he was being watched without his knowledge. No actual harm yet, that was.

But TJ really wanted to know the real reason Mr. Brown planned to continue reading the material without authorization. What was the man up to?

***

Mr. Brown

The elevator doors slid open, revealing Mr. Brown dressed in a recently purchased conservative dark-gray suit. A multicolor striped tie against a white cotton shirt rounded off the look. He stepped out and turned right, heading toward his office. The distinguished gray-haired woman behind the black marble-top desk, dressed sharply in a dark-blue pleated edge skirt suit highlighted with a paisley scarf and white gold shrimp hoop earrings, noticed Mr. Brown exit the elevator and stopped what she was typing.

"Mr. Brown?" she called to him.

Mr. Brown stopped and looked toward the receptionist, saying nothing.

"You wanted to be notified whenever security had plans to be in the offices after hours. The carpets are scheduled to be cleaned this weekend," she told him.

"My carpets are fine, Mrs. Jackson," he responded flatly.

"Yes, sir. I understand, but they are doing the entire floor," she explained.

"My carpets are fine. They don't require cleaning," Mr. Brown answered in the same uncaring tone and continued on to his office. As far as he was concerned, the matter was closed.

At the door to his office, he smoothly removed his keys from his pocket, slid it into the keyhole on the first try, unlocked the lock, and entered the office. He gently closed the door behind himself, making barely a sound. If somebody were watching, they would have sworn he was sneaking into his own office.

Inside the office, he removed his suit jacket, draped it over one of the two chairs in front of his desk, and then walked to the window that took up most of the wall at the rear of the room and turned the plastic handle opening the vertical blinds covering it. It was cloudy outside, and there wasn't much morning sun to let in, but he preferred whatever natural sunlight he could get to artificial illumination. His window looked out over the north parking lot, and off in the distance, he could just make out the outline of RFK Stadium. He could tell that traffic on Independence Avenue was backed up once again due to the morning rush.

After logging on to his PC, the Department of Homeland Security logo replaced the Microsoft emblem on both screens, and a row of icons appeared on the left-hand side of the left-most monitor. He used his mouse to navigate the cursor over an icon illustrated by a picture of a magnifying glass over a file folder and double clicked. Another small security screen popped up on the monitor to the right, asking for a data stream and badge numbers. He entered both pieces of information from memory.

Displayed on his screen, as the program loaded, was a window divided into three vertical sections with a row of icons across the top of the entire window. The folders and file names in the left-hand section were data that had been marked as viewed. The folders and files in the middle segment were unviewed data, including the last time the user logged in, and everything in the right-hand section was newly collected data since the last login.

After two hours of sifting through data, a particular email stirred his interest. He clicked on his desktop icon for Google Earth, which opened on his left monitor with a three-dimensional rotating globe and a box to the left requesting location by address, city, state, and zip code. He typed in all the necessary information from memory and clicked display. After panning and zooming on the map for a couple minutes, he reached over to pick up the phone and dial zero.

"Yes, Mr. Brown," Mrs. Jackson's voice answered.

"Mrs. Jackson, I need a direct flight to Memphis this coming Friday afternoon with an open return. I will also need a rental car while I'm there. Something in the midsize range but nothing flashy."

"Will you require hotel arrangements as well?" Mrs. Jackson asked.

"If I needed hotel arrangements, I would have asked for them," he answered flatly and hung up the phone.

Almost as soon as he hung up on Mrs. Jackson, he picked up the phone again and dialed a four-digit number.

"Repository, this is Bill Sneed," a high-pitched man's voice answered.

"Mr. Sneed, this is Robert Brown on the third floor. I need to ask you a question."

"You bet. Shoot."

"Is it possible to move individual parts of a data stream that have already been viewed off the main server and onto the archive server?" Brown asked.

"Sure, we don't get a call to do that much, but it can be done," Bill answered.

"Then I need everything from this past Sunday on data stream number 82547568 moved."

"Right now?"

"If possible."

"Hang on just a sec," Bill answered, and Mr. Brown could hear strokes on a keyboard in the background. Then, a second later, "I can't do it right now because it appears somebody is still accessing the old data."

Mr. Brown did not immediately respond, lost in thought.

"Mr. Brown?" Bill said after he heard no response.

"Thank you," he said and hung up the phone. Again, he picked up the phone and dialed zero.

"Yes, Mr. Brown," Mrs. Jackson answered in a perfunctory tone.

"I need to change my departure back one day to Saturday, Mrs. Jackson," Brown informed the receptionist. "I have a loose end to tie up first."

***

The Cat Lady

This was the fifth time she had returned to the coffeehouse, and the manager noticed her, despite the added sunglasses and floppy hat. She nervously scanned the tables, looking for one that was unoccupied, and spotted one in the rear next to a couple who were reading their respective magazines. She scurried back to it before somebody else grabbed it and deposited her backpack on top. Then, with her bag guaranteeing nobody would take her table, she took her place in line to submit an order.

This was further than any point she let herself reach during her five previous attempts that morning. Each of the other times, she'd talked herself out of going through with it. Instead, she'd driven aimlessly around the city until she changed her mind, then returned.

It had been several days since she initially had the urge to post a comment to his blog. At first, it was easy to discard the idea as impulsive and foolish. She went about her usual routines—work, church, health club, volunteering at the Humane Society and library for a couple of hours here and there—but her mind wouldn't let the idea rest. Every night she would return to the blog to reread it, along with the comments. The outpouring of comforting words and support in those comments was impressive, and she wondered, no, she hoped, that he found some sense of solace in them.

What did she really hope to accomplish by commenting, anyway? She knew it would be pointless. She also knew it was irresponsible and selfish. She knew all those things, nevertheless, here she was using an anonymous internet connection, poised in front of the keyboard, ready to write something she couldn't put into words yet. What could she possibly pen that would offer some level of comfort?

A series of chirps from her cell phone announced the receipt of a text message. She took the phone out of the pocket in her backpack and looked at the tiny screen.

SAM CELL: *When R U coming home? Want 2 see a movie this PM?*

She typed out her reply and set the phone on the table next to the cooling decaf coffee. She leaned back in her chair again and stared vacantly at the laptop. All the tables in the coffeehouse were full, and a couple of college-age girls were sitting on the floor against the wall near the front of the building.

Her phone chirped again. She picked it up and looked at the screen again.

SAM CELL: *Great! See you then. Luv U!!*

It came to her as she was putting the phone back on the table. She suddenly knew what she wanted to say. Had to say. Her battery was already down to forty percent. She quickly navigated her web browser to his blog before she lost her nerve again. She steered her way to the comment link, clicked the button, and an empty comment box appeared.

She smiled as her fingers flew across the keyboard.

| 14 |

Letters

Lee

He picked his head up off the throw pillow. Once the cobwebs in his brain had dissipated, he silently cursed himself for falling asleep on the couch again. Fortunately, his son was a late sleeper, allowing Lee to take a shower, change clothes, and return to his desk before Chase knew any different. Lee didn't want him to see his father sleeping on the couch and give him another reason to worry. The clock on the opposite wall read 7:16 a.m. He tossed aside the throw blanket partially covering him and swung his feet onto the floor. He was still wearing the cargo shorts and T-shirt from the day before.

After Terri had passed, he'd gotten into a habit at night of trying to stay awake as long as possible before transitioning to his bed to increase the chance he would fall directly asleep. If he wasn't exhausted when climbing into bed, he would lie there wide awake, unable to turn his brain off. The trick was to time it just right because if he fell asleep on the couch, he would end up sleeping there all night like he had just done.

He had been sleeping on the couch every night since he began writing "Slow Dancer."

After a shower and a change of clothes, he made himself a bowl of cereal from the kitchen and carried it to his desk. After his computer came to life, the stack of papers that had accumulated next to the monitor caught his attention. The documents were printouts of emails he had received regarding his "Slow Dancer" blog. At first, he printed the emails, not knowing why it felt good to hold tangible evidence that his craft was being appreciated. But as the emails kept rolling in, he had to abandon his printing efforts when he ran out of ink. He would concentrate on returning a brief note to as many as he could instead.

The tone of most of the comments and emails was supportive and highly complimentary. There was one comment that especially intrigued him. Most responders were equally divided between registered users with personalized usernames and those who posted anonymously. Someone using the username of Slow Dancer wrote the comment that drew his attention. The comment simply read, *Find the picture.* When he clicked on the username to display more detailed profile information, he found that every field had been left blank. What picture, he asked himself? Was somebody spamming his blog now? He printed the comment anyway and added it to his stack of papers.

Of all the comments and emails he'd received over the last several days, none were from the Knights. Not even Mark. It had only been a couple days since the blog had been posted and he sent the emails out, so maybe he was expecting too much to hear something this soon. Perhaps they didn't receive his email? Maybe they hadn't read the blog yet? Maybe they had read it and could not care less?

That may be the case for some of them, but not Mark. The two of them had kept in touch via email, postings on one another's Facebook page, and an occasional phone call over the years, so Lee was confident Mark would respond to the blog in some fashion. On the other hand, Mark had been out of the country, so it was reasonable to believe that he was still catching up from being gone and hadn't had a chance to read it yet. At least, that was what Lee chose to believe.

He set about straightening the area around his desk by gathering all the printed emails and securing the bundle with a rubber band, storing them in one of the vacant cubbyholes above the work area. Satisfied with his efforts, he next turned his attention to the area around his turntable and albums. Two cardboard boxes rested on the floor between the desk and the accent table, both half full, and a stack of a dozen records lay on the floor in front of the boxes. The soundtrack album still sat on top of the turntable, the cover and sleeve beneath it, exactly where he had left it. He hadn't played another album since.

Lee picked up the record and slipped it into the paper sleeve. When he tried to slide the sleeve into the cover, it hung halfway and wouldn't go any farther. Lee pulled the album back out and re-inserted it with the same result. There was something inside the cover preventing the sleeve from sliding all the way in. He peeked inside the cover and noticed that there was indeed something deep inside. He put the sleeve down, turned the cover on end with the opening facing the floor, then pinched the sides to make the opening bow open. Out tumbled a six-by-nine-inch brown kraft envelope.

Lee dropped the album cover on the floor and sat heavily in his chair. His eyes transfixed on the brown envelope.

It's the same envelope. It had fallen in such a way that the address label faced upward, and his old LSU PO Box was clearly written on it. *But how could that be? I burned it! I placed it in a garbage can and lit it on fire. How is it here, now?*

Lee felt light-headed. Flushed. He began to doubt his memories. This made no sense.

He bent over and picked up the envelope, handling it as if it was covered with germs. Turning it over, he released the metal clasps on the flap, flipped the flap open, turned the envelope on end, and shook. Out spilled two sealed white envelopes and a single piece of paper. His letters to Andi and the letter from her father. Lee's mind was reeling.

How can this be? I put the envelope in the can and set it on fire. But it obviously didn't burn. Who? Who was there when I made that bonfire? He couldn't remember... *Think, dammit.* He stared at the wall across from him, reliving that day. When he returned from walking, the trash can was where he'd left it, full of cool ashes. He'd dumped the ashes and carried the can back to his room. He walked to the bathroom to hang up the wet clothes, but Mark was locked in there.

Lee's cell phone was in his hand within seconds, dialing Mark's number. After it had rung once, he glanced at the wall clock—twenty past nine. A voice answered after the fourth ring.

"Hello," the voice said.

"You pulled the envelope out of the fire?" Lee blurted out unceremoniously.

There was a long pause, then "You found it?" The tone was that of relief.

"Why?" Lee asked.

"Why what?"

"Why did you stop them from burning?"

"Lee, I watched you carry the trash can out to the courtyard and start the fire, but by the time I got out there, you were already walking away. I was curious about what you were burning, so I put out the fire and pulled out the envelope. After I read Mr. Taylor's letter, I felt so bad for you. I knew you were hurting, but I thought someday you might regret burning them, so I hid them in my room. I also knew you needed that catharsis of setting them on fire, so I put the newspaper back in the can and let it burn. That way, you would think you'd accomplished what you set out to do. I figured that once you got over Andi, I would give you the envelope and you'd appreciate still having the letters," Mark explained.

"So why didn't you give them to me?"

"Because you dropped out of school, numbskull. I tried my best to get you to snap out of it and stick around, but there was no changing your mind. So, I just hung on to them."

"But how did they end up back in the album?"

"Remember when I visited you in Atlanta? The real reason I was there was to give you the envelope. But I couldn't do it. I sat there with you and Terri, and I just couldn't find a good way to bring it up. The two of you seemed so happy together that I didn't see the point. So, when you left me alone in your study to refill our drinks, I found the record you showed me with the song you and Andi first danced to and shoved the envelope inside. I figured you'd find it one day. Just didn't think it would take this long."

There was another long pause.

"You okay?" Mark asked.

"It was quite a shock when it fell out," Lee answered.

"For the longest time I've wanted to tell you it was there, but when Terri died, I couldn't find the heart to bring it up."

"Good call," Lee replied.

"Are you mad at me?"

"How can I be? You were just looking out for me."

"When I was reading your blog, I kept waiting to read the part about you finding the envelope in with the album, and when it never came, I figured you must have overlooked it."

"I just found it two minutes ago," Lee explained.

"Oh. So how you doin'?"

"Do the other guys know—about Andi dying?"

"They do now, if they read your blog, but I never told them."

"Why not?"

"I assumed you would tell us, eventually. I just didn't think it would be twenty-nine years later."

Yet another long pause filled up the airwaves.

"Mark, Andi died," Lee said, his voice softer now. It was the first time he had spoken about her death out loud.

"I know," Mark replied, his voice just as soft.

"Terri's gone, too."

"I know. I'm so sorry, buddy."

"I feel cursed." Lee's voice was even softer.

"You definitely have been dealt some cards from the short side of the deck, that's for sure."

Mark couldn't see the awkward smile that flashed across Lee's face.

"What did you think of my blog?" Lee changed the subject.

"I kind of knew the ending, so it spoiled it for me. But you left out the part where I slept with those three girls in one night."

"That's because I wasn't writing fiction."

"Ouch."

"You haven't heard from any of the guys?"

"No, but I wouldn't take that as a sign or anything. They're all probably like I was, not knowing what to say to you."

"Then I guess I'll just have to call them instead."

"I have a better idea," Mark offered.

"An idea would be good."

"Why don't you come to Lafayette for the weekend? I can have everyone come out to my dad's lake house, and we can hash things out then," Mark proposed.

"This weekend?"

"Sure, why not? I'll make sure my schedule is clear."

"What about the others?" Lee asked, his mood improving by the minute.

"I'll contact them and let you know if anybody has a problem with it."

"Sounds good."

"This is going to be awesome!" Mark sounded excited now.

"If nothing else, it will be great seeing you again."

"Same here. I'll send you an email with more details, okay?"

"Okay."

"Lee...I am very sorry. For everything."

"See you this weekend, Mark," Lee replied, and disconnected the phone.

He placed his cell phone on the desk, and when he swung his chair around, he saw Chase standing in the doorframe, looking as if he had just crawled out from under his bed.

"Are you going somewhere?" Chase asked, nodding toward the phone.

"I'm probably going down to Lafayette to see some old friends," Lee answered.

"Oh, okay," Chase replied, finishing it with an enormous yawn and disappearing back into the kitchen.

Turning his attention back to the two white envelopes and the letter, Lee didn't know how he should feel. The letters had been nothing but dust in his mind for so long that it was surreal to see them sitting before him. Although he had written about them in his blog and referenced the feelings he had put in them, he couldn't remember exactly what he'd written. It tempted him to give in to his curiosity and open them. What would a twenty-year-old version of himself sound like? Would he sound stupid? Would he sound lovesick? Maybe he should do what he tried to do in 1992 and burn them. Yes, he wanted to honor Andi's memory and their brief time together, but did keeping the letters around serve that purpose, or was it just another painful reminder? He told himself that Andi wasn't in those words, no more than Terri existed in his home any longer. Still, he wasn't planning on moving anywhere soon. What should he do?

"What are those?"

Chase had walked up behind him, carrying a bowl of cereal, looking over his shoulder.

"These...are...letters that I wrote a very long time ago," Lee answered.

"But they haven't been opened. Did you never send them?"

"It's a long story, but the short answer is that the person I sent them to never read them."

"They're love letters, aren't they," Chase continued, not letting the topic drop like Lee hoped he would.

"As a matter of fact, they are."

"Can I read them?"

"No," Lee answered firmly.

"Why not?"

"They're personal."

Chase chomped on a spoonful of cereal for a moment, not moving away.

"They're not to Mom, are they?" he asked finally.

"No, they're not."

"Why do you still have them?"

"Honestly, I just found them hidden in one of my albums."

"Cool. Let me read one."

"Why on earth would you want to read one of my old love letters?" Lee swiveled around and asked his son.

"Three reasons. One, it's a good way to get to know you better."

"The old me. These were written twenty-nine years ago."

"Even better."

"The second reason?" Lee prompted.

"Maybe I can learn some tips about what to put in my own letter when it comes time to write one."

"I doubt that. And the third?"

"Because I'm really curious."

Lee stared at his son, contemplating his own feelings. He made up his mind and opened the desk drawer, pulling out the letter opener. Picking up his first letter, he inserted the tip of the opener into a small opening in the upper seal and ripped the envelope open. Then he handed it to his son.

Chase put down his bowl of cereal on the accent table and started pulling out the paper inside the envelope. Lee picked up the second letter and ripped it open as well.

"What are you doing?" Chase asked.

"I'm just as curious as you are. Like I said, I wrote these twenty-nine years ago," Lee answered.

Lee put down the letter opener and slid the folded paper out of the envelope. He straightened out the folds, and they both read in silence.

A couple minutes later, Lee looked up from the letter with a puzzled look on his face. He reached for the envelope and looked inside. Then he started looking around on the desk and floor at his feet. Not finding what he was looking for, he again picked up the envelope and looked inside more thoroughly.

"Dad, what's wrong? You look like somebody stole your lollipop," Chase observed.

"I think somebody did," he answered thoughtfully. "I'm missing a cherry stem."

| 15 |

Knights Reunited

Lee

Lee packed up his 2011 Jeep Cherokee and departed Conway for the six-and-a-half-hour drive to Lafayette.

When Mark emailed him to let him know everything was set and all the Knights, except for Ebe, would come to the camp, Lee felt the first of many knots form in the pit of his stomach. This was what he wanted, this was what he had asked for, but now that it loomed ahead, he couldn't help but be nervous about what his old friends would be like now and what their reaction to him would be. Nevertheless, he took it as a good sign that all of them had agreed to come. The weekend was going to challenge him emotionally. He knew it would require that he be expressive and outgoing, which never came easily for him. But if he was going to make amends and change his life, this was something he must do, and he needed to step up.

He pulled into the Walmart parking lot across from the North-gate Mall and spotted Mark's black Chevrolet 3500 HD extended cab off by itself right away. He pulled his Jeep into the slot to the right of Mark's truck and killed the engine. Opening the door and getting out of his car, he heard the door shut from the truck's driver's side. He met Mark as they both rounded the front end.

Mark wore his age well, at least on the outside. He had put on weight since Lee last saw him in Atlanta, but nothing dramatic and not what he thought somebody who'd had a heart bypass would look like. Mark's face and arms were deeply tanned from time spent at construction sites, and the hair on his arms was sun-bleached blond. His nose, which seemed so much more prominent when he was younger, now magically fit his face perfectly. His straight thin hair had receded, and he'd chosen to go with the fully shaved look which made his face a little chubbier than Lee remembered it. He was wearing a jean shirt with the sleeves rolled up, blue jeans, and a pair of fancy cowboy boots with silver metal tips.

The two of them bear-hugged, unconcerned about who might be watching and what they might think.

"Shit, how do you do it?" Mark asked when the two of them separated, looking Lee over.

"Do what," Lee answered, playing stupid.

"You look like you could pass for forty. You and Billy both," Mark responded, jamming his fist into Lee's shoulder.

"What can I say, clean living," Lee boasted. It always amazed people how Lee's face had maintained its youthful appearance while those around him were changing. If it weren't for his own receding hairline and bald spot on the back of his head, he could probably still pass for thirty. "You're not looking too shabby yourself."

"Better living through pharmaceuticals is my motto. I think I'm taking every drug known to man. How was the drive down?"

"Nice. Uneventful. Been waiting long?"

"I pulled up maybe ten minutes ago. You estimated your time well."

"I'm pretty good at that. So, what's the plan?" Lee asked.

"We load up with some booze and grub here, and then head on out to the house. I told the guys to show up around seven," Mark answered. Lee looked at his watch.

"Everybody still coming?" Lee asked, turning and walking with Mark toward the front entrance.

"Nobody's canceled that I know of. We still haven't found Ebe, though. He really pulled a vanishing act."

The two of them walked along silently for a bit, then Mark said, "It's good to see you again, Lee."

"You too, Mark, you, too."

An hour later, they loaded up their respective vehicles with enough groceries to feed a small army, complete with four cases of beer and a couple of bottles of hard liquor. Mark insisted on paying for everything, even though they'd agreed to split the expenses for the weekend. Finally, they pulled out of the parking lot and headed east toward Henderson Lake.

Mark's lake house was down a long, winding, gravel road. Their two vehicles pulled up onto a paved driveway which began fifty feet from the house and continued past the garage to a covered boat dock, housing what looked like a bass boat and two Jet Skis. The two cars parked in front of the extra-wide garage. Lee exited his Jeep and looked around. The house was surrounded by thick woods on three sides and the lake on the fourth, with no signs of civilization anywhere. Mark signaled for Lee to follow him, and he started a tour of the house and grounds.

"I'm impressed," Lee said when they ended up where they'd started.

"Dad put a lot of time and hard work into it. Mom did all the furnishing and decorating, of course. I've just left it like it is."

"Do you get to use it much?" Lee asked.

"I only come up here a couple times a year, but my sister and her family are out here a lot. We'd better get that beer iced down and the grill fired up before everyone shows up."

Lee heard the first car pulling down the gravel road around six thirty, and the knots in his stomach returned. A charcoal-gray Acura pulled in next to Lee's Jeep, then sat there with the engine running for several minutes. Finally, the engine died, and a short man wearing slacks, a sports coat, and sunglasses jumped out of the car. He pulled a suitcase from the back seat and began walking toward Lee and Mark.

Kent had put on considerable weight around his midsection, his hair was still disheveled, with a fair amount of gray sprinkled in, and he now wore a full beard with gray hairs as well.

"We were wondering if you were planning on sleeping in the car," Mark remarked as Kent approached, stoking the charcoal in the smoker one more time.

"My mom called just as I pulled up. Can't hang up on Mom," he called back. His voice had more bass and was more resonant than Lee remembered.

"How is she doing?" Mark asked.

"Pretty good. We moved her into an adult living community a couple months ago, and she's still adapting. More phone calls than usual," he answered, now standing right beside Mark. The two of them shook hands and then hugged briefly. Kent looked past Mark to Lee.

"Hi, Kent," Lee said.

Kent set down his suitcase and walked over to face Lee, his expression unreadable.

"I have just one question for you, mister."

"Okay," Lee answered, bracing. Mark stopped what he was doing and looked at the two of them.

"What is the airspeed velocity of an unladen sparrow?"

Lee stood silent for a couple seconds, then responded with, "African or European swallow?"

A wide smile broke out on his old friend's face. "Lee! You're back!" he exclaimed loudly, and the two of them embraced. The tension in Lee's body was suddenly gone.

"Shit, even I forgot that one," Mark stated, returning to preparing the food. "I can tell I'm going to have to brush up on my Monty Python."

Kent stepped back and looked at Lee. "Damn, have you invented a time machine or something? You look great!" he said.

"It's good to see you, too. How have you been?"

"I've got no complaints. I'm teaching first-year psychology at LSU. I'm married and have two kids, both in high school. How're your kids?"

"Both of them in college and trying to figure out who they are. I don't get to see them as much as I'd like, but you know how that goes."

"I do, I do."

"You want a beer, Kent?" Mark interrupted.

"You know it. Let me put my bag away first." He pointed to his suitcase.

"Pick out a bed in one of the downstairs bedrooms," Mark instructed him.

"Just as long as I'm not sleeping in the same room as you. Do you still wake up the neighbors with that snoring?" Kent commented as he picked up his bag and walked around to the stairs leading up to the back deck and then into the house through one of the glass doors.

"When's the last time you saw Kent?" Lee asked, returning to his chore of putting the beer and ice in the chests.

"Ummmmm...five years ago. We went to the SEC Championship Game together," Mark recalled. If you ever need LSU tickets, Kent's the one to talk to."

The two continued talking about LSU football, joined by Kent when he returned. Mark continued prepping the food, while Kent and Lee enjoyed their beers and talked.

A few minutes past seven, a red Dodge Ram 1500 came racing down the driveway.

"There's Billy," Mark commented without even looking up from the table where he was applying barbecue sauce to the chicken breast.

The red truck veered off the driveway onto the grass to park next to the other cars. Shortly after that, doors on opposite sides of the truck opened, and men stepped out from each.

"He's got somebody with him," Lee observed.

"That's just Raymond," Kent pointed out.

Raymond was no longer as thin as he once was, but it was an improvement. He appeared to have gained an inch or two, making him the tallest of their group, and his full-bodied black hair was still perfectly combed. He wore a red polo shirt, jeans with a crease down the pant legs, and a pair of black New Balance running shoes. Even though his face had filled out, he could have been a perfect Jay Leno impersonator with his exaggerated jawline.

Lee now understood why Mark made a comment regarding Billy's appearance earlier. He could easily pass for somebody still in their upper thirties or early forties, and his body maybe even younger than that. He still maintained a definite V shape in his upper body, with broad shoulders and a barrel chest sloping toward a skinny waistline. He was wearing a pair of brown hiking shorts, Merrell hiking boots, and a tan Hard Rock Cafe Cancun T-shirt that bulged over the muscles he had no doubt preserved through hours of dedication at a local health club. His curly locks were less noticeable with the shorter hairstyle, and there wasn't a speck of gray anywhere. Lee could tell by the spring in his step that his boundless energy was still intact.

"Lee!" Billy yelled from across the yard, throwing both his arms up in the air, bringing a smile to Lee's face.

"Billy!" Lee hollered back.

Lee walked out to greet the two of them. Billy broke into a jog and covered the fifty yards between them in no time. He raised his right hand in the air, palm facing Lee, and Lee reciprocated by giving his friend a high five that evolved into a semihug.

"Shit, it's so great to see you. Looks like you've been hitting the gym, haven't you?" Billy asked, squeezing Lee's upper arm.

"Three or four times a week. I don't need to ask you if you have," Lee observed.

"I only take off on Sundays and special occasions, like this weekend," Billy said, his boyish smile making Lee smile right back.

"Hi Lee," a voice said, and Lee noticed Raymond was now beside them with his hand out to receive a handshake. Lee grabbed hold of his hand firmly.

"Hi Ray, long time," Lee replied.

"Long time," Raymond repeated dryly. He let go of the handshake and stuck both his hands in his pockets. There was no smile on his face, and Lee immediately got the feeling that Raymond wasn't as glad as everyone else that he was there.

"Kent!" Billy cried out again and darted was off to greet his friend sitting in a lawn chair by the grills. Raymond and Lee looked at one another for an awkward moment, both with tight-lipped smiles. Mark walked up and stuck his hand out toward Raymond.

"Hey Ray," Mark greeted him.

"Hey, Sig," Raymond replied, shaking his hand. "I forgot how nice this place is. New boat?" he asked, gesturing toward the dock.

"It's not actually mine. It's my sister's husband's."

"Sig!" Billy shouted again as he appeared out of nowhere behind Mark and slapped his hand sharply on his back.

"Hey Billy," Mark replied, wincing slightly from the friendly attack.

"When are we going to eat? I'm starved," Billy asked.

"Everything's all set. I have a chicken smoking that is just about ready, and I need to throw everything else on the grill. So get yourself a beer and just relax," Mark answered.

"Don't you guys play music anymore? We need some music," Lee pointed out.

"Kent," Mark yelled, and Kent turned his attention toward the four of them. "Go put on some music."

Kent gave a thumbs-up sign and headed into the house. Mark walked back to the grill, leaving Lee standing there with Raymond and Billy.

"So, how long did it take you to drive down here?" Billy inquired, looking for something to break the silence.

"About six and a half hours."

"That's not very far," Raymond observed.

"And where is it you live again?" Billy continued, sounding a little confused.

"Conway, Arkansas. It's about forty-five minutes from Little Rock."

"Oh, I thought you lived in Atlanta," Billy explained his confusion.

"I used to, but we moved to Arkansas so we could raise our kids closer to family."

With the mentioning of Terri, his two friends fell silent, unsure of what to say. Just then, the unmistakable sound of Brian May's guitar was heard blaring from the all-weather speakers mounted on the walls at the corners of the deck. It was the first track from

Queen's *A Night at the Opera* album, and all three of them smiled at one another and said simultaneously, "Death on Two Legs."

They all took seats in lawn chairs circled around Mark, working hard on the grills, joined shortly by Kent, who received high marks for his music selection.

"So, nobody knows where Ebe disappeared to?" Lee asked the group.

It was Raymond who spoke up first. "Nope. He abandoned us, too."

If it weren't for the music of Queen playing in the background, the silence would have been deafening.

Lee was beginning to think that the upcoming weekend might not be as congenial as he hoped.

| 16 |

A Loss of Appetite

Mr. Brown

Before leaving the office, Mr. Brown changed into a dark pair of slacks, a navy-blue hoodie over the top of a plain black T-shirt, a Washington Wizards hat pulled down low on his brow, and black Nike running shoes. He also carried a small, nondescript backpack over his right shoulder, which he held tight. It was after hours, and the building was mostly empty, so any concerns Brown might have about being seen while leaving were minimal. He easily avoided the security cameras on his way outside, then once on the street he walked south eight blocks, passed two Metrorail stations, and then entered the third one.

He boarded the Blue Line train north toward the Metro Center, and then switched to the Red Line at the interchange. It was seven o'clock, and the early evening rush had subsided, all except the Friday night lingerers. He exited the train at the Tenleytown-AU station, intermingling with a handful of commuters, walked one block west along Albemarle Street to Thirty-Sixth, then turned left and began the five-block hike through suburban neighborhoods to the Connecticut Heights apartments.

Mr. Brown knew that the fat data specialist was dining with his mother tonight, as he did every Friday night, and wouldn't return home for at least another hour. There was more than enough time to prepare for his greeting when he returned home.

Brown's discovery of the snooping by the specialist in the Hamilton data only altered his timetable slightly. He had planned for every contingency and obtained the items required ahead of time. It was a shame the boy could not mind his own business. Not because he had any compunction about killing him, but his death would bring unwanted attention too close to home. Still, he could not allow Pickens to raise suspicions. His death needed to look like an accident.

He first thought about strangling the blob of a man with a plastic bag and then shoving a large, partially chewed piece of meat down his throat to make it look like he had choked to death on his own food. That had an ironic symmetry to it, but it had too many variables he could not control. A sharp assistant coroner might notice the petechial hemorrhaging in the eyes, which were a sure sign of strangulation. If they delved even deeper, they would find that there were no partially digested pieces of the same meat in his stomach. As appealing as the symmetry of his first plan was, he decided to go with a less risky method.

Plan B had its own share of risks. He had acquired the chloroform weeks ago from an online chemical supply house and the rusted pipe from a vacant home he had located a week before that. When Pickens returned from his last meal with his mother, Brown would be waiting for him with the chloroform. Once the specialist was asleep, he would remove the pipe feeding the gas stove and replace it with the rusted pipe complete with a large enough hole to allow the gas to escape. Because the apartments where he lived were past their prime and poorly maintained, the discovery of the rusted pipe wouldn't seem out of place. Once the gas was turned back on, Pickens would die in his sleep from accidental carbon monoxide poisoning. There were only two vulnerabilities to the plan. The first was after he turned the gas back on, he'd only have three minutes to exit the apartment because that was as long as he could hold his breath. He wouldn't be able to see his victim succumb to the gas. The second was the neighbors. They could smell the gas and take action, reviving the big man before his death. He considered both risks and dismissed them as negligible.

The Connecticut Heights apartment building was a twelve-story complex containing low to medium rent units. There was a single entrance monitored by a security guard twenty-four hours a day. The guard's sole responsibility was to screen traffic going in and out of the building to keep the so-called undesirables out. The only video camera in service pointed at the main door and the front lobby. Although the primary access was in the building's front facing the street, a service door in the rear, used solely by the superintendent, exited into an alleyway behind the building. They kept the service door locked, but the lock was old, and any third-rate lock picker could make easy work of it. Mr. Brown slipped on a pair of latex gloves he pulled from his front pants pocket and had no difficulty.

TJ Pickens's apartment was on the third floor, which could be accessed by either the elevator or two sets of stairs, each on opposite sides of the building. Mr. Brown stood at the landing of the north stairs, listening to ensure that no one was descending. Then, hearing nothing from above, he quickly sprinted the six flights to the third floor.

They had obviously upgraded the apartment locks in the building recently because they were the newer model Kwikset door locks with a secondary bolt lock that could only be secured from the inside. But Mr. Pickens must have upgraded the bolt lock on his door, at his own expense, to a commercial-grade SmartKey single-cylinder bolt lock that could be locked from the exterior of the apartment. Pickens undoubtedly took these added measures to protect the thousands of dollars of computer equipment inside his apartment. After spending just a few seconds working on both locks, he was in the apartment almost as fast as someone using a proper key.

Taking just a few moments to let his eyes acclimate to the dark, he followed a mental picture of the layout he had memorized. He was in a small hallway running parallel to the outside corridor. To his left was the entrance to the bathroom and, farther still, the master bedroom. To the right led to the kitchen and living area. He turned to the right.

In the kitchen, he unslung the backpack from his shoulder and placed it on the island bar separating the two rooms. He unzipped the main compartment and removed a linen cloth and a small, round metal cylinder with a screw-on lid. He reached into the compartment again and extracted the short, rusted pipe wrapped in clear plastic and a small tool kit.

He depressed a small button on his watch to illuminate the dial so he could check the time. He then started to work on the stove.

***

_TJ_

His mother had gone all out and prepared one of his favorite meals, stuffed chicken marsala, but TJ could not find the appetite to enjoy it the way it deserved to be enjoyed.

The lack of an appetite was something new for him. He did not know how to react. He could never recall feeling this way before. Even when he'd been ill because of seasonal flu or an occasional sinus infection, his desire for food had never been affected. And it had little to do with hunger because so much of his eating habits rarely revolved around his body's need for sustenance—it was more like a hobby to TJ. The pleasure he derived from an exquisitely prepared meal—such as the one that sat before him now—was curbed by his conscience. The more information he read about Lee Hamilton, the more his appetite diminished.

It had been several days since he began secretly reading the data stream that Mr. Brown had hijacked from him. TJ was more convinced than ever that Brown had some kind of personal vendetta against the man and was using the powers of Homeland Security to further his agenda, whatever it might be.

As far as TJ could tell, Mr. Brown wasn't toying with Hamilton's banking records, credit rating, or any of a dozen other electronic footprints he could disrupt his life with. Even so, it bothered TJ more than it should that such an apparently innocent citizen could be subjected to this intense scrutiny without cause or oversight. How could a data trap and the subsequent data stream ever have been approved in the first place? Only a person considered a viable threat of terrorism or detrimental to national security could come under this level of monitoring without a court order. TJ could find no evidence of that. Neither did he find any clues or inconsistencies that would lead him to believe that he was a threat to national security. A terrorist cell in Conway, Arkansas? Not likely.

So, what was he to do about it all? All of the options he considered ended with him either losing his job or, even worse, going to federal prison. He thought about communicating directly with Lee Hamilton to alert him of Mr. Brown's activity, but he rejected that idea. Sending a warning anonymously wouldn't guarantee that Hamilton would take it seriously. If TJ told him who he was, well, there was no assurance Hamilton would keep his identity secret, and that would put TJ in some deep shit. Besides, the Department of Homeland Security would deny all allegations, anyway. Still, even though Lee Hamilton might do nothing about it, he should be told to watch his back. If the situation were reversed, that's what TJ would want.

He looked at the pan holding the two pounds of oven-roasted chicken breast stuffed with prosciutto and fontina cheeses with sun-dried tomatoes, topped with mushrooms and a creamy marsala sauce. All TJ could muster was a sigh.

"TJ, you're not eating," his mother observed curiously when she returned from the kitchen with a basket of steamy crescent rolls. She was a spry woman for her age and weight, most of which she had put on after giving birth to her only son, TJ. At sixty-six years young, Elmira Pickens may have looked her age, but she didn't act it. Gray hair, age spots on her wrinkled face and arms, and a gimp in her step from the hip replacement surgery all betrayed her attempts to live as old as she felt, which was much younger.

"I'm waiting for Dad," TJ lied.

"He's not eating with us. He had a po'boy on the way home from work," his mother told him matter-of-factly. His father rarely ate with them on the ritual Fridays when TJ would return home. It seemed he didn't share the enthusiasm for food that TJ and his mother did, constantly asking his son a question he already knew the answer to. "How much weight have you lost?"

"Well, the truth is, I just don't have much of an appetite tonight," he confessed to her.

She sat in the chair opposite from him and adopted a concerned look.

"What's bothering you, darling? It's not like you to turn away from chicken marsala," she asked, avoiding hurting his feeling by pointing out he had never turned away from *any* food.

"It's something at work that I really can't talk about other than to say it has me in a quandary."

His mother dished some of the chicken marsala from the pan onto her plate. "Does it involve hurting somebody by your actions?" she asked, concentrating on the food.

"No."

"Does it involve hurting somebody by inaction on your part?" she asked again, now plopping a spoonful of mashed potatoes on her plate.

TJ paused a second before answering. "Maybe."

She looked into her son's eyes. "Then make it right," she stated firmly.

"I know that's what I should do, Mom, but by doing that, I may put my job at risk," he responded frustratingly.

"There's always a way, son. You just haven't thought of it yet," she counseled him, reaching for a crescent roll.

"I have been thinking about it for a week now, and I can't find a way," TJ countered, wishing he had kept his mouth shut so he didn't have to listen to her sage advice that never applied to the real world.

"If you don't, it will continue to eat at you, and you'll find no peace." She paused for a moment to fork a piece of chicken into her mouth. "Sometimes it helps to approach things from a different perspective, you know, like coming in the back door instead of the front," she offered, chewing slowly.

TJ sat back in his chair and folded his arms across his massive stomach. Anything he would say right now would just continue a conversation that was going nowhere and wasn't helping. He knew his mom meant well and was genuinely concerned for his well-being, but she really didn't have a grasp of how complicated life could be and tried to solve problems by using catchphrases from motivational posters. *There is no giant step, just a lot of little steps. No act of kindness is ever wasted.* Or his favorite, *When we all work together, We all win together.* What a crock! Tonight it's—*When the front door won't work, use the back door.* It was better to let the subject drop than to make her understand the situation. "Back doors, geez," he thought.

Back door. A flicker of thought suddenly flashed across TJ's mind. Back door. The more he thought about it, the more substance it developed, gaining a foothold in his thoughts. Was this a plausible idea? He turned it over in his mind, looking for holes and pitfalls, but could find none. It could work, he thought. It would be a long shot, but it was a chance. Now the idea had become a plan. But did he have the nerve to act on it? He stared at the chicken marsala in front of him and made up his mind. The plan now needed to become action.

"Mom, can I use your computer?" TJ asked, already rising from his chair.

"Now?" she replied.

"I thought of something that will help my appetite, and I need to do it now."

"Okay, sure." She watched him move as fast as he ever could to her PC.

TJ headed toward the den where the PC he had set up was kept, then stopped. He took a few steps back to the dining room.

"And Mom."

"Yes, honey?"

"Thank you!"

"Oh, you're welcome, darling." She went back to eating her meal.

The den was a combination library and living room with bookshelves on one side and a television on the other side. There was a leather sofa, a love seat, and a recliner facing the TV in the middle of the room. The PC was on a computer desk against a side wall near the bookshelves. Strolling into the room, TJ greeted his dad, who mumbled his response from the recliner watching a rerun of *Baywatch*.

The computer in his parents' house was more for TJ's use than it was for them. He'd convinced them they needed it to pay their bills online, and he could communicate with them via email more frequently. He knew they were set in their ways and wouldn't use it, but it would be there for him to use when he was bored. That was also why he persuaded them to install the broadband internet connection as well.

It took him just a few minutes to sign on and navigate to where he needed to go. When he finished, he measured his action against the expected result and decided that the odds weren't favorable enough yet, so he visited several other sites before finally signing off, shutting down the computer, and returning to the dinner table.

"Did you take care of what you needed to?" his mom asked when he returned.

"I'm starved. Does that answer your question?"

An hour later, with a full stomach and his mind at ease, TJ said goodnight to his parents and started his short walk to the Metro station.

After the fifteen-minute train ride, he trudged the seven blocks to his apartment complex. TJ gestured hello at Julio, the night security guard, as he walked by and climbed into the elevator.

As he exited the elevator, he pulled his keys from his pants pocket. He first slipped the key into the deadbolt and felt it release its grip on the metal plate, then inserted his other key into the door lock and twisted it open. *Home, at last,* he thought.

After making a beeline for the bathroom to relieve the pressure on his bladder, TJ wanted to get on his computer right away. He was curious to see if anybody had responded to his posts yet. He walked down the hallway, flipping the switch to the receded flood lamps above the island bar, and continued past the bar toward his computer desk on the far wall.

Suddenly, an arm grabbed him around the neck, and some sort of cloth was being jammed tightly against his nose and mouth. TJ flailed his arms around, but he could not connect with whoever was behind him. He tried to bend over to dislodge the arm around his neck, but that didn't work either. Dampness on the cloth in his face had a sweet smell. He tried to hold his breath, but the excitement and exertion of trying to fight off the intruder forced him to breathe heavily instead. He felt light-headed, and his arms suddenly felt like they weighed fifty pounds apiece. His vision blurred, and there was a ringing in his ears. He could feel the fight leaving him, and he could not resist when he felt himself being manhandled. Abruptly, the intruder, whose weight was holding TJ upright, was gone, and he collapsed face down onto his couch.

TJ was barely conscious but couldn't move or comprehend what was happening to him. He felt as if he were in a bad dream. He couldn't keep his eyes open and thought he heard footsteps, a noise in the kitchen, the sound a tire makes when you let the air out, and then nothing but the sound of escaping air. Then he was vaguely aware of something else. It wasn't a sound, but something different. A smell. He knew that scent. He felt his body cough involuntarily. Gas. He smelled gas. He heard footsteps again and what he thought was the front door opening and closing. His body coughed again. It was getting harder to breathe now. He had to wake up. He had to yell for help. The realization came to him that if he didn't, he might actually die!

With as much willpower as he could muster, TJ opened his eyes. His vision was still blurry. There were two and three of everything. His head was facing the hallway toward the front door. Summoning every bit of strength in his body, he rolled his massive frame off the couch and plummeted to the ground. He landed on his back with a tremendous thud, causing something on his bookshelves to fall over. Resting just a few seconds, he rolled over and got up on all four of his limbs. Crawl, he commanded his body. It didn't move. Crawl dammit! Slowly, he started moving toward the front door, but it wasn't fast enough. He could feel the gas starting to steal the strength. He had to call for help. It was his only chance.

Closing his eyes and redirecting his energy to his chest, he called, "Heeelllllppppp!" His attempt at a scream came out as little more than a whisper.

The walls of the apartments were paper thin, and his neighbors were probably home, but nobody could have heard that. Again, but much louder this time, he thought.

"Heeelll—" and he was cut off as a large hand covered in latex clamped over his mouth.

| 17 |

Confessions

Lee

He was beginning to wonder if this get-together was a good idea after all.

Things started out fine. Conversation during dinner and much of the early evening covered mature topics such as the state of the current economy, Hurricane Katrina, global warming, and the upcoming open primary election. The Knights all sat around in lawn chairs on the back deck, floodlights illuminating the space several feet into the backyard. Ice chests full of beer and red plastic cups used to mix the stronger drinks were conveniently nearby. The discussions were friendly and nonconfrontational, which was a little out of the ordinary from what Lee remembered when they were in college. He attributed this to the fact that Raymond, the one who was the most opinionated in debates, was hardly saying a word.

As they became more comfortable with each other, the conversation turned more personal. They talked a lot about their respective jobs, and family. Everyone was married, except for Mark and Lee.

Billy was the owner operator of an independent flight service. He had just the one plane, but business had been good two years in a row now and he was debating hiring a third pilot to take some of the load off himself and give him more free time with his family. He had one son who was a senior in high school and a second who was a sophomore, both all-conference athletes in football and baseball.

Kent, the professor at LSU, had a daughter who was a freshman at Tulane and wanted to become a neurosurgeon.

Raymond had become a lawyer, and a successful one at that. His firm had expanded numerous times over the years, setting up offices in major cities throughout the South, but he preferred to remain rooted in his hometown. He had a son in law school at LSU and a daughter who was a senior at the same high school that Billy's boys attended.

Mark had recently been promoted to vice president of site development for Rand Industries. He managed all of the company's considerable construction projects from South Carolina down to Florida and as far west as Texas up through Oklahoma. It was challenging work and something he admittedly always dreamed of doing, but it wasn't without its level of stress and frustrations. A triple bypass surgery, multiple ulcers, and a failed marriage were part of the price he had paid for his dream.

As the evening wore on and the drinks switched from beer to hard liquor, the talk evolved into other subjects. LSU football, LSU basketball, NASCAR, the degeneration of pure rock 'n' roll music since the mid-1990s, the emergence of grunge, and who the best guest host of *Saturday Night Live* had ever been. And still, Raymond sat off to the side, interacting only when asked a direct question.

Mark looked at Lee and asked, "What happened to the Braves this year, Lee?"

"Their pitching dried up and disappeared in the second half," he answered.

"That's something I'm sure you can relate to," Raymond quipped, triggering everyone to turn their heads in his direction.

That's when the night turned sour.

The sting in Raymond's comment took everybody by surprise and, knowing his history as a fierce verbal opponent, no one was eager to engage him. Mark finally spoke up by saying, "Raymond, why don't you eat another hot dog or something."

"I think you need to slow down with the drinking," Kent added, figuring there was safety in numbers. With his sunglasses now off, Lee could see that the discolored circles under Raymond's eyes had grown puffier and darker with age.

"I'm drinking Sprite, you dufus," Raymond fired back.

"Then maybe you should start drinking," Kent countered.

"It's okay, Kent. Raymond has had something to say to me since he got here. So, go ahead, Raymond, say what you want to say," Lee interjected, intending to redirect Raymond's anger away from the rest of them and toward its actual target.

The silence was Raymond's answer.

"Lee, Raymond just thinks that—" Billy started.

"I can talk for myself, Billy," Raymond cut his friend off. "Your right, Lee, I have had something to say to you. The only reason I'm here is that Billy insisted, although I wanted to see Kent and Mark again. But it seems nobody here wants to talk about the elephant sitting in the corner of the room. I have nothing to say. Rather, it's something to ask. We all have the same question—they just can't get up the nerve to ask it."

"Then ask your question," Lee offered.

"I want to know why you took off without saying a word to us. Not even goodbye. I read your blog and understand what happened to Andi. I'm sorry about that. But did we mean that little to you? Is friendship such a shallow concept to you?"

Raymond paused and looked around at the others. Billy and Kent were looking down at the floor. Mark looked compassionately at Lee, like a big brother who wanted to stop a bully from picking on his younger and smaller brother, but he wasn't sure what he could do to help.

"I know it hurt you," Raymond continued. "But that's what friends are for. You should have come to us, but instead, you ran away. So now here you are again, twenty-nine years later, wanting to pick up where you left off. So tell me, why should we welcome you back? Why?"

Lee stood up slowly from his chair and put his red plastic cup down on the patio table. As he was about to speak, Kent rose and walked up to Lee, putting a hand on his shoulder.

"Ray, I'm not trying to make excuses for Lee, and I know he'll give you his own answer, but I wanted to point something out to you. If I knew then what I know now, I could have predicted how Lee would react to receiving that news. He was raised a military brat, moving around year after year. What few friends he did have were constantly being left behind, and I would speculate that very few were close friends. Introverts look inward during times of emotional upheaval. He frankly didn't have the emotional toolkit to deal with that situation, and he responded the only way he knew how to. You and I have known each other since we started walking and most of our friends we've known forever. It was just easier for Lee to block out everything, including us, because that's what he knew how to do," Kent offered calmly.

"I appreciate you wanting to stand up for me, Kent, but that's not the only reason." Looking at Raymond, Lee said, "Ray, I have no excuse. It's as simple as that. I can't explain my actions other than to say that I had to get away. I wasn't thinking about you guys. More like I was running toward some sense of direction. I was hurt, lost, and confused. I made a mistake. Kent is right. My actions reflected my emotional immaturity, but not the value I placed on our friendship. I should have opened up to you, Mark, or anybody. I left instead. I have never learned how or when to ask for help when it comes to my emotions. I almost did the same thing with my own kids when Terri died, for which I will forever be ashamed, but they ended up being the ones who helped me through it. I am screwed up, and I know it."

"Saying that doesn't make it all right," Raymond responded, though less angry now.

"You're right. But I'm not here wanting to pick up where we left off because I know that can't happen. I'm here to apologize to all of you for what I did and tell you I know how unique our friendship was. We were the Knights Who Said Ni, for Christ's sake. If we could somehow become friends again, that would be great. But if not, then you'll at least know that I'm sorry."

They all sat there silently. Somewhere, a cricket chirped insistently, attempting to attract a willing female.

"I know how hard it is to control your emotions," Kent spoke up finally. "It's like at the end of *Field of Dreams* when the Kevin Costner character asks his dad if he wants to have a catch. No matter how many times I watch that, I lose it every single time."

The edge of Raymond's lips turned upward into a small smile. "And you teach psychology?"

Kent smiled back. "You know what they say, those who can't play, teach."

Raymond turned his attention back to Lee. "If I were you, I would get to know us better before you decide if you want to be friends again. You might disappear a second time after you do," he said.

"Absolutely," Kent piped up again. "Take me, for instance. These guys have ragged me for years about talking to my mother at least once a day and have every single day for as long as I can remember. Ever since cell phones became affordable, it's been multiple times a day."

"Kent, we don't really mean anything by it," Billy said.

"I know. But the thing is this, it's not just that we talk. My mother second-guesses every little thing in my life, including whether I should have come out here this weekend. My failure is that I'm not man enough to tell her to mind her own business and leave my family and me alone. How sad is that?"

Looking at Billy, Kent continued, "I know you guys were only kidding. But do you know how behind every sarcasm, there's a little bit of the truth? In this case, you were right."

After pausing for a moment to let his words sink in, Kent turned to Lee. "And you have missed nothing in the last thirty years anyway, at least not as far as I'm concerned. My whole life has revolved around nothing but college. First, I went there, now I teach there. I've never worked in the real world, and I don't know if I could. My whole life has been academics and theory." He raised his cup in a mock toast to himself. "I wonder if I can blame that on my mother as well."

The group sat in dumbfounded silence again, unsure of how to respond to their friend's revelation.

Billy was the first to comment. "Teaching is one of the most important professions there is Kent; you shouldn't take what you do so lightly."

Kent nodded slowly. He took another long sip of his drink.

"As far as your mom goes, I've never thought less of you or looked down on you because you talk to her more than most. My mom's been gone for five years. I'd easily trade a call every day to have her back," Ray added.

Kent nodded his agreement again.

"Then you have me," Mark spoke up, "who is the only one of us without children because I'm so wrapped up in my work that I don't know how to do anything else. I went to work for my dad straight out of college, and he intended for me to take over his construction business when he retired. But what did I do? I was so full of myself and driven to make it on my own that I took a job with a bigger company, Rand, and almost caused him to go out of business. I worked so hard and did so well that I ruined my relationship with my father, destroyed my marriage, stressed out my heart, and turned my stomach into a toxic waste zone. Let's face it—the only thing I'm good at is building things. I tear down everything else."

"You smoke a mean chicken," Kent joked.

Everyone chuckled at that.

"You should be glad that you didn't have kids," Billy observed. "You prevented them suffering through all the crap a divorced family goes through. Sometimes I wonder if Meg and I are going to make it and end up putting our kids through all that—like my parents did."

"What!" Raymond said in surprise. "You've never said you and Meg were in trouble."

"I said I just wonder, not that we are getting a divorce. We've been fighting a lot lately, and sometimes I worry that the only reason we're still together is because of the boys."

This somber version of Billy was something Lee wasn't used to. In fact, listening to all his old friends discuss everything wrong with their lives was unsettling.

"You're just going through a rough patch, Billy. We all do, but I know that you love Meg. You'll work it out," Raymond said.

"I hope you're right," Billy replied. "But I couldn't finish LSU. I couldn't hack the desk job my uncle got for me. And I couldn't cut the commercial flight school. My track record for finishing what I start isn't all that great," he added, now sounding more exasperated.

"How long have you been a pilot?" Raymond asked him.

"Almost twenty years now," he answered.

"And how's that working out?" Raymond questioned him further.

"We do okay. I'm out of town more than I'd like, but other than that, we make a decent living."

"Then it sounds like you're not planning on quitting that," Raymond continued.

"Shit, no. I love to fly. I'll never quit flying," Billy replied emphatically.

"And you love Meg, too. So you will not quit her, either," Raymond insisted.

"Ray, logic won't work on Billy," Kent said. "He's immune."

Billy threw a half-full beer can in Kent's direction, but it sailed over his head.

Mark got up from his chair and flung the remainder of his cup's contents off the deck. "Guys, look at us. We've all had personal issues and problems. Just a few minutes ago, we were giving Lee crap because he didn't turn to us for help thirty years ago, and tonight I discover stuff that we're all going through, but nobody has said a word. What kind of friends are we if we can't lean on each other?"

Silent nods were his response.

"What problems does Ray have? I didn't hear him spilling his guts like the rest of us," Kent said.

Raymond looked at Kent and said, "I do, just like everybody else. I started and developed a distinguished law career that's grown by leaps and bounds. Met and married a beautiful woman whom I love and adore and had two amazing kids. I did the coaching thing. They made me president of both our local soccer and baseball leagues.

And I'm respected by the community. So I admittedly have it all." Raymond stated to the group.

"Did I miss something?" Kent asked. "Where's the problem?"

Raymond showed Kent a weak smile. "I can't get rid of this feeling that something is missing."

"How so?" Mark asked.

"I don't really know. I feel unfulfilled. It's hard to put into words. Maybe it's just a midlife crisis thing. I find myself staring out the window in my office a lot at the kids playing basketball across the street and wishing I could be out there with them instead of prepping for court, like I should be. My mind wanders frequently, I'm unfocused, and I don't know why. I've told no one about this, not even my wife, because quite frankly, how can anybody who has everything complain about their life?"

Lee, the only one standing, looked around at his old friends.

"Damn," Lee broke the silence, "I'm glad to see I'm not the only one whose life is screwed up!"

The five of them broke out in laughter.

Lee continued, "Ray, let me suggest trying something like writing or anything else creative. Or take up mountain biking. The point is, try things until you find what you're searching for, or else that feeling you have will taint everything else you do."

Looking at Mark, Lee continued, "Sig, I guarantee you that you will find a woman out there who can either live with how you are or will motivate you to change—as long as you don't give up trying."

He turned to Kent. "Kent, if you consider your mom's opinions about what you do as butting in, tell her. But my feeling is that it doesn't bother you as much as you let on. It's comforting to have somebody hovering over you like that, and you don't realize it until it's gone," he offered.

Kent looked at Lee eye to eye. They raised their plastic cups in a toast toward one another.

KNIGHT RISE – 159

"Now I know why friends grow apart," Lee persisted. "It's because when we're younger, all we talk about is music, cars, and girls. And as we get older, it gets tougher to avoid the hard subjects. We choose to drift apart rather than talk about them."

"This stuff ain't fun," Billy offered.

Everybody nodded.

"Women eat this shit up, though," Kent said.

Everybody nodded again, more enthusiastically.

"Now I have a question for everybody. What happened to Ebe?" Lee asked.

Raymond, Mark, and Billy all looked toward Kent.

"Well, he graduated with Mark and me with a degree in computer science, and then he went to graduate school at ULL here in Lafayette and got a degree in software development. He got a good job with some accounting firm as their applications programmer and worked there for maybe eight years, then he just up and quit one day. Wouldn't say why. The next thing we know, he's moving to Dallas, and poof, he's gone," Kent recounted.

"We haven't heard from him in, what, seventeen years?" Billy said.

"Eighteen. But even before then, we started seeing less and less of him. You know his long red hair?" Raymond asked Lee, who nodded. "He cut it when he got that job at the accounting firm, but after quitting, he started growing it back and then some. After that, he looked like a redheaded Sasquatch."

"What about his family? Doesn't he come back to see them?" Lee inquired.

"His mom passed away in 1998 while he was working for that accounting firm, and his dad has since moved away," Kent answered.

"I had the girls in my firm try to track down his email address, and they ran into a dead end," Raymond commented.

"That's too bad. I really hoped that Ebe could be here too," Lee lamented.

"We all did," Billy added. "That would have been awesome."

A lull settled over the group.

"I need a refill," Billy stated, and everybody agreed. As they all moved to the ice chests to refresh their drinks, Raymond moved up next to Lee and poured some sprite in his cup.

"You sure I can't interest you in something stronger?" Lee asked him.

"What the hell, put some Seagram's in there for me," Raymond replied. "Listen, I'm sorry for what I said before."

"Don't be," Lee said as he poured some of the liquor into Raymond's cup. "You just forced me to say what I needed to say a lot earlier. Thanks."

One by one, they returned to their chairs. In the background, Pink Floyd played over the deck speakers. A slight chill had crept into the night, and a lone bullfrog could be heard croaking by the lake's edge.

"Lee," Billy started again, "your blog about Florida was incredible. It was almost like being there again."

They nodded in unison.

"I still can't believe that Andi died," Billy said solemnly.

"Well...that's something I'd like to talk to all of you about," Lee said.

"Ohhhhhh, that sounds mysterious," Kent commented.

"When I first found the album and remembered about Panama City, I got this urge to find out more about the accident. I thought that reading about it would somehow give me closure. So, I spent hours researching it over the internet. Do you have any idea how hard it is to find out if someone is dead...or alive?"

"You think Andi is alive?" Raymond sounded surprised.

"No...well...I have questions. The route Andi and her room-mates took going home, or at least the route I would have taken, passed through four states, four highways and two interstates, eight major cities, and nineteen counties. I couldn't find a single reference to a fatal car wreck in any of them during June 1992."

"But just because you couldn't find it on the internet doesn't mean it didn't happen. Like you said, they could have taken a differ-ent route," Mark pointed out.

"You're right, and by itself, I wouldn't have taken it any further." Lee paused for a moment. "But then there's the cherry stem."

"The plot thickens," Kent chirped again.

"You remember in my story the cherry stem Andi tied in a knot that I kept and put in the second letter I mailed to her?"

"Yeah, I remember that," Billy answered excitedly.

"Well, I opened the letters because I wanted to read what I wrote again, but the cherry stem was missing."

"Your story said you burned those letters!" Billy blurted.

"He thought he did," Mark interjected, "but he didn't."

"Now I'm confused," Raymond said. "You were lying?"

"No. Like Mark said, I thought I did," Lee clarified, looking at Mark.

"I pulled them out of the fire before they burned, and I hid them," Mark explained.

"Did you read them? Maybe the cherry stem fell out then?" Billy asked.

"No, I didn't read Lee's letters, just the one Andi's father wrote," Mark clarified.

"Wait a minute. That means you've known Andi was dead this whole time?" Raymond asked.

Mark nodded shamefully.

"Why didn't you tell us?"

"I didn't think it was my place. I thought Lee didn't want us to know for a reason," Mark tried to explain.

"Wow...this just gets better and better," Kent said.

"We're getting sidetracked," Lee said. "I respect what Mark did for me and don't hold any grudges. He hid the letters in the album, and I didn't discover them until after I wrote the story and posted it."

"Okay, so what is so strange about the cherry stem again?" Billy asked.

"I opened both letters, and the stem wasn't in the second one. That can only mean that somebody opened my letter and sealed it back without putting the stem back in," Lee explained.

"Well, maybe someone did. That doesn't mean anything," Raymond said.

"But it had to be somebody in Easley."

"So? It still doesn't mean that Andi wasn't in a genuine accident," Raymond reiterated.

"But doesn't it make you wonder? Why did Mr. Taylor say that he was returning the letters unopened, but at least one of them had been opened? Why? Add that to the fact I can't find any evidence of her accident. It's just all very curious," Lee explained, more adamant now.

"It was Mr. Mustard, in the den, with the candlestick," Kent announced.

"Lee, let's say you're right. Then why? Why would her father send you a letter telling you Andi was dead? And why did she not try to contact you?" Raymond asked pointedly.

"Her father did suddenly call them home early. Maybe he's one of those overprotective dads who found out she was seeing someone and wanted to break the two of you up?" Mark suggested.

"I don't know, maybe, but I need answers. I can't let it rest. I need to do now what I should have done back then, instead of folding up and running away."

"What are you going to do?" Billy asked.

"I'm doing part of it right now. I needed someone to talk to about this. Ever since I found that album and wrote the story, I've been turning this over and over in my head, trying to figure out just what really happened. I need someone to tell me if I'm obsessing over this and get a grip, or agree with me that something's fishy and help me figure out what to do next," Lee replied, looking at the four of them.

"Have you told us everything? Is there anything else?" Raymond asked.

"Just one other thing, but I don't know if it's really something or just someone pulling a prank."

"What is it?" Billy asked, leaning forward in his chair and placing his chin on his fists.

"There was a comment posted to my blog that said, *Find the picture*, and it was from a user registered as Slow Dancer," Lee said.

"I'll admit that is kind of strange, but what picture? Back then, it wasn't like it is nowadays, with cell phone cameras everywhere. Nobody was taking any pictures. And what does it have anything to do with your story?" Mark asked.

"I don't know. Andi never gave me a picture, and neither of us had a camera in Panama City," Lee answered, sounding deflated.

"I think I know."

Everybody looked at Kent.

"Remember in the Sunset Club, ladies' night, when we partied with Andi and her roommates?" Kent asked.

"Sure," Lee responded.

"Don't you remember? Andi and her roommates had our picture taken by the club. You know, you pay them fifty bucks, and they would hang it up on their wall."

Billy snapped his fingers and pointed at Kent. Lee stood up from his chair.

"Shit, you're right. I forgot all about that. We were all in that picture. If I remember correctly, the club put one on the wall and mailed the other to whoever paid for it. What are the chances that either of them still exists?" Lee asked everybody.

"Somebody thinks it does," Kent pointed out. "Who else would even know about the picture except the girls and us, and supposedly the girls are dead."

"I know what I have to do now," Lee announced.

"What?" Mark asked.

"I have to go to Panama City."

"What do you hope to accomplish there?" Raymond asked.

"I'm going to do what Slow Dancer suggested and track down that picture."

"I would think the smarter move would be to go to Easley, Andi's hometown," Raymond suggested.

"Why do you say that?" Lee asked.

"To find Andi's grave, if it actually exists, naturally."

The group let that sink in.

"I'll fly you to Florida if you want?" Billy offered.

"Count me in," Kent said.

"What? No. I can't let you guys do that. That's not what I came here for, and it's likely to be a colossal waste of time," Lee said.

"Are you kidding? This is cool. Were you not just sitting here listening to us tell you how dull and boring our lives are? This will be great, and I wouldn't miss this for the world," Kent explained. "It'll be like a quest. A holy quest. We are knights, after all."

"And after what we just spouted about friends being there for one another, it's time to put our money where our big mouths are. So I'm going," Billy stated flatly.

"I'm coming, too," Mark added. He, Billy, and Kent then all looked at Raymond.

Raymond shook his head and smiled.

"If we're going to do this, it might be smarter for us to split up. Half of us go to Panama City, and the other half head for South Carolina," Lee suggested.

"Why do we need to split up?" Mark asked. Everybody gathered around the grill area and either sat down or stood behind a chair. They all had a bottle of beer in their hands.

"Two reasons. First, by splitting up, we can cover what we need to cover and get the answers we need in half the time. It'll be quicker. And second, we might find something in Panama City that we have to follow up on in Easley or something we come across in Easley we need to ask questions about in Panama City. If half of us are in one place, and the other half are in the other, we can just make a phone call and take care of it."

"That makes sense," Lee said.

"But how likely is that?" Mark asked.

"I don't know, but let's plan for the possibility. Besides, we don't need all five of us to ask questions in either location. We are using our resources better this way," Ray answered.

"Okay, that sounds like a good plan. Who goes where?" Billy asked.

Lee didn't answer immediately. Instead, he looked around the room at his four friends. He realized then that the bond he formed so many years ago with them was still intact, and he couldn't find the words to express the emotion that he was suddenly overcome with. Tears filled his eyes.

It was Kent who broke the silence. "Can we save the group hug until I get back from the bathroom? I gotta piss."

| 18 |

The Quest Begins

Lee

He woke to the sound of the refrigerator door slamming shut. The sun was barely up on the horizon, and he guessed it was somewhere near six o'clock. Facing the lake, he could see mist slowly rising from the water, and far off in the distance, he could hear the soft hum of a boat's outdoor motor as it propelled itself through the gloom. He was still sitting in a lawn chair with his feet propped up on a second one, with a throw blanket covering most of his body. Behind him, he could hear the screen door slide open and shut. Then Billy came into view when he took a seat at the patio table with a glass of orange juice. He was wearing a Gold's Gym muscle shirt and a pair of black athletic shorts.

"Morning," Lee said.

Billy jumped as he realized he wasn't alone and looked at Lee in the lawn chair.

"Shit, what are you doing up so early?" Billy asked.

"I woke up and couldn't get back to sleep, so I came out here," Lee answered. "What are you doing up?"

"I wake up this early every morning to run. Care to come with me?"

"How far are you going?"

"Not far, three or four miles."

"Sure, let me change my clothes," Lee replied and started getting up from the chairs. As he rose, he discovered his legs and lower back were extremely stiff, and he already regretted agreeing to run.

After changing into T-shirt, shorts, and running shoes, Lee rejoined Billy, and the two of them stretched against the side of the house, then took off jogging up the driveway and down the gravel road. The cool morning air felt good on Lee's skin, and he could tell from how he felt it would be a good run. The stiffness in his legs and back were already growing fainter. He usually did his running on the treadmill at the health club, and it felt exhilarating to be out in the open, setting his own pace instead of keeping up with a machine. They ran in silence for the first mile, and then Billy started talking.

"So, you thought I was rambunctious, huh?" he said.

It took Lee a moment to figure out where Billy was coming from, but then replied, "I think I described you pretty accurately."

"You were right, I guess. It's just weird reading what other people write about you," Billy replied.

The two of them ran for another ten minutes, then Billy said it was time to turn around and head back. Lee was working up a good sweat when Billy spoke up again.

"You know all that stuff I said last night about not finishing stuff and my problems with Meg?"

"Yeah," Lee said, getting a little winded now.

"I didn't start thinking about all that until after I read your blog."

Lee stopped running, and after a few feet, Billy noticed that he had dropped out and stopped as well.

"Billy, that was me trying to remember what you were like after thirty years. I have no clue what kind of person you are now. People do change," Lee pointed out.

"Not as much as you'd think or hope."

"So, if you and your wife break up, I'm going to have that on my conscience?"

"All you did was make me take a hard look in the mirror. When is that ever a bad thing? I'm glad you wrote what you wrote. And besides, Meg and I aren't going to break up."

"You're not?"

"Nah, Raymond was right. I love her more than anything, and we're going to work through our issues. I promise you that!"

"That's great to hear."

"Can we finish this run now?"

"After you."

The two of them ran back the rest of the way at a quick pace, finishing with a sprint down the driveway all the way to the back deck. They both bent over with their hands on their knees, sweat falling onto the grass as they caught their breath.

"Was something chasing you?" They heard a call from the back deck.

Kent was seated alone at the patio table, wearing a navy robe and eating a pop tart.

"Where is everyone else?" Billy asked in between gasps for air.

"It's only eight o'clock. Where do you think?" Kent answered with his mouth full.

Turning to Billy, Lee asked, "Last night, didn't Mark say something about going fishing first thing this morning?"

"Was that before or after he blew chunks off the deck?"

The two of them looked toward an area in the grass just off the edge of the deck.

"Good point."

***

By late afternoon, the five of them had returned from fishing on the lake using the Triton bass boat belonging to Mark's brother-in-law. There were few bites, only one actual fish caught, and a couple of sunburned noses. But an entire cooler of beer was consumed, so they deemed the excursion a success.

During the day, everybody made phone calls, left messages, and took calls from people returning messages to clear schedules for the pending trip to Florida and South Carolina.

Billy only had a couple of flights booked for the upcoming week, which he had no problem handing off to another flight service he commonly exchanged favors with.

Mark was scheduled to return to New Orleans to oversee a project running behind, but he had confidence in the supervisor in charge of that site.

Kent, fortunately, had just administered his first semester test, and the next one wasn't due for another three weeks. So a teaching assistant would cover his classes while he was away. He joked it would surprise him if his students even realized he wasn't there. His wife, Cathy, would look in on his mother every couple of days for him, but he would keep his cell phone on and expect to receive a barrage of phone calls from her while he was away.

Raymond was due in court on Tuesday and Wednesday, but he contacted two of the firm's junior partners with instructions to request a continuance from the respective judges, citing a family emergency, which was almost always granted. Just in case it wasn't, both junior partners were well versed in the circumstances and could handle the court appearances in their sleep. Then he pushed all his other appointments off a week.

Lee was able to get in touch with his boss, who was also a good friend, to request a week's vacation starting Monday. As one of the higher-ranking adjusters for Corporal Indemnity, Lee pretty much made his own schedule, but his boss was curious about the last-minute request. Lee told him it was a personal matter that he would have to explain when he returned, which his boss understood.

After Lee hung up from his last phone call, everything was set. They all were ready to go.

"So, when are we going to do this, and who's going where?" Billy asked as he sat and watched Mark prepare yet another meal.

What Lee didn't say was that he had briefly considered calling the whole thing off earlier in the day. He worried he was overreacting. Now his friends were caught up in his conspiracy theory and taking time away from their jobs and lives to help him search for something that might be a delusion.

But then he remembered what had brought him to this point and still couldn't shake the feeling that there was more going on than he was led to believe twenty-nine years ago. Was it too much to want to have answers? And his friends thought enough about his questions to offer to help. The group may be headed off on a futile journey together, but maybe there was a way he could minimize the damage if it didn't go as he hoped.

"I'm thinking Mark and I will head down to Panama City, and you could fly Raymond and Kent to South Carolina?" Lee suggested, speaking directly to Billy.

"Why does Mark get to go to the beach?" Kent said, walking around from the back of the chair and sitting in it.

"Kent, this isn't a vacation," Lee replied sternly.

"Maybe not, but the scenery will sure be a lot nicer there," Kent countered.

"And Mark is single, and all of you are happily married. I don't want your wives coming after my head when they find out where you were heading off to."

"Lee's right," Raymond chimed in. "All they need to do in Panama City is track down the picture, and two guys can certainly handle that. In Easley, we'll be looking for a death certificate, talking to Andi's parents, and maybe talking to Gayle's and Trisha's parents as well. There's a lot more to do there, and it will take the three of us."

"How are you guys going to get down to Panama City?" Billy asked.

"We'll fly commercial?" Lee half-answered, looking at Mark.

"Sure," he agreed.

"So, when do we leave?" Kent asked.

"I need to drive back home tomorrow to pack some more clothes and travel stuff. Mark, maybe you can ride back with me, and we can just leave out of Little Rock?"

"Okay," Mark agreed again.

"Then how about we all take off Monday morning?" Lee offered.

Everybody looked at one another, nodding.

"Monday morning it is."

"The quest begins," Kent toasted, raising his beer in the air. Everybody else raised theirs as well, and as they brought them down to take the obligatory swig, somebody's cell phone started ringing. Kent dug in his pants pocket and came back with his ringing cell phone. He pressed a button and put the phone to his ear.

"Hi, Mom," he said, rising from his seat and walking away from the group to get some privacy.

"The A-Team we're not," Mark joked, eliciting chuckles from all of them.

Thirty minutes later, they were all sitting in a circle chowing down on the hamburgers Mark had grilled, joking about the one fish they had caught that afternoon. Lee's cell phone started vibrating in his pocket.

Looking at the caller ID, it told him his son, Chase, was calling. "Hello?"

"Dad, I think somebody is breaking into our house!"

| 19 |

Repercussions

Dianne

My run this morning wasn't having the desired effect, so for the last half mile I doubled the pace. I blew past the last clump of trees on the trail where I jogged and overran the park bench where I normally cooled down by a couple of yards. Circling back, I bent over and placed my hands on my knees, breathing heavily through my nose. After a minute, I stood straight, grabbed my right foot, and pulled it up behind me, feeling the muscle stretch.

The vigorous exercise would usually clear my head, letting me refocus and attack each day with a clear intent of what I needed to accomplish. But that wasn't happening this morning. What took place last Friday—Mack's firing—and the way they greeted Briana still bothered me. This was precisely why I hadn't wanted to take the job. I was used to only worrying about myself—and my clients—and turning a blind eye to office politics. The work was everything, and I liked it that way. So why had I let Tildy convince me I was the person who needed to make changes? Was a change even needed? I didn't think so until I saw the way the guys treated Briana. I'm sure they treated me the same when I came onboard, probably worse since I was the first female investigator hired, but that stuff never bothered me. I'm not stupid or insensitive. I know that just because I wasn't bothered, it didn't make the way they acted okay. The truth was, I was viewing their behavior differently now, and it made me feel ashamed. As a manager, their actions reflected on me, and I didn't like how they made me look.

Briana and I avoided talking about any of that during her first day, mostly because I didn't know what to say. But even if she was like me—which I doubted—things still needed to change. And like it or not, that fell on me now.

I switched over to stretching my left leg.

What was bothering me most was the way I handled letting Mack go. My temper had gotten the best of me. I called him unprofessional, which was ironic because what I did was exactly that. No matter what I thought of Mack, he didn't deserve to be dressed down in front of coworkers. And a new hire on top of it all. Not my best moment.

I bent over to grab my toes when my earbuds signaled an incoming call. I glanced at my smartwatch. It was six fifteen.

"Hello?" I said, after tapping my earbud.

"Good, you're up," Tildy's voice said.

"I'm up? Why are you awake this early?"

"Oh, honey, I've been up for hours. Sleep is overrated."

"I find it essential myself. What can I do for you?"

"I heard you had some excitement in the office on Friday."

"And how would you know that?"

"Evelyn. She knows everything that goes on there."

"I'm sure. But why would she tell you anything?"

"Evelyn's my cousin. Of course she tells me everything."

"Wait...what? Evelyn's your cousin? Why didn't I know this?"

"Aaron didn't like to advertise it. You don't think she got that job because of her glowing personality, do you?"

I chuckled as I walked over and sat on the bench. "I guess not. So, she must have told you about Mack then."

"She did, but that's not why I'm calling. Like I told you when you took the job, handle Mack as you think best, so it did not surprise me to hear he'd been let go. What does concern me is the secret meetings."

"What secret meetings?"

"They started about a week after you assumed control. It's most of the staff, and they meet at a tavern down the street from the agency. Evelyn says it started to bitch and moan about the changes, but recently they've grown more resolute. Cutting loose Norwood, Mack's firing, and now your new hire, they're all fuel for the fire."

"But you approved all those moves."

"I did, but I fear that's of little consequence now. I think you're about to have a full-blown mutiny on your hands unless something is done."

I let myself fall against the bench seat, ignoring the feeling of cold metal on my back, and stared up in the sky. This was helping my confidence level as I prepared for the day.

"What do you suggest?"

"Oh, I don't have any suggestions. That's why I handed everything over to you. I'm just giving you a heads up."

"Thanks, I guess. Why can't everyone just get over it and do the work?"

"It's the age of entitlement, my dear. We all believe we should have a say in every decision, and nobody trusts their leaders anymore."

"That's a bit cynical, don't you think, even for you, Tildy?"

"Oh, I don't know. I find that a little cynicism goes a long way these days."

"Any other gems of insight you want to pass along?"

"That's enough for now, don't you think?"

"I guess so."

I was about to press the earbud to disconnect from the call when I paused.

"You know, Tildy, I can't make them like me."

"They don't have to like you, Dianne. They need to respect you. Aaron sure did. I do. Make them see what we see."

The line went dead, leaving me there in the semidarkness alone with my thoughts...and a question.

How do I do that?

| 20 |

Unwelcome Visitors

Lee

Lee and Mark started their return trip back to Conway at six in the morning. Raymond, Kent, and Billy planned on sleeping a little longer before heading back and preparing for their trip to Easley, South Carolina. However, because of last night's phone call, Lee needed to get back as soon as he could.

Mark volunteered to drive, so as the landscape passed by unseen, Lee was going back over the phone conversations he'd had with his son the previous night. He had tamped down his panic and asked Chase where he was.

"I'm parked down the street from our house."

"Okay, what's going on?"

"So, I'm driving down our road to the house, and I see a light flash across our front window from inside. I slow down, and I see it again. I pulled over and parked in front of the McCoys' house, and I've been watching our house for a couple minutes now. I've seen the light a couple more times. I think there's someone in our house."

Lee could envision where Chase described parking. Lee's house was in a cul-de-sac at the end of a long road with four other streets jutting off it. The McCoys were a retired couple who lived four houses up the street from Lee's home.

"Stay where you are and call the police. Do not go anywhere near the house until they arrive, and then call me back!" Lee commanded.

"Yes, sir," was all Chase said and was gone.

"What's going on?" Billy asked.

"My son thinks somebody is breaking into our house."

"Is he in it?" Mark asked, concerned.

"No, he's parked up the street."

What felt like hours later was actually only fifteen minutes when Lee's cell phone went off again.

"Dad, it's me," Chase said.

"What's happening?"

"The police are here, and I'm in the house. They didn't catch anybody, but the back door onto the deck was open."

"Have you looked around to see if anything was taken?"

"Just briefly, nothing obvious. All the computer, video, and stereo stuff is still here. I really see nothing out of place."

"Good, maybe you interrupted him before he had a chance to get anything. I can look it over thoroughly tomorrow when I get back. But I want you to spend the night with one of your friends tonight. Got me? I'll be back home tomorrow before noon."

"You don't have to tell me twice. I'll be at Will's house. Call me when you get back in town."

"Will do. And Chase?"

"Yes, sir?"

"That was smart thinking. In real life, the heroes usually end up getting shot."

"I hear ya. See you tomorrow."

On their way home, Lee watched the moss-covered trees and numerous lakes, ponds, bayous, swamps, creeks, and rivers race by. The bright sunlight filtered through the trees and flickered upon his face as he stared out the car window. He thought about the fact that common crime had found its way into his little neighborhood and lamented the loss of innocence. An intruder breaks into one house and, in a way, enters everyone else's. Now the community will lie awake at night, listening for footsteps, cars stopping, dogs barking. The faith in humanity, in the safety of their homes, in simple goodness, had been vandalized. Trashed. There were maybe sixty older homes in his subdivision, and they built them all at least thirty years ago. It was in a very stable part of town with little turnover. Earlier in the year, Lee heard about some car break-ins that took place in a neighborhood bordering their own, mostly involving cars left unlocked, so he shouldn't have been surprised to hear that a dangerous element had found their quiet haven. He just wished it hadn't been his house first.

The drive back to Conway only took five hours and thirty minutes, mainly because of Mark taking liberties with the speed limit. Along the way, Mark questioned Lee extensively about his project of converting his albums to digital files, as he still owned quite a few himself.

Back in Conway, Lee's home was very similar to the other houses in the neighborhood, a single-story brick house with wood trim stained with dark brown paint chipped from age above the garage and on the sides. There was a large pane window next to the garage with a neglected flower bed underneath it, a couple of steps leading to a small, unassuming entranceway, then a pair of double-pane windows with a row of tall holly bushes in front. The lawn was green and well-trimmed, except directly underneath a couple of medium-sized pine trees where the grass was thin.

Mark pulled the Jeep into the garage and turned off the engine. Leaving their bags in the car, they entered the house through the door in the garage, into a short hallway past a laundry room on the right, and dead-ended at two doors. The door to the left led out into the kitchen, and the other went straight ahead into the recreation room. Lee led Mark into the kitchen and immediately dialed his son's cell phone number.

A couple of moments later, Lee said into the phone, "Hey, we're back home. See you in a couple of minutes," and he hung up the handset.

"Care for something to drink?" Lee offered Mark.

"Just some water would be fine," Mark answered.

Lee reached down into a cabinet next to where Mark was standing, pulled out a bottle of Dasani, and handed it to him.

"I'm going to take a quick look around the house to see if anything is missing. If you want to tag along, I can give you a tour," Lee said.

"Okay," Mark replied.

"This way is the living room," Lee pointed out, as he walked through a doorway directly across from the one that came from the garage.

Making their way through the house, Lee scanned each room, looking for anything out of place. Finally, they ended up in front of a row of glass windows, which was part of a room next to the main living area. There was a door that opened out onto a deck.

"This is our sunroom," Lee commented, as they entered the room. In the middle of the space was a small, round breakfast table with four chairs surrounding it. Looking to the left against the wall was a wooden gun cabinet with a pair of shotguns and a .22 caliber rifle visible through the glass display panels. Just past the cabinet was a closed door leading to the master bedroom. Off to the right side of the room, a glass door separated the sunroom from the recreational room beyond. Lee walked over to the gun case and looked at it for a moment.

"Nothing missing from here," Lee observed and turned to move on.

"You didn't say you hunted," Mark said.

"Not in a long time."

Mark reached out for the cabinet door, and to his surprise, it opened.

"You don't keep it locked?" Mark questioned.

Lee looked back at the cabinet. "Usually, it is. But Chase hunts more than I do now. He probably left it open." Lee walked back to the cabinet, pulled the keys out of his pocket, found the key he was looking for, and locked the cabinet shut.

Lee opened the door that led out onto a sprawling back deck, complete with a barbeque grill, storage bench, and a couple of deck chairs. The backyard was fifty feet deep and surrounded by a chain-link fence. On the other side of the fence was a gravel road and then nothing but woods.

"Nice and private back here," Mark pointed out.

"Yeah, that's one reason we bought the house. The convenience of a neighborhood inside the city limits, but you could walk out here naked if you wanted to. The city uses that gravel road to access a pumping station that's about a half mile down that way."

"This is really nice."

Just then, the door from the garage could be heard opening and closing.

"Chase, back here," Lee called out.

Chase walked through the doorway onto the deck dressed in an old T-shirt that advertised one of the local taverns at his school, some holey jeans, and a pair of Birkenstocks. He took notice of Mark and nodded in greeting.

"Oh my god, Lee, it's you!" Mark uttered.

Both Chase and his father smiled.

"Yeah, fortunately, he got most of his looks from me and all his brains from his mother," Lee said. "Chase, this is Mark Sigmar. He's my old college roommate from eons ago."

Chase took a couple of steps forward and took a firm grasp of Mark's extended hand. Mark still couldn't stop staring at Chase.

"Anything missing that you can tell?" Chase turned and asked Lee.

"No. I don't think so. I get this feeling that there's something out of place in the entertainment center, but I can't put my finger on what it is. But there's definitely not anything major missing."

"The police said you should come by the station tomorrow if you want to fill out a formal report, but either way, they will have patrol cars cruising the neighborhood for the next couple of weeks," Chase informed him.

"Lee, if you get me hooked up on your computer, I can set up our plane tickets for tomorrow," Mark said.

Chase looked at his dad. "Where are you going now?"

"We're flying to Panama City for a day or so, then South Carolina." Lee started leading the three of them toward the computer in the living room.

"Panama City, Florida?" Chase asked, surprised.

"The same."

"What's going on?" Chase continued to ask questions as he followed his dad and Mark.

"You know the letters that I let you read last week, the ones to Andi?"

"Yeah."

"Something is surrounding that whole matter that I have to lay to rest once and for all," Lee answered matter-of-factly.

He depressed the power switch on the computer, and the three of them waited for it to boot.

"How long do you think you'll be gone?" Chase asked.

"Hopefully, just a couple of days. You need to stay at school while I'm gone. I don't need to be worrying about you walking in on a burglar or being here alone while I'm gone."

"Don't worry about me. I'm outta here as soon as I pack up my stuff." Chase headed toward his room.

When Chase left the room, Lee sat down in the desk chair and logged on to his PC. Mark leaned against the back of the couch and looked in the direction that Chase had gone.

"He really looks just like you when you were at LSU. It's kind of eerie," Mark marveled.

When the computer was logged on, Lee stood up and surrendered the chair. Mark settled in and searched the internet to find the lowest fare to get them to Panama City. Instead of standing behind him watching him work, Lee asked Mark what kind of lunchmeat he preferred and then headed off to the kitchen to fix them a couple of sandwiches.

Twenty minutes later, they were both booked on a Southwest flight, leaving Little Rock at 6:50 a.m., connecting in Houston, and finally landing in Panama City at 1:22 p.m. local time.

***

Mr. Brown

The dark-blue Pontiac G6 was parked inconspicuously in the rear of the church parking lot. A few other vehicles still occupied spaces around the lot, so the Pontiac didn't stand out or seem out of place. The car was backed into an area that offered an unobstructed view of the road that ran in front of the Mormon Church, the road that was the only access to the small subdivision only a few hundred feet away.

Mr. Brown sat behind the wheel of the Pontiac with the seat pushed all the way back and a laptop computer in his lap. He was dressed in a lightweight dark-colored long-sleeve T-shirt and similarly colored slacks. In the passenger seat beside him was a medium-sized black canvas bag with a zipper opening on top and multiple Velcro pockets along both sides. Both sun visors were pulled down to prevent easy examination of the car's interior, but they didn't block his view of the road.

The sun had gone down almost thirty minutes ago, and he was aware that the illumination from the laptop screen reflecting upon his face made him more noticeable, but it was a risk he had to accept for at least a couple more minutes.

His operation from the previous night had only been partially successful before being interrupted. The son's arrival, whom he thought was supposed to be away at school, was unforeseen and unfortunate. But he had been careful and left no trace of his presence in the house apart for not properly shutting the door when he exited. He'd hopped the back fence, made his way through the woods to the access road, and followed that back to where he had left his vehicle. Even though he'd completed searching eighty percent of the house, the likelihood of finding anything useful from the areas left unsearched was minimal. Thoroughness was something he prided himself on, and it compelled him to wait for an opportunity to return. But the information he recently discovered may have since altered those plans.

One task he'd completed before fleeing the night before was installing monitoring software on Hamilton's computer. Being away from his office in Washington cut off his access to the information collected from Hamilton's IP address. To alleviate that problem, the program he'd just installed, a trojan that ran behind the scenes and was undetectable to the user, was designed to allow his laptop to view Hamilton's computer's screen output. The information viewed couldn't be saved or stored, but he could watch whatever was displayed on the other computer.

Mr. Brown watched as the computer at the Hamilton residence booked a pair of tickets to Panama City, Florida, for the following morning. Then, making a quick decision, he switched applications on his laptop and booked himself a seat on that same flight. He then closed the lid of his laptop, stored it away in the canvas bag in the next seat, and started up the Pontiac.

It appeared he wouldn't be returning to the Hamilton house tonight.

| 21 |

Panama City

Lee

"Welcome to Florida," Mark commented. "And I thought Louisiana was hot."

The two of them spotted a sign that read Budget with a small group of people standing by it. They made their way over, Mark carrying his duffel bag and Lee rolling his small suitcase behind him with his backpack slung over his shoulder. They could both feel the perspiration forming on their brows.

At the car lot, they quickly located the car and placed their luggage in the trunk. As Mark put the key in the ignition, started the car, and cranked up the air conditioning to the maximum, Lee pulled out his phone and opened Google Maps.

Mark looked to Lee. "Okay, where to first?"

Lee looked at his watch. It showed two fifteen. "Let's try the Sunset Club and see if they have a manager there in the afternoon."

"Do you have an address?" Mark replied.

Lee reached behind him and pulled his backpack up front with him. He unzipped a pocket and took out a sheet of paper. "It's on South Thomas Drive, 8843 South Thomas Drive, Panama City,

Florida, 32408," he stated while entering the address into his phone at the same time. A calm female voice then said, "Turn right in sixty feet."

"We have lift-off," Mark announced and steered the Taurus out of the lot.

Forty-five minutes later, Mark pulled into the first slot of an enormous parking bay and put the Taurus in park. Lee leaned forward to see the club sign on the roof, and Mark turned around to double-check the sign at the edge of the road. Then they looked at one another.

"This isn't good," Mark commented.

"I'll say," Lee agreed.

The vast parking lot occupied the space where the Sunset Club used to sit. The previous building, which was already past its prime in 1992, along with the other clubs on either side of it, had been completely torn down. The new structure was tucked between an enormous Hyatt hotel on one side and a considerably smaller resort on the other. It was a massive, multi-floored version of the Sunset Club with three different entrances.

"You think they'll still have the pictures?" Mark asked.

"There's only one way to find out. Let's go ask."

Mark pulled the car closer to the main entrance and killed the engine. Then, the two of them climbed out of the car, walked up a short flight of stairs to a landing, and tried the front door, which surprised them both by opening freely.

Inside, the club was shadowy and dark. As Lee's eyes adjusted, he could vaguely make out a thick, velvet-covered cord of rope hanging loosely about waist-high between two stanchions positioned against opposite walls of the hallway, passively preventing farther advancement into the building. Farther on past the rope, he could see multiple hallways heading off into different directions of the club. The two of them could hear muffled music playing from what sounded like a portable player emanating down a hallway that branched off to the right of the foyer.

Mark found a clip holding the velvet rope to the pole closest to them, unhooked it, and put it back in place after they had passed through. They both followed the music to a closed door with the word Manager stenciled across it. Lee knocked on the door, and when no one answered, he knocked again, this time with more force. The music from inside the room, an old AC/DC track, lowered in volume. Lee rapped again, and a few seconds later, the door opened to reveal a woman in her mid-thirties with blond hair shorter than Lee's, dressed in faded jeans and a well-worn Florida State University jersey.

"Can I help you?" she asked, having to look up to see Mark's and Lee's faces. She had a pair of reading glasses hanging low on her nose and a pen tucked behind her right ear.

"I hope so," Lee answered. "We are searching for a picture that used to be displayed in this club before they rebuilt it."

"What kind of picture?" she asked. She appeared impatient and disturbed by the interruption.

"A group photograph. They used to hang them on the walls of the old club." Lee spoke up again.

"Oh, those." Now she looked even more annoyed. "We sent most of those to the people who paid for them. We only display the ones that were never claimed or sent back to us as undeliverable in the Retro Lounge, which you can come back and see tonight during regular business hours," she informed them, and then started to close the door.

"Miss," Lee placed his hand against the door, preventing her from closing it entirely, "I know this is an imposition, and I understand you have work to do—"

"That's right, I do. I'm in the middle of closing out the accounting month, and I don't have time to help you just now. If you come back tonight at nine o'clock when the club normally opens, I will be more than happy to assist you, but now if you don't leave, I will be forced to call security and have you removed from the grounds."

Lee thought she was bluffing about calling security, believing she was here alone, but he lowered his hand anyway. She nodded a thank-you and closed the door.

"I guess we come back tonight," Lee said as he turned away from the door and started out the way they had come.

Mark remained standing in front of the door, looking down at the doorknob. When Lee realized Mark wasn't following him, he turned around. Mark looked back over his shoulder at Lee, shook his head slowly, and then turned back to the door and took hold of the knob. He gave it a turn and pushed the door open, remaining where he stood.

Inside the office, a pair of horizontal filing cabinets stood against the back wall, and on top of one of them was a portable speaker. The woman they had just spoken with was sitting behind an old metal desk with numerous notebooks and papers piled in front of her. Aside from the desk, most of the office was filled with filing cabinets and cardboard storage boxes.

The woman looked up from her work with a mixture of anger and fear.

"Please give me one minute. That's all, after that, we'll leave without a fuss. I promise," Mark said hurriedly, raising his arms and hands in a nonthreatening gesture.

The woman looked at Mark and then past him to Lee standing farther down the hall. She took a deep breath and laid the pen in her hand on top of her papers, crossed her arms, and sat back in her chair.

"One minute," she agreed.

Mark lowered his arms. "My friend and I flew here this morning from Little Rock, Arkansas, just to find this picture, so I don't have to tell you it has some special significance to us both. We aren't just a couple of reminiscing old farts."

The woman's demeanor seemed to relax. "What's so important about this picture?"

Lee had now walked up behind Mark. Mark gestured over his shoulder to him. "My friend Lee met and fell in love with a girl at your club in 1992. Unfortunately, the girl tragically died in a car accident driving home from her vacation that same week. The picture we are looking for is the only one that exists of the two of them together."

The woman's eyes instantly went to Lee, and she uncrossed her arms. Lee couldn't bring himself to return her gaze, choosing instead to look down at the floor.

"And you waited—" doing a quick calculation in her head, "twenty-nine years to come for it?" she asked curiously.

"Honestly, we only just remembered it," Mark answered.

She looked back and forth between the two of them and then shook her head.

"I would like to help you out, really I would, but I am absolutely swamped, and if I don't finish this paperwork by tonight, my boss will have my head. So if you come back tonight, I could probably help you," she said.

"Do you like football?" Mark suddenly asked, nodding at her shirt.

"Yes. What does that have to do with anything?" she answered hesitantly.

"The company I work for has season tickets to all the major college stadiums. We're talking box seats. If you help us out right now, they're yours."

The manager's eyebrows rose significantly, but then her expression switched from surprise to suspicion.

"How do I know you'll really give them to me?" she asked in a distrustful tone.

"I guess you'll have to trust me, but look at it this way. The worst thing that can happen is that you lose a little time. The best case is that I'm as honest as I look, and you get two Seminole season tickets for some awesome seats," Mark said convincingly. "Even if you're not a fan, you could sell them and make a load of cash."

The woman pondered the proposition for a moment, then stood up behind the desk. "Who actually paid for the picture?"

Mark and Lee looked at one another, neither one indicating that they knew the answer to her question.

"When the picture was taken, whoever paid for it filled out a form so we could send a copy to them at their home address. If the girl who died paid for the picture, then odds are we wouldn't be able to get in touch with her. Since we had so many pictures unclaimed, we rotate them between our Retro Lounge and storage," the woman explained.

"Can we look in the lounge?" Lee spoke up for the first time.

"Follow me," she said as she came from behind the desk and walked past them into the hall. Trailing behind her, Lee noticed a colorful tattoo of a mermaid on the back of her neck.

As they were walking, Lee looked at Mark and said, "You never told me you had tickets like that?"

"*Had* is the operative word now."

Navigating through a disorienting maze of hallways in near darkness, passing several of what must have been the theme rooms the club offered, they followed the woman, walking along at a brisk pace. She vanished into a dark doorway, then a flood of lights abruptly brightened the room and made them squint their eyes.

When Lee's eyes adjusted, he was standing in the Sunset Club from 1992. Before him was the huge dance floor in the center of the room. On the ceiling above the dance floor was a dizzying array of lamps, colored lights, strobes, even the requisite mirror ball hanging directly over its center. A bar ran along the wall to the right, with tables and chairs in the area between it and the dance floor. Olden-style tables and chairs were along the walls on either side of the dance floor. Various paintings of beach settings and different seaside paraphernalia, such as boat paddles, ring buoys, and so on, decorated the far wall. The opposite wall was covered with eight-by-ten-inch framed photos.

The room was an exact replica, albeit scaled down, of the club from the 1990s.

The manager appeared beside the two of them again. "We built this room to honor the original club," she explained. "It's one of our more popular rooms."

Shaking off their shock, Mark and Lee walked over to the photo wall and started looking at each one closely. Minutes later, they had seen them all, and the one with Andi in it wasn't one of them.

"It's not here," Lee told the woman, dejected.

"Don't give up yet. We still have the ones in storage."

They followed the woman through the room, past the DJ equipment, and to a small door at the back of the room. She pulled a set of keys from her front pocket, located the correct key, and unlocked the door. She flipped a light switch as she entered a room the size of a medium closet. Along the left wall were maybe a dozen columns of cardboard boxes stacked three high. On the front of the boxes was a handwritten four-digit number.

"What year was the picture taken?" the woman asked, stuffing her keys back into her pocket.

"Uh, 1992," Lee answered.

The woman walked down the row of boxes and selected one a third of the way along the wall in the middle of the stack. She pulled the box out and carried it back to where Mark and Lee stood.

"Have a look," she said, placing the box at their feet.

Mark and Lee kneeled and removed the top of the box. Inside were probably a hundred eight-by-ten-inch photographs. They both grabbed a handful and started looking at them slowly.

Mark was the one to find it. He froze when he discovered it, letting the rest of the pictures in his hand slip back into the box. He looked up from the image.

"Lee," was all he said.

Lee raised his head up from the photographs in his hand and saw Mark holding a single picture, smiling. He also let his pictures fall back into the box and reached slowly to take the portrait from Mark.

The picture showed ten people with various crazy expressions and exuberant poses gathered around one of the club's tables. Lee's eyes focused on just one person. There she was. Although he could describe numerous aspects of how she looked in bits and pieces, he had lost the ability to see her face long ago, relegated to a few flashes of memory that could never be sustained for more than a few seconds. Now there she was, pictured with Lee as they hugged one another in the middle of the group. Lee's heart ached all over again.

Lee smiled back through mist-filled eyes at Mark. The smile on Mark's face suddenly disappeared, and he appeared shocked.

"Lee, look at the back of the picture," he said.

Lee flipped the picture over, and on the back was drawn a large heart in red ink. Written just outside the upper left side of the heart were the words "Andi and Lee" to the lower right side. Lee looked at Mark, confused.

"Look at the date," Mark almost yelled.

Four numbers were written directly below the heart—2000.

| 22 |

Revelations

**Lee**

After thanking the manager for all her help and exchanging contact information to ensure she would receive her season tickets, Mark and Lee returned quickly to the car to plan their next move. The two of them sat there now, still parked in the empty lot with the engine running so the air conditioning could battle the afternoon heat that was steadily rising.

"She's alive, Lee. She's _alive!_" Mark repeated for at least the tenth time since leaving the club.

Lee sat there, staring at the photograph and nodding.

"Why aren't you more excited?" Mark asked, excited enough for them both.

Lee looked at Mark. "I don't know. It makes little sense. If she's really alive, then why all the cloak and dagger shit? Why not just send me an email? And why did her father say she was dead? I just have this feeling that something majorly screwed up is going on."

"And we're going to find out what," Mark said.

Lee stared at the red heart again, contemplating. "You know, we don't know for sure Andi wrote this. Somebody else could have written that."

"Why in hell would somebody do that? For what purpose?" Mark asked.

"Maybe it's an elaborate trick," Lee guessed. "Somebody could have put that on the back of the photo and then written the comment on my blog, making me think that she's alive."

Mark thought for a moment. "The only people who knew about the picture's existence were us."

"What about Gayle or Trisha? They knew. They could have done it."

"Again, I ask why? More importantly, they're supposed to be dead, remember. If they're not, then neither is Andi," Mark pointed out, becoming exasperated.

"I don't know, but that is one of the many questions that we need to find out. I'm just saying that we shouldn't assume this is Andi's writing," Lee explained.

The two of them sat in silence for a moment, Lee unable to take his eyes off the photograph. Then he said, "You know, somebody else knew about the picture and actually had easier access to it than anyone."

"Who?" Mark asked.

Lee turned the picture around to face Mark and pointed to a person at the back of the group.

"Mike. Andi's family friend Mike. He was there. He knew about the picture. I think he should be our next stop," Lee suggested.

"And how are we going to locate him?"

"His last name was Stevens. Mike Stevens."

Mark made a sour face. "That's not going to help much. He could be anywhere. How many Mike Stevens do you think there are?"

"Then we need to go see the manager again," Lee answered, opening his car door.

Turning off the car and catching up to Lee, Mark asked, "And how is it you think the manager can help us find him?"

"I remember Mike knew most of the bartenders and waitresses working here. I think he was a regular, and maybe, just maybe, somebody might still know him," Lee explained.

They continued talking as they walked in through the front door and stepped over the velvet rope. "The manager doesn't look old enough to have been working here back then," Mark pointed out.

"I know, but maybe she knows somebody who did. In either case, she's got to be our first step."

They found themselves in front of the manager's door again, and they could hear that the music had resumed from the other side. Lee reached out and knocked on the door firmly. A short moment later, the blond manager opened the door again.

"Let me guess," she said when she recognized the two of them, "you changed your mind, and I can't have the tickets?"

Lee grinned. "No, I need to ask you a couple more questions, if I can."

"Please make it quick. I really am under the gun here."

"How long have you worked here at the club?"

"This is my fifteenth year," she stated proudly.

"We are looking for someone who we believe was a regular here in 1992 and maybe beyond that. Is there anybody still working for the club who might remember somebody from that far back?" Lee asked.

"I'm sorry. I'm the most senior employee here now. I started out behind the bar and worked my way up to bar manager."

"Well then, can you look at this picture and see if you recognize this guy?"

"Sure. But I've got to warn you I'm terrible with remembering faces."

Lee held up the picture and pointed to the man in the back of the group. The manager adjusted her reading glasses and peered closely at the photo. She smiled and then removed her glasses.

"That's Mike Stevens. He's more than a regular now. He's one of our regional alcohol distributors."

Both Mark's and Lee's eyebrows went up. "Then you know where we can find him?" Lee asked.

"Sure, he has a warehouse and office here in Panama City, but he may not be in town today. However, I have his cell phone number for emergencies." She unclipped her own cell phone from her hip and pushed a couple of buttons.

Lee saved the number into his own cell phone as she read it to him. "Thank you very much," Lee offered, pausing momentarily, then stepping forward and giving the woman a gentle hug.

"I hope you find what you're looking for," she said as they broke apart. Finally, they all said goodbye once again, and she closed her office door.

As they returned to the parking lot, Lee pulled out his cell phone and dialed the number he had just saved.

"Hello," a voice on the other end of the line answered.

"Is this Mike Stevens?" Lee asked.

"It is. Who's this?"

"My name is Lee Hamilton, and I work for an investment firm looking into the possibility of purchasing a nightclub here in the Panama City area. I have been told by several contacts that I needed to speak to you regarding the alcohol distribution in this area," Lee lied.

"That's right. I'm the one you should talk to," Stevens agreed.

"I'm in Panama City today, and I was wondering if we could get together in person," Lee continued.

"Sure, come by my office anytime. I'm about to head out for the day, but I'll be here at eight in the morning."

Lee got the address before saying goodbye and ending the call.

The two friends were standing by the car now. Lee put his phone away and noticed the curious look Mark was giving him.

"Why did you lie to him?" Mark asked.

"I didn't want to freak him out over the phone and have him hang up on me. I need to talk to him face to face so I can see his expression when we ask him the questions we need to ask."

"So, what now?" Mark wanted to know.

"I guess we find someplace to stay for the night and get something to eat."

"Any preferences on where we bed down?"

"How about we check out the Regency?" Lee suggested, smiling.

They climbed into the Taurus, started it up, and pulled to the edge of the road. Lee was about to gun the engine and merge with traffic when his cell phone started ringing. He took it off his hip and answered it on the third ring.

"Hello," he said.

"You guys do know you're being followed, right?" an odd-sounding voice on the other end of the line said.

***

Twenty minutes later, with the help of Google Maps, the Taurus was pulling into the Regency parking lot.

En route, Lee couldn't believe how much the strip had changed. The Regency, however, was the one structure that was just as he remembered it, except now it had degraded into a second-rate hotel that was probably one of the least expensive choices for students during spring break. Its seven floors dominated the hotels surrounding it at one time, but these days it just couldn't measure up compared to the glass towers that overshadowed it.

The two of them entered through the swinging doors of the main entrance, carrying their luggage into a spacious lobby still decorated by large tropical plants. The fake antique furniture in the corners of the room had been upgraded to more modern decor. The twenty-seven-inch television on a stand was replaced by a forty-two-inch LED mounted on a wall.

Lee walked up to the check-in desk while Mark stood in front of the plasma watching a local news broadcast.

"I'd like a room for the night with two double beds," he asked the young woman behind the desk.

"Yes, sir," she replied as she entered keystrokes into her computer. "Smoking or nonsmoking?"

"Nonsmoking, and as a matter of fact, is room 322 available?"

The young woman continued mashing buttons on her keyboard. "That room is indeed free. Your name, sir?"

"Lee Hamilton."

He finished giving the woman more information and an imprint of his credit card, and she handed him two scan card keys to room 322. He motioned to Mark that they were ready to go up, and they made their way around the corner to the elevators.

Stepping off the elevator on the third floor, they quickly threw their bags in their room, and then stopped in front of room 320 and knocked on the door. A couple of seconds later, the door opened, and a man with long red hair stood before them.

"Ebe," Mark exclaimed, embracing his old friend.

"Hey, Sig," Ebe replied, slapping Mark's back.

When the two of them were finished, Mark stepped past him into the room, and Ebe turned toward Lee.

"Hey Ebe," Lee said softly, grinning broadly.

"If it isn't the man who's causing all the fuss," Ebe replied, smiling also. The two of them hugged tightly.

They all stepped into Ebe's room and shut the door behind them. Mark took a seat in the desk chair near some curtains that covered the sliding glass window, which led out onto a small patio. Ebe walked to the second double bed and sat down, straddling the corner facing the first bed. Lee remained standing, leaning against the dresser on the front wall.

"That was a good idea, sending me here to get a room before the two of you arrived," Ebe said. "That way, your mysterious follower wouldn't see me check in."

"Why did your voice sound so weird on the phone?"

"I used a voice scrambler, and it was a burner phone. Just in case your phones are tapped."

As Ebe spoke, Lee made notice of the changes in his friend. His red hair was almost as long as he remembered, although his freckles had seemed to mellow. Ebe seemed slimmer, considerably so, with sunken cheeks and loose hanging skin on his neck. He now sported a red goatee with streaks of white weaving through it, accentuating his face's thinness. He wore a plaid long-sleeve shirt buttoned tightly around his neck and tucked into a pair of faded Levi jeans. Plain white socks covered his feet, and Lee could see a set of hiking boots sitting against the base of the bed.

"Okay, Ebe, time to tell us what the hell is going on," Mark stated from his chair. "How do you know somebody is following us? How did you know we were here in Panama City? And *where the hell have you been?*"

Ebe smiled at Mark and then at Lee. Then, addressing Mark, he said, "Which of those questions would you like me to answer first?"

"How about you start at the beginning?" Lee answered for Mark.

"Actually, I counter propose that I start at the point that is most relevant to our concerns at this moment," Ebe suggested.

Lee glanced at Mark, who returned the look.

"I had forgotten how hard it was to have a conversation with you sometimes," Mark said.

"Fill us in how you see fit," Lee offered.

"Fine. My work sometimes involves the unauthorized circumvention of computer security via wide-area communication networks. I have been associated with this area of expertise for almost ten years now, both formally and informally."

"Wait a minute," Mark interrupted. "You do what?"

"He's a hacker," Lee explained.

"An ethical hacker, to be specific," Ebe explained further.

"I'm lost." Mark was more confused.

Lee looked directly at Mark. "He breaks into computers over the internet. He does it professionally to debug or fix security issues in large systems."

"Gotcha," Mark said, nodding with understanding.

Ebe nodded as well. "You need to know that to understand how I came to be here. Because of what I do and my total immersion in everything internet related, my presence in numerous forums, communities, conventions, and certain social networks provides me with a unique opportunity. It funnels certain information to me that involves governmental misuse of technology."

Ebe paused when he noticed Mark's eyes were glazing over again. "In other words, I always have my ear to the ground listening for information that the government, local or federal, is abusing the internet freedom we all share.

"A couple of days ago, a warning was circulated across several sources from a user known as LL&P. This is a gamer with a considerable web presence and a respectable reputation in the circles he frequents. His warning suggested that an innocent citizen was being targeted by a government agency, and this citizen's internet activity was being tracked and cataloged. I'm quoting this next part word for word from his post. *If anyone out there knows a Lee Hamilton in Conway, Arkansas, warn him!*"

Lee pushed off from the dresser he was leaning against and stood straight up. He shot a look at Mark, whose mouth was now wide open.

"He's gotta be talking about somebody else," Lee said.

"Another Lee Hamilton in Conway, Arkansas?" Ebe countered.

"Someone from the government is watching what I do on the internet? What for? What did I do?" Lee exclaimed excitedly.

"I believe that is blatantly obvious to even the most casual observer," Ebe answered cryptically.

"You want to explain it to those of us who are denser than the most casual observers?" Mark said.

Ebe looked at Mark. "Somebody is very concerned about Lee remembering and now questioning the circumstances of Andi's death."

Mark stood up and started pacing in front of the closed curtains. "Andi's not dead," he said, almost to himself.

"We don't know that for sure," Lee quickly countered. Then, looking back to Ebe, he saw that his friend's eyebrows were raised. "We found a picture at the Sunset Club. All of us were in it, taken in 1992. On the back, there was writing that made it appear that Andi wrote on it in the year 2000."

"Why are you so set on believing that Andi is dead?" Mark asked with irritation in his voice. He had stopped pacing.

"I'm not," Lee responded. "We just have too many unanswered questions, and I don't dare get my hopes up."

The three of them were silent for a minute, and Mark resumed his pacing.

"Do you think this warning you read is true?" Lee finally asked Ebe.

"I know it is."

Mark stopped pacing again. "How do you know?"

"Because as soon as I found out, I ran a check on Lee's computer. I found a trojan embedded in the operating logic."

"What's a trojan?" Lee asked the obvious question, knowing that his friend would just assume everybody knew what it was.

"It's a piece of code hackers use. In this case, it sends a mirror image of your screen to another IP address."

"Could you tell where the data was being sent to?" Lee asked.

"This was a sophisticated piece of code, and I would need more time to crack it."

Lee thought for a moment. "How did you know my IP address?"

Ebe smiled. "I read your blog regularly."

Mark stopped pacing and peeked through the curtains out through the window. The room they occupied faced the hotel's front and overlooked a good portion of the parking lot.

"I wouldn't do that, Mark," Ebe suggested to him. "We don't want to tip off whoever is following you that we are aware of him."

"And how do you know somebody's following us?" Mark asked back.

Ebe stood up and stepped to the dresser where there were a couple of bottles of water. He picked them both up and offered one each to Mark and Lee, who both accepted.

"As soon as I confirmed the trojan, I phoned the one person in Lafayette I have kept in touch with."

"And who would that be?" Lee asked.

"Kent," Ebe answered simply.

Mark's head snapped around. "Kent has been communicating with you all these years?" he asked incredulously.

"Yes," was Ebe's one-word answer.

"Why didn't he tell us?" Mark asked again.

"Because I asked him not to."

"Why? And why did you disappear like that?"

"The reason I moved away is simple. Being gay in Louisiana wasn't any picnic. My work allowed me to live anywhere I wanted, so I did. And it was because of the work that I chose to keep everyone in the dark except Kent. I had to keep a low profile, and the more people who knew where I was or what I was doing, the more dangerous it was for me."

"Can we discuss this later? How do you know someone is following us?" Lee asked, attempting to get him back on track.

"I live in Atlanta now, which is only a six-and-a-half-hour drive. When Kent told me about your excursion down here, I decided to surprise you when you got off the plane. It wasn't difficult to ascertain your flight information. I arrived at the airport in plenty of time and found a place to watch the car rental kiosks, assuming you would choose to rent a vehicle instead of taking a taxi everywhere. When the two of you appeared, I noticed a man trailing you, paying particularly close attention to your movements."

Once again, Mark and Lee exchanged looks.

"The man carried only a small bag and didn't seem to be heading anywhere with a purpose, other than anywhere the two of you went. So I postponed our reunion for a while longer and watched the gentlemen for a bit. He rented a vehicle from the same company as you and rode the bus to the car lot with the two of you. I followed the bus to the lot, watched the two of you pick up your car, as well as our mysterious stranger, and when you left the lot, he followed you all the way to the Sunset Club, where he parked across the street and watched while you were inside," Ebe related.

"What does he look like?" Lee asked.

"His most distinguishing feature is his military haircut. I believe it's called a crew cut," Ebe answered.

"I remember that guy from the bus," Mark exclaimed excitedly.

"I do too," Lee confirmed, "but who is he and what does he want?"

Mark and Lee looked at Ebe.

"I can't tell you yet, but I did get the license plate from his rental car."

"Do you think there's somebody following the guys in South Carolina?" Mark wondered aloud.

"I don't know, but let's not take any chances," Lee said, pulling out his cell phone and selecting a number from his contact list.

"Hello," the voice on the other side of the line responded after a couple of rings.

"Raymond, it's Lee. How's it going there?" Lee asked.

"Lee, we were just about to call you guys. You won't believe what we found out already," Raymond stated excitedly.

"Same with us," Lee responded, "starting with the fact that we have somebody following us."

"Following? Do you mean like tailing you? For real?" Raymond said.

"As real as a heart attack. And there's more, a lot more," he continued, looking directly at Ebe. "But what did you find out first?"

"I don't know what we've gotten ourselves into, but whatever it is, it's way over our heads. We didn't find a death certificate for Andi, but we found one that was kind of surprising. Two actually," Raymond said cryptically.

"I'm not following," Lee admitted.

"We found death certificates for Mr. and Mrs. Taylor, Andi's parents."

"Why is that significant?" Lee replied, still confused.

"Lee, they died in 1992, the same day that Andi drove home from Florida."

| 23 |

Deep End of the Pool

Lee

"Lee, are you still there? Lee?"

The hand holding Lee's phone had dropped from his ear and now was hanging limply at his side. His expression was blank. Raymond's voice could be heard coming from the cell phone in his hand.

After the shock had worn off, Lee's brain re-engaged. He saw the concerned looks on Mark's and Ebe's faces.

"What is it?" Mark asked.

Lee put the phone back against his ear. "Can you say that again, Ray?"

"We found death certificates for Andi's parents, and they died the same day Andi drove home from Florida."

Lee repeated the information to Mark and Ebe.

"Shit the bed," Mark exclaimed loudly, looking at Ebe and then back at Lee.

"Nothing about Andi being dead?" Lee asked.

"No, nothing. You said someone is following you?" Raymond asked.

"It's true. And we also found out that some government agency has hacked into my computer and is tracking my internet activity," Lee went on. "That's why we called. To warn you. Somebody may be watching you."

"How do you know that?"

"Hang on," Lee said, then turned to Ebe. "You drove your own car down here, right?"

Surprised, Ebe had to think a moment. "Yes, a Chevy Blazer."

"Can you drive to Easley, South Carolina tomorrow?"

"Sure, whatever you need," Ebe answered.

"Raymond," Lee turned back to his phone, "we will be in Easley late tomorrow."

"Do you need Billy to come down there and fly you back?"

"No, we'll just change the return of the tickets we already have. Just find out all you can by tomorrow and watch your backs," Lee warned.

"Don't worry about us. You two be careful," Raymond responded.

Mark stepped over and leaned his mouth near Lee's phone. "Tell Kent I'm going to kick his ass when we see him."

"What was that about?" Lee heard Raymond ask.

Lee looked at Mark, who had returned to his seat on the bed. "We'll explain when we get there. See you soon." He disconnected the line.

"What now?" Mark asked.

Lee shook his head. "I don't know about you, but I'm feeling like I've fallen into the deep end of the pool, and I can't remember how to swim."

Mark got up and paced. "Tell me about it."

Ebe spoke up, "We need to get something to eat and then formulate a plan. Maybe somebody should pick up some takeout? We can't take the chance of letting our mystery guest see the three of us together and losing the advantage we have over him."

"I'll go," Lee volunteered. "I'm getting squirrelly anyway, and then, Mark, you can catch Ebe up while I'm gone," he reasoned. "What does everybody want?"

"Do you think it's safe to go out by yourself?" Mark asked, looking at Ebe.

"I don't see why not. So far, whoever this is seems content just monitoring your movements," Ebe answered, shrugging his shoulders.

"That makes me feel better," Lee deadpanned.

"I saw a Subway a couple of blocks up the street on our way here. That okay?" Mark suggested.

Both Mark and Ebe agreed with the suggestion, and after he jotted their orders down on a piece of stationary, Lee headed off toward the lobby.

He walked through the parking lot outside the hotel to the sidewalk, paralleling the street, and looked to the north. He saw the bright lights of hotels, novelty stores, T-shirt shops, putt-putt golf courses, and numerous liquor stores, but no Subway. He turned toward the south and spotted one across the street, a couple of blocks away. He started walking.

The sun was just about to disappear behind the horizon, and the heat was slowly losing its grip. Lee could smell the salt air from the Gulf only a couple hundred feet from where he was walking and had a sudden urge to go swimming. He had forgotten how intoxicating the beach could be. Recently, there never seemed to be time for vacations, even before Terri got sick. However, the allure of the sandy beach and the outgoing tide were still powerful, and he felt maybe he could genuinely unwind here if given the opportunity.

Crossing the street at the light, he could now see into the Subway storefront and was relieved to see that there was only one customer being served, so he anticipated his wait would be a short one. As he pushed open the front door, a soft chime came from the rear of the store. The customer he had seen from the street, a thin, lanky teenager with a shaved head and arms covered with tattoos, was paying for his sandwich.

Lee walked down to the end of the counter and waited for the employee to take his order. He guessed she was probably in her early thirties, and her skin was a white as cream, which was incredible for someone living in a Florida beach community. She was a little on the plump side, and the dress that looked two sizes too small for her didn't help any.

He gave her the order for the sandwiches, and as she worked, he let his eyes wander to the menu on the wall behind her. He was vaguely aware of the chime that sounded as the front door opened. Instinctively, he glanced at the new arrival and saw a man entering wearing a Florida State Seminoles hat and a red windbreaker. He returned his attention back to the menu.

Lee watched the woman employee through the glass divider, and when she reached to her right to pick up something, his blood ran cold. Reflected in the glass, standing just behind him, was the man in the Florida Seminoles hat and red windbreaker. The face underneath the cap belonged to the man with the crew cut.

Lee's head snapped up and stared straight ahead. He could feel his heart pounding in his chest. Its thumping filled his eardrums, drowning everything else out. His mind was racing so fast that he couldn't find a coherent thought to latch onto.

"Sir?"

He suddenly realized the woman behind the counter was speaking to him.

"Uh...what...I'm sorry," Lee sputtered.

"What toppings do you want on your sandwich?" she asked.

"Uh...everything," he managed to get out.

He was glad that his hands were in his pockets so the mystery man behind him wouldn't see them shaking.

What should I do? What if the man intends to kidnap and torture me, to find out whatever information he's after? Stop it! Now you're letting your imagination run wild, he told himself.

Bam!

Lee jumped and whirled toward the loud noise. A skateboard was rattling around on the floor in front of the booth where the teenager was sitting. He must have dropped it. The pounding in Lee's heart was now more like a machine gun.

He stepped down to the register at the end of the counter and waited for the woman to complete his order. *Don't look at him,* he had to keep telling himself. *Don't do anything to make him suspicious. But what if not looking at him is suspicious? What would he do if he didn't know who he was? Would he glance at him again? Wouldn't that be normal?* Maybe so, but he didn't trust himself to not look awkward. *Just give me my damn sandwiches and let me get out of here.*

The woman wrapped up the three subs and put them in a thin plastic bag. As she started ringing up the bill, Lee thought differently about the situation. This could be an opportunity. Maybe he should confront the guy and find out what was going on? Once the crew cut guy knew they had blown his tail, perhaps he would leave them alone. Mark and Ebe would be proud of him.

Maybe he could do this.

"That'll be eighteen dollars and fifty cents," the woman informed him.

Lee grabbed the bag and threw a twenty-dollar bill on the counter. It was all he could do to not run all the way back to the Regency.

***

Tuesday morning, Lee and Mark checked out of their room around eight thirty and made their way to the Taurus. Ebe stayed behind to find out all he could about their mysterious shadow.

The night before, they'd stayed up late talking about Lee's encounter with the crewcut man and trying to figure out who he was and why this was all happening. None of them had a theory that made even the slimmest amount of sense. Eventually, the conversation drifted toward Ebe and where he had been the last eighteen years.

Ebe informed them he stayed in Dallas for six years and then moved to Portland, Oregon. He said that the climate on the West Coast didn't agree with him, so he moved back to Dallas for another three years before settling down in Atlanta, where he'd been for the last seven years.

His foray into hacking as a profession started out literally by accident. His job in Dallas was for a large credit card company, managing their conversion from a distributed network to a centralized one. This chore took nearly two years to complete, then he became the manager of their overall data processing facilities.

Although by day Ebe's work was wholly legitimate and his salary paid the bills, at night, he sought a different reward—respect. Even while he was still working in Lafayette, Ebe was obsessed with a compulsion to develop his computer skills to identify and create shortcuts for computer break-ins and dirty tricks. He admitted it was a misguided way to bolster his self-esteem among his computer peers. Nevertheless, he loved the attention and the mystique the growing notoriety brought him.

One night, he was performing a random search for access to financial records he intended to distribute indiscriminately among his fellow hackers when he broke through a particular security profile that appeared familiar to him. It was the data files from his own company.

Realizing that his processing facility was so vulnerable and that such an intrusion was more of a personal affront than a random act, Ebe set about to reverse engineer his company's security footprint so that it was impenetrable. His combination of application-layer firewalls, stateful packet-filtering, and circuit-level gateways performed as expected and earned him a positive reputation within the financial information network. Soon, he was receiving offers from other firms to act as a consultant and install similar systems in their networks. At first, he took these on as side jobs, not for the money, but for the challenge. Before he knew it, he was making almost as much money as a consultant as he was at his regular job. He quit his job, leaving them as secure as the current technology allowed, and started his own business as a network security consultant traveling all over the US.

Ebe told them that with the license plate number of the mystery man's rental car, he could find out some information about him using his laptop and his wireless data link card, but it might take some time to dig up something useful. He would work on that as long as it took. In the meantime, Mark and Lee would visit Mike Stevens at his office before their flight.

The two of them arrived in front of the Southeast Unified Distributors office just before nine o'clock. Lee and Mark walked in the front door and entered an open office with three separate desks facing the front of the room. There was only one person in the room, and he was sitting at the desk in the middle.

"Lee Hamilton?" the person behind the desk asked, rising. Lee recognized the man immediately as Mike Stevens, despite him now sporting a mustache and being nearly thirty years older. He was several inches taller than Lee, short-cut black hair, sharp features, and still looked thin and in shape. Lee took the extended hand.

"Mike Stevens?" Lee pretended to question.

"That's me," he said as they shook hands.

Lee pointed to Mark. "This is my associate, Mark Sigmar."

Mike shook Mark's hand as well.

Mike pointed to a couple of metal chairs with plastic seats in front of his desk. "So, you are interested in some club properties in Panama City?" he asked, also taking his seat.

"Not really," Lee answered.

Bewilderment showed on Mike's face.

"I'm sure you don't remember me," Lee explained, "but we met at the Sunset Club twenty-nine years ago."

Bewilderment turned into bafflement on Mike Stevens's face. Lee pulled out the photograph from his backpack and laid it in on the desk in front of Mike. At first, he looked at it as if it were an alien object, and then slowly came the recognition. Mike looked between the picture and the two of them several times. Lee could tell from how Mike looked at the picture that this was the first time he'd seen it. Obviously, he wasn't the person who made the notations on the back of the picture.

"Why are you here?" Mike asked finally.

"We were wondering if I could ask you a few questions about Andi," Lee asked.

"Sure, but I don't know how much help I can be. I haven't seen or heard from her since the day this picture was taken," Mike replied. "How is she?"

"You didn't get word that Andi died in an automobile accident driving home from this trip?" Lee asked, gesturing toward the picture he was holding.

Mike sat up straight in his chair, genuine confusion now on his face.

"Wait. What did you say?"

"Andi died in an automobile accident driving home from Panama City. She never made it home," Lee repeated.

Mike was deep in thought and didn't reply right away. Finally, he said, "No, that can't be."

"Why not?"

"The police spoke to Andi's dad after she went home, and nobody mentioned anything about an accident," Mike explained.

Mark and Lee exchanged looks. "Why were the police talking to Andi's dad?"

Mike handed Lee back the picture and then started shifting some papers aimlessly around his desk, now appearing uncomfortable. "My dad went missing that week, and the police wanted to talk to Andi about her meeting with him," Mike said.

The memory of seeing Mike's dad in the Regency talking to Andi flashed through Lee's mind.

"Your dad disappeared that week?" Lee asked.

Mike's expression turned somber. "Yes. We never saw him again. My mom called the police, but I'm not convinced anything sinister happened."

"Why's that?" Mark asked.

Mike was now stacking papers in different piles. "My parents were having problems, fighting all the time, and my dad owed a lot of money to some people. I think he just ran off."

"Did the police speak to Andi directly?" Mark asked.

Mike thought for a moment. "I'm not sure. I don't think so. They only spoke to her father, but he confirmed Andi saw my dad, and everything was fine when he left her."

"You don't know on what day the police made that call, do you?" Lee asked.

"Shit, that was thirty years ago," Mike replied, waving his hand as if he was shooing a fly away.

"Why did your dad come over to see Andi while she was there?" Lee continued.

"Well, back then, my family lived in Tallahassee. I was coming over to see Andi and was supposed to pick up a package from her to bring back to my dad. Unfortunately, we both spaced out and forgot about it, so my dad had to drive over here the next day to get it," Mike explained.

"What was in the package?" Mark asked.

Mike squinted his eyes and appeared to be looking off to the horizon. "I...can't...recall. It was a long time ago. Actually, it was something that Andi's dad was sending to my dad. Why is that important? And who told you that Andi died in an automobile accident?"

"You haven't heard from Andi since then?" Lee continued to question Mike, ignoring his questions.

"Not since the night that picture was taken. My dad and Andi's dad were roommates in college, and their family came over to our house whenever they were in Florida, but we lost touch after my dad disappeared."

"We need to get to Easley," Mark said to Lee, who nodded.

The two men rose from their seats, but then Lee hesitated. "Where did your dad work, Mike?" he asked.

"He worked for the county, in the district attorney's office."

The phone on Mike's desk rang. He apologized for the interruption and picked up the handset. As he was talking, Lee gestured his head toward the front door. When the two of them started to leave, Mike slapped his hand over the mouthpiece.

"Wait a minute. Where are you going?" Mike called out to them. "Somebody needs to explain to me what's going on."

Mark and Lee walked out the front door, ignoring his appeal.

"Frank, let me call you right back," Mike said, then put the receiver back on the base. He got up and walked to the windows at the front of the office, just in time to see Lee and Mark drive away.

Returning to his desk, Mike sat in his chair and leaned back as far as he could without tipping over. He drummed his fingers on the desk as he appeared to be contemplating something, then abruptly leaned forward and opened the bottom drawer on the right side and removed a notepad. He flipped through the pages, quickly searching for something within it. When he came across what he was looking for, he immediately picked the phone up and dialed a number he read from the notepad.

"Yeah," a voice on the other end of the line answered.

"Is this Paretti?" Mike asked.

"Yeah, this is he. Who's this?" the gruff voice responded.

"This is Mike Stevens. You told me once that I should call you if anybody ever came around asking about my dad's disappearance."

| 24 |

Easley

**Billy**

"Damn, Raymond, you give the phrase *high maintenance* new meaning!"

Billy was sitting on the edge of the double bed, yelling his remark to a seemingly empty hotel room. The dull roar of a hair dryer coming from the bathroom around the corner suddenly stopped.

Raymond stuck his head out of the bathroom door, his hair contorted and disheveled. "Did you say something?"

"No, just hurry," Billy hollered back.

It had been so long since he had shared a bathroom with Raymond that he'd forgotten how vain his friend could be with his appearance. Face scrubbers, moisturizers, shampoos, conditioners, styling gels, hair dryers, toenail clippers, tweezers. He had it all. It had been that way since the day they first met, and it looked as if time had eroded none of his idiosyncrasies. Billy couldn't knock the results because Raymond still looked good, at least his hair did, but the time he spent in the bathroom could frustrate, especially if you'd been set to leave for at least an hour.

"I'm almost ready," Raymond yelled back, and the roar of the hair dryer started anew.

Billy walked next door to see if Kent was ready. He grabbed his room card off the dresser and slipped into his jeans pocket, walked by the bathroom, and then stepped out into the hallway.

The town of Easley, where the motto is *You Can Easily Do Better in Easley*, had a population of 21,126. They named it after Confederate General William King Easley, who in the late 1800s persuaded officials from the Charlotte-to-Atlanta Air Line Railway to lay a track through the town. The town was surveyed, and lots sold on August 3, 1873, shortly after the railroad was finished.

Easley was home to four different hotels, three of which were within walking distance of one another, just off the highway running along the outskirts of town. They could have driven and stayed the thirteen miles down Highway 123 into Greenville, where Billy had landed his airplane. Greenville was a much larger city with a broader variety of overnight accommodations to choose from. Still, Raymond insisted everybody stay in town to have quick access to their rooms and not have to work out of their rental car. Raymond and Billy shared a room and gave Kent the single to have privacy whenever he talked to his wife or mom.

Billy walked the couple short steps to Kent's room and banged louder than necessary on the door. The door flew open, and Kent stood there wearing a purple polo shirt, jeans with a sharp crease down the legs, and holding a toothbrush in his mouth. Without saying a word, he turned around and returned to the bathroom, leaving Billy to enter the room and close the door behind him. Kent's room was arranged completely opposite of theirs, with the dressers and TV on the left wall, and instead of two double beds, a king-size bed occupied most of the room. The bed had already been made.

"Housekeeping has been here already?" Billy asked, wondering why they had been to his room so early. It wasn't even eight thirty yet.

"No," a garbled voice answered from the bathroom, spitting afterward.

"Then, did you actually sleep in the bed?"

"Yes," Kent's disembodied voice said matter-of-factly. "I made it this morning."

Billy looked at the bed and then toward the bathroom again. "Did you flip the mattress also?"

"Raymond ready?" Kent asked as he walked into the room, ignoring Billy's comment.

"Probably by now, but it'll take him thirty minutes to pack up all his cosmetics," Billy answered, sitting on the neatly made bed.

Kent grinned at Billy's comment. "What's the plan?"

"Raymond wants one of us to go to the library and pull the microfilm of articles from June 1992 to see what we can find. Somebody else will go to the police station to see what information they will tell us that won't be in any newspaper article. Last, somebody will need to track down Andi's roommates, Gayle and Trisha."

"But, aren't they supposed to be dead?" Kent asked.

"You would think, but since it's looking more and more likely that Andi didn't die in a car wreck, then they didn't either. So, somebody needs to see if they can find one or both."

"Do we get to choose which one we get to do?" Kent inquired, walking over to the window and opening the curtains. A steady, misting rain was coming down outside.

"I'm guessing that Raymond will take the police, seeing as he's a lawyer, which means it is looking at film or making lots of phone calls for the two of us."

Still staring at the falling rain outside, Kent said, "Tell me again why we didn't get to go to Panama City?"

A knock on the door brought Billy up from the bed to open it, letting Raymond into the room.

"Anyone try the breakfast yet?" Raymond asked. He was wearing a pressed white button-down shirt, a blue tie, tan slacks, and loafers.

"Why so fancy?" Billy asked.

"I'm going to see the police. Jeans and a T-shirt will not get us the information we need," he pointed out.

"I left my pocket protector, Clark Kent glasses, and Keds sneakers at home. Does that mean I don't get to go to the library?" Kent queried.

Raymond put his hands on his hips and blankly stared at Kent.

"The breakfast is pretty good," Billy interjected, "and the coffee is damn good."

Raymond looked at Kent. "Have you eaten yet, wiseass?"

He shook his head. "But I'm not hungry."

"I guess I'll pick something up later. So, who wants to stay here and track down Trisha and Gayle?"

"I'll stay," Kent volunteered, raising his hand.

"Okay, but no watching pay-for-view movies. You have a job to do," Raymond warned.

Kent lowered his hand. "Then I want to go to the library."

Looking at Billy, Raymond asked, "You okay trying to track them down?"

"Sure."

"Then let's go, Kent," Raymond commanded and headed out the door. Following behind Raymond, Kent turned toward Billy and gave a mock salute, and then disappeared out the door.

Billy sat on Kent's bed, wondering what he should do next. It embarrassed him to tell Kent and Raymond that he had no clue how to track down two people, much less trying to do it with only their first names to work with. Not one to sit in front of the TV and watch shows like *Matlock* or *Magnum, PI*, and the only thing he read was sports magazines and not mystery books meant he felt ill-equipped.

Slapping his hands together and rubbing them rapidly as if he were trying to warm them up, Billy got up from the bed and walked over to the desk. He opened the drawer and removed a large phone book, placing it on the desk and moving the chair around so he could sit down.

***

Raymond

The Easley Law Enforcement Center was located two blocks from city hall on Second Street and only three blocks from the Market Square. The steady rain had slowed to a soft mist, but Raymond had stopped at a Walgreens on Main Street and picked up a five-dollar umbrella, which he now held over his head as he walked across the cobbled sidewalk.

Reaching the Law Enforcement Center, he checked his watch before pulling open the door. It was nine thirty.

Inside the building was a small waiting area with a row of a dozen folding metal chairs lined across the wall to the right of the entrance. A man wearing jean shorts and a dirty t-shirt was the only person seated. A waist-high wall with glass extending to the ceiling was at the front of the waiting room, with a door at the far-right end. Behind the wall directly across from the front entrance on the left side was a reception desk with a woman wearing a blue uniform sitting behind it, typing on a keyboard. Raymond stepped up to the glass in front of the desk.

"Can I help you?" she asked without looking up, her voice carrying through the circular collection of tiny holes in the glass.

"I need to speak to a detective," Raymond announced.

"Regarding?" she asked again, still not taking her eyes off her computer screen.

"An old crime committed here in Easley."

The police officer looked up at Raymond. "You have information regarding the crime?" She asked.

"Yes," Raymond lied. He knew that the truth would never get him in to see a detective.

"When did the crime take place?" she inquired, looking back at her computer screen again.

"June 1992."

She typed the information into her computer. "Name of the parties involved?"

"The Taylors, Richard and Sandra," Raymond told her.

The policewoman finished typing, sat back and waited a couple of seconds. Raymond saw her eyebrows go up, and she looked in his direction again. Then, picking up the phone, she dialed four digits. He couldn't make out what she was saying when she spoke into the handset, but she quickly set it back on its base and looked at him again.

"Someone will be with you in a moment," she said and returned to typing on her keyboard.

Raymond said thank-you to the woman even though she appeared to no longer be listening to him. He swung around and noticed that the man in the jean shorts was now lying across three chairs in a pseudo fetal position. Raymond grabbed his iPhone off his hip and checked his emails. He was about to respond to one when he heard somebody call out.

"Are you the gentleman with the information about the Taylor case?" a man, slightly older than Raymond with a receding hairline and a bulging beltline, asked. He was wearing a white dress shirt with a bland color tie knotted loosely around the neck.

"Yes," he lied again. "That's me."

"Can you come with me, please," the man asked and held the door for Raymond to enter through.

After walking through the door, the man with the pudgy waistline let the door close and then extended his hand to Raymond.

"Detective Walsh."

"Raymond James," Raymond replied, shaking the detective's hand at the same time.

"This way," the detective said, walking through rows of desks toward offices in the back of the room. He entered one with the door already open, stood to the side to allow Raymond to enter, and then closed the door.

"So, are you a reporter or writing a novel?" Detective Walsh asked as he made his way around his desk toward his leather chair.

Raymond stopped in midmotion as he was taking a seat. "Excuse me?"

"Are you a reporter or a novelist?" the detective asked again, his expression serious. "This investigation goes back more than a few years, and usually after so much time, only reporters doing a story about unsolved murders or somebody writing a book looking for morbid details is what we see."

"I'm neither. I'm a lawyer," Raymond answered, sitting down. He could see a collection of family pictures arranged aesthetically atop a credenza behind the detective. A dozen framed certificates and awards hung on the wall above that.

The detective's expression changed slightly, a little more relaxed. "Interesting. And do you really have information about this case?"

"I'm not really sure," Raymond answered honestly, shifting uncomfortably in his seat. "Let me be honest with you, Detective Walsh. I'm a friend of the Taylors' daughter, Andi, from a long time ago, and I'm just trying to find out what happened to her. We were told that she died in a car accident while she was driving back from

Florida. Apparently, the same day her parents died," Raymond admitted.

"And who told you this?"

"That's the weird thing—her father," Raymond stated.

Detective Walsh's eyebrows rose, and he appeared more interested. "You spoke to Mr. Taylor?"

"No sir, it was in a letter sent months after what I now know was the day of his death."

The detective sat back in his chair and took a deep breath. "It sounds to me like you were the brunt of a very terrible joke," he finally said.

Raymond smiled uneasily. "I think you may be right. But do you know what happened to Andi? Where she is now?"

"Regardless of how many years it's been, this is still an ongoing murder investigation, and as a lawyer, you know I can't comment about open cases." The detective sounded like he was reading from a script.

Raymond debated with himself how far he should push this. Was the information worth pissing off the detective? Could he tell Lee he had learned all he could know with a clear conscience?

"Detective, when was the last time you or anyone else in this precinct looked into this case?" Raymond pushed on.

Instead of the glaring stare or angry retort Raymond was expecting, the detective instead remained leaned back in his chair with a semi-amused expression on his face, saying nothing. All his years of taking depositions or time in a courtroom questioning witnesses led Raymond to realize that the detective's demeanor meant that he needed to adjust his approach from his normal combative mode. He needed to appeal to the man's compassion.

Raymond moved to the edge of his seat expectantly. "Please, detective, we have spent nearly thirty years believing Andi was dead. Can you kindly tell me what you know?" Raymond almost begged.

Detective Walsh sat forward in his chair and placed his forearms on the desk in front of him. He stared at Raymond as if he were exposing him to some form of visual lie detector test. Raymond noted the detective's left eyelid drooped.

"Well, since technically it isn't even our case, I can tell you what I know. An unknown assassin murdered the Taylors and one of their employees, Pamela Goodwin, in their shop during an apparent robbery. This took place before their daughter had returned from Florida. She was taken into protective custody when she arrived in town."

"Taken into protective custody by whom?"

"The Feds. Listen, all I can tell you is this. The bodies were discovered by a customer in the morning. On that same day, our office received a call from the Greenville FBI office wanting us to send a patrol car to the Taylors' home to check on them because Richard Taylor didn't show up for a scheduled meeting with them. We informed the FBI of their deaths, and before you could blink, they were here swarming the place. The FBI are the ones who took Andi Taylor into custody."

"Then I guess I need to be talking to someone at the Greenville FBI," Raymond said.

The detective smiled and shook his head. "They won't tell you anything. It's an open investigation, and they invented the term tight-lipped. I shouldn't have told you as much as I did."

Raymond sat back, dejected. "So that's it? Three people are murdered, Andi Taylor disappears, and that's all the answers we have?"

"Mr. James, my guess is that Miss Taylor knows something about the person who killed her family and was placed in witness protection for her own safety. If I'm right, you probably won't see Andi again," the detective informed Raymond.

Raymond rose from his chair, and Detective Walsh did the same. They shook hands once again. Raymond thanked him for his time and information, and then he turned to leave. At the door, he paused before opening it.

"I know one way we might see Andi," Raymond told the detective.

"How is that?"

"If they catch the killer."

| 25 |

Unanswered Questions

Mr. Brown

At times, he had doubts that following Hamilton and his companion to Panama City was the right decision. Maybe his time was better spent completing the search of the house, but this last-moment venture was intriguing. His instincts were right.

Not that they were difficult to trail, because quite the contrary was true. The task was borderline tedious, and thinking back on it, he should have remembered that assignments like this are where mistakes occur. He regretted toying with Hamilton when he picked up sandwiches, but not because he feared being spotted. No, it was sloppy and unprofessional. He chastised himself and swore to not let his guard down again.

Interestingly, they visited two key locations from Hamilton's blog, the Sunset Club and the Regency Hotel. But, unfortunately, nothing Mr. Brown learned from those destinations would be relevant and help him find what he was after. Hamilton had gotten his hands on a photograph at the club that the two of them seemed particularly keen on. Surely that wasn't what this trip was about? Reminiscing? Their choice of hotel gave him hope it might prove otherwise, theorizing that they chose it so they could access where the girl stayed back in 1992 to search it. But he knew that would be a fruitless endeavor, having torn it apart himself many years ago.

Things got interesting the next day when they drove out to visit Southeast Unified Distributors. At first, Mr. Brown was unsure of their intentions, so while they were inside, he called his office and had a quick background check run on the business. He confirmed the distributor serviced the Sunset Club, but the business owner's name made him take notice. Mike Stevens. Stevens. He didn't believe in coincidences, and this would have to be a huge one to not be what it looked like. A quick online search confirmed it.

The two men he was following were across the street, talking to the son of a man he had killed.

He was unclear the extent of the younger Stevens's involvement, but it made sense why the pair were here talking to him. Would they be able to make the connection between the elder Stevens's disappearance and the girl vanishing? How about the death of her parents? He doubted that last bit. He had effectively thrown off the police investigation in Florida, and it was all due to luck. It was happenstance that he was still in the Taylors' residence when the police called to question their daughter about her meeting with Stevens. Hearing that it was the police when the answering machine picked up, he made a split-second decision and grabbed the phone before they hung up. He pretended to be Mr. Taylor and answered their questions, putting their minds at ease. As far as anybody in Florida was concerned, the Taylors were alive and well.

Even though this recent development still didn't bring him any closer to finding what he sought, it reinforced his suspicion that Hamilton and his cohort were doing more than reminiscing. The man could make waves in the investigative waters that had been calm for such a long time. Still, he was confident that whatever they dug up would only satisfy their own curiosity and couldn't be linked to him. However, it always paid to be sure.

When his targets were getting ready to leave, Mr. Brown briefly debated whether he needed to pay Mr. Stevens his own visit, but the boy had never come in contact with the item and the likelihood he would have it now was slim to none. He decided Stevens wasn't worth losing track of his quarry, so he waited until the Taurus built a four-car lead on him and then pulled out after them.

From their direction, it didn't take long for him to guess that their next destination was the car rental agency and a return to the airport. They were heading home. Of course, that was an assumption, and he needed to confirm it before he relinquished his surveillance, which could be tricky. If they were going to change their flight, it would most likely take place at the airline desk in the terminal, at which point he could call his office. In Washington, they could access live updates to all airline travel. That meant that he needed to keep a close enough eye on them to react quickly if they changed their plans.

He had already decided it was too risky to drop his rental car off at the lot and ride the same bus with them back to the airport. Instead, he would use the more expensive option of dropping the vehicle directly at the airport, putting him there approximately fifteen minutes ahead of them.

He picked up their trail at the departure terminal, stepping off the blue and gold bus, and watched as they walked to the ticket counter to check in. Then, he pulled his cell phone from his front pocket and speed-dialed his office.

"Department of Homeland Security, how may I direct your call?" a youthful female voice answered. Mr. Brown found it ironic that the woman who belonged to that voice was actually forty-seven years old.

"Air Transportation," he stated, and the woman responded by asking him to hold.

As he waited, he continued to watch Hamilton and his partner as they stood at the ticket desk.

"Good afternoon, Air Transportation, Williams speaking," a cheerful male voice spoke into his ear through his cell phone.

Mr. Brown recognized the voice of the person on the other side of the line. Jim Williams was one of those annoying people who continually brought his children's fundraising activities to work and pushed them on his coworkers in the break room or cafeteria. Tins of popcorn, cookie dough, candy bars, even Pampered Chef fliers were constantly being thrust into people's faces. It reached the point that if somebody spotted him in one of the common areas, they would turn around and walk away rather than be subjected to the guilt-inducing sales pitch. He despised the man.

"Jim, this is Robert Brown from the cybercrimes division, badge number C20254J. I need a flight destination check," he said to the man.

"Certainly, name and flight number?" Williams responded, all the peppiness disappearing from the tone in his voice.

"Hamilton, Southwest flight number 1930 from Panama City to Little Rock." As he spoke, he watched Hamilton and his friend leave the ticket counter and head toward security.

He could hear some keystrokes being typed through the phone connection, then finally, "I now show him booked on Southwest flight number 5779 bound for Greenville, South Carolina."

Mr. Brown unceremoniously closed the cover of his cell phone, cutting Williams off. He had the information he needed.

They were heading to Easley.

***

Lee

Lee and Mark returned their car to the rental agency, caught the shuttle to the airport, and hopped on their 1:14 flight to Greenville, South Carolina via Atlanta uneventfully. They were focused and businesslike as they moved from destination to destination, speaking only occasionally, each staying in their own thoughts about the mystery they had unwittingly found themselves in. Not once did they look over their shoulders for their mysterious follower, even though they were sure he was there, taking care to be invisible.

Ebe had reminded them before they parted in the morning to be careful what they said when they made calls because their cell phones might have been tapped. They definitely shouldn't call him, as he was still flying under the radar. Lee was learning quickly that a bit of paranoia could go a long way.

Stepping out of the walkway from the concourse into the baggage claim area of the Greenville-Spartan International Airport, Lee spotted Kent standing by the exit, waving his arms. He and Mark headed directly for him, and as they approached, they could see Kent looking past them, scanning the arrivals for somebody else.

"Ebe's not with us. He's driving up," Mark said flatly.

Kent nodded his understanding and gestured toward the loading zone outside.

"Raymond stayed in the car, so we didn't have to park," Kent said, leading them outside where he veered left and started jogging toward the Impala. He climbed into the passenger seat and was finishing buckling his seat belt as Lee and Mark threw their bags into the trunk. Lee slid in behind Kent and Mark behind Raymond, the sound of their doors slamming shut serving as a signal for Raymond to pull away from the curb.

"Have you guys seen any sign of somebody following you?" Lee asked as he wrestled with his seat belt.

"Right now, I think everybody is following me," Kent answered.

Raymond sped up onto GSP Drive, heading toward I-85. Rush hour traffic had thinned considerably in the thirty minutes between the time they had driven into Greenville from Easley and now. The rain had finally subsided, and the clouds appeared as if they were becoming lighter.

"Where's Billy?" Mark asked.

"He's still at the hotel trying to track down Trisha and Gayle. Kent and I left directly from the library," Raymond answered, keeping his eyes on the road.

"I believe we each have a lot of information to share, but let's wait until we are *all* together first, okay?" Lee asked.

Raymond glanced back over his shoulder briefly. "Okay. But can I ask you one question first?"

"Go ahead," Lee answered.

"Did you find anything that explains what kind of shit we've stepped into?"

"No," Lee answered simply and lapsed into silence. *What have I dragged us all into? What are they thinking about me right now? I pop up out of nowhere after thirty years, and suddenly we're involved with government agencies and have mysterious figures following us. We have murders and disappearances and deceptions and who knows what else?*

He looked at Mark, who had become unusually quiet since leaving Mike Stevens. Now every glance or muttered word took on a new meaning, one that painted Lee in a very negative light.

Mark nudged Lee on the elbow as they grabbed their bags from the trunk, making a subtle head motion toward a black Chevy Blazer parked a couple of cars away.

They all entered through the rear door with Raymond and Kent leading the way and walked up a brightly lit hallway leading to the front lobby. They turned right in the lobby and proceeded down an adjoining hallway with guest rooms on either side. Raymond stopped in front of a room on the right, watching Kent use his key card and open the door.

The four of them entered the empty room, hearing the air conditioner at the base of the window humming steadily.

"Billy must be in our room," Raymond speculated. "It's just down the hall. Why don't you guys just throw your stuff on Kent's bed until we can get another room."

Mark and Lee did as they were instructed, Lee keeping his backpack slung over his shoulder, then all of them retraced their steps out the door. Continuing down the hall in the same direction, they stopped at the next door on the right. Raymond used his key card to open the door.

When the door swung open, the group could see Billy in the room straddling the desk chair, speaking to somebody who was sitting on a bed, partially blocked by a wall. As they moved farther into the room, they could see that person was wearing an unbuttoned brown plaid oxford shirt over a gray T-shirt, a pair of severely faded jeans, and some nondescript black sandals. But the person's shoulder-length red hair was all that anybody could see that would hint toward his identity.

"Ebe!" Raymond exclaimed, freezing in his tracks, shock smeared across his face.

Ebe smiled widely. "Hi, Ray."

Kent stepped past Raymond and embraced Ebe as he rose from his seat. Mark and Lee continued into the room, giving Billy a knuckle crunch as they passed by, both taking a seat on the second double bed.

Lee noticed Raymond watched Mark's and Kent's lack of reaction to Ebe's presence, then his friend put his hands on his hips. "You knew he would be here?"

"He was with us in Florida," Lee answered.

Raymond looked at Ebe for a moment, then at Kent. "This is what they meant about going to kick your ass?"

Kent offered a sheepish grin.

Raymond looked at Billy, but before he could open his mouth, Billy said, "Hey, I was as surprised as you were when I opened the door."

"Raymond," Ebe interjected. "Allow me to explain."

Ebe told Raymond about his work and how it led to discovering the government eavesdropping on Lee. Then he recapped his phone conversation with Kent informing Ebe what the group's plans were, his decision to drive to Florida and warn Lee and Mark, and finally stumbling across the person following them.

Looking back to Kent now, Raymond said, "You've known where Ebe's been all these years?"

"That's right, and don't anybody give me any shit about it either," Kent replied forcefully. "Ebe asked me not to say anything, and I didn't. Lee didn't say a word about Andi being dead. Mark never said a word about Lee's letters and knowing Andi was dead, Billy said nothing about his marriage being in trouble. You never said anything about feeling empty." Kent looked around the room slowly before continuing. "I'm not the only one keeping secrets."

The six of them let silence fill the room.

"Why don't we," Mark said, breaking the stillness, "go over what we've found out so far?"

"Good idea," Raymond said, nodding. "I'll start. Like we told you on the phone, yesterday we discovered that there isn't a death certificate for Andi Taylor, but we found ones for her parents, with the date of their death listed as the same day Andi left Panama City for home. Lee, are you sure about the dates you wrote in your blog?"

Lee nodded.

Raymond nodded back to Lee and continued. "What I failed to mention was the cause of their deaths. They're listed as gunshot wounds. Today I talked to Detective Walsh of the Easley police and discovered that an unknown assailant murdered the Taylors and a third person during an apparent robbery of their shop. Andi was not there. It turns out that Mr. Taylor had been in contact with the FBI for unknown reasons, and when they learned of his death, they took over the crime scene."

The group sat there in stunned silence as Raymond let everything sink in.

"The local police, who know very little because this is an FBI case, suspect that Andi somehow knows or can identify the killer and was taken into protective custody."

"So, she is alive?" Billy blurted out.

Ray looked at Billy. "It appears so. But all we know for sure is that no death certificate was ever filed for her in Pickens County."

Kent spoke up. "The local paper didn't have much more except that a customer discovered the bodies at ten o'clock and they had been dead less than twenty-four hours. We found another story about a high school girl who went missing a week after the bodies were discovered, but we don't know if it's connected or not."

Lee reached into his backpack lying at his feet and took the eight-by-ten photograph from the pocket. He handed it to Billy.

"Here is the picture, just like the comment on my blog talked about," Lee started. "You can see on the back where somebody wrote on it in 2000. We thought that it might have been Andi's friend Mike, you know, the guy who partied with us that one night. He's there in the picture."

Billy was looking at the writing on the back of the picture, and when Lee mentioned Mike, he turned it over in his hands and looked closer at the photograph, nodding when he recognized him at the back of the group.

"We went to see him this morning. We could tell from his reaction when we showed him the picture that he had totally forgotten about it, or he's an excellent actor. But what we learned from him is that his dad went missing that same week we all were there. On top of that, he told us the police called to inquire about Andi's meeting with Mr. Stevens. According to Mike, the police talked to Andi's dad, and he told them Andi had confirmed the meeting and Stevens was fine when he left to return home."

"But according to Raymond, the police said that Andi hadn't made it home before they killed her parents," Billy pointed out.

"Exactly," Lee agreed.

"Then who did the Florida police talk to?" Billy asked what was already on everybody's mind.

"There's something else," Lee continued. "Mike's dad went to see Andi to pick up something that Andi's dad had given her to pass along to him. Mike couldn't remember what it was. But you can start connecting the dots. The Taylors are murdered, Mike's dad goes missing, and the person who brought the unknown package to Mike's dad, Andi, is also missing."

"That still doesn't answer the question of who sent the letter to you about Andi's supposed death." Kent pointed out.

Yet again, the conversation paused while everybody in the room looked at one another with serious faces.

Lee couldn't hold it in any longer. "I don't know what I've gotten you into, but it needs to end here. I started this because I wanted to find out what happened to Andi. But now I know she might not want to be found because she is hiding from someone. People are dead—murdered—and we're being followed by who knows who. We need to go back to our own lives and leave this alone."

Billy started to voice an objection when Ebe cut him off. "I might be able to help with some of that," he said.

"With what?" Lee asked.

"I believe I know who is following us."

| 26 |

The Tip

Dianne

I was feeling haggard. Not a term I would usually use to describe myself, but one that certainly fit the bill at the moment.

The last couple of days had been rough. Two of my investigators called it quits, with no notice or reason given. That meant more cases to spread around, and now I had the extra task of interviewing to fill those vacancies. You could almost feel the tensions in the office, and each day I expected to see a plank appear, sticking out of a second-floor window, and a mob waiting to see me walk it.

So, I did what I usually did—put my head down and worked straight through until I collapsed. Now I was parked in front of the house of an investment banker suspected by his life partner of two-timing him with his own sister. It was boring, but at least I was out of the office where the only person who was glad to see me was Briana.

When my cell phone rang, I briefly considered letting it go to voice mail. It was a momentary lapse. I looked at the caller ID, and although I didn't recognize the number, I answered it anyway.

"I understand you're trying to get ahold of me," the gruff voice said. There was static in the connection.

I glanced at the number again, and that's when it clicked. I had been calling the number for almost a week with no response. "This is Antonio Paretti?"

"That's me. Who is this?"

"Mr. Paretti, my name is Dianne Williams, and I work for Silent Sleuth Investigations in Charlotte, North Carolina."

"So?" Antonio responded flatly.

"Several years ago, someone from our agency," I paused a moment as I flipped a page in the file I kept in the seat next to me and scanning quickly continued, "a Dave Bishop talked to you regarding the disappearance of Craig Stevens. I believe he offered to reward you for any information you could provide us about that incident. I am just following up to see if you might have any new information we could use," I blurted out, my eyes trained on the entrance to the house I was watching.

There was nothing but silence on the line.

"Mr. Paretti, are you there?" I asked.

"I remember now. What happened to Cobb? I'm used to dealing with him."

"Aaron passed away earlier this year. I've taken over the running of the firm."

"Too bad. He was an okay guy. Listen, I need to call you back. Can I reach you at this number?" the gruff voice finally spoke.

"Yes," I answered, and suddenly the line went dead. My gaze turned from the house to my cell phone. I shifted in my seat.

Ten minutes later, my cell phone rang again.

"Hello?" I answered.

"What did you say your name is?" Antonio Paretti asked without introduction.

"Dianne Williams."

There was another long pause before the voice spoke again. "How much dough are we talking about?"

I paused momentarily, shocked. Could there really be new information about a thirty-year-old murder? I weighed the fact that whatever amount I quoted wouldn't be charged back to the client this time, as I had promised a free pass.

"Does that mean you have something for me?"

"Maybe. How much?"

"A hundred," I offered.

"Shit, are you kidding me? That won't even cover my cell phone bill for a month," the voice barked.

"Okay, five hundred."

After another long pause. "And how you gonna get it to me?"

"I'll wire it anywhere you want first thing tomorrow morning."

Another long pause followed.

"Do you have any information or not, Mr. Paretti?" I prompted again.

"It just so happens two guys showed up in Panama City yesterday asking questions about the Stevens guy," the voice answered, noticeably quieter now.

"What was their interest?"

"All I know is they seemed surprised to hear he was missing."

"Would you know their names?" I asked, my heart beating faster now.

"Yeah. Lee Hamilton and a Mark something."

I scribbled down the names on a sheet in the file. "Is there anything else you can tell me?"

"I know where they were heading next."

"And where might that be?"

"Your neck of the woods. They were headed to a town called Easley in South Carolina," the gruff voice said, sounding almost cheerful.

Now it was my turn to be quiet.

"Did you hear me?" Antonio asked.

"You'll have your money first thing tomorrow, Mr. Paretti," I responded and disconnected the call.

All the exhaustion, weariness, and lack of concentration I'd been experiencing lately were suddenly gone, and I felt sharper than ever.

Whoever these guys were, they'd asked questions about a person connected to Pamela Goodwin's murder and were now headed to the city where she was murdered. This wasn't a coincidence.

I debated what I should do next. The agency was shorthanded, the office was in turmoil, and oh yeah, there was this promising new hire who was receiving very little guidance. I needed to be here right now. So why was I waffling?

I knew why. If there was even a glimmer of a chance a desperate woman could get closure about her sister's death, even after three decades, wasn't that worth pursuing?

I made up my mind. I was headed to Easley.

| 27 |

Unmasked

Lee

"Using the license plate I copied down from the car that was following Lee and Mark, I was able to find out quite a bit of information about the person who rented it," Ebe started explaining to everybody.

"All the information on the rental form was fake, which I suspected, but he slipped up. The rental agreement was changed before the drop-off to an airport return instead of a lot return. When that happens, it creates a subsequent internal document in the rental company's system and whoever initiated that form made a note of the phone number the change came from. That cell phone is registered to a Robert F. Brown with a driver's license issued from the District of Columbia. His actual residence is in Silver Spring, Maryland, where he owns a two-bedroom home in a quiet middle-income neighborhood surrounded by newly developed affluent condos. He doesn't have a vehicle registered in his name, which suggests he is a user of the mass transit system in Washington." Ebe allowed everything to sink in before continuing.

"According to his driver's license, he is six feet tall and weighs two hundred and five pounds, which I can collaborate."

"I can, too," Mark interjected.

Ebe nodded at Mark, and then continued. "Our Mr. Brown was born in Birmingham, Alabama, to an Emily Brown and her husband, Lieutenant Colonel Patrick Brown. His father was in the army," Ebe said, looking at Lee.

"He has one brother two years older than him. Growing up, the two of them hopped from station to station with their father, finally graduating from high school at Fort Benning, Georgia. From there, Robert Brown followed in his father's footsteps and served in the military, enlisting in the Marines right out of high school.

"He served two and a half years in the service as part of the military police unit before being dishonorably discharged in 1987. Although the report and all other details of the incident have been removed from the public record, I found out it involved another marine's death. He avoided criminal charges but was forced to leave the service.

"In 1988, he started working as a patrolman on the Atlanta police force, eventually rising to the level of a senior detective in their major case squad. He left the Atlanta PD, unexpectedly, according to the records, and moved to Tallahassee, Florida, in 1991, where he became a detective there before being promoted to chief of detectives in 1995. He served in that capacity until he moved to Washington in 2002 and accepted a US Immigration and Naturalization Service position. He was there for fifteen years until he moved into his current position in 2017." Ebe finished and fell silent.

"So, who does he work for now?" Billy asked anxiously.

"The Department of Homeland Security," Ebe answered solemnly.

Nobody had anything to say for a short time.

"You got all that from a license plate number?" Billy inquired.

244 - DL HAMMONS

Ebe shrugged his shoulders. "Homeland Security did most of the work for me. They do comprehensive background checks," he answered.

"When I get home, I'm throwing my computer in the trash," Kent commented.

Lee shook his head. "Like I was saying, guys, we need to drop this now and walk away. I couldn't live with myself if one of you got into trouble, or hurt, because of my wild goose chase," he pleaded.

"You say that, but are you going to stop?" Mark asked him. "If we all go home, what are you going to do? Are you going to quit?"

Lee's silence was his response.

"Okay, then let's think this through," Raymond suggested. "Lee is being followed, and his computer is being watched by the Department of Homeland Security. According to Ebe, this scrutiny started when he posted the story about our trip to Panama City and meeting Andi on his blog. So what could he have said or done that has anything to do with national security?"

Nobody offered an idea.

"I have a different theory," Ebe announced.

"By all means. We're all ears," Raymond said.

"What if Lee isn't being followed by the Department of Homeland Security?"

"Huh? You just told us he was," Billy said.

"Actually, Robert Brown is the one doing the following. What if he's using his position to do that?" Ebe postulated.

"What makes you think that?" Billy asked.

"Two reasons. The first is that the person responsible for alerting me to the scrutiny on Lee has a reputation for standing against government overreach, which is surprising because he works for the government. Anyway, it wouldn't be a stretch to think that the overreach we're talking about is personal, not governmental. And second, in doing my research of Mr. Brown, I came across a surprising coincidence that is hard to ignore and I believe is worth exploring."

"Explore away," Raymond encouraged him.

"Robert Brown's younger brother went to college in Tallahassee, Florida and ended up going into politics. He was a circuit judge there in 1992, the same time we were down there. He ultimately became the mayor at approximately the same time Mr. Brown started working for the police department in Tallahassee. When his brother became a US senator, Robert Brown moved to Washington, DC, and got a job that his brother could have easily helped him land," Ebe explained further.

"How is that relevant to any of this?" Kent asked

"It might not be at all, but Robert Brown's brother is Senator Theodore Brown."

Lee sat down heavily, and Mark's head fell forward, his chin pressed against his upper chest.

"Who is Theodore Brown?" Billy asked, clueless.

Lee looked at Billy and answered, "He's the Republican running mate with Jack Fallon, candidate for president of the United States."

Billy stared at Lee for a moment, then at everybody else in the room.

"Oh, crap!" he said succinctly.

Determined not to be overwhelmed, Raymond looked at Ebe and asked, "So, why do you think Mr. Brown is acting on his own? What is his interest in Lee?"

Ebe thought for a moment before answering. "I believe Mr. Brown suspects that Lee might have something he is searching for."

A surprised look appeared on Lee's face. "Huh. What? What would he think I would have?"

"I don't know. But consider the facts. We know that Andi's father sent something, via Andi, down to Mike's dad, a man who worked in the DA's office in Tallahassee. That same DA went missing that same week. Andi's parents are dead, and Andi herself is missing. My guess is that somebody, maybe our Mr. Brown, is after that item and eliminating the people who have come into contact with it. You spent time with Andi while she was down there, so for whatever reason, he now believes you have it. Or at least thinks you can lead him to it."

"But Andi gave it to Mike's dad. I wrote that on my blog. How could anybody think that I would have it?" Lee questioned.

"Oh...Lee," Kent uttered as if he had just remembered something. "The envelope."

"What envelope?" Lee asked.

"Yes," Mark jumped in. "You're right, Kent, the envelope."

"What is everybody talking about?" Billy wanted to know.

"The envelope that Andi gave Lee when she left Florida. The one she told him not to open until she specifically asked him to. That one," Kent explained.

"Do you still have it?" Raymond asked.

"I think so, maybe up in the attic somewhere. We put the boxes with our old college books up there. It should still be in my yearbook. But you can't possibly believe that is what this guy's looking for? And whatever it is, why would Andi give it to me?" Lee pondered.

A cell phone started ringing somewhere, and Kent dug in his pants. He looked at the caller ID on the screen, gave everybody a sheepish grin, and disappeared into the bathroom. As the door was closing, they could hear him saying, "Hello, Mom."

Raymond continued where he left off. "We need to get that envelope and open it for no other reason than to eliminate it as the possible item."

"I don't know, Ray," Lee said, sounding unsure of himself. "She told me not to open it."

Raymond stared at Lee for a moment, then Mark, Ebe, and Billy.

"Lee, this might be the key to everything that's going on here. You can't possibly be thinking of keeping that promise even now. That's just plain ridiculous."

Lee shook his head, staring down at the floor. "You can't understand, Raymond."

"Then explain it to me, Lee," Raymond barked back, his frustration clearly showing now.

Lee's head snapped up, and he glared at Raymond.

"Because what if that envelope is totally innocuous, which I believe it is, then the opened letter will be just one more reminder of how I let Andi down," he snapped back, his eyes returning to the floor.

"Listen, we will not figure this out tonight," Mark interjected, attempting to diffuse rising emotions. "Let's book ourselves a room, get some grub, get some sleep, and tackle this again in the morning."

Raymond nodded.

"I'll sack out with Kent on his floor," Ebe suggested.

"Okay. Lee, let's go check in."

Lee rose from the bed and followed Mark out into the hallway. As soon as the door was shut, Kent emerged from the bathroom and looked around the room.

"What'd I miss?"

| 28 |

Taken

**Dianne**

Whoever this Lee Hamilton guy is, he's a wild card, a complete mystery, and that is something I really dislike. There was no mention of him in the Pamela Goodwin case file. Nada. So why was he in Florida asking questions about Craig Stevens, somebody who disappeared twenty-nine years ago? A coincidence? Not likely. Plus, in this line of work, there was rarely such a thing. No, Hamilton was a new player in this mystery, and he needed to be questioned.

I found Hamilton registered at the third hotel I called in Easley. I asked to be put through to the room.

"Hello?" a male voice said.

"Is this Lee Hamilton?" I asked.

"Just a second," the voice said. Then, after a pause, a different voice took over.

"Hello?"

"Lee Hamilton?"

"It is. And you are?"

"My name is Dianne Williams, and I am an investigator from Silent Sleuth Investigations in Charlotte, North Carolina. I was wondering if we could meet so I could ask you a few questions?"

"Questions about what?" the voice asked.

"Specifically, Craig Stevens."

After a momentary pause, "Okay, sure. Where are you located in Charlotte?"

"Actually, I'm pulling into the entrance to your hotel right now."

"Well then, I was just on my way out to get some coffee. Would you care to talk over a cup?"

"Sure, that would be fine. I can drive us."

"Uhhhhhhh, if you don't mind, I'd rather take mine. You can ride with me if you'd like."

He's cautious, I thought, which is unusual, but not much. "Okay," I agreed.

"I'm parked out back if you want to pull your car around. I'll be standing next to a black Blazer."

"I'll be right there," I said, and the line went dead.

I directed my Lexus down a thoroughfare next to the hotel and emerged into a second parking lot. I quickly located the black Blazer where a man in his forties was just unlocking the door. I parked a row behind him and killed the engine. Stepping out of the car, I got a better look at Lee Hamilton. He was five foot nine, about two hundred pounds, had a shaven head, a snub nose, and a serious expression. He appeared in excellent physical condition, dressed simply in jeans, a yellow polo shirt, and off-brand running shoes.

"Mr. Hamilton?" I said as I approached, my hand extended.

"Guilty. But call me Lee. Miss Williams, or is it missus?" Lee answered, taking my hand.

"Miss. But I'm Dianne."

Lee gestured to the passenger side door. "Well, Dianne, climb on in, and we'll head out."

I walked around the rear of the Blazer and opened the passenger side door, slipping gingerly into the seat. Lee climbed behind the wheel and slid the key into the ignition.

"You know I probably have as many questions for you as you do for me," Lee stated as he turned on the ignition and fired up the engine.

"We can help each—" I started to say when the Blazer's rear doors flew open, and two men jumped inside. I whipped my head and shoulders around, only to have the barrel of a black handgun shoved in my face.

"Turn around and face forward, both of you," one man barked.

I turned around and looked forward. Lee did the same.

"Cell phones. Pass both of them back here," the man commanded.

We did as we were instructed without turning around. The man on the right took them both, turned their power off, and let them drop to the floorboard.

"Friends of yours?" Lee asked under his breath.

"Shut up!" the voice shouted again. "Let's get this rig moving and drive where I tell you."

"Listen, I have cash in my wallet. Why don't I just leave it on the seat, and you can have the car, no problems," Lee tried to negotiate.

Suddenly, a hand holding a gun delivered a hard blow to the side of Lee's head, stunning him.

"Hey, that's unnecessary," I yelled, which resulted in the black handgun making a second appearance in my face.

"I said drive," the man bellowed.

Lee put the Blazer in reverse and backed out of the parking spot.

The man told Lee to get on the highway heading south. When Lee looked to his right to check oncoming traffic, his eyes met with mine. In that split second, I saw a combination of worry and resolve on his face. It was clear that the men in the back seat were as much a surprise to him as they were to me.

After twenty minutes of silent driving, Lee was instructed to exit the interstate. We were now on a two-lane road, and I spotted an old truck coming at us from the opposite direction. I frantically tried to think of a way to signal the occupants about our predicament without alerting our abductors. But, unfortunately, everything I could think of would also put the people in the truck in harm's way. As the truck passed by us, I silently cursed my futility.

After another ten minutes of driving through the open countryside, we turned right on a dirt road which led to a large red barn a half a mile farther. Lee was told to park the Blazer behind the barn so it wasn't visible from the road, then kill the engine.

"Out," our captor ordered. "Leave the keys in the car."

Lee and I opened our doors simultaneously, and the men behind us did the same.

"Into the barn," came another command.

As I walked toward the barn door, I scanned my surroundings, looking for anything I could use to my advantage. There was a four-foot-long two-by-four leaning against the corner of the barn, but it was too far away to help. A gravel drive led from the dirt road to the barn entrance, but the rocks on the path were too small to do much good. I kept looking.

At the barn door, one of the two men stepped ahead of us and swung it open. I estimated he was five-feet, ten-inches tall, two hundred thirty pounds, muscularly built with thick black hair and several days' worth of stubble on his chin. He had a face that reminded me of a boxer, probably because part of his right eyebrow was missing because of an ugly scar. There was no weapon in his hands, but I could see a holster underneath the gray sports coat he wore.

Walking through the barn door, I immediately noticed a lone metal chair sitting in the middle of the open floor. Empty stalls with closed gates lined both sides of the barn's inner area, except the one in the far right-hand corner filled with stacks of baled hay.

The guy trailing Lee prodded him in the middle of his back with the gun. That guy was as tall as his partner but weighed much less, probably two hundred pounds. His hair was also very dark, a little longer, but slicked straight back with gel. He was wearing a tan sports coat over the top of a black T-shirt. Whereas his partner resembled a fighter and most likely had the intelligence to match, this one had eyes set close together and an intensity that concerned me.

"Have a seat," Slick said to Lee.

I watched Lee walk to the chair and sit down slowly. He was facing the door we had entered through. The thug with the scar took me by the elbow and dragged me over to one of the stable gates. I could still see the resolve in Lee's eyes, but now there was concern as well.

Slick slipped his gun into his waistband as he walked up beside Lee on the left-hand side and put his right hand on Lee's shoulder. Then, with blazing speed, his left hand slammed into Lee's stomach, driving up into his solar plexus and forcing out all the air in his lungs.

I lunged forward to help but was quickly restrained by the boxer.

Caught unaware, Lee doubled over and rolled off the chair onto the dirt floor. He writhed around as he tried to regain his breath. Slowly, the vacuum in his chest eased, and his breathing returned to seminormal. Slick grabbed him by his shoulders and muscled him back into the chair.

"That was to let you know what to expect if we don't get the co-operation we expect. Answer our questions truthfully, and that's all you'll have to suffer," Slick said.

It was a few more seconds before Lee could speak. He then said, "Whatever happened to just saying please?"

That made me grin, but it didn't amuse Slick much.

"Just remember, friend, if you make this more difficult than it needs to be and you don't tell us what we need to hear, your lady friend will sit in this chair next."

Lee glanced at me, more worried now. When I looked back, I spotted movement at the barn door. Being careful not to give anything away, I kept my eyes on Lee.

"What do you want to know?" Lee asked evenly.

Slick walked behind the chair. "Why were you asking questions about Craig Stevens?"

I could tell Lee was pondering the question. "I wasn't, exactly. I was talking to Mike Stevens about an old girlfriend. Mike is Craig Stevens's son."

From my peripheral vision, I could see the shadows of two, maybe three, men on the other side of the barn door. Luckily, the boxer hadn't noticed them yet. The way they were sneaking around gave me hope they might be intent on a rescue. But who were they?

Slick continued walking around the chair Lee was sitting in. "Then why were you so curious about his father's disappearance?"

"I didn't know he had disappeared until Mike told me. He vanished the same time my girlfriend did. It seemed like a massive coincidence."

"I would have to agree. How do you know Neville Scranton?"

Lee looked over his shoulder at the man as he came around from behind the chair. "I don't know who that is," Lee answered.

"How did your girlfriend know him then?"

"I don't know that she did. Listen, you're asking me questions about things I don't know anything about."

Slick stopped in front of Lee.

"And you were doing so good up until then."

"Listen, really, I have no clue who Neville Scranton is or why you would think I would have any information that would help you," Lee explained earnestly, bracing for what was no doubt coming.

Slick reached into the pocket of his sports coat and came out with a straight razor.

"Let's just say I don't believe in coincidences either," he said, walking around behind Lee.

"Nobody move!" an unfamiliar voice suddenly bellowed. "FBI."

When the boxer turned toward the voice, I raised my leg and brought my foot crashing down on his. Howling in pain, he bent over and reached for his damaged foot, but his head met my knee as I drove up into his temple, sending him stumbling back into the stable gate. Without missing a beat, I spun around three hundred sixty degrees, spinning on one foot while I let the other whip around and slam into my opponent's ear. His head jerked around from the force of the kick. He stood there motionless for a second, then fell face forward to the floor.

My attention went to Lee just in time to see him grab the chair from under him and swing it at Slick in one fluid motion. The chair struck Slick's hand, knocking the razor across the room.

Slick must have seen the others come rushing in through the barn door and decided the odds were against him, so he raised his arms high above his head. Lee took one step forward with his left foot and swung up into Slick's groin with his right foot. Slick doubled over in pain and Lee swung the chair in an uppercut motion, sending it crashing into Slick's head with a clang. He flew backward and landed spread eagle, unconscious on the dirt floor.

I removed the gun from the boxer's holster and watched as Lee flung the chair into the corner. We exchanged knowing smiles.

"You sure know how to show a girl a good time."

| 29 |

Questions

Dianne

After hours of questioning by the local PD, during which I gave them little information because what happened confused me as much an anybody, a lanky gentleman I recognized as one of our rescuers met me coming out of the station.

"Miss Williams?"

"Dianne."

"My name is Raymond James. I'm friends with Lee."

"You were with the group that rescued us, right?"

"Correct. Lee is still being interviewed, but I know he has questions for you."

"And I for him."

"Perfect. We wondered if you'd like to join us for a coffee while we wait. There's an establishment just up the street."

"That would be great," I responded.

We turned and started walking. The sun was fading, and with it, the afternoon heat. The two of us were the only people on the street, the rest of the world having already packed it in for the day. I could get used to the early evening pace of Easley.

"How do you know Lee?" I asked as we walked.

"We're old friends. We knew each other in college at LSU."

"What is it you do when you're not out saving damsels in distress?"

Raymond chuckled. "I'm a lawyer in Lafayette."

"Interesting. Is Lee a lawyer as well?"

"No, hardly. He's an insurance adjuster. Listen, I think it would be better if we hold off on the Q and A until Lee joins us, if you don't mind?"

"Not at all," I answered, and we continued strolling along in silence.

The Market Square Chess Café was a combination coffee shop, eatery, and chess club, all set in a rustic background smack in the middle of downtown Easley. Sandwiched between a real estate office and an old-fashioned toy store, the café presented a very unassuming front that could easily be missed if you weren't looking for it.

After entering, I followed Raymond toward the back of the café. All the tables in the rear were long and wooden, like extended picnic tables with only bench seating on the sides. Other than a couple of older men carrying on a chess match in the corner of the dining room, the only other customers were seated at the table Raymond was heading toward.

A curly-headed, muscular man—someone else I recognized as one of our rescuers—and a man with long red hair sat with their backs against the wall. Opposite them was a man of Asian descent. Except for muscleman, they all looked to be in their fifties.

Both Raymond and I sat down facing the wall.

"Thank you for what you did this afternoon," I said to the muscular man, then, turning to Raymond, "Both of you."

"Hey, I was there too," the Asian man exclaimed.

"And it was Ebe here who tracked you," the muscular man said, jerking his thumb at the redhead.

"Well, thanks to all of you. And out of curiosity, how did you find us?"

"You were driving my Blazer, which has a LoJack installed," the man they called Ebe replied. "I just hacked into their system, and the GPS did the rest."

"Impressive. I could use a man with your skills at my agency."

Raymond smiled. "I'm not sure you can afford him."

"I'm Kent, by the way," the Asian man said. "That's Billy and Ebe."

"And you're all friends from college, like Raymond?"

"That we are. And you're a private detective?"

"I am."

"Guys, we all have questions," Raymond reiterated, "but we need to wait until Lee and Mark get here."

"Mark? There's another one of you?"

"He's the last, promise," Raymond said.

"So, know any good jokes?" Kent asked.

We made casual conversation for about an hour until Lee and another man, dressed in a distinctive western style, arrived.

"We finally made it," the cowboy, who I assumed was Mark, announced as they approached.

I watched Lee take notice of the coffees in front of us.

"That looks good."

"I'll get us both one," Mark offered, already heading back to the front of the café.

Lee took a seat next to Ebe with his back against the wall.

"I'm glad to see you stuck around," Lee directed to me. "Have these guys introduced themselves?"

Everybody around the table nodded.

"They haven't been a pain, have they?" Lee asked.

I smiled back at him. "Well, I've been spending most of my time trying to talk this guy into coming to work for my agency. What he did with his laptop was impressive."

Lee extended his fist to Ebe, who reached out and returned the fist bump.

"Hey, I was the one who called the police," Kent objected.

"Yeah, thanks for that," Lee said. "That's four hours of my life I'll never get back." Then, he turned his attention to me. "How long did the police question you?"

"Maybe three. But most of the police knew me. I've done some work around here before."

Mark returned with the coffee and sat at the end of the table.

"So, before we were so rudely interrupted, you were going to tell me about your involvement in all this," Lee stated.

I took another sip of coffee before beginning.

"My agency represents a relative of Pamela Goodwin, a girl who was murdered here in Easley twenty-nine years ago. She died at the same time as a Mr. and Mrs. Taylor. Pamela worked in their shop on a part-time basis. After the police stopped actively working on the investigation, Pamela's sister retained our firm to re-investigate the murders. She comes to us every year, always on the anniversary of her sister's death."

"And you take money from her?" Kent asked rudely.

I bristled and looked across the table at Kent. "Not this year. I recently took over running the agency, and I'm doing it on my own time."

Kent looked down at his coffee, sufficiently chastised.

"I'll be honest with you. For the past several years, the person who had been handling this case was just going through the motions. In his defense, it is a twenty-nine-year-old murder case with no witnesses and zero leads."

"None of that explains why you're here now or why you contacted Lee?" Raymond asked plainly.

"That's true, but before I go any further, I think it's your friend's turn to explain how he's involved?" I responded.

I could tell by how Lee was looking at me that he was sizing me up, trying to reach a decision. Finally, a crooked grin told me he had made up his mind.

"I'm not sure you will believe me. I can hardly believe it myself."

"I'm pretty open-minded," I replied, intrigued.

"Fine, I'll give you a quick summary," Lee started. "Our story started in 1992, when the six of us took a summer vacation to Panama City. We were LSU students looking to have some fun before we started working for the summer. While we were there, I met, and...fell in love with Andi Taylor."

"Taylor...as in—"

Lee nodded. "She's the daughter of the Taylors, the same Taylors who were murdered with your client's sister. Andi and I only spent four days together, but the two of us really connected. Anyway, we both went our separate ways. Over a period of several months, I wrote her a couple of letters, with no response. I called the number she gave me, but it was disconnected. Finally, I received a letter from Mr. Taylor, along with my unopened letters, informing me that Andi and her roommates had died in a car wreck on the way back home from Florida."

My interest was piqued even further, but I still couldn't see how any of this fit in with the murders.

"I kind of lost it and shut down emotionally. I dropped out of school for a couple of years before I finally got my act together. I got married, had kids, and life went on. Then about three weeks ago, I stumbled across something that made me remember my time with Andi. The more I thought about her, the more I wanted to know the details of how she died. But I couldn't find any. Not one article about a car wreck killing three college co-eds. I also discovered that someone had opened the letters I sent to Andi and read them, so somebody hadn't been completely honest with me."

I sat there transfixed, allowing my coffee to get cold. "So, what made you go back to Panama City now?"

"I write a blog, and I posted a story about our 1992 trip and how I met Andi. On that post, I received a strange comment from an anonymous reader instructing me to 'find the picture.' At first, I didn't know what that meant, but after I reconnected with these guys, they helped me remember we had taken a group picture while we were in Florida that could still be at the club where it was taken. The only people who knew about that picture, or so we thought, were us, Andi, and her roommates. So, the comment on my blog seemed mysterious. Mark and I flew down there to find that picture. These guys came out here to find out what they could about Andi's death."

"Did you find it?" I asked, absorbed. "The picture?"

"We did, and that was what sent us looking for Mike Stevens. On the back of the picture, somebody had drawn a heart and dated it the year 2000. It turns out Mike Stevens was in the picture with us. Mike's and Andi's families were close."

"So, you met Mike Stevens in 1992?" I prodded.

"Briefly. He works in Panama City. We went to see him about the picture and find out what he knew about Andi's car accident. He knew nothing about it. Nothing about a car wreck or that Andi was missing at all. That's when we learned his dad had vanished the same week in 1992, when we were in Panama City. Meanwhile, these guys here in Easley discovered that Andi's parents had been murdered on the same day she returned from Florida. That meant somebody other than Mr. Taylor must have written the letter to me. That's when Mark and I flew up here."

"You didn't tell her about Mr.—" Billy started to say, but an elbow in the side from Ebe silenced him. Lee gave him a stern look as well.

I looked at Billy, then back at Lee.

"That's some story, Mr. Hamilton."

"Lee."

"That's some story, Lee. I guess this is your lucky day."

"Considering we both were kidnapped today, I'm wondering why you would say that?"

"Because I have something for you."

"And what's that?"

I took another sip of my now cold coffee.

"Answers."

| 30 |

Answers

Dianne

I sat back in my chair and waited to see what Lee's response would be.

"Answers are something that has been in short supply recently, and the ones we get always seem to lead to more questions," Lee said cautiously.

I let my eyes drop as I thought about how much I should share. The past twelve hours had really thrown me for a loop, and I reminded myself to be careful. What had started out as a nuisance case and an act of kindness had blown up in my face. Forget about the expenses I'd never recoup; someone kidnapped me, for Christ's sake. The silver lining of it all was meeting these men. They were an unusual group. What I had pieced together while we waited for Lee to be released was that they were all from Louisiana, at least initially, and their story about tracking down a lost love—although strange—rang true. So did the bond they had for one another. I was serious about trying to recruit the redhead into my firm. Maybe telling them everything I knew could help with that.

"What our agency learned when we first got involved was Richard Taylor, Andi's father, contacted the FBI office in Greenville twenty-nine years ago. He had information, and evidence, about a corrupt judge in Florida being blackmailed by his bookie. But, unfortunately, the person at the FBI who took the call that night dropped the ball. Instead of getting somebody out here to take Mr. Taylor's statement right away, he made an appointment for Mr. Taylor to come to their office the following day. When Taylor didn't appear, they tried to contact him by phone several times, and when that failed, they called the local PD. That's when they were informed that the Taylors had been murdered.

"According to our sources, the proverbial shit hit the fan after that. Andi Taylor arrived home later that day and was immediately taken into protective custody. The FBI had already screwed up once, and they weren't going to take any chances with her safety, so they placed her in witness protection until they caught the murderer," I explained.

"So, she's still in witness protection?" Lee asked quickly.

I hesitated for a moment. I didn't want to build up Lee's hopes only to see them dashed later. "As far as I know."

"What was the evidence Mr. Taylor was going to give to the FBI?" Mark asked. "And who was the judge involved?"

"Unknown. The bookie was a guy named Neville Scranton. He was also murdered. Scranton was the guy those thugs who kidnapped us were asking you about. He was a midlevel player in organized crime in Tallahassee. Taylor told the FBI he had voice recordings between Scranton and this unidentified judge. He also said he sent a copy of the recordings to a friend in the Tallahassee district attorney's office—Craig Stevens. Something must have gone wrong because Stevens disappeared. When Taylor couldn't reach Stevens, he became concerned and called the FBI."

"That must have been when he called Andi and told her to come home early," Lee said.

"So, the goons that kidnapped you and Lee work for organized crime in Tallahassee?" Kent leaned forward and asked.

"That's my guess," I answered. "Those guys have long memories when it comes to killing one of their own, and revenge is a moral imperative for them."

"So how did they know I was in Florida asking questions or that I'd be here in Easley?" Lee wanted to know.

"My guess is, Mike Stevens was offered an incentive to let them know if anybody came asking questions about his father's disappearance. I found out in much the same way, via an informant. It wouldn't be hard after that to pick up your trail."

I looked at Ebe, who nodded his agreement.

"What do you think they'll do with those guys?" Kent asked.

"Kidnapping, aggravated assault, they'll definitely be seeing some jail time."

"So that's it?" Mark said. "Andi didn't die in a car accident. Instead, she disappeared because the FBI placed her into witness protection because of a murder her father had evidence of. How did her father even stumble across any of that here in South Carolina?"

"He owned an antique store and pawnshop. The prevailing theory is someone pawned the device that had the recordings on it," I explained.

"Was there information about the person who pawned the recorder? Don't you have to fill out something when you pawn something?" Ebe asked.

"There's nothing. Whoever murdered the Taylors stole the inventory book as well."

I watched them all ponder what I had just dumped on them. It felt good supplying them some answers, but I also couldn't help but feel depressed. Now that I knew their role in this drama, I realized nothing would help me deliver my own answers to my client, Mrs. Bennett.

"Then Mark's right, that's it," Raymond announced.

"Now that you know what happened, will you be heading back to Lafayette?" I asked, looking around at them all.

Lee stood up and walked a short distance away, thinking, then returned to the table.

"I'm not, not yet. I still want to find out who wrote that letter telling me Andi died and signed Mr. Taylor's name to it," Lee said, still pacing. There was an undercurrent of hostility in his tone.

"I would have thought that was obvious," I said.

"What?" Lee exclaimed, stopping his pacing. "Who?"

"One of her roommates. That's who'd I put my money on."

"Gayle or Trisha?" Lee said.

"Oh...I was supposed to be tracking them down," Billy offered. "But I came up empty."

Although I believed everything Lee and the others had told me, my intuition wasn't satisfied. Lee was holding something back. There was an element to his story he was keeping to himself, and that bothered me. I didn't like loose threads.

On the other hand, I had given them all I knew and had learned nothing in return, so I should really get back to my backlog of cases in Charlotte and the brewing mutiny.

But still.

I made a quick—some might say irrational—decision.

"Would you like some help?"

***

Raymond guided the car out of town, following the GPS directions, with me, Lee, and Mark as passengers.

It didn't take long for me to locate the first roommate Lee mentioned—Gayle—even though we didn't have her last name. Knowing that Easley was a small town and Gayle had known Andi since they were youngsters, I first went online and accessed the Easley yearbook from 1990. There were only two Gayles in that senior class, and Lee quickly pointed out the correct one. Gayle Poskey. From there, we got lucky. Accessing the Pickens County Public Record, which was a breeze for Ebe, we found out that Gayle Poskey had married right there in Easley and become Mrs. Gayle Robinson. And as luck would have it, her family owned a home close to the hotel.

A few miles out from the city limits, the GPS instructed Raymond to turn onto Country Club Road. The group had decided that only Lee, Mark, Raymond, and I would make the trip, leaving the others at the hotel. Lee didn't want to overwhelm Gayle. I offered to stay behind, but thankfully he thought it fitting that I come along.

Even though it was dark, I could make out the massive homes and the expansive lots they stood on as the Blazer made its way toward our destination. SUVs and sports cars occupied the driveways we passed, and it became apparent that Gayle had married into money.

When we arrived at the house, I noted it was conservative compared to the homes we observed on the drive in. It was a large white Victorian with a wraparound porch and a separate four-car garage with a room over the top.

The four of us exited the car. Motion-controlled flood lamps illuminated the driveway and front yard, causing Raymond to shade his eyes. Solar track lights also lined the walkway from the driveway to the front porch, making it easy to find our way to the front door. Lee reached out and pushed the glowing doorbell button. Inside the house, we could hear chiming.

KNIGHT RISE   -   267

Yellow porch lights sprang to life, and the front door behind the glass outer door opened. An older woman with blond hair hanging loosely around her shoulders peeked her head from behind the door. I'm not sure why, but a sense of anticipation was building inside me.

"Can I help you?" she asked timidly.

The woman was the same height as me, but considerably heavier. From the look on Lee's face, he recognized the woman.

"Gayle, do you remember me?" Lee asked through the glass storm door.

Gayle looked at him carefully, but there was no recognition in her eyes.

"No, I'm sorry, should I?" she replied.

"It's me, Lee. From Panama City in 1992. I met you and Andi there," he said, trying to jog her memory.

Gayle's eyes appeared to focus more intensely on Lee's face, and then recognition came. Her eyes grew large, and her mouth dropped open. She stepped out from behind the door, and we could see she was wearing a white tunic and light-blue twill pants. She looked at each of the three men standing there, then to me. Her hand went to her mouth.

"Can we come in and ask you a few questions?" Lee asked.

Gayle lowered her hand from her mouth and unlocked the storm door, pushing it open. Lee took hold of the handle and held it open for us to file in through.

"I'm Mark," he reminded Gayle, giving her a gentle hug. Raymond followed suit, then Gayle turned and hugged Lee. Their embrace lasted considerably longer. When the two of them parted, she looked at me, and there was confusion in her glistening eyes.

"I'm Dianne," I said. "I'm a private investigator helping these guys out."

We followed Gayle into a huge living area with hardwood floors and a giant Persian carpet beneath a large leather sofa, two antique end tables, and a similar coffee table. The couch faced a fireplace lined in brown marble with an impressive piece of art deco hanging above it.

Though she remained standing, Gayle gestured for us to take a seat. Mark, Raymond, and I sat on the sofa, and Lee took the edge of the piano bench. Gayle remained standing.

"Can I get any of you something to drink? Water, tea, a beer, maybe?" Gayle asked us.

We all shook our heads. "No, thank you, we're fine," Mark answered.

In the light of the living room, I could see from Gayle's long black lashes and bright red lipstick that she was a fan of makeup.

"I can't believe you all are here in my living room," Gayle commented, still moving her eyes from person to person.

"It has been a very long time," Lee agreed. "It is good to see you again."

"Why are you here, now, in Easley?" Gayle asked, focusing on Lee.

"We came to find out what happened to Andi."

The expression on Gayle's turned serious and a bit sad. She sat down on the edge of the reading chair, facing us all.

"Why now? After all these years?"

"Gayle, somebody sent me a letter in 1992 that I thought was from Mr. Taylor telling me that Andi, you, and Trisha died in a car wreck driving back from Panama City," Lee explained.

A look of genuine surprise appeared on Gayle's face. "What?"

"I've thought that Andi died in a car accident for all these years," Lee reiterated.

Gayle looked from Lee to us on the couch, then back to Lee. "Why would somebody do that?"

"That's one question we're here in Easley to get answers to."

Raymond spoke up. "Gayle, can you tell us what really happened?"

"How much do you know?" she asked.

"We've found out just today about her parents and the FBI putting her in protective custody," he told her.

Gayle lowered her head, clasping her hands together. "I still remember that day like it was yesterday. That was the day that my life changed forever. Andi and I had grown up together—grade school all the way to college. We were constantly together, through everything, good and bad. We were closer than some sisters. When they took her away, it was as if she really died. It devastated me."

We all remained silent as Gayle fought to keep her composure.

"When we got back from Florida, we went to our apartment at Clemson first to unpack. After a while, Andi tried calling her parents, but somebody from the FBI answered instead. Maybe thirty minutes later, they were picking her up. That was the last time I ever saw her."

"Did they ask you any questions, Gayle?" I asked.

"Not then, but the next day they came back and asked me about Andi meeting Craig Stevens at the hotel and giving him a cassette tape," she recalled slowly.

"I was there, remember," Lee reminded Gayle.

"That's right, you were. Mr. Stevens showed up out of the blue, asking Andi for the cassette. She went up to our room and got it, gave it to him, then he left. That was all there was to it," Gayle recounted. "They asked me if I remembered seeing anybody with Mr. Stevens, but I didn't."

"Gayle," Raymond now addressed her, "did you know then that it was a cassette tape Andi was giving Mr. Stevens?"

Gayle thought for a moment. "No, I didn't know what it was until the FBI asked me about it."

"I need you to think about this carefully. Gayle, do you know where Andi kept the tape before she gave it to Mr. Stevens?" Raymond continued.

"No," she answered quickly. "As I said before, I didn't even know the tape existed until the FBI told me about it."

"Let me ask you this, then. Do you remember Andi handling multiple cassettes at once in your hotel room?"

"That was so long ago," Gayle said, staring off into space while she mined deep into her memories. She shook her head after a moment. "No."

Raymond ran his hand through his hair and looked at Lee. Then, suddenly, he looked back at Gayle. "What about on the drive down to Florida?"

Gayle looked off into space again, started shaking her head slowly, then abruptly stopped. Her eyes narrowed and then became wide as saucers. Her right hand covered her gaping mouth.

"What is it?" I asked.

Gayle looked at me and then Ray. "Andi didn't...but I did."

"What do you mean?" Lee asked now.

She looked stricken. "Andi was driving, Trisha was in the front seat, and I was alone in the back. We were driving through Dothan. I was bored with our tapes and looked for something new to listen to, so I went into Andi's bag. I found an unlabeled tape, so I tried to listen to it on my Walkman. All that was on it was two people talking. I was putting it back when Andi slammed on the brakes to avoid hitting somebody who pulled out in front of us, and all the tapes got dumped on the floorboard. I thought I put them all back the way they were, but I might have switched some. Oh god...is this all my fault?" Gayle half cried.

"What happened to those tapes, Gayle?" I asked.

She was no longer listening to anybody.

"Gayle, this is important. What happened to those tapes?"

"Someone stole them from my car in Panama City. I just now remembered that," she answered, trancelike.

Mark looked at Lee. "The tape that Andi gave you, the one with your song on it. It might be the tape everybody is looking for. That's why Brown is following you. That's why he broke into your house."

"Who's Brown?" I asked, which caused Lee to shoot Mark an angry look.

Gayle was talking again. "You do know…she loved you," she whispered, her eyes glistening again. "She cried during half the drive back from Florida, and the other half she spent talking about you."

Mark and Raymond looked down at the floor. My heart ached for my new acquaintance.

Lee looked back at Gayle and smiled weakly. "I loved her too, Gayle," was all he could say.

Gayle held his gaze for a moment, then she used her fingers to comb her long blond hair back behind her head, where she funneled it into a circle and then flipped the end over her right shoulder.

"She loved your blog," she said unexpectedly.

All our heads jerked up.

"You've talked to her…after she was in witness protection?" Lee asked excitedly.

"We communicated…occasionally," she answered hesitantly.

"Isn't that against the rules for people in witness protection?" Mark asked.

"Yes," I answered for her. "Most definitely."

"When was the last time you spoke with her?" Lee wanted to know.

Her expression turned somber again. "Two years ago. She suddenly stopped sending me messages. I haven't heard from her since."

Everybody was quiet for a moment as we considered that last bit of news.

"In the months right after Andi was taken away, did you receive any letters from me?" Lee continued.

Gayle looked shocked. "No. In fact, it crushed Andi when I told her we never heard from you."

"I sent two letters. Somebody got ahold of them and sent them back to me," Lee pointed out, exasperated.

"How did the two of you communicate, Gayle?" Mark asked.

"The first time was a note in a letter, no return address, telling me to look at the personal ads in the Sunday edition of the *New York Times*. I found an ad from AT with a date, time, and phone number. After that, I would check the newspaper every Sunday, looking for an ad, which would usually be there two or three times a year. The phone number was always different. I was pretty sure they were public phones because I could usually hear a lot of people in the background," Gayle explained.

"So, you could never get in touch with her directly?" Mark asked.

Gayle shook her head.

"And the ads stopped two years ago?"

"Yes. With no explanation. Just nothing."

"Gayle, whatever happened to your other roommate, Trisha?" I asked.

"She married a football player before she graduated and was content being a housewife for several years. Then she got her real estate license and did that for a while. Unfortunately, she died from ovarian cancer three years ago," Gayle answered solemnly.

"My wife died from ovarian cancer," Lee said matter-of-factly, which made my heart ache for him even more.

"I know. I read your blog," she responded, smiling. Lee smiled back.

"Do you think that Trisha could have written the letter?" Raymond asked.

Gayle made a sour face. "I seriously doubt it. She hardly ever got mail and never checked the mailbox."

"Somebody got them," Lee pointed out the obvious.

Gayle pondered that for a moment, then said, "I wonder if Lynn could have..." she started, her voice trailing off. Her expression showed she was deep in thought.

"Lynn? Lynn, who?" Mark asked.

"Lynn, our other roommate," Gayle announced.

| 31 |

The Green Monster

Dianne

From Lee's reaction, I could see that a fourth roommate was a surprise.

"I thought there were only three of you?" Lee asked.

Gayle rose from the reading chair and disappeared into the next room, continuing the conversation.

"There were only three of us who went to Panama City." Gayle's voice could be heard from the other room. "But there were four of us rooming together in our apartment at Clemson. Lynn couldn't make the trip because she had a summer internship starting that week."

Gayle reappeared with a cigarette in one hand and a lighter in the other.

"Does anybody mind if I smoke?" she asked, and we all shook our heads. She lit the cigarette and blew out a billowing stream of white smoke. She already appeared much calmer. "I can't help myself, I smoke when I get nervous. My husband and son hate it. They're at soccer practice."

"Do you think Lynn could have intercepted the letters?" Lee asked her when she seemed ready to continue.

Gayle hunched her shoulders and took another drag of her cigarette. "I don't know. Maybe. She was kind of weird. After she moved in, she kind of became obsessed with Andi. I mean, she dressed like her, used the same perfume, even had her ears pierced like Andi – two studs in her right ear."

"What happened to her?" Raymond asked now.

"About a month after Andi left, Trisha and I got our own apartment. We didn't ask Lynn to move in with us because, well, like I said, she was creepy. I think she moved into a single. I heard she got a job in Atlanta with the company she interned with after she graduated."

"That explains why the phone number Andi gave you was disconnected," Mark pointed out.

Lee nodded. "You wouldn't know what company Lynn got a job with, do you?" he asked hopefully.

"No, I'm sorry. I don't," she answered. A cloud of smoke now encircled her head.

"That's okay. What was Lynn's last name?"

"Coleman. Lynn Coleman."

Lee looked at the three of us. "Maybe Ebe can find out where she is."

When Lee rose to his feet, the rest of us followed his lead. "I think we got what we came for. Thank you so much for talking to us, Gayle. You've been a great help."

Gayle rose also, and we all started making our way toward the front door. At the foyer, Lee turned around, and Gayle gave him another hug, being careful of the cigarette in her hand. When they separated, she looked deep into his eyes.

"Tell me I didn't cause all of this," she pleaded.

When Lee didn't respond right away, I stepped in. "Gayle, the person who did this would have killed the Taylors whether or not he had the right tape. What you did was give us a shot at catching him."

Gayle smiled at me weakly and nodded.

Mark and Raymond each gave her a light hug, and then we all said goodbye.

Back in the car, as we pulled out of the drive, Mark looked at me over his shoulder.

"Do you really believe what you told Gayle about not causing of all this?" Mark asked.

"I do. I think that anybody who could have possibly listened to those recordings had to die. That means the Taylors, Craig Stevens, and even Andi. That's why they placed her in witness protection," I hypothesized.

"So, what do we do now?" Raymond asked from behind the driver's wheel.

"That's a good question," Lee mumbled.

***

Back at the hotel, I listened carefully as the men took turns summarizing the information they'd learned from Gayle for the others. When there was finally a lull in the conversation, I took the opportunity to ask the question that had been bothering me the whole way back.

"Who is Mr. Brown?"

Their response was no response. Instead, heads swiveled back and forth as they exchanged looks with one another.

"I promise I didn't say anything," Kent finally chimed in.

"Look, I'm just here to help. That's kinda hard to do when you don't have all the facts."

"You should tell her, Lee," Mark spoke up. "What could it hurt?"

Lee leveled his gaze at me, then nodded. "I'm not sure how it fits into all of this, but Mr. Brown is somebody who works for Homeland Security and has been tailing me ever since my blog about Andi was posted."

"But he's unaware that we know he's following Lee," Ebe quickly pointed out.

"He broke into your house?"

"We think so. He also planted a piece of software on my computer to spy on me."

"He's after the cassette and thinks Lee has it," Raymond blurted out. "He might even be the man who killed this Neville Scranton guy, Mike Stevens's dad, Andi's parents, and their store clerk. He could be behind all of it."

I could feel my heartbeat quicken. Could it be that this group of friends stumbled across something to flush out a murderer and lead to answers for my client? It seemed too farfetched.

"What about the envelope?" Ebe stated. "The one Andi gave you. Do you think that's involved somehow?"

"What envelope?" I asked, confused.

"It's something Lee wrote about in his blog. Andi gave him a plain white envelope before she left Panama City, with instructions not to open it until she told him to," Mark answered.

It was becoming clear that I needed to read this blog everyone kept mentioning.

"I'm not sure about anything anymore," Lee said.

That's when an idea popped into my head. It was something that I was usually dead set against, civilians taking matters into their own hands, but in this case, it might be justified.

"There could be a way to find out," I blurted out before I could change my mind.

Everyone's attention was now squarely on me.

I laid out the plan for catching Mr. Brown. It was audacious, dangerous, but workable.

Raymond was the first to speak. "We are not the police. We are not the FBI. We're not qualified for this. We need to let the professionals handle this."

"I like it," Lee commented, looking at me.

"So do I," chimed in Billy.

"But Lee," Raymond continued, "we should let the FBI handle this from now on. You've done enough."

Lee appeared unswayed. "Raymond, this guy works for the government. We don't know who else might be involved."

"But like we said before, he could be working on his own."

"That's true, but we still have too many unanswered questions, and I'm inclined to work with what I know," Lee said, then pointed at me. "I know that she's authentic. I know her motivation for being here. And I know she wants to help."

I offered Lee a faint smile.

"I understand it if you want to go home. In fact, I hope you will. That goes for you all. I don't want to see anybody hurt, and I believe this is a dangerous person we are dealing with. I can do this by myself, but it isn't a suicide mission. Dianne and I will take precautions to ensure our safety, so don't feel like you're obligated to stay."

Lee was standing in the center of the room now. Ebe and Kent were on the edge of one bed, Mark and Raymond were on the other, and Billy was straddling the desk chair. I was leaning against the desktop. As Lee spoke, he looked each of us in the face.

"Not long ago, I was a man feebly trying to get over the loss of my wife. It was the second time that I had faced grief, and the second time I shrank away from it. I have flaws, and I'm ashamed to say that letting people down when things matter the most is the worst of them."

Lee paused for a moment before continuing.

"I stand here now, barely able to contain my anger about that flaw, but it pales compared to the rage I feel toward the person who is ultimately responsible for all this. I intend to see this through to the end."

It was an impressive speech. I looked at the others, but nobody was saying anything.

"I'm in," Billy finally said.

"Me too," Mark followed quickly.

"Fellas," I commented, "I want to make sure you've thought about what you're getting yourselves into."

"You guys really don't have to," Lee said.

"What do we do first?" Billy asked, looking at Ray defiantly.

Raymond looked at the ceiling, then shook his head. "In for a penny, in for a pound."

Lee smiled. "We have one last errand before we kick this plan off. Ebe, I need your help."

"At your service. What do you need?" Ebe inquired.

"I need you to locate Lynn Coleman."

***

The next afternoon, Ebe's Blazer pulled into the driveway of a simple one-story house in what might have been one of the oldest neighborhoods in Lilburn, Georgia. I was in the back seat next to Mark, with Ebe behind the wheel and Lee in the passenger's seat. After Ebe switched off the engine, nobody seemed in a hurry to exit the car.

Locating Lynn Coleman was almost anticlimactic. Back in Easley, I watched as Ebe first accessed the online phone directory for Atlanta and the surrounding areas, quickly finding that six Lynn Colemans were living there. Once he had addresses, he researched each one until he came across the mortgage holder with a degree from Clemson. Lynn had apparently never been married. That or she reverted to her maiden name after a divorce. It was only a two-and-a-half-hour drive to Atlanta from Easley, so the four of us hopped in Ebe's Blazer and took off.

Lynn's house was on a hilly road off one of the primary thoroughfares, the small subdivision consisting of a single street that wound back through a wooded area and had maybe fifty modest-sized houses on it. Newer developments that bookended the one-street subdivision were building homes twice as big, but worth probably four times the older homes.

There were two foreign-model cars parked inside an open carport. After mentally preparing myself for what we might face, I eventually climbed out of the Blazer, following the others. Confrontation, regardless of how vested you were, was never easy.

The four of us ascended the short stairwell onto a narrow porch on the front of the home. As we walked along the porch, we passed in front of a large pane window with thin curtains partially obscuring the view inside. I could make out two people sitting on a couch. Lee pushed the button for the doorbell.

A couple seconds later, a blonde woman in her mid to late forties, wearing a pink cotton appliqué top with a split neck, opened the door.

"Yes?" she asked.

"Excuse me, are you Lynn Coleman?" Lee asked her, adopting a rigid smile.

"No, just a moment," the woman answered, then turned her hips slightly so that she faced back into the house. "Lynn, it's for you," she called.

A couple of seconds later, a woman a little older than the one at the door appeared beside her. She had long wavy hair that was so dark it seemed black, and she wore a simple gray T-shirt over jeans.

There was a pair of gold studs in the woman's right earlobe.

"Can I help you?" the woman asked, an inquisitive look on her face. The blond woman remained beside her.

"Lynn Coleman?" Lee asked again, still smiling.

"Yes," she answered.

"The Lynn Coleman who attended Clemson University?"

"Yes." Her curious expression deepened.

Lee glanced quickly at the three of us standing behind him, then said, "My name is Lee Hamilton, and I am an old friend of Andi Taylor."

All of the color left the woman's face. She looked as if we had just delivered the news about the death of a close relative.

Lee's pseudosmile evaporated.

"I was wondering if I could ask you a few questions about Andi," Lee continued, even though the woman no longer seemed to hear him.

Both of Lynn's hands went to her face, covering it. Her friend, seeing her reaction, put her arm around her shoulder and glared at Lee.

"What's this about?" she asked. Her tone was hostile.

"I need to ask her some questions," Lee said sternly.

"I don't think so. You need to just get—" the friend started, reaching to shut the door when Lynn put her hand out to keep the door open.

"No, Sam. I need to talk to him," Lynn said, stopping her friend.

Now it was the blonde woman, the one called Sam, who looked confused. Lynn stepped back to clear a path into the house. "Please come in," she said.

Inside the house, the two women, holding each other's hand, led us from the foyer into a rectangular living area bordering the house's front wall. Opposite the large pane window was a cloth couch with two end tables on each side and a wooden trunk serving as a coffee table. A recliner sat just to the right of the window, and a pair of old-fashioned rocking chairs faced one another against the far wall opposite the room entrance. A medium-sized television sat on a knee-high stand on the other side of the pane window, tuned to the local news station.

Cuddled deep into the right corner of the couch lay a white Persian cat.

Lee took the recliner, and the other guys claimed the rocking chairs. I remained standing behind the recliner. Lynn and Sam reclaimed their seats on the couch.

Lynn picked up a remote control and turned off the television.

"Will somebody please tell me what's going on here?" Sam asked the room, a nervous tone in her voice.

Lynn patted Sam's hand she was still holding.

"Samantha, honey. This man is here to get an answer to a question, and it's an answer that I have been dreading telling for a very long time. It's something I am incalculably ashamed of. A low point in my life. I was a different person then. I can only hope and pray that you won't think less of me after I'm finished," Lynn said calmly, almost detached.

I watched as Sam's expression turned worried.

Lynn looked across the room at the men in the rocking chairs. "You must be Ebe and Mark?"

The two of them nodded.

Turning her gaze to me, she said, "I'm sorry. I don't know who you are."

"It's not important."

On our drive over, I'd taken the opportunity to read Lee's blog, so I knew the circumstances now and just what this meeting meant to Lee.

Lynn turned her gaze to Lee and said, "You write excellent descriptions."

Lee smiled weakly.

"I met Andi in the spring of 1991 in a freshman psychology class. We became friends almost at once. We were both sociology majors and had a lot of classes together. I was from Atlanta, at Clemson on scholarship, so I didn't have any friends at school until I met her. I followed her and her friends around like a puppy, but they were all nice and made me feel like I belonged, especially Andi.

"Andi was incredibly special. She was never fake or pretended to be something she wasn't. She knew exactly what she wanted and how to go about getting it. At the end of our first semester, Andi asked me to room with her and her other roommates, Gayle and Trisha. Their fourth roommate dropped out of school, and they needed someone to take her spot. By the end of that next semester, I knew I was in love with her.

"And I honestly believed that Andi felt the same way about me. She just hadn't realized who she was yet. At least that's what I thought. I mean, she wasn't interested in boys, preferring to hang out with us girls when she didn't have her head buried in a book. I did everything I could to help her realize what the two of us meant to one another. I could afford to be patient because...I loved her enough for the both of us.

"It crushed me when I found out I wouldn't be able to go to Florida with them. However, the summer internship was too important to pass up. I was even more disappointed when Andi chose to go with Gayle and Trisha instead of visiting me in Atlanta. It was our chance to have time alone and grow our relationship. But she turned her back on me.

"Then the betrayal of all betrayals came when she returned home from Panama City. I drove all the way back from Atlanta to welcome her back. But when I saw her, she was different. Happier. Radiant. But also sorrowful. I was confused. She came running up to me when I saw her, and for a moment, I thought it was because she'd missed me, but then she told me about...you."

I glanced at Lee to see how he was handling Lynn's story. He was stone-faced.

"Andi went on and on about you. How the two of you met, telling me about every minute of your time together. How she felt when she was with you, like she had never felt before. It made me sick. I was devastated.

"Then the FBI came and took her away. I was so miserable and angry about what she told me, I was actually glad she was gone. Looking back on it now, I can't believe I became the person I did, or that side of me even existed. I postponed returning to Atlanta. Instead, I stayed and sulked in my room. Gayle and Trisha thought I was depressed about Andi being gone like they were, but they hadn't a clue.

"When your first letter arrived, I was the one who pulled it from the mailbox. As soon as I saw the postmark, I knew it was from you. I almost ripped to shreds, but I took it to my room and hid it instead. I don't know why. I knew there would be other letters, so I made it a point to pick up all the mail. Sure enough, a second letter arrived. It had been months since they had taken Andi away, but the hurt in me was still fresh. I decided to read your letters, to find out what kind of boy stole Andi's heart from me. I steamed them open and read them over and over, and every time I did, the hatred for you grew. I knew that if I didn't do something, the letters would keep coming.

"So, I wrote a letter. A letter I knew would keep you from looking for her and hurt you at the same time. Because that's what I wanted, to hurt you. But the letter had to be from someone you wouldn't question, so I made it sound like it was coming from Andi's dad. I included Gayle and Trisha in my make-believe tragedy so you wouldn't try to seek them out. It was perfect, and it worked."

Lynn stopped speaking. Sam had let her hand slip out of Lynn's and was now sitting a little farther away.

"I don't really know when I realized the gravity of what I had done, but it was years later. It has weighed heavy on me ever since. For a while, I convinced myself that a different person, someone far removed from who I am now, had done such an awful thing. But I know that isn't true. I did this."

Lee still showed no emotion. I wondered if I should be worried that he would go after this woman.

"Eventually, I went searching for you on the internet. I found your blog, but I couldn't bring myself to contact you. I fell in love with your writing and continued reading it, believing one day that I might work up the courage to apologize. Then you posted your story about Andi, and it all came rushing back. I did at least take one small step. I posted a comment on your blog. I assume that's why you're here?"

"That was you?" was all Lee said.

Lynn nodded. "I hoped it helped."

Lee's face was still expressionless. He stood up from the recliner slowly and headed toward the front door. When the three of us realized he was leaving, we rushed to catch up.

Lynn jumped up from the couch and rushed after us. As Lee opened the door, she called out to him. He turned around slowly and gazed upon her with the same expressionless face.

"I know this can mean absolutely nothing coming from me now, but I need to say it, anyway. I'm so deeply sorry," Lynn pleaded, the pain evident in her.

I watched Lee open his mouth to say something, then stop and look away. The muscles in his jaw tensed and relaxed continuously as he ground his teeth. Finally, he looked at her again and said simply, "There is no way the meaning of that word, sorry, could hope to erase the anger inside me right now. My rational mind tells me you were just a confused kid, much like I was, and you could not have envisioned the depths of your deceit. But my heart won't listen to that. It can't. Someday it might. But not today."

Lynn Coleman broke down in tears as the four of us walked away.

| 32 |

The End Game

Mr. Brown

He waited at the tiny grocery store across from the entrance to the wooded subdivision where the black Blazer and its occupants had gone. He desperately wanted to get out and stretch. All of the driving over the last few days, coupled with his age, was wearing on him. He doubted he would learn anything here to tell him where the cassette might be, but he couldn't afford to lose track of his target. He twisted his neck and felt it crack.

Learning that Hamilton had apparently recruited the men from his blog, the ones he deemed the _Knights Who Say Ni,_ to help him pursue answers was unsettling, and it was compounded by the fact that a female private detective was now involved. Had Hamilton hired her to help him? No matter. The man could invite his entire church choir if he wished if it led to finding the cassette. However, Mr. Brown knew he couldn't keep tabs on all of them, which made him anxious. If this were a proper operation, there would be multiple teams in place, one for each tangent, but that was a luxury he couldn't afford in this case. He had to set priorities.

His tail of Lee Hamilton had been entertaining, and with all the miles he was putting on the rental car, expensive. Watching him and the detective be grabbed by those two goons was certainly unexpected, but thinking about it more, not surprising. Asking around about Craig Stevens in Panama City surely set off some red flags with the syndicate, so their own questions needed to be asked. Subtlety was never their strong suit. Mr. Brown was just glad he didn't have to intervene and spoil the advantage he had.

Now, as he waited for the Blazer to appear, he let his mind wander to his time spent here in Atlanta. Starting out as a beat cop in downtown Fulton County, the training he'd received as a military MP served him well, and he quickly had his superiors funneling him the challenging assignments. More importantly, the detectives started explicitly asking for him when backup was needed for high-profile arrests. He gained a reputation as a no-nonsense cop who didn't shy away from the use of force. His eye for detail and an analytical mind combined with one of the highest test scores on the detective exam the department had seen for quite some time garnered him his own gold shield well ahead of the average time for promotion. Of course, the time he spent hanging around the detective division didn't hurt his chances, either.

Despite the apparent qualifications and experience working as a detective, he exhibited a problem his first year in his new position. It revolved around the most important criteria the job was measured against, the ability to clear cases. That was, until he found out how things really worked, and that was when his proper education began.

It started with coercion, intimidation, planting evidence, and false testimony. Showing a proclivity for bending the rules in the pursuit of the greater good was the unwritten rule. Over time, the lines blurred, and bribery, shakedowns, and muscle for hire became part of what it took to get the job done. And Brown was good at it.

But he never regretted leaving Atlanta for Tallahassee when the opportunity arose. His brother needed watching.

After forty-five minutes, he spotted the Blazer coming back up the road. He fell in behind their car and followed them on the winding roads onto the Stone Mountain Highway, and then to the I-285 loop heading south. When they crossed over I-20 into south Atlanta, he knew they were heading to the airport.

He knew Southwest would likely have the most direct flights to Little Rock, but it would force him to make yet another calculated risk. He was confident they were returning to Hamilton's home in Arkansas, so he would abandon the tail and take steps to get a direct flight to Little Rock. That would leave him vulnerable in two ways. They could go on another airline, which would be okay because his direct flight would arrive before any competitor's flights. Or they could fly to a different destination altogether, in which case he would be screwed.

Walking away from the Southwest counter with a ticket on the 6:45 p.m. flight, he spotted Hamilton, the private detective, and his other traveling companion talking to one another near the back of the line. He made his way to A concourse and disappeared into the corner of a coffee shop near the gate, planning to wait until the last minute before boarding the flight.

He suppressed a smile when he saw three of them take seats at the same boarding gate. The long-haired redhead wasn't with them, but there was no reason for concern. Mr. Brown deduced that the man either lived in the Atlanta area and dropped off his passengers or was flying to a different destination. Either way, his primary focus was only one hundred feet away.

This would all be over soon.

***

The plane was almost empty before Mr. Brown got off. There was no reason to hurry any longer because he was confident he knew where everyone was heading. Securing another rental car, he casually set out toward Conway and what he hoped would be the last chapter in this silly game of cat and mouse.

He had concluded that although the last three days had been interesting and challenging, it was a complete waste of his time. Hamilton hadn't led him anywhere or to anyone who could have had the tape, and whatever part of the mystery he had uncovered was still that, a mystery. But in retrospect, he knew he had to follow his instincts and ensure that would be the case. Even though nothing came from the time he'd devoted, nothing was still an excellent result. All he needed to do now was wait to revisit the Hamilton home to complete the search previously interrupted. Either way, if he found the cassette or not, he could close the book.

Now driving down York Lane, Mr. Brown could see Hamilton's Jeep was the lone car in his driveway. Turning around in the cul-de-sac, he began to return to the Mormon Church parking lot he had used before, then he noticed a dark house on a corner with numerous newspapers strewn on the front lawn. The house's driveway faced back down York Lane in the direction of the Hamilton house. He backed his car into the driveway and killed the engine.

After taking bites on the burger he had stopped to pick up while driving from the airport, he removed his laptop from his travel bag. He wanted to check Hamilton's PC activity to see what correspondence he may have received while en route.

Thirty minutes later, he watched as Hamilton uploaded a new entry to his blog.

| 33 |

Slow Dancer (Revisited)

TUESDAY, JULY 27, 2021
SLOW DANCER (Revisited)

First, let me apologize.

I've ignored *Cruising Altitude* and, in turn, my readers, and for that, I'm genuinely sorry. I can only tell you it wasn't planned or anticipated, but once you hear the reason for my absence, I believe you will forgive my neglect.

Thank you! Believe me when I tell you that the combination of those eight letters has never said so much and encapsulated so little. The response to my latest story has been nothing short of phenomenal. Your words of support and heartwarming stories of similar experiences via all the comments and emails have touched me beyond my capability to communicate back to you.

Some of you left me questions, quite a few actually, so many in fact that I've decided to post this follow-up to answer them and detail what has happened to me since I first posted my story. I think you will find this as interesting as the original story. I know I did.

The most popular question, or technically questions because the one always went with the other, was, do I still have Andi's white envelope, and did I ever open it? The first answer is yes. I do still have it. It was still in my college yearbook where I placed it so many years ago, which I rescued from a box in my attic just recently. And the second answer is no, I haven't opened it. Why not? Because Andi hasn't told me to, per her instructions.

I wrote in my story that I burned the letters I wrote to Andi along with the letter from her father, or so I thought. Soon after I posted my story, I found those letters stuffed inside the album cover. That was just the first of a series of discoveries that would rock what I thought I knew about what happened to Andi.

I won't bore you with all the sordid details. The bottom line is this: Andi and her roommates didn't die in a car wreck, as I was told by her father. In fact, the letter wasn't even written by her father. It was sent by a hurt, angry, jealous friend of Andi's as a way of keeping me away from her, and it worked. I realize now that a stronger person would have seen through the deceit and found the truth, but I wasn't that person. At least I wasn't then.

So, if Andi didn't die in a car wreck, where is she? The answer to that question is even more bizarre. Andi's parents were murdered while she was in Panama City, and when she returned home, she was immediately placed into the witness protection program by the FBI because she was also in danger. That is why she never tried to contact me. She couldn't. The murderer of her parents has never been caught, and the fleeting hope I had of ever seeing Andi again disappeared with each new piece of information I uncovered.

I know it all sounds like a crazy murder mystery novel, but I couldn't make this stuff up if I tried. And if I did try, I certainly wouldn't end it with the bad guy getting away, the girlfriend missing and probably dead, and the hero more depressed at the end of the book than he was at the beginning. But at least I found a silver lining.

I have reconnected with the Knights Who Say Ni. Mark, Raymond, Billy, Kent, and Ebe. I spent a glorious weekend with all of them in Lafayette, and then we went on a sort of *quest* to answer my questions about what happened to Andi. I have just detailed that for you above. It was a bittersweet process, enjoying getting to know them all again—even if it meant uncovering truths that may have been better left alone. But going forward, I know that I have at least atoned for one of my mistakes, and I have realized how deep the bond of friendship can go.

This journey all started with a song, and it will end with one as well. Thanks to Mark, I now have the tape that Andi gave me on our last night together. Fearing that I would destroy the tape, he took it from my room and hid it. He returned that tape to me when we all met in Lafayette, but I haven't had the nerve to listen to it yet. There was a time when playing that tape would have made me feel as if my insides were collapsing in upon themselves, but I believe that I'm past that point now.

Don't worry, I will be fine. I have all of you to thank for that. But for now, I need to take a short break and distance myself from recent events. I thought I owed you some answers and an explanation before I disappeared again.

Don't go far. I will be back.

Lee

| 34 |

House Guests

<u>*Dianne*</u>

"I could use a cup of coffee," I said, rising from the couch. "Anyone else?"

Lee was still sitting at his desk, doing something with his computer. "None for me. Keeps me up at night."

Mark was sitting in the corner. "I'll take some, as long as it's not instant."

I hesitated before moving to the kitchen, watching Mark nervously tap his fingers on the armrest.

"It's not too late to call this whole thing off," I said. "You can delete what you just posted, and we'll think of something else."

"Dianne, I don't know your—" Lee started to say when the doorbell chimed.

I turned toward the front door, where the porch light cast the shadow of someone on the doorstep through the glazed glass.

Lee rose from his chair. "This is it," he said, then moved to the front door and pulled it open. Standing on the landing was a tall, middle-aged gentleman with sandy-colored hair and a military-style crew cut. He had intense green eyes. Although the wrinkles around his eyes and leathery skin indicated an age slightly older, his physique was that of someone who kept excellent care of himself. Despite the warm night, the man was wearing a wrinkled brown sports coat over a black polo shirt and tan pants.

"Can I help you?" Lee asked.

"Lee Hamilton?" the man asked in a low, gravelly voice. His smile could easily be confused with a grimace of pain.

"Yes."

"My name is Brown, and I wonder if I might have a word with you for a moment?"

"Regarding what?" Lee inquired.

"Someone you used to be acquainted with. Andi Taylor."

"Oh...yes...absolutely, please come in," Lee responded, holding the door open for Mr. Brown to walk through. I tensed when the man stepped inside.

Standing in the foyer, Brown took notice of Mark and me. He nodded.

"These are my friends, Mark Sigmar and Dianne Williams," Lee introduced the two of us as he closed the door.

"Pleased to make your acquaintance," Mr. Brown said.

"This is Mr. Brown, and he says he has some information about Andi," Lee said, directing his comment to Mark and me.

"I'm not interrupting something, am I, because I can come back," Mr. Brown asked, turning slightly toward the door.

"No, now is fine. They both knew Andi," Lee insisted.

"Did you know Andi well?" I asked.

"Not actually," Brown said, boldly stepping into the living room. His smile had disappeared, but his eyes had a look of mild amusement. "I'm really here to get back something she possessed at one time. It belongs to me."

Lee looked puzzled. He was playing his part well, I thought.

"I'm sorry, I don't understand. What is it of yours you think I have?"

"A cassette."

Lee glanced at me, then back to Brown.

"A cassette tape? I'm still confused."

"I don't think you are. The tape that Andi Taylor gave you in Florida." Mr. Brown's expression hadn't changed.

"A mix tape of music? How could you possibly think that could be yours?"

"You have the tape, right?" Brown asked, ignoring Lee's questions.

I didn't like the way this was playing out. Brown was way too confident. I moved over and stood next to Lee.

"I do, but I think you need to answer my questions," Lee responded, adopting a more serious tone.

"If you can just show me the tape, I can prove to you it belongs to me," Mr. Brown said evenly.

Lee looked at me, then Mark, and then began making his way back toward the sun-room. I followed him over to the round breakfast table where he had previously placed the cassette tape. He picked up the tape, and when we turned around, Mr. Brown was there, standing directly behind us. He was quiet as a cat when he moved.

Brown held out his hand for the tape. Lee made a motion like he would give it to him, and then he pulled it back.

"I think you need to tell me how you know Andi and answer my questions before I let you have this," Lee said firmly.

The amusement vanished from Brown's face. He looked hard at Lee and me, then over his shoulder at Mark, who had remained by the chair. Our visitor appeared to be mulling something over. Then, as quickly as it disappeared, his amused look reappeared.

"You know, I've read your blog, *Cruising Altitude*," Brown said.

"I gathered that," Lee replied smartly.

"It was an interesting read. Really. And I can tell from your writings that you enjoy telling stories. You have a very keen eye. It just so happens I have a story as well, one that will answer all your questions about Andi and the tape. Maybe we could all take a seat. I can tell it to you," Brown said.

Lee exchanged looks with Mark and me. "What do you think, guys?" he asked.

"It couldn't hurt to listen to his story," Mark answered, shrugging his shoulders.

"I'm curious," I seconded.

"Okay then," Lee agreed, and we all gradually moved to take seats around the breakfast table. I noticed how Mr. Brown moved quickly around to the opposite side of the table so he would be facing the front door, his back to the sun-room windows. He was a smart cookie.

"My story begins around the same time as yours actually, in 1992, just a couple months earlier, though. Back then, I was a detective in the Atlanta Police department. Life was good, and my career was looking promising. Then, one day, I received a phone call from my older brother. He was a circuit court judge in Tallahassee, Florida, and it seemed he had gotten himself in a little bit of trouble. He had run up a bit of a gambling debt, and his bookie was blackmailing him to gain favor on a case in his court. Incriminating recordings were involved. My brother didn't want to ask for anybody's help locally, so he contacted me, his brother, the cop. He wanted me to speak to this bookie and convince him that pursuing his current course of action wasn't in his best interest. Naturally, I couldn't turn my little brother down, so I flew to Tallahassee and visited this bookie.

"This bent nose was a genuine piece of work. He got under my skin almost from the start. Unfortunately, he wasn't the rational type, and things got out of hand. He had brought a couple of thugs with him, and that gave him the nerve to pull a knife." Brown chuckled softly to himself and shook his head. "Well, let's just say it was the last time any of them pulled a knife."

Mr. Brown paused for effect.

This guy is really enjoying himself.

"Would the bookie's name be Neville Scranton by chance?" I asked.

Brown looked at me as a teacher would have looked upon his prized pupil. "Very good. You get a gold star, missy," he said mockingly. I clenched my fists underneath the table.

"All of this didn't go over well with my brother, even though I was simply defending myself and liberated the incriminating recordings for him."

"I can imagine," Lee deadpanned.

"This next part...well...I'm embarrassed to admit. You see, I pride myself on paying close attention to details. It's one of my strengths. However, I put the recorder in my briefcase—it was one of those new fancy digital ones. At least it was new at the time. My flight back to Atlanta made a connection in Greenville on the return. There was a fifty-minute layover, so I bought a paper at a newsstand in the concourse. I set the briefcase down beside me to pay when suddenly a customer in line next to me started having some kind of seizure. When I returned my attention back to the counter, my briefcase was gone. By the time I figured out it was all a diversion, the fake epileptic customer was long gone. Not one of my finest moments, unfortunately."

"Now, you must bear with me for this next part of the story because it's a combination of deduction and supposition, as these events took place when I wasn't present. I believe whoever took my briefcase broke into it and took the few items of value, including the digital recorder, and pawned them. They used a pawn shop in Easley, South Carolina—the shop owned and operated by a Mr. Richard Taylor."

Mr. Brown paused once again.

"I believe that Mr. Taylor inspected the device before putting it up for resale and happened across the recordings. Hearing the conversations between my brother and Neville Scranton, he must have figured out what they represented. Although the judge's name was never spoken on the tape, you could surmise by other remarks that it involved activities in Tallahassee.

"It was Taylor's next decision that led to his demise.

"Mr. Taylor was an ex–college roommate of a man who happened to work in the Tallahassee district attorney's office. Craig Stevens. Taylor figured he could kill two birds with one stone by giving his friend a copy of the tape, which would see justice done and help his buddy's career at the same time. So, he called his friend and played the tape over the phone. What Mr. Taylor didn't realize was that his friend recognized the voice on the tape, the judge, because he worked with him day in and day out. Unbeknownst to Mr. Taylor, Craig Stevens decided there was another use for the tape. Blackmail.

"After making arrangements to have the tape sent down to him in Tallahassee, Mr. Stevens contacted my brother and asked for an exorbitant amount of money. Of course, there was no way he could pay this blackmail without his wife finding out, so he called on me once again to clean up the mess that he said I'd helped create by letting the recorder get taken. I told him I had the money to pay the blackmailer and to arrange a meeting with Mr. Stevens.

"I showed up at the meeting with Mr. Stevens in place of my brother, which, not surprisingly, caused him much distress. I showed him the money, he showed me the tape. Now I knew the original recording was on a digital device, so the tape he showed me must have been a copy. Still, I insisted on listening to the tape before I handed over the money, and what do you think I heard?"

We remained silent. I could see sweat beads breaking out on Lee's brow.

"Music. Specifically, love songs. You should have seen the flabbergasted look on Stevens's face. When he saw my gun, he started blabbering like a baby about how he got the tape and where it came from. He really was a pitiful specimen right up to the moment when I put a bullet between his eyes. I wouldn't do that."

I had begun to casually slide my right hand inside my front pants pocket, then froze. Mr. Brown's eyes were still on Lee, but when his head slowly turned toward me, I removed the hand from my pocket.

"You know," Mr. Brown continued, "telling you all of this is sort of cathartic. I don't get to talk about my line of work that often. Well, actually, never. So, this is rather refreshing. So, please don't interrupt me again."

I shot a glare at Lee, but he wouldn't look at me. He was keeping his gaze fixed on Brown.

"Now, where was I? Oh yes, I buried Mr. Stevens in the Florida marsh and then went looking for the tape and my recorder. I searched the girls' hotel room when they were out and took all of the cassettes from their car. Still no tape. Unfortunately, my time had run out because I needed to get to South Carolina before Mr. Taylor found out that his friend had gone missing. I got there just in time, as it turned out. I arrived in the morning when he opened his shop, eliminating him and his wife along with some pimpled-face schoolgirl. I searched the shop and found my recorder. Then I drove to his home and explored there but didn't find the copy.

"Weeks after all the fuss had died down from the Taylors' deaths, I returned to search Andi Taylor's apartment at Clemson for my tape, still with no success. You can imagine how frustrated I was because the only person who could tell me where my tape went was now in witness protection, and I had run out of ideas."

Brown fell silent. He looked around the room slowly, his gaze ending on the cassette tape in Lee's hand.

"Of course, the whole incident did have a side benefit. My brother makes sure I'm taken care of when properly motivated. And I get to work for the federal government with almost total autonomy. Yet, I never fully gave up on finding my tape. I've always kept my ear to the ground, listening for clues. I'm not really sure how, but I believe the cassette you hold in your hands is the very one I've been trying to get back for twenty-nine years, so if you don't mind, I would appreciate it if you gave it to me now."

Mr. Brown extended his hand toward Lee, but Lee made no move to give it to him.

Lee grasped the cassette by the edge of his fingers, then held it up, showing it to Mr. Brown. "This isn't your tape," Lee said simply.

Brown lowered his hand. "And why would you say that?" he asked, scowling now.

"This *is* a tape of slow songs, but it's one I made about fifteen years ago. The tape you are looking for no longer exists," Lee said smugly. "We have a new one now."

"I'm afraid I don't understand," Brown said, frowning.

"Ni," a voice uttered as the door to the master bedroom swung open. I was happy to see Billy step out of the room carrying a pump shotgun, with Kent trailing behind him.

I turned my attention back to Mr. Brown, who didn't move, both of his hands resting casually on top of the breakfast table. The man's head turned one hundred eighty degrees when the door on the other side of the room opened, and Raymond stepped out brandishing another shotgun. I quickly got to my feet and stepped away from the table. Mark and Lee followed suit.

Mr. Brown's eyes drifted to the near-empty gun cabinet against the wall. Then, when he looked back at us on the other side of the table, there was amusement in his expression again.

"You got everything?" Lee asked, not taking his eyes from Brown.

"Every word, recorded for posterity," Kent answered, holding up his cell phone. "Hi, Dianne."

"You sure waited long enough," I said, to which Kent simply shrugged.

"I lost track of the real tape a long time ago. It's probably at the bottom of some landfill somewhere," Lee said. "No tape meant no evidence against you, so we decided to make our own recording. All we needed to do was lure you here and get you to talk, which you were pretty helpful with. Thank you."

Kent's cell phone began chirping. He pulled it from his pocket, then pressed a button to silence the noise. "A reminder to take my anti-anxiety medication. How ironic is that?" he said, smiling weakly as he slid the phone into his pocket.

"To satisfy my curiosity, how did you know I was onto you?" Mr. Brown asked calmly.

Lee paused before he answered, "I'll answer that if you answer one for me."

"That's acceptable."

"Another friend of ours, the one we left back in Atlanta, spotted you tailing us in Panama City. He's a computer genius, and he found out everything about you, Robert," Lee answered. "Now it's my turn. Did you kill Andi Taylor?" Lee asked.

The look in Brown's eyes gave me chills. Eventually, he gave a one-word answer, "Yes."

Lee's expression did not change.

"She should have taken the witness protection policies more seriously. You have some loyal and brave friends here, Mr. Hamilton," Brown commented, looking slowly around the room at us all.

"Technically, I'm not a friend yet," I said, winking at Lee. "I'm just an interested third party who represents that pimply faced girl you so casually murdered. Her name was Pamela Goodwin."

Mr. Brown grinned at me. "Then it's a shame that you'll have to die with the others."

Billy pumped the slide on the shotgun roughly, ejecting a cartridge that bounced against the wall and then tumbled onto the tile floor. Then he pointed the barrel directly at Brown's head.

"What did you do that for?" Kent asked nervously.

"Shut up, Kent," Billy said. His voice was guttural.

"I thought they just did that in the movies. There was already a live round in the chamber, so why did you waste a shell and pump in another one?" Kent continued. "Dramatic effect or something?"

"Will you shut up! I should have dropped you off in Lafayette," Billy barked.

"And miss seeing you doing your Rambo impersonation?" Kent retorted.

"Will you two clam shut," Raymond snapped.

"Has someone called the police yet?" I asked with a sense of urgency. I didn't like Mr. Brown's demeanor one bit.

A quiet chuckle from Mr. Brown made us all go silent. He lowered his head, shook it side to side a of couple times, and then rose from his chair. As he did, his left hand slowly slid into his left pants pocket.

Both Bill and Raymond took a half step backward and re-adjusted the shotguns against their shoulders.

"You don't want to test me," Billy warned.

"That's right, he's been the paintball champion of Lafayette Parish for three years running now," Kent added.

"Kent! This isn't a joke. Call the police." I half shouted.

"That won't do you any good," Mr. Brown said menacingly, holding up a small black object in his hand.

"What is that?" Lee asked.

"This nifty little device disables cell phone coverage within a twenty-five-yard radius," Brown advised us with a voice that now sounded more menacing. Slowly twisting his right arm behind him, reaching underneath his coat with his hand, he drew it back with a black handgun with a silencer attached to the barrel.

"He's right," Kent stated, looking at his cell phone now. "I have no coverage."

I checked mine as well. "Mine, too."

"I want to go home now," Kent said.

Suddenly, Billy lowered the shotgun barrel until it pointed at Mr. Brown's leg and pulled the trigger. The only sound was the dull click. Billy quickly pumped the slide and chambered a different shell, but Mr. Brown made no move to get out of the way. Billy pulled the trigger again with the same result.

"Shoot him in the leg, Raymond," Billy shouted.

Raymond swiftly did as Billy commanded, with the same result.

"On my first visit to your lovely home, I took the precaution of removing the firing pins on all your weapons," Mr. Brown said calmly, "just in case I needed to return. Did I mention my attention to detail?"

What have I done? This is my fault. People will die because I had to tug at a loose thread and couldn't keep my mouth shut. But what could I do? Brown was on the opposite side of the table, and there was no way I could get to him in time before the shooting would begin.

Billy turned the shotgun around and took hold of the barrel, holding it now like a bat. I scanned the room in search of something to use as a weapon.

The expression on Mr. Brown's face turned dark.

"Six of us against only one of you," Billy growled.

"This is a SIG Sauer P226 tactical handgun with fifteen rounds in the clip. That's obviously more than enough. I like my odds."

As the gun shifted in Billy's direction, Lee screamed, "No!"

Suddenly the plate-glass window at Brown's back shattered inward, stunning everyone. The murderer fell face forward onto the breakfast table.

Shocked by what had just happened, none of us moved, frozen in place. Then, gradually, we started coming around, realizing that nobody was hurt, and that Mr. Brown was motionless on the table. I moved closer to inspect him and was almost sick by the sight. A trickle of blood seeped from a wound on the back of the man's head, while a grapefruit-size piece of his skull was missing from the front.

Mr. Brown was dead.

We all looked at one another silently, then turned to stare out the shattered window into the vacant night.

| 35 |

The Final Chapter

**Dianne**

I stood next to Lee in the Capital Suite. I wasn't sure why he wanted me here, but it didn't feel right to say no. Lee was doing something on his phone, which was all right because I wasn't sure what to say. The secret service agent standing by the door was sort of a conversation killer.

A minute later, the door opened, and another dark-suited secret service agent entered, followed by somebody I recognized from the television ads. Senator Brown nodded at both agents, which must have been a signal for privacy as both men left the room and closed the door behind them.

The historic Capital Hotel in downtown Little Rock, situated near Arkansas's first state capitol building (now known as the Old State House), had been part of the city's history since 1876. Once the most luxurious hotel in the state, it often served as an unofficial political headquarters, where decisions, as well as political careers, were made. In 1974, the hotel was listed on the National Register of Historic Places. It was completely renovated in 2007 at a cost of nearly forty million dollars.

To be honest, I wasn't impressed.

The senator extended his hand. "Teddy Brown," he said.

Lee took the hand and shook. "Lee Hamilton."

Then I followed. "Dianne Williams."

Senator Brown reached into his coat pocket and pulled out a cassette tape. "Quite an interesting invitation you passed along, Mr. Hamilton. What can I do for you?" the senator asked.

Lee put his hands back in his pockets.

"I just wanted to meet the man who saved our lives," Lee answered glibly.

Senator Brown looked at me, then Lee with mild surprise.

"I'm not sure I understand what you're talking about, Mr. Hamilton," the senator replied.

Lee shuffled his feet.

"Senator, please don't pretend that you don't know who we are and why we're here. I've had enough lies and deception to last me a lifetime already," Lee said pointedly.

The senator grinned slightly. "Then you would never make it in politics."

Lee smiled back at the senator.

"Is this what I think it is?" Senator Brown asked, holding up the cassette tape.

"No, not actually. That's just a blank tape I used to get you to meet with us."

The senator's face turned hard.

"The tape you are referring to doesn't exist any longer. I lost that a long time ago," Lee told him.

"So, all the trouble my brother went through was for nothing?"

"Basically, yes."

The senator walked a few steps to the railing that prevented guests from plummeting to the lobby floor several floors below. He put his hands against the shiny hand guard and looked out across the impressively decorated surroundings. Lee and I followed him and stood just to his right.

"How much do you know?" the senator asked, still looking out over the open space.

"Your brother told us everything before he—" I said, before letting the rest of the sentence trail off.

"I don't suppose he mentioned that I never wanted any of it to happen. When I asked him to help me, I thought I was at the lowest point of my life. I didn't know what to do or who to turn to. My brother and I weren't on the best of terms, but he was a police detective in Atlanta, and I thought he could convince the person blackmailing me to go after bigger fish.

"But I knew my brother had a problem controlling his emotions. When I was twelve, he broke my arm when I wouldn't give him back his baseball glove. They dishonorably dismissed him from the Marines because he severely beat a fellow marine who was resisting arrest. The marine ended up dying. I knew all of that, nevertheless, I asked him for help. I was that desperate.

"When I found out he had killed my blackmailer, the bad dream I was hoping to wake up from only got worse. Things spiraled out of control when Craig Stevens from the DA's office called me about the recordings. I found myself on the edge of an unspeakable abyss where there would be no salvation."

The senator turned his gaze toward Lee and me. His face was sullen and gaunt.

"I know I should have turned myself in then and suffered whatever consequences would have befallen me because doing so would have saved innocent lives. But I was young, I was scared, and I was desperate. I still clung to the belief that I might crawl out from under the whole mess if I could somehow pay off Craig Stevens. Because of that, I called my brother again.

"He promised me he would pay the money for me, and I believed him. But, to this day, I don't know what would have happened if Craig Stevens had brought him the right tape. Would my brother have given him the money and walked away, or would he have killed him, anyway? I guess that's a question I'll never know the answer to. But Stevens didn't have the tape, and what happened after that I'll have to live with for the rest of my days."

The senator bowed his head and became silent.

Lee finally spoke up. "We've looked up your career, Senator, trying to find something to help us make up our minds about what to do. I have to say it impressed me, what I saw. I'm not a Republican, but I respect what you have accomplished and most of the ideologies you believe in."

The senator turned and looked squarely into Lee's eyes. "I know this sounds hollow coming from me now, but every moment since the day I learned what my brother had done has been devoted to public service and making amends. I have not been able to rest, take comfort in, or sit on my laurels and simply enjoy my accomplishments because I am driven by my guilt to do even more whenever I do. That is why I am here today. And that isn't just a politician doing what we so easily become accustomed to, telling you what you want to hear."

Lee looked at the senator carefully, then at me. I knew what Lee was silently asking, so I nodded my agreement. He reached into his pocket and pulled out a cell phone.

"I believe you, and that is why I am giving you this," Lee said, handing the senator the phone.

Senator Brown took the phone and stared at it. "What is this?" he asked.

"That phone contains a recording we made of your brother confessing to his crimes. It's not been copied or forwarded," Lee explained.

The senator's eyes moved from the phone to Lee.

"Oh, and you owe a friend of mine a new phone," Lee added, which made me smile.

"Why are you giving me this?"

Lee shrugged his shoulders and looked at me.

"The people who showed up at Lee's house after your brother was shot—before we had a chance to call anyone—offered no identification. They weren't the FBI or any other law enforcement agencies I recognized. They removed the body quickly and efficiently, erasing all forensic evidence. It was a professional who took the shot that killed your brother. There was only one other person who could have known what he was up to. You did save our lives, Senator. We felt we owed you one."

The senator slipped the phone into his pocket with the tape.

"When my brother informed me he was starting his investigation again, I thought it only prudent to have him monitored and intercede if or when it became necessary."

Lee grinned. "I would definitely say it became necessary."

"Yes. There's a chubby computer programmer in Washington I believe shares that same sentiment."

"How are you going to explain his disappearance?" I asked.

"Oh...he'll turn up in a week or so, the victim of a hunting accident. The ticket might even get a few sympathy votes because of his death."

Lee grinned again. I turned toward the senator and extended my hand.

"We know you have a busy schedule today and don't want to interfere any more than we have to. It was a pleasure meeting you, Senator Brown," I said.

The senator gave my hand a hearty shake. Then he shook Lee's hand, holding on to it just a couple of seconds longer than was necessary.

"It's my understanding that this whole thing started with a search for an old flame. Did you find her?"

"No, sir. Your brother murdered her two years ago."

A sliver of pain seeped into the senator's face. "I'm so very sorry," he said.

"Just keep making amends, Senator," Lee responded seriously.

The two of us started walking toward the staircase. Just before we started descending the steps, the senator's voice called out to us.

We looked back to the hallway entrance and saw the senator standing there. He was holding the phone Lee had just given him in his hand.

"Just so you're aware, we'll be keeping tabs on you. All of you. It's not that I don't trust your intentions, but I've been in politics a long time."

Lee nodded, but the disappointment was there in his eyes.

"Maybe too long," Lee said.

We both turned and went searching for the nearest exit.

| 36 |

The Penultimate Chapter

<u>*Dianne*</u>

The drive from the airport during midday traffic was easier than I'd predicted, so I arrived back at the office a few minutes before I'd told Evelyn to expect me. When I walked through the door, the look on her face was more dour than usual. Something was wrong.

"What's the matter, Evelyn?"

"They're waiting for you in the break room," she said.

She didn't need to explain what she meant. I sighed deeply and dropped my carry bag in the closest waiting room chair. Evelyn looked like she wanted to cry.

"I want you to know that I'm not part of this," she said. "I might not have agreed with Tildy's decision at first, but I'm loyal if nothing else."

"Thank you for saying that, Evelyn," I said. Then added as I walked past her, "To tell you the truth, I didn't agree with Tildy's decision at first either."

The break room was almost full. The eight male investigators were spread out, some sitting at tables, others just milling around.

KNIGHT RISE - 313

Briana was at the back of the room, leaning against the wall, a look of intense displeasure plastered across her face.

John and Henry were sitting at the table nearest the door. John rose to his feet as soon he saw me.

"Dianne, we think it's time we make some much-needed changes around here."

"Is this about the weak-ass coffee that machine keeps spitting out? I told Evelyn to complain to supplier last week."

"You know very well what this is about. Tildy made a severe error in judgment when she put you in charge, and the business is suffering. We think you should step down and let someone else assume control."

I noticed head nods from half the people in the room. The other half refused to make eye contact with me.

"You do, do you?"

"That's right."

"Have you spoken to Tildy about your concerns?"

John shook his head. "Tildy doesn't understand this business, which she has made abundantly clear by putting you in charge. No, this is between us."

"All of you feel the same way?" I asked the room.

Again, only half of those present responded with a nod. I guess the saying was true. *There was safety in numbers.* What I found interesting was what the expression did not mention. Often the ones being protected...were cowards.

"And I'm guessing you want to be the one to take my place?" I asked John.

"What's important right now is that you relinquish the manager's position. Who takes over after that doesn't matter."

"I'm sure. And if I refuse?"

"Then we all walk."

I folded my arms across my chest, scanned the room again, then nodded. "Okay, make your case."

That seemed to confuse John. "What?"

"You say that I'm ruining the business, so state your case. Tell me how I'm doing that. If you can convince me, I'll do what you ask."

John looked around the room, seeking support. When nobody spoke up, he pointed his finger at me.

"Norwood Construction. They were one of our biggest clients, and you pulled the plug on them. We're certainly going to feel that in our wallets."

"Clients. Okay, let's talk about clients. Maybe you're not aware of this because I just heard it myself driving here from the airport, but the DA Office will be slapping Norwood Construction with half a dozen indictments by the end of business today. That's not a good look for them or anyone else in business with them. On the other hand, Rand Industries, one of Norwood's principal competitors, has just signed an exclusive five-year deal with Silent Sleuth for all its security business. I'd call that a win-win, wouldn't you?"

John was suddenly looking unsure of himself.

"But I'm not through. I have also recently formed a relationship with Corporal Indemnity, a major player in the insurance industry based in Arkansas for all their investigative needs, and a law firm out of Louisiana with branches covering the southern states. Overall, even with the loss of Norwood's business factored in, I project our revenue to increase sixty to seventy percent by the end of the year. That's if I can hire enough people to keep up. What's your next point?"

John looked positively flustered now. "Well, speaking about new employees, you hired someone green around the gills with no experience when we need people who know how to do the job."

"Briana, what was that you were telling me about cannabis security compliance the other day?"

Briana straightened up, welcoming the attention.

"It won't affect our revenue stream this year, but it is a growth market that Silent Sleuth has yet to explore, and there's a ton of money there."

"And remind me again, what is your area of expertise?"

"Cannabis security compliance," she replied, smiling.

"What's your next point, John?"

"You're a woman," came a voice from behind me. I turned to find Mack Green, but he seemed different. He was clean-shaven, and his eyes were clear.

Mack strolled into the room, and as he did, a few of the faces that had avoided looking at me before now appeared hyperinterested. Again, I could feel the momentum swinging back against me.

"Being a woman shouldn't make a difference," I said.

"Your right. It shouldn't, but it still does, doesn't it? That's why I'm here. I have something I need to say to you, and now seems the perfect time to say it."

I swallowed hard. I'd be within my rights to have Mack escorted out of the building, seeing as he was an ex-employee, but playing a heavy hand like that would probably work against me in the long run. So, I let it play out.

"Go ahead, say your piece."

Mack scanned the room, then looked me directly in the eyes.

"I'm sorry."

I blinked several times. *Did I hear him right?*

"And I'm sorry to you as well, Briana," Mack continued, gesturing toward our new hire.

The expression on John's and Henry's faces told me they were just as confused as I was.

"When I got home last week after you...you know...well, my wife was pissed. Not about me being fired, because she's been wanting me to retire for a while now. No, I upset her about something else. Evelyn had called her and spilled the beans on some things I said. My wife was livid. That's when she asked me a simple question that changed everything for me, and it made me see things in a whole different light. I'm a big enough man to admit when I'm wrong, so, I've come here to apologize to you both."

"What was the question your wife asked you?" I heard myself ask.

Mack gave a sorrowful smile. "What if that was your granddaughter?"

The silence in the room was deafening. It was the first time I had ever seen Mack look...uncomfortable.

"She's still just a baby, but I...uh...when I imagine someone treating her the way I did to the two of you, I just—"

Mack lowered his head, and the room grew silent again.

"Dianne, you were right to fire me. I've been listening to these guys at the tavern do nothing but bellyache for the last couple of nights, but all I could think about was what you said about me and how true it was. I've been coasting along for years. Everyone knows it, but you're the first person to call me out on it. I may not like you personally, but you've always been a straight shooter, and that's all anybody can ask. I bear no hard feelings."

"Mack," John finally spoke up. "We were hoping you'd—"

"John, put a clamp on it," Mack barked, then looked back at me. "Don't listen to this bunch of momma's boys. Tildy knew what she was doing when she put you in charge."

I didn't know what to say, and even if I had, I couldn't say it. My throat felt like I was being strangled, constricted with emotion.

I heard Evelyn call my name from the doorway.

"Yes, Evelyn?" I struggled to say.

"Mrs. Bennett is here to see you."

"Can you show her back to my office please?" I asked.

I looked back at the room. "Listen, I've got to take this meeting. What do you say we all just get back to work? Anybody have a problem with that?"

This time, everyone in the room shook their head, even John and Henry.

A few minutes later, I was back in my office, and Mrs. Bennett was sitting in the same captain's chair she used during her earlier visit. She was dressed once again in her yellow work uniform.

"Mrs. Bennett, thanks for coming in," I greeted the woman warmly.

The woman's expression was that of concern and bewilderment.

"I understood you to say that you would mail me a report when you finished your investigation, Miss Williams," she pointed out. Her long hair was straining mightily against the black plastic headband on her head.

"Normally, that would be true, Mrs. Bennett, but this time I felt it prudent to give you the results face to face," I explained.

"Oh, I see."

"Mrs. Bennett...Emily...I wanted to tell you in person that the individual who murdered your sister Pamela was apprehended several weeks ago."

Mrs. Bennett did not move, nor did her expression.

"Furthermore, he was shot and killed during his apprehension," I continued.

The woman's eyes glistened.

"You're...sure...it was...him?"

"Yes, ma'am. I personally heard his confession before he died."

At first, it appeared as if Mrs. Bennett was not reacting, but soon her bottom lip began to quiver.

"Why?" The question was barely audible.

"All I can tell you is that the Taylors were trying to do the right thing, and your sister got caught in the middle."

The shaking that had been slowly building took over the woman's whole body, and her head dropped into the hands in her lap. Sobs, ones I'm sure had been building for decades, shook her body. The only sound she made was a low, sorrowful moan.

I got up from my chair and walked around the desk. I bent down and gave the woman a gentle hug around the shoulders.

"Take all the time that you need," I whispered in her ear, then left the room and closed the door behind me.

Epilogue

<u>*Lee*</u>

Two weeks following his trip to the Capital Hotel in Little Rock, Lee finally got around to installing a new window in his sun-room. He was tired of looking at a cardboard patch in the hole. He had bought the replacement glass pane that morning and was waiting for his father-in-law to arrive and show him what to do.

Reading the paper in the sun-room while he waited, he heard the doorbell ring. He wondered why his father-in-law didn't just let himself in like he usually did.

"Come on in, Gary," Lee yelled, flipping the page of the newspaper.

When the doorbell sounded again, Lee realized that Gary might have his arms full and couldn't open the door. So, he got up from the chair and made his way to the front door.

His jaw dropped when he pulled the door back.

"Ebe!" Lee shouted, confused and happy at the same time.

Ebe stood on the porch smiling widely, which always made his face redder than it already was. His goatee was gone, and he was wearing a dark-blue T-shirt with a white shield in the style of a coat of arms imprinted on it. The words *Knights Who Say Ni* were emblazoned at the bottom of the shield.

"What are you doing here?" Lee asked excitedly. "Nice T-shirt, by the way."

Ebe looked down at the front of his shirt. "You like it? I had a bunch of them printed for all of us. I have yours in the car."

"Come on in," Lee encouraged, and Ebe stepped into the foyer and stopped.

"So, what brings you to Arkansas," Lee asked a second time.

"A bit of unfinished business. I kept thinking about what Lynn Coleman said when we talked to her. What she said about leaving the comment on your blog," he said.

Lee's expression exposed his puzzlement. "Yeah?"

"She told you she hoped her comment helped. I was wondering what she meant. I mean, how could she have known about the picture? It just made me think, so I went back to your blog and reread every comment. I found another comment posted several days after the one from Slow Dancer you'll find interesting."

Ebe pulled a folded piece of paper from his back pocket and handed it to Lee, who still looked puzzled. Lee unfolded the paper and recognized it as a printout of comments from *Cruising Altitude*. Ebe had highlighted the one in the center of the page in yellow. It read:

Lee,

I am a longtime reader and a first-time poster. I could no longer sit back and watch you suffer without doing something to try and ease the hurt you feel because your pain is mine as well.

I knew Andi better than most people, and I loved her as well. But my feelings couldn't compare to those she had for you. That kind of love never dies, and it didn't in June of 1992 either. Trust me. You can be at peace with the knowledge that Andi's love for you lasted much longer than a paltry four days in the sun.

I hope this helps in some small measure.

Anonymous

Lee looked up from reading the comment.

"That was submitted from an internet café in Lawrenceville, Georgia, which borders the city of Lilburn, where Lynn Coleman lives. The Slow Dancer comment was submitted from a Starbucks in Chicago," Ebe explained further.

Lee's mind knew what that meant, but it wouldn't allow him to see the truth. He suddenly felt unsteady. He wanted to go back to putting in the window. He wished Gary would get here so they could get started. He couldn't let himself think about what Ebe was trying to tell him. Too much heartache. He couldn't afford to get his hopes up, only to have them crushed to pieces yet again. Better to do something safe, something normal.

"The rest was rather easy. I flew to Chicago and visited the Starbucks the post was made from. I got all their credit card receipts from the day the post was made, which they were happy to give me for a sizable amount of money. Then I ran a background check on each one. As soon as I found one with a history that only went back for two years, I knew I was on the right track."

Lee was only half listening, wondering what was keeping Gary so long.

"For this next part, you have to come outside," Ebe told him, going to the front door and opening it.

Lee stepped through the door onto the front step, moving like a zombie. In his driveway were two minivans, an Escalade, and Mark's truck, all of them loaded with smiling men, women, and children waving at him. Lee recognized Kent and Billy, each behind the wheel of their own minivan, Raymond behind the wheel of the Escalade, and Mark in his truck. Dianne was there as well, sitting in the passenger seat of Mark's truck.

"Everybody wanted to come. We're all going out to eat for a while, but we'll be back," Ebe said as he walked off toward the vehicles. He jogged around to the passenger side of Mark's truck and climbed in after Dianne slid to the middle.

One by one, all the cars and trucks backed out of the driveway and headed down the street. Mark's truck pulled out last, and when it did, Lee could see that somebody had been left standing behind. As the person began walking in his direction, Lee became light-headed. It was a woman.

The woman was wearing jeans and an incredibly old LSU T-shirt.

Tears flooded his eyes, impairing his vision, but there was no mistaking who she was.

She was still the prettiest woman in the room...or street, in this case.

It was Andi.

She had taken diligent care of herself, adding only five or ten pounds to what she once weighed. Her hair was longer, but there was no mistaking the button nose and her distinct facial features, despite the few wrinkles she had gained. Her smile was just as he remembered. Magical.

When they were six feet apart, she came to a standstill. Her eyes were also filled with tears.

"Hey you," Andi said.

"Hey, you," Lee struggled to say, trying to overcome the lump in his throat.

Her smile disappeared. "You broke your promise."

Lee tilted his head. "Huh?"

"You broke your promise," she repeated. "You told me you would never tell anyone about our night on the beach."

"Oh, that. We were kids when I made that promise, barely out of our teens. I didn't think you would mind," Lee explained. "Besides, I kind of thought you were dead."

"A girl has got to protect her reputation, even from the grave," she said as she crossed her arms.

"You want to talk about reputation? Do you know what the locker room at the health club was like when the guys found out I was a virgin until I was twenty?" Lee countered with a smirk.

Andi's smile peeked out again.

"I understand that you still have my white envelope."

"I do."

"And you never opened it?"

"Nope. Do you think now you can tell me what's in it?"

"Nothing."

"Nothing?" Lee repeated.

"Nothing. It was just a childish girl's test of trust. Something my mom taught me. If you opened it before I asked you to, I would have known it, and you would have failed the test," she explained.

"I could have steamed it open," Lee offered.

"No, you couldn't. I super glued it shut. The only way to get inside was to open it," she countered, smiling brightly again.

Lee couldn't help but smile back at her smile. Then slowly, both of their smiles faded as they became lost in one another's eyes. Finally, Lee couldn't fight the urge any longer, and he moved forward and took her in his arms.

They hugged one another so tightly it became impossible to tell where one ended and the other began. The embrace turned into a longing kiss. They stood there silently, alternating between sobs and laughter, without regard to their surroundings and whoever might be watching.

They broke apart, standing with just a foot of space between them, holding on to each other's hands.

"I'm so sorry for what Lynn did to you, making you think I died all those years ago," she said. "I couldn't believe it when I read it in your blog."

"I actually lost you twice. I was told that you were murdered two years ago," Lee told her.

"Somebody lied to you, obviously. They moved me to Chicago when the marshals found out I'd been communicating with Gayle. They suspected someone was on my trail again."

"I'm just happy that you're here now." He took a couple of strands of her hair that hung in her face and tucked them behind her ear.

"Thank you for catching the bastard who killed my parents."

"It was the least I could do...after abandoning you," Lee said, suddenly unable to look her in the eyes.

"I don't look at it that way, and neither should you. You did what you had to do," she said. When Lee didn't respond right away, she added, "I was so sorry to read about your wife."

"I appreciate that," Lee answered, looking at her again. "Are you married?"

"I was close once. Awfully close. Left him standing on the altar, in fact. I just couldn't find anybody who fit the role." Pausing for a moment, she then said, "I wasn't as lucky as you were."

"I'm sorry for you."

An uncomfortable pause slipped between them.

Andi looked deep into Lee's eyes. "Thank you for giving me my life back," she said. Her voice cracked as she spoke.

"What's left of it you mean," Lee joked.

"I don't know about you, but I'm planning on being around for quite some time," she said with mock annoyance.

Lee's face turned serious again.

"Care for some company?"

Andi's smile gave him the answer before she spoke the words.

"I thought you'd never ask."

THE END

ACKNOWLEDGMENTS

How do you write one of these? I mean, to try and thank the seemingly endless number of people who've all had a hand in delivering on a dream—and doing so without leaving someone out or feeling slighted because of a malfunctioning brain cell of mine. Seems impossible. But okay, I'll take a stab at it anyway.

It's a bit of a tired phrase—*It takes a village to raise a child*—but since I consider this book my unruly child, I can confidently state that it felt like the entire eastern seaboard had a hand in its development. The path to landing it into your hands is so full of twists, turns, diversions, abandonment, and revitalization that it could make its own an entertaining story. Although the number of people directly involved in bringing **Knight Rise** to fruition is limited, those instrumental in my development as an author are far more widespread. So many people believed in me, even when I didn't believe in myself, and they each deserve mention.

First and foremost, I must recognize a nebulous force...the blogosphere. Never has there been such a knowledgeable and supportive environment for an aspiring novelist. I stumbled into that arena while doing research for this book. The community embraced my innocent naivete before eventually pointing me in the right direction. I visited and interacted with hundreds and hundreds of sites, far too many to list here, but there is one that stands out for his unwavering backing of efforts. **Alex J. Cavanaugh** is a successful author in his own right. Thank you, Alex, for showing me how blogging is done right.

Next in line are the folks who took the time to read my early drafts of all my manuscripts and supply insight on how they thought I could improve. Critique Partners, Beta Readers, Friends, the list goes on. It has been their efforts through the years that have molded me into what you see today. Thank you, all! In alphabetical order – Angela Brown, Patricia Burroughs, Lindsay Carlson, Sonja Cassella, Alexia Chamberlyn, Kristi Chestnutt, Crystal Collier, Gerardo Delgadillo, Julie Dao, Patti Downing, Melissa Embry, Elise Fallson, Chris Fries, Anne Gallagher, Sierra Godfrey Fong, Aaron Green, Christy Hinz, Donna Hole, Solange Hommel, Hannah Kincade, Liz Larson, Lori Lopez, Laura Maisano, Linda Masterson, Alex Perry, Summer Poole, Flor Salcedo, Jessica Salyer, Lola Sharp, Tiana Smith, Portia Stewart, Tara Watson, and Nancy Williams.

Special recognition is reserved for these following individuals as their contributions significantly impacted the trajectory of my progress. In one way or another, each of them boosted my morale or propped up my self-confidence when it needed it most. A most heart-felt thanks to Lisa Regan, Dianne Salerni, Barbara Poelle, Shelly Stinchcomb, Sarah Negovetich, and Tina P. Schwartz.

And then there's my editor for *Knight Rise*, the awesome Penni Askew. She took what was a promising start and helped me shape it into something that I'm extremely proud of. She guided me in such a way that it never felt intrusive or forced, allowing me to figure things out for myself while all-along leaving a trail of breadcrumbs to ensure I never got lost. Thank you, Penni!

Brianne van Reenen – the owner of Wild Lark Books – by selecting me as the first original author her new business pursued showed a trust in me that cannot be quantified. Never did I imagine that our meeting at a writers conference years ago would lead to this delightful collaboration. The respect I have for her, and this business venture, is immense. Thank you for the opportunity to realize my dream, and I can only hope this book moves the needle in the right direction for you.

Last, but most assuredly not least, is my family. My kids—Cody, Jaime, Casey, Dakota & Disney (yes, the dog and cat – don't judge)— and especially my best friend and wife, Kim. She has always been much more than my number one cheerleader. She is my sounding board and brainstorm partner. Thank you all for believing in me and allowing me to pursue this dream. It means the world to me. Love you!

Oh...wait...there's one more! You, my faithful reader. I can't forget about you. Thank you for taking a chance on Dianne and the Knights, and hopefully, I'll be able to provide more of their stories to you.

Much love!

A LETTER FROM DL

I want to say thank you for choosing to spend some of your hard-earned income on Knight Rise. If you enjoyed reading it as much as I did writing it, consider signing up for my newsletter at the link below. It's the perfect way to keep up to date with news about future Knights adventures and all my latest releases. Your email address will never be shared, and you can unsubscribe at any time.

https://www.dlhammons.com

This was my first attempt at writing a novel, but it ended up being a dozen years in the making. Any error you can think of that aspiring novelists run up against, I did that here. Too long, too bloated, too unfocused, too many grammar issues, too... too... too! I ended up putting it on the shelf and continuing my development as a writer with other projects, but the Knights have always stayed with me. The book sat, waiting patiently, until I felt confident enough to fix its problems. When I finally found time to give it the attention it deserved, the result was uplifting. They say that fine wine tastes better with age, and I guess the same is true with some manuscripts. The final product is a far cry from where it began, but the time it spent waiting in the wings was well worth it.

If you feel the same, I'd really appreciate it if you'd leave a review or recommend it to a fellow booklover. Reviews and word-of-mouth recommendations are the best way to introduce new readers to one of my books for the first time. No joke. These things make a difference. It doesn't have to be much. Even something like *This book **ROCKS*** is enough.

I'd also like to hear from you. You can usually find me hanging out at one of the social media places below, as well as my website listed above. Tell me what your reading experience was like, or just say HI. I don't bite (unless you're covered in caramel – then all bets are off).

https://www.facebook.com/DLHammonsauthor
https://twitter.com/DL_H
https://www.goodreads.com/DLHammons
https://www.instagram.com/dl_1956/
https://wildlarkbooks.com/dl-hammons/

CPSIA information can be obtained
at www.ICGtesting.com
Printed in the USA
BVHW060946291221
625055BV00019B/1984